AN ABSENCE SO GREAT

Other Books by Jane Kirkpatrick

NOVELS

Portraits of the Heart Historical Series
A Flickering Light

Change and Cherish Historical Series
*A Clearing in the Wild**
*A Tendering in the Storm**
A Mending at the Edge

*A Land of Sheltered Promise**

Tender Ties Historical Series
*A Name of Her Own**
Every Fixed Star
Hold Tight the Thread

Kinship and Courage Historical Series
*All Together in One Place**
No Eye Can See
What Once We Loved

Dreamcatcher Collection
*A Sweetness to the Soul**
Love to Water My Soul
A Gathering of Finches
Mystic Sweet Communion

NONFICTION

A Simple Gift of Comfort
Homestead
*Aurora: An American Experience in Quilt, Community, and Craft**

*finalist and award-winning works

AN ABSENCE SO GREAT

A NOVEL

JANE KIRKPATRICK

WATERBROOK
PRESS

An Absence So Great
Published by WaterBrook Press
12265 Oracle Boulevard, Suite 200
Colorado Springs, Colorado 80921

Scripture quotations or paraphrases are taken from the King James Version.

This book is a work of historical fiction based closely on real people and real events. Details that cannot be historically verified are purely products of the author's imagination.

ISBN 978-1-57856-981-6
ISBN 978-0-307-45927-5 (electronic)

Published in the United States by WaterBrook Multnomah, an imprint of the Crown Publishing Group, a division of Random House Inc., New York.

Library of Congress Cataloging-in-Publication Data
Kirkpatrick, Jane, 1946–
An absence so great : a novel / Jane Kirkpatrick. — 1st ed.
p. cm. — (Portraits of the heart)
ISBN 978-1-57856-981-6 (alk. paper)
ISBN 978-0-307-45927-5 (electronic : alk. paper)
1. Women photographers—Fiction. I. Title.
PS3561.I712A64 2010
813'.54—dc22

2009040201

Printed in the United States of America
2010—First Edition

10 9 8 7 6 5 4 3 2 1

To Jerry,
who is the loving eye behind the lens.

CAST OF CHARACTERS

Jessie Ann Gaebele	a photographer
Lillian Ida Gaebele	a seamstress and older sister to Jessie
Selma Selena Gaebele	a singer and younger sister to Jessie
Roy William Gaebele	a budding musician and younger brother to Jessie, nicknamed "Frog"
William and Ida Gaebele	parents of Jessie and owners of a drayage in Winona, Minnesota
**Voe Henderson*	friend of Jessie's
Frederick John "FJ" Bauer	owner of Bauer Studio
Jessie Otis Bauer	wife of FJ and professional photo retoucher
Russell, Donald (deceased), Winifred, Robert	children of FJ and Jessie Otis Bauer
Augie and Luise Staak	FJ's sister and brother-in-law
Violet and Freddie	children of Augie and Luise Staak
Lottie Fort	milliner in Winona
Ralph Carleton	a Winona evangelist and confidant of Mrs. Bauer

**Mrs. Suzanne Johnson*	owner of a photographic studio in Milwaukee
Henry and Mary Harms	Jessie's landlords in Milwaukee
Marie Harms	daughter of Henry and Mary
**Joshua Behrens*	business student at Marquette University, Milwaukee
***Hilda Everson*	Jessie's employer in Eau Claire
Virginia Butler	Jessie's employer in Bismarck
Herman Reinke	FJ's North Dakota ranch partner
Charles Horton	president, First National Bank of Winona
George Haas	owner of Polonia Studio in Winona

The photographers identified in the text, including those at the photographer's association meeting, are actual historical figures.

* Characters are created from the author's imagination.

** Jessie Gaebele's actual employer's name in Eau Claire was Johnson; the name of her Milwaukee employer is unknown.

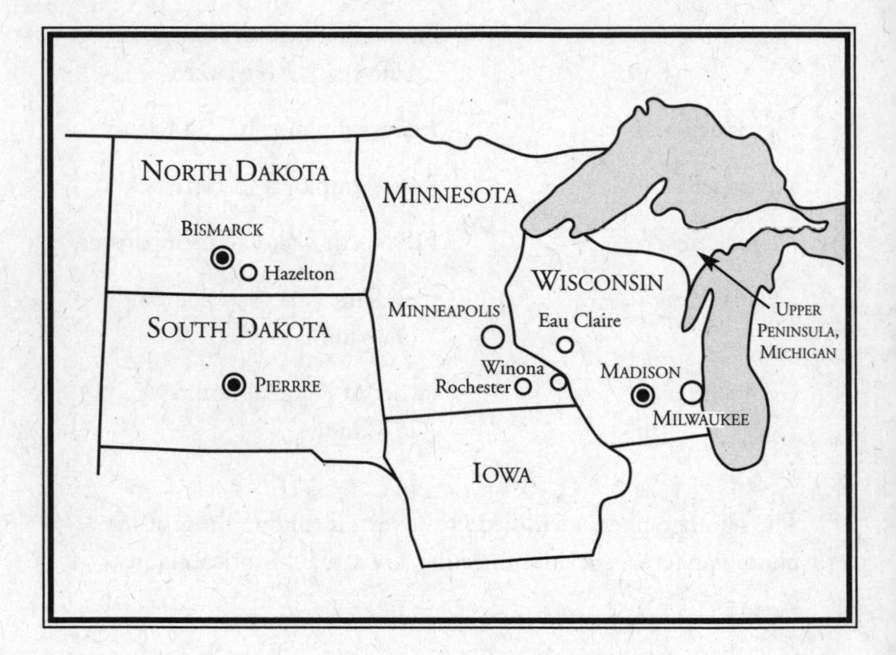
North Dakota
Minnesota
Bismarck
Hazelton
Wisconsin
South Dakota
Minneapolis
Eau Claire
Upper
Peninsula,
Michigan
Winona
Rochester
Pierrre
Madison
Milwaukee
Iowa

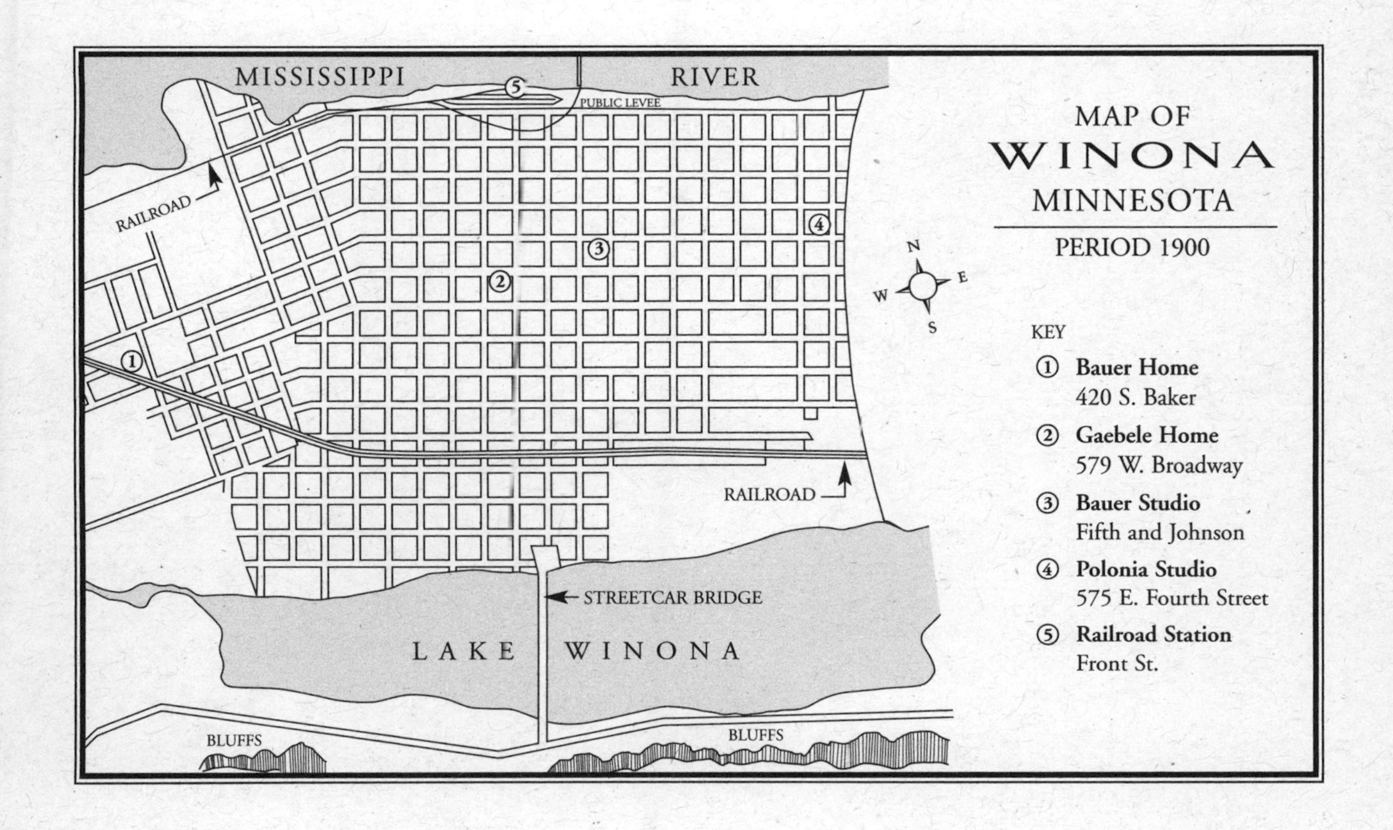
MAP OF
WINONA
MINNESOTA
PERIOD 1900
KEY
① Bauer Home
420 S. Baker
② Gaebele Home
579 W. Broadway
③ Bauer Studio
Fifth and Johnson
④ Polonia Studio
575 E. Fourth Street
⑤ Railroad Station
Front St.
MISSISSIPPI
RIVER
PUBLIC LEVEE
RAILROAD
RAILROAD
N
E
S
W
STREETCAR BRIDGE
LAKE WINONA
BLUFFS
BLUFFS

How could I ever prepare for
an absence the size of you?
—adapted from *Coastal Home* by MARK DOTY

Absence is to love what wind is to fire;
it extinguishes the small, it enkindles the great.
—COMTE DE BUSSY-RABUTIN

And into whatsoever city or town ye shall enter,
enquire who in it is worthy;
and there abide till ye go thence.
—MATTHEW 10:11

Baby Misha
December 1910, Johnson Studio, Milwaukee
5 x 7 Graflex

Loneliness

A photograph, like life, often reveals as much about who's absent as who's there.

This child's name is Misha, the son of Russian immigrants who arrived at the Johnson Studio in Milwaukee, Wisconsin. The woman, the mother and wife, or so I assumed, wore a brightly colored headscarf tied beneath her square chin. The cloth framed a somber face the color of a toddler's first tooth. A thick shawl with fringe shimmered as she whispered, comforting the baby wrapped in her arms. The man's hat and suit and upright stature, with his dapper look and gentle eyes focused on the child, reminded me of Fred.

They were a contrast, the man appearing much older than she, and I wondered if he might not be the woman's father rather than a husband, perhaps grandfather to the child; but from their interactions I decided they were married with some age between them. Age differences always intrigue me, what with Fred's being twenty-six years older than I.

From within the cocoon of her clothing, the woman brought the child out, holding him up to me with two hands beneath the baby's arms, which stuck straight out like a scarecrow, wearing a red wool jacket and a knitted cap of yellow, red, and black yarn.

"You take? Pho-to-graph," she demanded, spreading the last word as though each syllable merited the same weight.

"Yes," I said. "But not today." I closed the door they'd stepped through so I could shut out the swirling snow set free from the porch I tried to keep swept. "But not today." I didn't want to lose the commission, but by late afternoon of a Wisconsin December, night consumed more of the day than a photographer liked. I shook my head, waved my hands palms down. "Not today."

"No?" the man asked. "No?"

The woman pulled the child back into her woolen shawl, shrugged her shoulders at the man.

I pointed up toward the window. "No light," I said. "I could use the flash, but it casts deep shadows on the subject."

The Johnson Studio wasn't anything grand like the Bauer Studio of Winona, Minnesota, the one I'd been trained in. It lacked the skylights that brought in the very essence of a photographer's life: warm natural light. "You come early tomorrow," I told him. "Your son can wear the christening dress again."

"Today. We must do it today," the man said in accented but better English than the woman's.

A hard jaw expressed the woman's displeasure, and the child began to fuss. The woman was definitely the mother. The eyebrows on the child stretched in soft brown lines over blue eyes just like those on the woman who held him. The child's mouth derived from the man who spoke in Russian now. A pleading tone carried his words.

They argued. Agony threaded his posture with palms outstretched, pleading. He wanted this photograph more than she did.

I picked up the appointment book and showed them an empty space, then pointed to the Seth Thomas clock sitting on my desk. "Nine. In the morning," I repeated, all the while looking at the child's face, the expressive eyes so full of trust and yet with a hint of concern, as though he could feel the tension between these adults.

"Today." The man turned back to me. "Even with poor light. It must be today. Tomorrow she goes away." His voice cracked as he averted his eyes.

"You might not be happy with the result," I told him.

"It will be all I have," he said. "They go back. The photograph is all she leaves me."

The emotion in his voice was likely more than he wanted to share with me, but I found that this often happened in my studio. Photographs could expose discomforts, which often led to confessions.

I nodded assent and brought them into the operating room, that place within a photographer's studio where light and living begin their journey onto paper and posterity.

The woman advanced as I moved the chair around to capture whatever I could of the fading light. I set up a lamp.

It was not an easy exposure. I thought of what Fred, my mentor, would do in the same circumstance, then stopped myself. I'd not compare the results. I tried my best not to allow thoughts of anything Fred did to come into my head, though I failed at that more often than not. A human weakness. I was here in Milwaukee to learn what I needed to pay attention to, and it wasn't memories of Fred.

I turned to see the woman remove the child's woolen jacket and cap and waited for her to remove her own, as I thought they'd all be in the photograph. But she handed me the child.

"Just Misha," the man said.

That decision, too, revealed more than they perhaps intended: the mother and child were leaving, but only the child was to be captured for his memory.

Misha's weight was no more than a watermelon. Delicate tatting stitched its way up the skirt. The flounced collar emphasized the roundness of the infant's face. My sister Lilly, a seamstress, would have approved of the fine handstitching on the child's garment, quite likely a christening gown. Misha looked angelic with those trusting blue eyes staring into mine.

"It will be better if you hold him," I said. "He'll look more relaxed."

The man shook his head. "Just the child."

The woman pointed to a plant stand with a turned pedestal of maple and a flat seat that held a large fern. I moved the child to my hip. I had a younger brother and sister and carried infants that way, my arm around Misha's waist, his stocking legs dangling loose. Did the mother want the plant in the photograph? To my surprise, she removed the fern, set it on the floor, then brought the pedestal to sit in front of where my camera focused. The mother took the child from my arms and plopped Misha on the plant stand, allowing the skirt of the dress to flow down onto the turned pedestal. The woman smiled for the first time, revealing a single dimple and one broken tooth.

I had to admit, Misha's milk white dress against the dark pedestal presented a lovely contrast, but also a precarious sight, with the child barely able to sit by himself balanced on the stand. He'd have to be braced, and I wasn't sure he'd like the discomfort of the posing stand. It would be so much better if the mother just held him on her lap or we placed the child in a chair, safely propping him up.

"You can't let him be by himself," I said. "The photograph will take too long; he won't be able to sit still. It will blur." It would be unsafe too.

The woman misunderstood and released her hands at that moment, allowing the child to simply be.

"No!" I shouted as I reached for the baby. Misha's eyes grew wide, and he made a small catlike sound of anxiety, turning to his mother.

"I'll have to brace him," I said. I turned to the man. "Tell your wife she'll have to hold the child steady until just before I take the picture. To be safe, even with the brace."

The man nodded, spoke to his wife, who secured the child while I brought the posing brace from the wardrobe where I kept photographic equipment not often used. The infant kicked his feet and smiled. How little it takes to appease us when we trust those around us to keep us safe.

I secured the brace, which looked like large tongs of a tuning fork, slipping them around the slender ribcage of the child and attaching the base to the plant stand. I fluffed the dress out to cover the contraption. It would be there just long enough to expose the film. "You stay holding him until I signal," I said. The man translated, and the woman nodded.

I worked fast then, racing against the light and my own anxiety about the security of the child. I rolled my Graflex to the best angle, checked the position in front of a dark backdrop, then lifted my hand up as I bent beneath the cloth. I held my breath.

But the mother appeared to have great confidence, for she stepped back before I signaled, and farther than necessary to be out of the picture. Her husband spoke to her, and she returned as the child wiggled. I straightened up, took a step forward, but the brace held firm. For how long, I couldn't know.

I glanced up at the feeble light then and whisked back behind the camera, pushing my own long skirt to the side with a swish. Who knew the story behind the separation of this family? It was something I'd never know, even if the language didn't barricade such a conversation. How we put people we love in awkward poses is not a subject easily discussed even among intimates, let alone a photographer and her subjects.

The mother's choice of the plant stand was an odd one, and yet it created a lasting impression. As I looked at the child through the lens, Misha sat perfectly apart, a singular image of innocence detailed with delicate eyes and nose and ears and hands balled into soft fists. I wondered if I'd ever give birth one day to such perfection, if from my body would come a child created out of love, and if I did, would I one day put her into a fragile position even for a moment? Would I trust what I loved to an unseen brace?

Time and light faded. I lowered my hand as the signal. The woman stepped out of the picture. I exposed the film.

She had let happen what might, trusted in a strength she could not see.

It's what I think of each time I see this portrait; it's the wish I cherish for my life.

PART 1

SETTING

ONE

Setting Things Right

Milwaukee, Wisconsin, four months earlier

JESSIE GAEBELE'S THOUGHTS AT TIMES behaved like a toddler's: one moment they stayed safely hidden in the pump organ's shadow, and the next minute they popped up to pull out all the stops, increasing in volume, shouting in her head, underscoring the aching loneliness that defined her days.

Today, as she stood in this men's refuge permeated by the scent of oil and grease and gasoline, she flicked away those toddler voices. She had good reasons to be here. She was eighteen years old, it was 1910, and young women alone were going places they'd never gone before. She didn't need to bc embarrassed or afraid. Why had she come to Milwaukee if not to prove to herself and others that she could make wise choices and pursue a dream? One day she'd have her own photographic studio back in Winona, Minnesota, where her family lived. Her future beckoned, but she would return only when she'd proven to herself that she was in control of her heart.

"It might be best if you had your father look at it, Fräulein," the proprietor cautioned.

"I'm not purchasing it for my father," Jessie told him, a man her father's age she guessed.

"Ach, I'm sorry. You look so young. Your husband then."

Jessie took a deep breath. "It's for my own use."

The proprietor's eyes widened. "Ah, well, do you have"—he looked over her small frame—"the stamina to make such a purchase? Riding an Emblem's not like riding a bicycle or a horse, if you know what I mean."

She didn't know how to ride an Emblem or a Pierce or any other kind of motorcycle. She didn't know where she'd learn or practice, or where she'd keep it once she figured out a way to afford the gas. But it was the perfect accoutrement, so much more distinctive than a certain kind of hat or a new pair of shoes. Jessie needed inspiration with fall closing in on her, the days soon shortening into long, lonely nights. Winter always made her dreary, and this first one away from her family promised to weigh her down like the pile of wool quilts on the bed that she no longer shared with her sisters.

"I'm a photographer," Jessie told him, "and stronger than I look. I have my own income too. I assure you that I can afford to buy it." This wasn't quite the truth, but close. She planned to pay small portions each month. She'd read that some businesses did that now, calling it *credit,* from a Latin word meaning "to believe." The proprietor had to believe she would make the payment.

"Take a closer look then, Fräulein," the man told her, moving aside so she could step closer.

Don't do it. Don't do it.

She was here in this motorcycle shop because she'd seen the *Milwaukee Journal* photographer, Robert Taylor, making good use of such transportation. Unlike the Winona newspaper, the *Journal* printed photographs not just of disasters like the fire at the flour mill but of everyday things: people picnicking, ships easing along the Milwaukee River, the country's first kindergarten class. Studio shots they weren't. Nor were they tramp photographs, as Fred referred to photographs taken outside of the staged, controlled setting of a proper studio. To Jessie, spontaneous photographs of everyday life demonstrated the vibrancy of a people and a place. It was the kind of photography Jessie preferred, a view of the world through a commonplace lens, reminding her that ordinary ways were worthy of remembering.

As a photographer, one needed to be distinctive, and that certainly made Robert Taylor so: his motorcycle, and the blue and white polka-dot cravat he always wore. A photograph of him had brought her to this place. Art did move people, Jessie thought wryly.

This purchase would allow her to get out into the countryside, where the fields and trees and streams of this southern Wisconsin landscape would fill the void she'd brought with her. Would Fred approve? She shook her head. Forgetting Fred was another reason she'd come to Milwaukee.

Fred. She would not give up control of her feelings to imagine a life that could never be. She'd buy this motorcycle and create new memories.

Don't do it!

"It's a good price, Fräulein. And I'd wager there's a young man who would be more than willing to train a student such as you how to use it." He grinned. "I'm assuming here that you don't know how to ride one."

"You've assumed correctly," Jessie told him. She moved the camera case to her other hand as she ran her gloved hand across the Emblem's shiny surface. "But that's a temporary state."

Two hundred dollars was a lot of money, and she'd committed herself to saving all she could so she could one day purchase her own studio instead of always working for someone else. Still, with a motorcycle she could leave the city on weekends, get away from the often overbearing kindnesses of her boarding family, the Harmses.

The proprietor cleared his throat in what sounded like impatience.

If she spent money on a motorcycle, she'd have to settle any guilty feelings over not sending more home to her family and accept that a little joy in her life didn't mean she was being lax. The machine would be an investment; that's how she'd think of it. It would make her focus on her work with greater effort. Wasn't that the truth?

"I've heard of females riding bicycles. Seen a few around the city too. But a woman on a motorcycle? That would be a first in my experience. And I'm a man of experience, if you know what I mean." He winked.

Jessie didn't, but being the first female to ride a motorcycle around Milwaukee did not appeal; an innovative way to make money did. Yes, the motorcycle would allow her that. The newspaper would buy her prints. She didn't know for certain that was the case, and she was trying to be honest with herself these days. At times that balance between what was and what could be felt precarious indeed. That, too, was part of her reason for being in Milwaukee, to practice being forthright. The newspaper might only want Robert Taylor's work. But there were dozens of other newspapers from outlying towns she could approach.

Don't do it!

If she could sell her prints, she could contribute to the Harms household, if they'd accept her money.

"You're thinking the price isn't fair, Fräulein? I can tell you that even Schwinn's motorcycle is that price, and it isn't half as sturdy as the Emblem. Or are you just using that pretty head of yours to calculate?" He grinned, then added, "Maybe you like my company on this Saturday afternoon."

"I'm sure it's a fair price." Jessie stroked the blue gas tank on the side with the Emblem label painted in black. Her fingers lingered over the smooth leather of the seat. She set the bag holding the 3A Graflex on the box above the front fender to see if the rectangular camera bag fit in front of the handlebars. It did.

Her eyes stopped at the chains and tires. She'd worked for a bicycle shop owner in Winona, cleaning and sorting bicycle parts, so she knew there'd be more than just the cost of the machine to worry about. There'd be expense to keeping it up too. Was her talent enough to pay for all this?

But, oh, how she'd love the independence! It would help fill up the hours of doubt that marked her arrival in Milwaukee. Who was

Jessie Gaebele if she wasn't Lilly and Selma and Roy's sister, her parents' child, the apple of her grandparents' and uncle's eyes? Who was she if she wasn't Fred's…what? Student? Employee? Past paramour?

Paramour. She'd read a story employing that word in *Woman's Home Companion.* She and Fred hadn't been lovers, but she had been the "other woman," a weight as heavy as her camera case. Who was Jessie Gaebele when she was separated from those who had defined her? Her mouth felt dry.

"Wind rushes across your face and you feel like you're flying on one of these babies, if you know what I mean," the proprietor said. "You will feel as though you are in love."

"Absence is to love what wind is to fire; it extinguishes the small, it enkindles the great." A French writer had written that. She hadn't meant to say it out loud.

"Ah, love," he said and eased closer to her, and as he did, he shifted the wad of tobacco that pouched out his lower lip. He turned his head, and Jessie decided he'd moved to reach the spittoon sitting on a nearby bench. She wrinkled her nose, turned back to the Emblem.

"Men who ride these are in love with their machines," he said. He scratched at his arms, large, with muscles thick and twisted like old lilac trunks. "I can tell now that you've a good head on your shoulders…seeing as how you're taking such time to weigh the merits of this machine and know it'll take you to exceptional places." He moved closer to Jessie. "Maybe a pretty young thing like you just needs extra reassurance about such a big purchase."

"I know I wish to buy it, but I need to discuss whether you would allow me to purchase it on…credit. I'd give you a portion of the price now and then a sum each week."

"You want me to trust you? I'd need a substantial deposit for that."

He was beside her now, ignorant of the proper space between a gentleman and a lady. She could smell the day's sweat on his striped shirt, and she stepped sideways, putting distance between them but still steadying her camera perched on the machine.

"I'd have to be certain of your good intentions." His voice sounded lower now, his gaze moving like a slow flame up from her size three shoes to the glasses on her face. He stared into her eyes. She felt her face grow hot. "You give me something and I'll give you something, if you know what I mean." He nodded toward a door near the back. "Let's take this negotiation into my office."

Don't do it!

Jessie's hands felt damp inside her gloves, and she was alerted for the first time to the danger she was in.

"Come along, Fräulein," he said. He lifted her chin with his oil-stained fingers. "It's perfectly safe. You need a man of my experience is all, precious little thing like you, to teach you about business ways. Credit indeed." He grinned.

She stumbled back from him, one hand still clinging awkwardly to her camera. There was no one else in the shop; it was situated in a district with other industries frequented by men but few women. It was late on a Saturday afternoon. No one would hear her cry of distress even if she shouted. Her heart pounded. She never should have come in here, a woman alone.

"I'll give you a special deal on the machine, if you know what I mean," he persisted.

You know what he means.

She finally heard the words inside her head, the ones meant to keep her safe. "I've made up my mind," Jessie said, hoping she wouldn't give him reason to persist so she could make as dignified an escape as her leaden feet would allow.

But he reached for her then, squeezed his wide paws at her cheeks. He lowered his face toward hers. Dark tobacco juice glistened in the corner of his mouth. He pushed her against the Emblem.

Get out! Get out!

How could she be so foolish! Jessie hefted the only weapon she had and struck him with her camera case, the force of it twisting her and the case to the ground. Only then did she consider what she'd destroyed and just how long it would take to earn her way back home.

Two

Out of the Shadows

JESSIE HEARD THE PROPRIETOR'S GROAN. She hoped it was more from surprise than pain as he staggered back and she scrambled to stand, her hand slippery on the leather handle.

"Little I may be, but I'm not defenseless," Jessie told him, her breath coming fast and deep. "And I'll not be needing credit, if you know what I mean." She held the bag in front of her and pushed her way past him. "You, you...you're no gentleman," she finished, looking back at him. "You should be ashamed."

"I should have my head examined," he whined. He rubbed his shoulder with one greasy hand. "You've wounded me." He was just like the bullies who troubled her younger brother on the playground.

"It's the state of my camera I'm worried about. You're lucky I don't call the police."

She fast-walked out the door, turning back only once to see if he followed. He didn't. She rushed a good three blocks before she lowered herself onto a wooden bench, where she sat, shaking. A few maple trees dropped leaves as red as dried blood as she collected herself. "You're all right," she said out loud. "You're all right. No damage." No smudges on her gloves or her yellow suit jacket or skirt, but she still felt dirty. She brushed at the linen. What had she been thinking, going in there by herself? She shook her head, reached for the case and carefully shook it. Nothing rattled. She opened the suitcaselike bag holding her camera.

The lens was intact. No tears to the bellows when she opened it. Nothing on the casing appeared cracked. She pointed the camera at a building across the street, clicked the shutter. It sounded all right, but she'd have to develop the film to be certain there wasn't any hidden damage. Her hands shook as she put the camera away, words of gratitude whispered.

In all her eighteen years, nothing like this had ever happened to her. Oh, there'd been that time at the wedding she'd photographed, but she was only out of sight of the revelers for a moment, and the young man who approached her there came with the influence of rye on his breath and proved easy to manage. But what had happened now was nearly an assault. It *was* an assault. She shouldn't minimize it.

Maybe she should call the police and report the proprietor. What would she say? She started to shake again. Would they think *she* attracted such behavior? She hadn't batted her eyes or dipped her feathered hat in a coquettish fashion, had she? She tried to think. No, she hadn't. She'd been businesslike. She did not flirt. It wasn't like her. Her older sister had warned her about being out in the world and to be careful of simple acts that could flummox a man. Jessie thought she had been careful, though who would believe a woman's word spoken against a man's, and in a motorcycle shop? The mere fact that she had entered it, a young woman alone, suggested something to him she'd never meant. Was this what a woman's independence was all about, having to defend against intentions others imagined?

Tears filled her eyes after the anger passed. She blinked. Jessie sat up straight, wiped her cheeks with her gloves. It would be nice to talk this over with someone. Fred. He'd brush away the tears and speak endearments about how she'd handled herself well, maybe give her words of advice about money, machines, and men. But Fred was no longer in her life, could not, would not be. That had been her choice.

She stood, placed the camera back in the case, and closed the latch. She adjusted her hat and leaned out from the walk to see if a streetcar approached or if the proprietor followed. Neither. At least she hadn't made him so angry that he pursued her.

Jessie always felt better moving, so she began to walk, nodding at shopkeepers locking up their stores, careful not to keep her eyes on theirs too long. More people strolled now in the afternoon, stepping over leaves that skittered across the boardwalk. What was she to think of this episode? Marie Harms, the boarding family's daughter, was younger and wasn't a woman of the world. Confiding in her would only alarm the girl, maybe make her less trusting of people. Telling Mrs. Harms about it would certainly make the Harms family question her thinking. How could she afford to buy a motorcycle but not pay room and board to them? Though they'd insisted that boarding her at no cost was their pleasure, people could be funny about costly gifts if they disapproved of the recipient's other expenditures. Jessie wouldn't want to tell her employer, Suzanne Johnson, either. She too might question Jessie's judgment in going to that motorcycle shop in the first place, and that question might affect her perception of Jessie's work. Jessie hoped to do well running the studio for the young widow. If she sustained their clientele and Suzanne liked her work, Jessie could save up money for her own studio. Best to keep personal errors and episodes to herself.

She was alone in this, something else to remember about the freedom of living in a new place, separated from family and friends. One day, perhaps, she'd share the stories, recall memories when she wrote to her family. But such events needed time to give up all their insights. She thought of Fred again. She missed him.

She didn't like memories that forced her to deal with them daily.

The sidewalks in this section of the city weren't swept clean, and tiny pebbles pressed into the thin soles of her shoes. She looked again for the streetcar. Maybe she'd write to Voe, her companion at the Bauer Studio before Voe had married and Jessie had been exiled to Milwaukee. Voe would probably make light of the episode and remind Jessie that she could be "thick" in the ways of men. And she didn't want Voe to write back and raise unwanted memories.

Jessie recalled the progression of her episode, examined clues to what she'd overlooked in the sequence. She'd ignored the signs, even the small voice inside telling her not to enter that shop. She'd been thinking of how she could make money, negotiate business, fill in the gap of her loneliness. How odd that she could notice the fine details in a photograph, yet when her own safety was at stake, she dismissed the particulars that informed.

She wouldn't go home to Winona until she met three self-imposed conditions: save enough money to buy her own studio, prove to herself that she could make wiser decisions, and tell herself the truth about her feelings for Fred. Her appearance in that motorcycle shop didn't bode well for meeting any of those criteria.

At least *this* time her not being truthful hadn't hurt anyone but herself. That was progress. In the future, she'd pay more attention to what was happening around her and not settle on a single explanation for the small things that inner voice told her about. That's what an independent woman did in order to survive: she learned from her mistakes.

The clank of the streetcar rolling along the tracks announced its arrival. Jessie hurried to the stop, then stepped on board and took a seat, placing her camera case beside her. She gazed out the open window, letting the breeze cool her face. Before long they'd replace the open cars with closed ones and people would bundle up for winter, shutting out the cold winds off Lake Michigan while closing in the coughs and smells of winter.

Bits of paper on the floor ruffled in the breeze. The brim of Jessie's hat brushed against the window frame as she turned to look at the lake. Small boats shimmered and skimmed across the glassy surface, their sails unfurled. She loved the water and missed settling into a canoe for a glide across Lake Winona. She'd missed this year's canoe races, leaving for Milwaukee when she did. That couldn't be helped.

Today, Lake Michigan acted more like an ocean, Jessie imagined, though she'd never seen one. She couldn't see across this lake, had to imagine what waited on the other side. Government Pier, with its concrete walk, came into view. She liked to walk this pier that took her out into the water, where she could stand with the lake on three sides of her. It was almost as though she floated. Jessie adjusted her glasses. She watched a sail dip toward the waves and right itself. The sailboats were probably owned by the presidents of Briggs & Stratton, the Milwaukee engine manufacturer, or maybe Harley-Davidson's chairman. Harley-Davidson manufactured motorcycles in Milwaukee at a price much too high for Jessie to consider. Not that she would now.

Would there ever be a time when she didn't think about money: how to earn it, how to increase it, how and where to spend it? Her parents worked hard. Each of their daughters had held jobs from the time she was thirteen and finished the eighth grade and thereafter contributed to the family expenses. Her youngest sibling, Roy, had special needs that required extra. They weren't rich like the Harms family or the sailboat owners, but they'd been happy. Their small Winona garden included not just needed vegetables but lovely asters and zinnias, lilies and lavender, with only the last doubling as practical and fragrant. Family had given them richness—that and their faith. Jessie's disgrace had marred both. But they hadn't exiled her to Milwaukee; Jessie had done that to herself.

"May I sit here, miss?"

Jessie looked up as a young man tipped his boater at her and nodded toward the seat her camera rested on.

"Of course." She lifted the case, then stopped herself. She set the case back down. "No. There are plenty of other seats. I suggest you take one of those."

"I believe we've been on this same car before," he persisted. "I'm Joshua Behrens. And you are?"

"Not wanting to be bothered," Jessie said and turned to face the window.

She didn't mean to be rude, but empty seats dotted the car and she didn't trust her ability to assess whether this man was being kind or heading her toward another "episode."

She watched him grip the ceiling handhold for a bit, and then he moved past her, the scent of distinctive cologne lingering in the air. She'd never been unkind to a stranger, but she'd had enough challenges sorting out good intentions from bad for one day. And maybe what she'd done wasn't rude but appropriate for setting limits; independent women needed to know how to do this.

The streetcar slowed as the next stop approached. It was hers, but she considered staying on board, riding to the end of the line. She might have if not for the sweet-smelling gentleman behind her. At least he hadn't persisted in conversation. Besides, riding to escape wouldn't change anything today. She sighed and pulled the cord over the window, signaling the driver, and at the next stop, she stepped off to an empty street. She still had a few blocks to walk to Stowell Avenue. Summer would soon change its clothes into autumn in the gardens of Milwaukee's elegant homes. Despite her good intentions, she turned to look back as the streetcar rolled away. Joshua Behrens smiled down at her from his seat and waved. She didn't wave back.

She met a horse-drawn taxi, nodded at the driver, then rounded the corner. She stopped. Fred walked up the porch steps, talking to Marie Harms. No, it couldn't be. She saw what she wanted to. It was probably a friend of Henry Harms, who removed his hat as he stood. She squinted. The figure did actually resemble Fred, his back a slender soldier stance. She swallowed a mixture of fear and anticipation. She'd earlier imagined talking over her episode with Fred, and now her imagination confused him for someone else. She lifted her hand to her throat, felt the rapid pulse.

Marie spied her then, jumped up, swung her chubby arm in welcome. "Hurry up, Jessie," she shouted. "Gottlieb's here."

THREE

Of Shadow and Light

GOTTLEIB. THE FAMILY CALLED FRED by his given name.

Fred turned then, straw hat in one hand, the other wiping at his thinning hair before hanging loosely at his side. His smile widened his mustache as he looked at Jessie, urged her up the stone steps, reaching to assist by taking her camera. She couldn't breathe. Her feet moved her forward without her knowledge.

"He's come for the photographic conference next week. Isn't that grand?" Marie said. "You two can talk about cameras and whatnot. Want some iced tea?"

"I…I wasn't aware of the conference," Jessie said. "And, no. No tea. Thank you. I can manage the camera, please," she said, holding tight to the case. She could ask him to look it over, to make sure it wasn't damaged. But then she'd have to tell him what had happened, and in truth, she'd decided she didn't want to talk about it to anyone, least of all Fred.

"Next year it'll be in Minneapolis," Fred said.

"What? Oh, the conference." She'd been so busy at the studio, she'd been unaware of the photographers' association gathering. "How unfortunate that you had to travel so far from Winona to attend this one."

"I'm receiving an award," he said. "For the double exposure I took. You remember, yes? Seemed I ought to pick up the plaque in person."

"Oh." Jessie had been his model for that award-winning photograph.

"He showed us the print, and you look smashing," Marie said. "You never told us that you modeled." Marie shook her adolescent finger at Jessie. "You're holding out on us."

"I don't usually. Model. Or hold out on you," Jessie said. She didn't dare look at Fred's walnut-colored eyes for fear he'd see the confusion and pain within her own. "If you'll excuse me, I have things to attend to." She pushed past them, mumbling as she moved the camera case between Marie and Fred. "I hope your meetings go well."

Behind her she heard Marie say, "Jessie works hard. She must be tired to leave so quickly. So tell me, Cousin, what will the conference be like?"

"Educational," Fred said. From the sound of his voice, Jessie knew he stared after her. "That's the real reason I came for the conference. Education."

Jessie waited as long as she could before joining the Harms family and their newly arrived relative for supper. She changed her clothes three times in her third-floor bedroom, deciding on a simple yellow shirtwaist, a tight high collar despite the warm evening, and a dark linen skirt over her whalebone corset. She hooked a tiny gold pencil on a chain at the waistline to look as professional, as mature, as confident as she could.

The meal of roast pork and hot potato salad with mounds of carrots and parsnips from the Harmses' garden kept Jessie from having to speak much, though she ate little, pushing her food to the gold-rimmed edge of the china. The room felt warm despite a breeze lifting the lacy window sheers. Jessie barely tasted the vinegar bathing the potatoes as Henry and Fred discussed such invigorating topics as incandescent lamps in vehicles replacing carbide flame jets and what affect the formation of local conservation agencies would have on rivers and streams.

"World's changing," Henry said. "May as well get used to it."

Fred turned to her. "Are you enjoying your work with Mrs. Johnson?"

"It keeps me quite busy," Jessie said. "It's a much smaller studio than yours, but she serves a lot of clients. And she doesn't make the photographs herself. Her husband did that."

"Maybe she'll attend the association meeting," Fred said. "The classes are quite instructive."

Jessie dreaded the week ahead, remembering that most photographers' conferences began on Monday and lasted through Friday. Would he stay at the Harmses'? *Oh please, God, no.* She needed to keep as far from Fred's path as possible.

"I… She hasn't mentioned it," Jessie said.

"Will you be staying with us?" Mary Harms asked Fred then. "We'd love to have you."

Fred looked at her, included Jessie in his gaze. "Thank you, Cousin, but no. I'll stay at the conference hotel. Without my car, it's easier."

"You could always ride in with me," Henry said. "And I'd be happy to pick you up evenings. Or you could take a cab. But maybe you prefer hotel beds to Mother's feather ones." He chuckled, winked at his wife.

Fred looked at Jessie as he spoke to the Harmses. "Your hospitality is welcomed, yes," he said. "But I can meet with salesmen and other vendors after the sessions. And you have a houseful."

"Oh, there's always room for family," Mary said. "And I'm sure Jessie would like to hear about the day's events at the conference, wouldn't you, dear?"

"I'll encourage my employer to attend," Jessie said. She fabricated that possibility. "She could use the time of refreshment. She still grieves her husband's death."

"They'll publish minutes," Fred said, turning to Mary. Then to Jessie: "I'll bring you a copy if you like. Or send you one," he added when Jessie's eyes grew large in alarm.

She dropped her eyes. "That would be fine. If you sent it. Thank you."

"If you change your mind," Henry said, "door's open; a comfortable bed awaits. Let's take our cigars on the porch, shall we?" And with that the two men stood and left.

Jessie sat with Mary and Marie in the living room, the ticking clock background music to their embroidery. Jessie held a book in her hands but couldn't read, her mind constantly drifting to the conversation on the porch, the scent of smoke a lifeline to the men. She hoped her parents would never know that he'd been here, and so soon after she'd arrived. She hoped she wouldn't ever be alone with him, then ached for a moment with just the two of them. *All light casts a shadow,* she thought. His presence brought a touch of home and with it a lessening of loneliness, and yet he'd added to the strain of his absence. Greater effort would be needed now to set her back on track.

"I'm going to run Gottlieb to his hotel," Henry said as the men came back into the living room. "Would you like to ride along, you three?"

"I would," Marie chirped. She plopped her embroidery hoop into the basket beside her chair. "I bet Jessie would too."

"Would you?" Fred said.

"I...I think not."

"The award will be given on Friday evening," Fred said then, gathering up his hat. "A boat ride is scheduled on Lake Michigan in the afternoon. Perhaps you'd join me? They display the week's work then, too, and the award photographs."

"Oh, Jessie, wouldn't that be grand? They'd see you as the model. Maybe you'll get an award too," Marie said.

"Isn't it nice that our Gottlieb offers advancement for your professional growth, Jessie?" Mary said, continuing to stitch.

"Yes. Mr. Bauer's been of great influence in my life," Jessie said. "I can never repay him."

"Not necessary," Fred said. He stiffened as he spoke. She could tell she'd offended him, keeping the conversation strictly business, but that's what it had to be. "I thought you might like to see how the association works. Some other time."

"I'll hope to attend a conference myself one day," Jessie said. "But I thank you for the invitation and regret I cannot accept. I'm working on Friday, and the evening is already filled. I congratulate you on the award. It's always nice to have one's work recognized."

He clicked his heels together and bowed slightly at his waist. "Miss Gaebele," he said.

Jessie rose, the book sticky in her sweating palms. "Good evening," she said.

"Mary, Marie. Thank you for a lovely evening," Fred said. "Henry? I thank you for the lift to the hotel."

"Wait," Marie said. "Aren't we coming with you?"

"Yes, of course," Fred said, turning to her. He looked at Jessie, but she shook her head. "Until our paths cross again then."

Jessie walked straight-backed up the stairs and didn't let herself look back through the banister to see if Fred watched her go. She heard the car start up, Marie's happy laughter lifting through the window. She reached her bedroom and stared at the image in the mirror. "You did well," she said. "You did well." Her voice shook, but she'd kept her dignity in this dangerous situation. She'd made the wisest choice, though she longed to take a ride on the lake, to immerse herself in photographic images and talk. She flung herself on the bed and wept.

August 30, 1910

Dear Sister,

How are you? I am fine.

I miss you. The summer drags without you here, when it used to move so quickly. I'm working hard at Lottie Fort's now, making new hats, learning to shape the felt and everything. Mrs. Bauer came by. I know I shouldn't mention her, but she's a good customer of Lottie's. She wasn't so sad looking as when I worked for them, so maybe Melba Laehn, that new girl they have, has brought her happier thoughts. She picked out an ostrich fan. Lottie trades them now, and I trained Mrs. Bauer in fan language, showing her how fanning slowly meant she'd marry someone, which she said was ridiculous, as she was already married, didn't I know? Well, I said of course I knew, but this was how one talked with a fan, giving information without words. She urged me on then, though I could see she thought me daft.

A closed fan says, "Don't be sassy," and an open fan against the cheek drawn slowly says, "I love you." A half-open fan against the lips invites a kiss. The pink feather tickled so much when I did that that I sneezed three times in a row! She laughed at that, and I saw how nice it was to hear her laugh, and I realized how seldom I heard it when I worked for the Bauers.

There was one last fanning word, and that was how to tell someone to keep a secret. You place the open fan over your left ear. That means, "Don't tell."

I'm sorry I told your secret, Jessie. I know that's why you went away to Milwaukee, and I'm sad for that. Maybe if I'd known this language, then you could have reminded me what to do before I did it and you could have stayed home forever instead of moving away to forget Mr. Bauer.

Lottie also sells gloves and hankies and scarves and parasols and purses. She says it's necessary to branch out in uncertain times. She even sells hatpins I just love, with intricate flowers at the top, and one has a metal butterfly so while it's holding a hat, the butterfly sits nestled inside a cluster of dried flowers. I have to learn all about each hat or pin or parasol so I can match them up with their new owners. That's how Lottie puts it. I eavesdrop while women are searching, or I find ways to talk about what they like in life so I can hand them the perfect accessory. Lottie says dresses are fine, but it's the small things, the accessories, that distinguish us as unique and that everyone, even me, needs in order to feel special.

After all my sneezing, Mrs. Bauer decided against an ostrich feather fan and bought instead a cream silk gauze embroidered with tiny flowers. The ivory sticks are pieced and look like small picket fences holding the gauze. She said she liked the little blue flowers and that it would go with her blue hat, the one like you have. She was wearing a blue hat, and it certainly looked like yours, but I didn't dare ask to see the label to be certain that Lottie had made it. I do wonder what makes me distinctive. Do you wonder what makes you special?

Roy wants chickens. Mama says we have enough, but he wants them as pets, he says, since Mama doesn't want dogs or cats around. It's what they argue about over supper, though Mama always wins because Roy can't get the words out. Since you've gone, Mama has forgotten not to finish his sentences for him, so I try to remember when we're alone. I always wait, even though it seems like hours, especially when I know that what he wants to say is "r-r-rooster."

What are you doing in Milwaukee? I just wonder. Are you still at that nice place you sent a note to us about? Lilly said you shouldn't have such a lovely home when you're supposed to be there for your "mea culpa." I had to ask her what that word meant. Lilly says it's two words. She spends time with Catholic girls, so maybe that's where she got the idea we're each to carry blame for our mistakes, all the way to Milwaukee. But I think there's a time for everything; isn't that scriptural too? If being in Milwaukee shortens the time it takes for you to feel forgiven, then your being away will be worth it.

That's all I have for now. I hope you're well and that you'll write soon. When we receive your letters, we read them out loud over supper because they paint a picture, Roy says, though he isn't the one who gets to read them to us. I am. You share pictures even when you don't send a single photograph, so we can see how you are. I'm fine too.

Your little sister, Selma

FOUR

Delegate of Change

"CAN YOU HANDLE THE RAYMOND SITTING this morning?" Suzanne Johnson asked. "I've a terrible headache, and the smell of Mr. Raymond's cigar aggravates it."

"Of course," Jessie told her employer. It was Suzanne's studio, after all; she could ask Jessie to do anything she wanted. The tall, slender owner of the photographic business often had headaches. In the five months since Jessie had started working for her, Suzanne had excused herself several times a week, rubbing her temples with her fingers, shaking her head ever so slightly, as though the movement could brush away the pain. Jessie remembered Fred's telling her that Mrs. Bauer often suffered from headaches. She wondered if there was something in the air at the studio that caused them, in the same way that mercury poisoning from the developing solutions made photographers ill. She had occasional headaches but hadn't associated them with chemicals. She needed to be alert to that possibility. Suzanne often colored prints. Perhaps the lead paint contributed to her headaches, though at least Suzanne didn't put the brushes in her mouth the way Mrs. Bauer once had, to keep the brushes moist.

Suzanne had not attended the photographers' gathering. She said she had no desire to learn to photograph the way her husband had. As the holidays approached, Jessie hoped Suzanne would feel well enough to bear more of the load though. As it was, Jessie often returned to the studio on Saturdays to work on retouching or reordering supplies. Not that she minded. The work kept away thoughts that shouldn't develop. Besides, the walk back and forth was good for her. Despite the cold winds off the lake, she stayed healthy, hadn't even had a sniffle. Of course, each morning she followed the health routine suggested by her women's magazine. She ate two poached eggs with dry toast, then exercised by lying on the floor and rolling first right, then left, while keeping her feet off the floor. She repeated it twenty times. Even if the actions didn't keep her healthy or slender, she'd continue them just to be free of her whalebone corset a few minutes longer.

Jessie watched Suzanne run her hand along the back of the chair, stop a moment at the edge of the desk as though waiting for pain to pass, then open her apartment door and disappear. Jessie wondered what sort of treatment Suzanne used to ease her discomfort. Her employer still grieved the death of her husband, and that could well be why she had those nagging pains. Everything in her life had changed with his death, creating in her a gasp of distress rarely followed by a satisfying breath. No one Jessie was close to had died, but Fred had lost a child to an accident, and she'd seen in him death's deep burrow into the world of "what might have been." She'd met Fred years after the boy's passing, and yet Fred still grieved. She could see it huddled there in his dark eyes. One needn't have faced death to feel so great an emptiness. There were other kinds of losses that Jessie knew well. She still ached from Fred's unexpected visit just as she'd started to move past the memories. Handling the encounter without complication built her confidence, but it also required starting over again, facing the truth of what could never be.

Jessie watered the ferns, brought in fans and muffs and vases for possible use in the upcoming sitting. Suzanne needed more time, Jessie decided, as she went about opening the linen drapes, letting pale December sunlight pour in. It couldn't be easy for her to share her studio with another. The Bauer Studio didn't have an apartment attached; Suzanne's did, so she lacked the luxury of getting away from the memories at day's end. Maybe that added to her headaches.

Mr. Johnson had been the photographer, the developer. He did a fair postcard trade as well. Suzanne made the appointments, stocked the developing room, worked on ads to run in the paper, and assisted with retouching as needed. "Except for answering the phone, I did the private things," she told Jessie when first they'd met back in July. Suzanne folded her hands in her lap during that initial interview. Her soft voice forced Jessie to lean forward to hear her. "My husband was the charmer. He could make a nasty child sit still and like it, and convince any customer who was unhappy with their portrait that it really was the perfect picture of them." She shook her head, a wan smile lifting her lips. She twisted the gold ring on her finger. "He was very good at convincing people of things."

"Changing how they saw themselves."

"Yes. Exactly. And not just the patrons." She'd looked away, fluttered her hands at her cheeks, and moved on to show Jessie the appointment book, discuss procedures. Suzanne's last comment brought Fred to mind. Perhaps all successful photographers possessed a quality that reshaped reality, and not just upon glass plates. Kodak had it right promoting photography as camera "witchery," without knowing they spoke too of a photographer's alchemy of the spirit. More magical than the process of photo development was the change photography produced in people who evaluated what the lens had captured about them.

Jessie had hoped that Suzanne's personal comment that first day would mark the beginning of a friendship and that one day the two would share a deeper conversation about Mr. Johnson, what it had been like to work together day after day. They could compare stories, in a way. Jessie thought they might talk over tea about being unmarried women now, alone in a city, and how each fared when they weren't busily at work. That day hadn't come. Only words of weather or supplies filled the silences between the clients coming to the Johnson Studio. Jessie's job involved blending in with the owner's wishes, not becoming friends with her.

Jessie waited for the first client as she listened to Suzanne moving around in her apartment. In general, Jessie's work at the Johnson Studio wasn't unlike the work she'd done for Fred at the Bauer Studio. Here, too, clients acted hesitant as they walked into the reception area, looked around at the horsehair couch, wiggled their noses at the scented candle Mrs. Johnson liked to burn. Peacock feathers in large vases stood like statues on the floor, drawing children, as did other props included in the final sitting. Jessie would give clients a tour, show them the operating room, and point out the developing room and the door that led to the small apartment Mrs. Johnson lived in. If the darkroom wasn't occupied, she'd open the door to let them see the shelves of chemicals, the rectangular tubs filled with water where they bathed the prints. The children always giggled at the idea that pictures took baths. The line over the tubs, she'd tell them, was the clothesline. "We hang the prints there to dry just as your mother hangs up your flannels." They'd giggle more.

Giving clients a sense of their surroundings, aligning the strangeness with the familiar, put people at ease. But the adults still often acted shy of having their portraits made. Jessie had to gentle them into the idea that spending money on their families in this way wasn't frivolous but preserved a memory, recorded change. At the same time she had to reassure them that what appeared on the glass negative was only a moment in time; it wasn't the sum of who they really were.

Fred had told her that the Indians he photographed in his North Dakota studio said their elders didn't approve of photographs. They believed that such prints stole a part of their souls, trapping it on the paper. She marveled at the silver-tongued photographer who had first wiped away generations of deep spiritual belief, permitting the next generation to have their portraits made. Changing a person's vision of the soul was no small thing. Fred had captured Chief Red Cloud, a portrait he'd been quite proud of.

Like the Bauer Studio, the Johnson Studio had a retouching room that was nothing more than the back of a closet where they hung shawls and capes. Jessie spent a fair amount of time in that darkened room removing blemishes from a person's face, inking out lines at his or her eyes. She wouldn't describe that task to potential patrons as she gave the tour. Some might find the practice false, manipulating truth. Yet they'd like the results: a prettier picture than when they looked at themselves in the mirror.

Most people didn't pay attention to the tiny lines at their eyes as they used the mirror to set their hats or collars straight, but they noticed it in a print and did not find it pleasing. It was the craft of the retoucher to retain everything that signified the essence of a person, such as a mole on Grandpa's chin that everyone would notice if it was absent. But small things—a reflection on a woman's eyeglass, a stray strand of hair, a tear glistening on a baby's cheek—could be removed and not detract from the image. In that way, a photographer mimicked a portrait artist, painting an image of a person over time and perhaps revealing a bit of the artist herself within the oils.

As with the Bauer Studio, time with clients went quickly. She enjoyed meeting new people, hearing their stories. She also imagined the stories they didn't tell, how they arrived in Milwaukee, what struggles they faced, if there was a reason they were having their portrait made other than what they said. Most of the Johnson clients came from the north and east sides of Milwaukee and were German, though Yankees lived in that section of town too. While Jessie didn't speak German, she could understand bits and pieces if clients lapsed into that first language. But most spoke English they would have learned at the settlement houses or the country schools they attended before moving into the city. Thick accents still marked them as newly arrived.

After Christmas, Jessie planned to suggest to Suzanne that they expand to the South Side patronage and maybe even lure their neighboring "Yanks," as Suzanne called them, English descendants. Milwaukee attracted people of all persuasions, who settled into distinct neighborhoods and yet mixed throughout the city as a whole. Jessie loved that about Milwaukee: in the fall, she'd walked through different neighborhoods and known the nationalities of the residents by the smell of their strudels, kielbasa, lefse, and lox.

Jessie was certain the studio could attract more business if they sought permission from a few of the finer clients to use their portraits in newspaper ads. The cost would be more, but the images would attract interest and the *Journal* appeared to like using photographs. The small text ad Suzanne placed each week—"Portraits by Johnson. Serving the North Side"—just didn't have the flash Jessie thought it needed. So far, Suzanne had been reluctant to adopt suggestions. She had kindly put Jessie's portrait of a young girl named Pearl in the front window. That was the only change Jessie could see. Doing so must have caused distress; all the other portraits there had been done by her husband. But Suzanne was fond of Pearl's portrait. She'd looked wistfully at it, and Jessie wondered if the absence of a child was another grief the woman carried. Suzanne was bound by the desire all have when faced with grave emptiness: the yearning to keep the old routines, hoping they might wash away despair. And yet they couldn't because something—everything—*had* changed. Jessie knew that firsthand. To manage her sadness, she'd found it best to seek new ways of doing things, even if it meant "episodes" brought experiences one didn't care to repeat.

The Raymonds arrived on time and were easily posed because the man told Jessie exactly what sitting he wanted. His wife appeared much younger than he, and Jessie thought there might be a story there, of this white-haired and obviously successful man sitting as he wished, with a comely young woman standing behind him, her diamond ring sparkling on the finger that rested on his shoulder. His wife silently did whatever he directed.

"You've had your portrait made before, Mr. Raymond," Jessie ventured as she turned the wheel on the camera stand, raising it to the proper height. Her skirts swished as she moved about the device, focusing, setting. Her slippers slid easily across the carpeted floor.

"Why do you ask?"

"You know what you like," Jessie said.

"Aye, he does know what he likes."

It was the first time the woman had spoken, and Jessie judged from her words and missing eyetooth that she was not of her husband's social class. Jessie wondered how the two had met, what circumstances had brought them into marriage. Maybe they weren't married, but why would he give her such an extravagant gift or go to the expense of having a portrait made together? Fred had given Jessie gifts, but the two of them had never been in the same photograph. The woman wiggled the finger bearing the ring, the morning light flashing against the small diamonds set around a larger white stone.

"Keep your hand on my shoulder," he told her. "The photographer will need absolute stillness, won't you?"

Jessie nodded as she manipulated the lens, prepared the glass plates that would slide into the frame in the belly of the Johnsons' portrait camera. The woman placed her hand against his expensive wool suit and stiffened her standing pose. Her smile disappeared into plumping cheeks.

"You've taken a few photographs yourself," Mr. Raymond said. "Yet you can't be much older than what, eighteen? Are you the Johnsons' daughter?"

People often wanted to know personal things about photographers. Perhaps asking them to reveal a bit of themselves equalized the vulnerability of being exposed to film. It also gave people subjects to talk about while they waited in that awkward setting. Jessie usually complied. She wanted people to be comfortable, as they'd be more inclined to like the final results.

"Nearly nineteen," Jessie told him. "In just a few months. And yes, I've been doing this since I was fifteen. I'm pleased a certain level of experience shows."

"And are you a Johnson?"

"Oh no. Mrs. Johnson is widowed. I've been hired to help her run the studio until she feels she can manage it on her own or perhaps sell it to another photographer. My plan, though, is to have my own studio one day." Jessie thought that the more she spoke her dream out loud, the greater the likelihood it could happen.

He looked around. "This one could use sprucing up, be more inviting."

"Oh, don't move," Jessie said. "That's it. I'm almost ready here." She straightened, moved the camera slightly to take advantage of the light. "I rather prefer taking pictures as Robert Taylor does, of the *Journal*," Jessie said.

"Of disasters?"

"No, more ordinary things, outside. The Indian Mound at Olmsted's Lake Park or people picnicking at River Park. Could you turn your head to the right, lower your chin just a thread, Mrs. Raymond? Thank you. But those photographs don't pay well unless you're Robert Taylor, working for the *Journal*. I think we're ready now."

"So you enjoy 'gardens of the poor'?" Mr. Raymond said.

"Is that what the parks are called?"

"It's what Olmsted called them when he designated the land. He wanted park space always free and open to the public, with both active and passive areas."

"I like active areas," his wife said. "Watching the golf."

"Watching golf," her husband corrected. "Not 'the golf.' That's how we say it."

"All right. Hold that pose. Mrs. Raymond, you're a natural," Jessie said, hoping to erase the look of a woman chastised for her grammar. The woman smiled without showing her teeth, but it lacked enthusiasm. Still, she had distinctive features, pleasing to the eye. Jessie took the shot at the crest of the smile easing up toward her eyes.

"I wonder if you might be willing to have a few other poses," Jessie asked as the Raymonds let their shoulders relax. "You have such lovely eyes, Mrs. Raymond. I'd like to try images of just you if that would be possible. I wouldn't charge you for them unless you decided to take one. I'm always looking for subjects for character studies. Most photographers are."

"Minnie," she said. "Call me Minnie." She looked at her husband, awaiting his answer.

"I have a lovely gown that I believe would highlight your wife's creamy skin tone," Jessie said. "May I get it for her?"

The gowns were unique to the Johnson Studio, a series of props Jessie thought inventive. A few of the gowns could be slipped on from the front right over a patron's dress with a tie on the back to keep it closed long enough for the photograph. Others were gowns that Suzanne had acquired in various sizes, beautifully stitched. Jessie brought two out for Minnie and her husband to look at. "I prefer this one with the lace and silk ribbons and the ruche on the sleeves. There's even a bow for your hair," Jessie pointed out.

"I like that one too," Minnie said.

Her husband nodded. "That one then, with the large flower in front," he said.

Jessie motioned for Minnie to change behind the folding screen. Soon her maroon dress draped over the stork painted on the panel.

"If you're inclined," Mr. Raymond said, "you might consider photographing gardens since you enjoy outdoor images. There's quite a market for them, from what I hear, in Chicago and back East. That sort of thing eventually makes its way to Milwaukee. We don't like to be outdone. You couldn't do it until summer, of course, but it might be an option. Sell them to the owners."

"Like Jessie Tarbox Beals," Jessie mused.

"Don't believe I know her. Is she local?" Jessie shook her head. "Here's my card," he said. "Come spring, look me up. I like helping young ladies succeed."

Jessie glanced at him, to see if his words carried more meaning. They didn't seem to. His address was on Lake Drive, one of the finer sections of the city.

Minnie came out from behind the screen then, looking lovely as she ran her hands over the ribbons and lace. Jessie posed her and took the shot.

Minnie still wore the pensive look, and Jessie suspected that her eyes reflected the strain of her journey from a settlement house to the fine halls of the homes along Lake Drive. Finished, Jessie said good-bye to the Raymonds, told them when the prints would be ready, then developed the prints immediately.

Minnie's face formed slowly on the glass plate. The woman reminded Jessie of Suzanne, of all working women trying to make their way. She'd have to peer more closely at herself in the mirror to see if her own eyes revealed emotions she hadn't imagined they would.

Minnie Raymond
December 1910, Johnson Studio, Milwaukee
Johnson 5 x 7 Graflex portrait camera

Resignation

I love this photograph. Not just because it required so little retouching, but because the viewers' eyes are drawn into the eyes of this woman, Minnie Raymond. I was her in many ways. A common girl, "shop girls" you might call us, with limited schooling, finding ourselves connected to older men perhaps in ways we'd never imagined. Good men, men who liked women, enjoyed being helpful to them, and who didn't always realize how their well-intentioned instruction could wipe away a girl's confidence as swiftly as the proper brush could erase a blemish on a glass plate.

The pose I chose had Minnie looking off in the distance, not staring at the camera, as though she pondered. Her expression to me says, "So. It has come to this, a mixture of blessing and unease." Fred took several photographs with the subjects avoiding the lens, but he preferred they look directly into the camera. He had a special talent in poses set that way that captured the best of a subject. With photographs he took of me, it was almost as though his care for me spread like warm butter onto the glass plate, giving my eyes a sensual look they really didn't have, making me appear more beautiful than I am. Loving eyes can do that. Fond eyes. It was important, especially in those first months after I moved to Milwaukee, that I minimized the intensity of my feelings for him, repositioned memory and hope by using neutral words to trick my mind, if not my heart. He was fond of me, nothing more.

So in this photograph I didn't want her looking directly at me as I closed the shutter. She struck me as a sister, a girl who found herself in an unusual situation of the heart. Her shoulders are set firm and forward toward the camera, but her eyes—her eyes reveal a sadness, looking back.

Minnie didn't photograph as sensual, yet you could see it in the fullness of her face, the arch of her lips. I minimized the shadow against the left side of her throat, the light softening her jaw line and serving as camouflage to a plumping chin. That chubbiness appeared recent to me, and I could imagine her as a girl as thin as spaghetti, handing off portions of her own food to younger brothers and sisters at their settlement house. She just didn't seem accustomed to affluence.

Of course, I made that judgment in part on the day I photographed her, for when she came out from behind the screen, having put on the elaborate gown, she tugged at the sleeves, wearing a surprised look that the material pulled against her arms and bodice. Her eyes held wonder for just a moment.

When Minnie came alone to pick up the prints, I was surprised. But she affirmed what I'd imagined about her past. She told me that her frizzed hair was new for her. "Siegfried tooked me to a parlor. They had a machine. Called it a Nessler perm machine. It took six hours. Aye, I looked like a lamp with dozens of tubes out of my head. The things lifted my hair from my scalp." She put her fingers into her hair to demonstrate. "So my hairs weren't burned. I was scared though." She laughed when she told the story, but I could imagine it wasn't terribly funny at the time. "I got only the frizzles left." She touched the frizz at her temples and lowered her eyes. "Siegfried, he's fond of newfangled things."

"That he tried out on you," I said.

She shrugged. "I like trying new things too."

I wanted to ask her what she was thinking about the day I took the picture. It's one of the fascinating things about a photograph: when people see one of themselves, they often remember what was on their mind, whether they were happy or impatient, the context of their exposure. Sometimes they even talk about who wasn't in the picture and why they were absent. I never outright asked, but occasionally people volunteered such information. Minnie did.

"I don't look so happy there, do I?" she said.

"You look…thoughtful," I offered. "Resigned."

Minnie frowned.

"Accepting," I corrected. "Willing to submit to something uncomfortable. Posing can be…awkward for some people. Others take to it like cats lap milk."

"So much money he spends on frivolous things." She flashed the ring again. "While others scrape and save. I'm glad my hands aren't in the photograph. He's did so much for me. I make mistakes. You noticed. Siegfried corrects them so's I won't sound bad. Or...what's the word? Embarrass him."

"I don't see how being who you are would embarrass him," Jessie said.

"I was thinking when you took that picture that I weren't worthy of such finery. That dress. And on top of that, I make mistakes."

"Seems to me that Siegfried, Mr. Raymond, cares for the person who makes mistakes, the person you are. And that dress looked lovely on you. If you lived in Winona, I'd give you my sister Lilly's card. She'd sew up the perfect dress for you. Looser in the arms," I added. From the expression on her face, I was sorry I'd spoken.

"The sleeves was too tight. Does it ruin it, you think?" She held the portrait in her hands.

"Not at all. You can't tell. It looks natural as a baby's smile. I shouldn't have mentioned it at all. That's my mistake."

"I'll be embarrassed to show this to my mother. I've put on such pounds since Siegfried and I married, while she's still so thin. He gives them money," she defended. "He does. He's very generous." I wondered what had brought them together. "We should just take the photograph of the two of us, leave this one behind. I told him I'd bring back the proofs so he could decide which he wants."

"I suspect your mother would be pleased to see you looking well, that you've made a good life for yourself with a man who loves you." I told her that because I believed it and not just because I feared I might lose the commission. "I think it's a lovely portrait. I was about to ask you if we might use it in a new advertisement we're considering. To show quality portrait shots to promote the studio."

"You'd want one of me?"

"I'll need to check with Mrs. Johnson, but yes, you." A smile lifted Minnie's lips.

In the end, Minnie wasn't certain whether Siegfried would approve, but she took the print with her, saying she'd ask his permission. It's what women do, seek permission from those who have authority over us. I'd resisted such seeking from my parents, doing things they later disapproved of. And here I was, in another state, far from any earthly authority.

I did have the authority of my employer, I supposed, realizing I'd offered something to Minnie without Suzanne's approval. But by the time Siegfried had rendered his agreement to our using Minnie's photograph in the newspaper ad, so had Suzanne. "It's a fine rendition of my wife," Siegfried said when he came to pay for the final prints. "I'd like the world to see it. You've a fine talent, Miss Gaebele," he added.

I remembered that the pastor had said the word "talent" came from a Roman coin and was a currency. "If I could just learn how to spend it wisely," I said. Wise choices proved a constant challenge to my days, a position I was resigned to.

FIVE

Surprises

"LOOK WHAT I'VE GOT FOR YOU, JESSIE!" Marie Harms met her at the door. "It's a surprise!"

Marie spoke in exclamation points, Jessie decided. Everything was worthy of note.

"You'll have to let me take my hatpins out and remove my coat," Jessie said as she closed the door behind her. Her eyeglasses fogged up in the transition from the December cold into this well-heated home. Mr. Harms liked it warm, and the coal delivery came weekly to ensure his comfort. The house smelled of cinnamon, and Jessie considered making a detour through the kitchen, but Marie stood right in front of her, wearing enthusiasm.

"I'll just follow you up to your room and bring the surprise with me," Marie told her, pulling a large string-wrapped box from the table behind her. "Go on," she urged Jessie as she started up the stairs. "Oh, I'll go first." Marie pushed past Jessie, who grabbed the banister to keep from falling. "Oh, I'm sorry," Marie said at the landing. "I'm just so excited." Her expression changed. "Are you all right? I forget how much room I take up on these stairs." Jessie thought to correct the girl's self-criticism, but Marie motioned for her to proceed. "I'll be waiting for you upstairs," she sang.

Jessie rested a moment on the landing, gazing out through the round stained-glass window that looked over the trees and onto the lake. Whitecaps dotted the water like whipped cream on cupcakes. Jessie couldn't hear the girl racing up the carpeted stairs, and it surprised her that a young woman of Marie's size was as light as poppy seed on her feet. At seventeen, Marie had the vibrancy of Jessie's younger sister, Selma. Marie's love was participating in activities with her friends. At least that's what she chattered about whenever she and her mother, and sometimes Jessie, were alone together. Lately her chatter had been about the first dance of the season.

"You must come with us," Mary Harms, Marie's mother, had told Jessie. "You'd be the belle of the ball with your tiny waist and winsome ways."

Jessie gracefully declined, said she lacked the proper dress for such lovely events. Truthfully, she hated denying these kind people anything at all, as they'd been so good to her, but she had never been to a dance in her life. Her parents had strictly forbidden such a thing as a principle of faith, and Jessie accepted their view. Having once been held closely by Fred, she realized how dangerous a dance could be. The Harmses didn't push Jessie further even though Marie spoke often of her "real grown-up" event. Jessie encouraged the girl as she swirled her dresses across the bed or considered what powder to purchase to smooth out the occasional bump on her skin.

At the top of the last flight of stairs, Jessie caught her breath. Her camera was heavy. She'd taken it with her to work that morning, though she usually didn't. New snow had fallen, and she couldn't resist the chance to capture crystal on the tree branches etched against an azure sky. She'd even caught the streetcar afterward so she wouldn't arrive late at the studio, looking carefully around but not seeing Mr. Behrens, who claimed to take this route often enough to have seen her before. Jessie decided that had been his "I'm a potential beau" approach.

In her room, she found that Marie had turned on the gaslights and now moved from side to side in happy anticipation, pointing to the bed. Jessie set down her camera, pulled off her gloves, removed her muffler; the hatpins she placed in the porcelain holder on her dresser. She unbuttoned her suit jacket, deliberately taking her time, teasing as she would have with Selma back at home.

"Open it, open it! I told Mama I wouldn't wait until she got home. Oh, I hope you like it."

"Your family is much too kind to me," Jessie said. "It's an awfully large box. And early for Christmas."

She lifted it with both arms, shook it, and slowly untied the string. The box had no label, but it was large enough to house new bed linens, and Jessie wondered if that might be what it was. With winter coming, flannel sheets would bring welcome warmth. The coal heat didn't rise efficiently to her third floor. The box was heavy.

"Shall I guess?" Jessie said.

"Yes! But quickly." Marie hopped onto the bed, bouncing the box.

Jessie stabilized the box. "Piecing for quilts. That would be perfect for me. I need something to do with my hands in the evenings."

"No, it's not piecings. What else?"

"Hmm. Books? I don't have many to read. Books would be pleasant."

"Just take the cover off," Marie said. "Oh, here. Let me."

Marie leaned forward and whisked the box from Jessie's hands, pulling it onto her crossed legs as she sat on the bed. She shook the cover loose. Pink tissue covered whatever was inside until Marie folded it back. Hundreds of beads glistened in the gaslights. Marie pulled the cream-colored gown out of the box and held it before her.

"It's… I…"

"Close your mouth, silly," Marie told her. "It's a pleasure to behold, isn't it? Mama's seamstress is just the most marvelous of anyone we know. Madeleine makes all my dresses, but this one will look wonderful, which it must for a woman with a tiny body like yours. Try it on."

"I couldn't. I can't accept it."

"Of course you can. People accept presents all the time."

"But you've already… Your family has already done so much for me, letting me stay here, feeding—"

"Oh, we receive payment for you being here," Marie bubbled.

"I'm certain that the time I spend helping you learn about your camera is insufficient payment for all your family has done for me," Jessie corrected.

"Maybe," Marie said. "See if it fits. I guessed at the size, but I think I captured it. I'm pretty good at judging dimensions."

Jessie took the gown from her and held it to her breast while looking in the mirror. "I'd say your guess was quite accurate," Jessie said. She felt as though she held butterfly wings in her fingers.

"Slipping Madeleine one of your own dresses helped get the sizing right," Marie said and smiled. "I bet you didn't even notice it was gone. Well, she only had it for a day."

"You gave your seamstress my dress?"

"Mama gave it to her. I collected it and put it back."

Jessie had wondered if the Harmses' maid had brushed her suit when she noticed the hangers hung differently. She'd been grateful, though now the action felt invasive.

"I'll have to be more aware," Jessie said.

"Oh, Madeleine has your measurements now, so I won't need to revisit your closet."

"Well, it's certainly...elegant," Jessie said. "But..." She put the dress back in the box, or tried to.

Marie grabbed her wrists. "You at least have to try it on, see if it fits." Jessie shook her head. "So I can admire Madeleine's work. Didn't you say your sister was a seamstress? Wouldn't she want her work worn once? It honors the maker."

That made sense. Jessie laid the dress over the screen panel, then stepped behind it to finish unbuttoning her jacket, to remove her clothes and corset. The dress was beautiful, of delicate workmanship. Each tiny bead that covered the bodice would have been stitched on by hand. The whole must have taken hours to secure. She ran her hands over the beads that flowed out like streams onto the skirt, felt the material beneath it. Silk. So grand. It slipped like warm water over her head, settled onto her shoulders, surrounding her lower limbs. Its weight surprised. She stepped out from behind the screen, and Marie gasped, her hands clasped beneath her chin.

"Oh, Jessie, it's like a slipper on your foot, it fits so perfectly. Swirl now. Pick up the train. It has a bracelet tab you can use. That's it. Mama's seamstress took the tucks in just where they needed to be. She probably had enough material leftover to make you a matching purse." Marie pawed inside the box while she said, "You're slender as a chicken leg."

"I'll receive that as a compliment," Jessie told her.

"Oh, it's meant so," Marie assured her. "I'd loan you a pair of my slippers," Marie continued, "but I declare, you have feet smaller than a rabbit's. You'd drown in my shoes. What size are they?"

Jessie looked down at her toes. "They're a three. Not that it matters. They hold me up and take me walking; that's all I care about."

"And now dancing. You'll set all the boys to whistling, Jessie."

It would be lovely to wear, but...

Again those toddler thoughts reached up and screamed, full stops out, *Don't do it!*

Though she knew she shouldn't, Jessie admired herself in front of the long oak-framed mirror. The Harmses' seamstress had witch's fingers. She must've turned one of Mary Harms's older dresses, three sizes too large for Jessie, into this creamy tubular sheath, the very style Jessie had read about that had caused a stir in Chicago papers. If she wore this in public, her mother would gasp, as the dress not only revealed a bare neckline and marked her slender waist, but the material fit tightly over her hips, conforming to the back of her thighs and widening only slightly at her calves and ankles before pouring into a pool at her feet. The neckline was suggestive; the tinsel-wide straps left her shoulders bare. Her sister Lilly would shake her head. Selma would smile and clap, and Roy would grin. She wasn't sure what her father would feel: probably a mixture of admiration and concern.

"Now you have no excuse, none at all. Oh, and look, here's a jacket and a purse." Marie held them up, one in each hand. "Try this on too. Mama will be home soon and you can give us a fashion show."

"Marie." Jessie turned from the mirror. "I just—"

"No one else will be able to wear it, so you may as well accept it. It was meant for you. You didn't ask for it; it arrived unbidden, the very best kind of gift. It would be rude to reject it."

"I know this may sound strange to you since you've grown up around...dancing, but I've never been to...one. It wasn't just the lack of clothing keeping me from your plans. I should have said that before you went to all this effort."

"Never danced? How could you not? As pretty as you are? You must have had a dozen invitations. Didn't you ever go to barn dances at least? Rebecca usually goes home to Cedarburg in the summer to help with harvest, and she says there are lots of barn dances in the country."

"Winona isn't in the country," Jessie said.

"Even I have invitations this year," Marie continued.

"You should have. You're a lovely girl, Marie. Most of the boys I know are just chums," Jessie said. "We went on hayrides, but always with others around from our church." She cleared her throat. "I can't wear it. It's just too stylish."

"You can and you will." Marie crossed her arms over her chest the way Selma might.

"Marie. I don't dance be—"

"Because you don't know how. I'll teach you! Papa will help. It's good fun, Jessie. It is. Here I am, younger than you, but about dancing I'm wiser."

"In a dance there's nothing to separate a man and a woman..." She felt her face grow hot with the memory of being so close to Fred once that she could feel his heart beating against hers. The fabric that separated them had seemed to melt, only cloth and good intentions keeping skin from sizzling skin. She cleared her throat, "I'd be uncomfortable that close to, well, doing movements that—"

"Is that what you're worried about? It's not one of those sporting dances," Marie said. "Goodness, Mama wouldn't let me go to those places either. We have chaperones and no alcohol at all at our dances, and girls and boys only touch their hands together. Surely you could do that."

"It's the idea of it," Jessie said. "Knowing my family wouldn't approve."

"I declare." Marie thumped a pillow on the bed. "There's nothing wrong with dancing, Jessie. There just isn't. Papa and Mama wouldn't do it if there was."

It wasn't Jessie's place to tell the story of Exodus and how angry Moses became when he came upon men and women cavorting about. That's the story her parents told her in explanation, along with vague descriptions of the iniquities of the dance halls, where girls earned a dime for a dance. Her sister Lilly said those dimes bought more than dancing. But even the chaste dances sponsored by the Eastern Star or other civic groups were off-limits to Jessie's family.

Still, Jessie was a guest here, and guests did what was expected of them. She hadn't put others first often enough, but here in Milwaukee she was doing her best to ride a different canoe across a murky lake.

"It's… My parents have always forbidden it."

"I can quote you psalms and verses in Jeremiah telling about young girls dancing and old men being merry and mourning no more," Marie said. "Dancing helps people from being sad, Jessie."

Jessie thought there might be more to those verses than a call to swing and sway, but she didn't pursue the subject. "My family, my mother, would be disappointed in me if I showed up in this. I'm sorry, Marie. I should have stopped you before Madeleine spent so much time making the alterations."

"They weren't alterations," Marie charged. "Mama bought the material new. Just for you."

Such finery! The gift had no ulterior motives. Yes, they hoped she'd join the family at dances, but there was nothing sinister in that, not for those who found nothing wrong with men and women moving cheek to cheek. Jessie had read about the newest dances, like the Bunny Hug and Grizzly Bear.

Marie looked close to tears. "I've already promised my friends, nice young men, that you'd be there. They've seen you at church. You can't disappoint them." Whining was an annoying habit Marie had that her parents indulged and that usually worked for the seventeen-year-old.

Jessie sighed. "It's what I do best. Disappoint. They'll get over it. Besides," she said, brightening as she pulled the dress up over her head, "You'll be there. That's all that matters. And you can tell me all about it. I'll wait up for you."

"It is not all that matters. I've given my word."

"Then you'll have to take it back," Jessie told her, regretting that she'd even tried the dress on.

"Papa said I couldn't go unless you did, that it would be rude to leave a guest at home while I went off partying. This is the first big cotillion of the season, Jessie."

"Let me talk to your father," Jessie said. "I'm sure I can make him understand that I won't mind being left here while you're off dancing."

"How will you explain the expense of the dress?" Marie said. She lifted an eyebrow.

"Guilt does not work on me," Jessie lied. "I'll find a way to pay for it. It'll take time, but I'll do it. I can't have your family supporting me any more than they already do."

"Gottlieb pays for all that," Marie snapped, arms crossed over her chest.

"What?" Jessie felt silk and beads slipping from her palms.

Marie's eyes grew large as a gargoyle's, and she pressed her hands to her mouth. "I wasn't supposed to tell about Gottlieb!" she whispered.

"What does Fred—Gottlieb—have to do with my expenses here?"

"Don't tell Mama that you know. Please, please. Gottlieb said to keep it secret. It was just a kindness, he said, for his past employee, and he was afraid you wouldn't accept it, so he gives the money to

Mama. Oh, oh, oh. Mama will be furious! I probably won't be able to go to a dance until I'm fifty!" Marie threw herself back onto Jessie's pillow. This time the tears Jessie saw were real, the girl genuinely sorry for having let the secret slip out.

"It's all right," Jessie told her as she sat beside the girl on the bed, brushing tear-drenched hair from her cheek. "It'll work out." Confusion made Jessie's stomach hurt. She wiped at Marie's eyes with her handkerchief, her own heart trying to make sense of this truth.

"Can we wait to tell Mama and Papa? Until after we talk about the dance?"

"Deciding when to tell them is the least of my worries," Jessie said. Whatever was Fred thinking, paying the Harms family for her care? What was his intention? She couldn't ask him. But she didn't like it, that was certain.

SIX

Dressing Up Disappointment

JESSIE TOLD MARIE SHE'D KEEP the secret until Sunday. It gave Jessie more time to think. That morning she dressed for services she'd attend with the family. Visiting their German Lutheran congregation worked better than trying to find an Evangelical Reformed church, the denomination she'd grown up in. It seemed kind to share the Harmses' services, and Jessie liked their pastor.

In the quiet reverence of the sanctuary, she hoped to resolve this complication of Fred's payments on her behalf, which made her the "kept woman" her mother had once charged she was. Her parents would be horrified at Fred's generosity. It wasn't right, and yet his kindness warmed her, made her face hot when she thought of his wish to care for her. She didn't deserve his generosity. That's all his offers had been when he'd visited. He'd violated no borders, never even returned for a final supper with the Harmses, just attended the conference and must have taken the train home. But paying for her room and board...

The choir sang, and Jessie let the music wash over her. When had Fred worked out this payment plan with the Harmses? She shook her head. Marie looked at her. Jessie patted the girl's hand to reassure her. Maybe staying with the Harms family helped Suzanne Johnson in an indirect way. Suzanne didn't have to worry about sharing her small apartment with Jessie or what influences might plague a young woman alone in a big city. Most working girls her age stayed in boarding houses or lived with the families they served. Yes, staying with the Harmses might help Suzanne, but it didn't sever the thread that now attached to Fred.

The pastor spoke of "listening to the Lord," then from the book of Matthew, chapter ten, he read, and Jessie turned her thoughts there. " 'And into whatsoever city or town ye shall enter, enquire who in it is worthy; and there abide till ye go thence.' We are told to seek out worthy people, but even more, to abide with them, allow them to cover us, the original meaning of the word 'abide,' and comfort us until we go." Maybe that was all she was doing by accepting the goodness of the Harmses and, by extension, Fred. Allowing them to cover her, to help her to remain safe until she left.

Just before the collection plate passed by her, Jessie decided she'd find a way to repay Fred's gift, costly as it may be. Even if it meant not being able to save as much for her own studio, repayment was the right thing to do. Depending on how much it was, in the end she might have to move out, find a less expensive place to live. Maybe the Young Women's Christian Association could house her. It was quite a distance from the studio, but she could likely afford the YWCA. Maybe she should assess the Milwaukee Settlement House. She would pay him back. Doing this on her own turned one of the wheels on the train that would eventually take her home.

After church, a light snow covered the REO's top. Henry sat at the wheel, Marie already in the backseat with quilts wrapped around her. They could almost walk home from church. It wasn't that far away, but Henry loved to drive his car.

"Come along, Jessie," Marie shouted to her. The girl lifted the quilt, and Jessie slipped in under it, her hands warm in her muff.

"I already told Mama that you know about Gottlieb," Marie whispered to her. "I just had to confess."

One problem was already resolved then, Jessie thought. They'd surely understand when she refused to accept the dress, which she'd decline over dinner. She'd whisper another prayer and hope the rest of the complications would take care of themselves. "Don't borrow trouble," her mother had told her more than once.

"He specifically didn't want you knowing," Mary Harms told Jessie after raising the subject over pot roast. "Just like Cousin Gottlieb to do it that way. He's a generous man."

"He is that," Jessie said. "He bought my Graflex for me." Mary nodded, dotted the corners of her mouth with the pressed linen napkin. "It was a thank-you gift. I'd done extra work for him, while he was ill," Jessie explained. "Photographers often become sick from the mercury poisoning; that's why he gave me the camera."

Henry Harms brushed away her defense. "We know Gottlieb. He's done some foolish things in his life, leaving that good employment he had with his great-uncle in Buffalo, but he's made a name for himself since. Fine wife and family he has too. Good citizens." Jessie picked at her beans, kept her eyes on her plate.

"His uncle helped him during his youth. He's just passing that on," Mary said. "And you're the recipient, Jessie. Nothing wrong with that at all."

"Sometimes people like to give gifts as a way of saying they're sorry," Henry mused, holding his fork halfway to his mouth. "Gottlieb's been known to lose his temper." Jessie looked up at him. She'd never seen evidence of it.

"Oh, I'm sure that isn't the reason Gottlieb secured Jessie's stay here," Mary said.

"I wasn't implying," Henry defended. "Just thinking of why people give gifts. People have motives. I certainly prefer a necklace to speak for my stupidity than having to say, 'I'm sorry,' don't I, Mother?"

Mary Harms nodded. "Yes, you do, even if it does distress me not to hear words of contrition."

Jessie fidgeted. This conversation was much too personal for her ears and not at all like the conversations she'd spent her life around. Besides, it turned her thoughts to home, and she needed a tether keeping her here. *Abide till ye go.* She recalled the morning scripture. The words might also be admonishment to keep her mind on this moment rather than wandering into the future or the past.

"I've decided to pay Gottlieb—Mr. Bauer—back," Jessie said. "It will take time, but I will. And I'll look for another place to stay so he doesn't expend any more on my care than he already has."

Mary frowned. "That would put us in a terrible state, Jessie. We couldn't return the money to him because then he'd know that you know. If you pay him directly, he'll know too, and we'll have disappointed him. And ourselves." She glared at Marie, who lowered her eyes and picked at her peas. "No, your best hope is to just let him help you. You'd be doing us a huge favor, you must know that. The dress and jacket and purse are yours to keep anyway. Marie said you might reject them too— Now let me finish," she said when Jessie opened her mouth to protest. "The dress gave work to Madeleine, so you see, you contributed to her family. By receiving, you are giving."

"We make contributions to the settlement house and the church with Gottlieb's money," Henry said. "You don't cost nearly as much to keep as he sends us."

Would accepting their explanation put other people first, or would it justify her taking undeserved treasures while burrowing deeper into bad prospects?

"Let me think about this," Jessie said. "But can we settle this one issue today? Please don't restrict Marie from her first grown-up dance because I'm not willing to be there. It would be one less weight I'd carry knowing I wasn't the cause of such disappointment."

"Marie told us of your position about dancing. We had no idea," Mary said.

"Dancing is to a German as kielbasa is to a Pole," Henry said.

"Not in my family."

"These dances are merely social gatherings with a Virginia Reel thrown in to wear off energy," Henry told her.

"It's just not right to leave you here alone while we go off," Mary said.

"Couldn't you at least come along and watch?" Marie pleaded. "Wear the new dress for Madeleine's sake? Maybe you could help serve the cakes, couldn't you? There must be something."

What could I do there?

The idea came like a flash-light explosion.

"Do you think people might be interested in purchasing a print of themselves at a dance?"

"A fine idea all around," Henry enthused. "I'll get the organizers' permission for you to photograph people for a small fee." Jessie would have to speak with Suzanne about developing the film. She'd need the studio's darkroom. Maybe she could give Suzanne half the commission. That way she'd make money, and so would Jessie. She'd be working at the dance. It wouldn't be as though she was...dancing.

She'd have to make up a listing so customers would know how much a print might cost and how soon they could expect it back. She'd need a way to get addresses and phone numbers for those who had telephones. She began thinking about the kind of backdrop she'd want, to create portrait shots rather than photographs of people dancing. With the extra funds, she'd be able to set aside money to reimburse Fred. And she could put off the decision about moving to a rooming house, at least until after Christmas. Why, she might even have more to send home for Roy's treatments.

Only one problem remained: Jessie would have to work out why she couldn't wear the dress. A beaded sheath wasn't at all what a professional photographer would wear while she worked.

Jessie entered the Johnson Studio excited. Suzanne sat at the appointment desk as she usually did in the morning, a cup of tea no longer steaming near her fingertips. Dark shadows lingered beneath her eyes, which she lifted to Jessie's.

"Good morning," Jessie said. "Isn't it a lovely day?"

"You're in a cheery mood," Suzanne said.

"I am," Jessie said. She shook the snow from her coat and removed her rubber boots from her shoes. "I have an idea that could make us both extra money, and it wouldn't take any of my time away from the studio."

"Continue," Suzanne said.

"I can meet my other obligations, I'm certain." She pulled the pins from her hat and decided right then that she would buy a different hat, one with a much smaller brim that needed only one pin at the most. Something like a man's hat, without plumes. That would work. She could leave it on while she photographed the outdoors without having to worry about the feathers getting in her way. Maybe she could wear it indoors too, when she photographed professionally off site.

"I've been offered the opportunity to participate in the Lake Drive cotillions held through the winter. The people I stay with, the Harms family, attend those events with their daughter. I've never been to a dance, but they thought people would like having their photographs made when they're all dressed up and looking beautiful."

"It's been years since I've been to a dance."

"Oh... Well, sure." Jessie paused. "I didn't think about your wanting to photograph people. I thought I'd do that. I wanted to use the developing room here to make prints and all, but of course you might want to do this sort of thing yourself."

"What did you have in mind?" Suzanne asked.

"I could pay you half of the fees, and I think we'd both come out ahead. But if you want to do the photographing..."

Suzanne shook her head. "No. I never took pictures." She sighed, picked up the teacup, and sipped, wrinkled her nose at its tepidness or maybe its taste. "I wouldn't be here now if I hadn't married a photographer and he hadn't...died. I have so few photographs of us together. He was always behind the lens. Photographs at a dance," she mused. "Harold and I used to love to dance."

It was the first time Suzanne had mentioned her husband by his first name; she'd always referred to him as Mr. Johnson. "Did you?"

"Harold was very lithe on his feet, considering he was a big man.

Over six feet tall, he was. He'd whisk me around the dance floor, and I felt like a princess, flying." Her eyes filled, and Jessie faltered, not knowing whether to change the subject or allow Suzanne to remember even though it brought her sadness. "Please send me your last pair of shoes, worn out with dancing, as you mentioned in your letter, so that I might have something to press against my heart," Suzanne quoted, holding her clasped hands to her breast. "Goethe," Suzanne told her, blushing. "The German poet. He was a favorite of Harold's."

"We could do it together," Jessie said. "We could." She reached for Suzanne's hand, held its coolness in hers. "Young Marie Harms says the dances are lovely."

"Harold told me that Socrates took up dancing in his old age, saying he'd been missing something essential, but I suspect going to one now would be too painful," Suzanne said, pulling her hand back. She circled the ring around her finger.

"It could be fine advertising for the studio, bring in more clients, people wanting family photographs taken, things like that. I'd need backdrops, something I could carry easily. Maybe a few props. People attending such things would be good clients for us, don't you think?"

"Of course, we never attended a cotillion."

"Come with me," Jessie insisted. "It wouldn't be the same as when you danced with Harold, but—"

Suzanne stood. "No. I don't think it's a good plan for the Johnson Studio either," she said. "The truth is, we have all the work we can handle, just the two of us, and I don't want to consider adding a third person. It's just too tiring for me to work on the accounts, retouch, get the ads out." She rubbed at her forehead again.

"Didn't you ever want to be a photographer yourself?" Jessie whispered. "Doesn't the idea of making pictures and seeing how they develop make you want to see each morning come? Wake up looking forward to what the lens will show you?"

Suzanne stared at her. "I've nothing to look forward to. If you outlive your husband, if he dies on you, you'll know what I mean. You'll introduce yourself as a widow for the rest of your life. It'll be the defining word for you. All your interest in cameras and lighting and such won't carry you any further than the morning light. After that, you'll spend all your time in the darkest of rooms."

Jessie thought then about how Suzanne *did* always introduce herself to clients as the Widow Johnson rather than as Mrs. Johnson or the owner of the Johnson Studio. Surely it put potential suitors off.

Jessie wasn't sure it was good to have an absence affect your life forever and ever, the way Suzanne described it. But Fred's absence now shaped her life. She didn't want to think of that. Instead she wondered what her own mother would do if her father died first. How would she support her siblings still at home? She couldn't run the drayage firm; she'd have to hire an assistant as Suzanne had. Or she'd have to sell the company and maybe move them all in with her grandparents. Women often depended on the kindness of family.

Jessie was fortunate indeed to have a way of supporting herself... well, almost by herself.

"What if I don't mention the Johnson Studio? Could I still use the darkroom in the evenings? Maybe Sunday afternoons? You'd earn half the fee."

Suzanne looked thoughtful, but in the end she shook her head. "Maybe you can set up a darkroom at the Harmses' home. I...I don't want to sound ungrateful, Jessie, but it's difficult to have someone always around. My evenings... I don't know how to explain it." She pressed her fingers against her temples, and Jessie thought a headache might be making its way into the conversation.

"Are you feeling all right? You haven't been working with the chemicals, have you?"

"No. I'm just tired," she said. "I hate to put water on your fire, but if you could have a darkroom where you live, it would save you traveling here. It would be much easier for you. For both of us. I really do want to have time when it's just me here, alone."

That was that, then. Jessie would have to dance to another tune.

SEVEN

Poetry of Feet

IF SHE DIDN'T SEND MONEY to her family this week, well, maybe for two weeks, Jessie would have enough to buy chemicals for the developing solutions, as well as paper. At least Suzanne had said it would be acceptable for Jessie to purchase those from her. Once she was paid by the dancing clientele, Jessie'd have money to send home again. She planned to ask the Harms family to allow her to use one of the attic rooms as a darkroom. She'd have to bring the film down to the second floor to bathe it, but aside from that, it wouldn't take much at all to make the room dark enough to work in.

On the other hand, it might be better to forget the cotillions, focus instead on finding an inexpensive place to live and storing up funds for when Suzanne sold the studio. Jessie would be let go and would have to find a new place to work. She could sense Suzanne's disinterest in maintaining the business. Perhaps the headaches made her decisions for her. Jessie would look at possible openings closer to home. She wondered if Eau Claire or La Crosse, across the river from Winona, might have need of an independent photographer to help run a studio.

"Just when I think I have a plan, life jumps up to tell me I don't," she said out loud. Her day had been like a ride on Mr. Ferris's wheel: one moment she felt on top, and the next she was swooping toward the bottom.

The idea of buying the Johnson Studio niggled at her mind. But

Jessie couldn't imagine making enough to buy out Suzanne, and while she might believe that Jessie would pay her back, Suzanne probably couldn't afford to extend credit. Jessie could ask a bank for a loan, but no one in Milwaukee really knew her to put in a good word for her. She would not ask the Harms family to speak for her. Truth was, she hadn't thought about living the rest of her life in Milwaukee anyway.

There was much to like about the city, especially the Mitchell Park Conservatory, where flowers bloomed nearly all winter inside the cavernous greenhouse. The Harms family had taken her there to see the ten-year-old building that demonstrated the city's love for year-round foliage. But she'd always imagined she would own a studio in Winona, close to home.

The idea of photographing at the dance had given her such a jolt of excitement that she just had to make it work. Photographing people at dances wouldn't be allowed in Winona, that was certain. Her parents would be appalled. She swallowed. If things worked out, she'd find a way to tell them, to ease any worries they might have. She couldn't find another place to live in Milwaukee with such short notice, however, so remaining with the Harmses made sense. A new line of income would allow her to put money aside, however small the amount. Meanwhile, she felt excited about the attic darkroom. She would take Mr. Ferris's wheel up and see what happened from there.

Six inches of new snow fell on the Saturday of the cotillion. Mr. Harms said they'd have to take a cab because his REO touring car wasn't built for snowdrifts or the winds pushing at high speeds across the lake. As a help to Jessie, they'd planned to arrive early so she could set up her camera and allow the lens to warm up, because moving from the cold to a warm room would cause it to fog over.

She didn't want to make the Harmses have to wait for her, but she'd lost track of time. They'd agreed to her darkroom plans, and she'd been setting up, making the large attic area on the other side of her room her own. Her attic had one narrow window at the end, which she'd covered with several layers of black cloth. She'd have to sit hunched because the wall sloped, but it was otherwise perfect. Chemical tins lined a shelf above the developing trays. The chimney ran up through the space, providing precious warmth.

"Haven't you dressed yet?" Marie asked, fanning herself nervously. All day the girl had been skittish as a gopher being hounded by a dog. Rebecca, the maid, had piled Marie's thin hair up on her head, then flattened it with a black velvet bow. Still, she looked lovely. Marie fidgeted with the clasp on her black velveteen cape. "You have to wear the new dress so you'll look like you belong there."

"I'm wearing this suit, Marie."

She wailed her disappointment: "You'll look too stuffy!"

"Marie…"

"You have to wear the dress Mama had made for you! You have to. If you don't, they'll remember that I told you about Gottlieb, and Papa will be angry all over again and not let me go to the dance."

"All right, all right." Jessie relented, though she couldn't imagine Henry Harms stopping things at this point; he probably waited in the cab. "I'll take the dress with me and change once I get everything set up. Your parents are waiting, and I can't pick up the train and carry my camera at the same time."

"Can you hurry?"

Jessie pressed her hat against her curls, grabbed her camera case and the dress from the closet, then padded down the stairs to where Henry waited in the foyer. He took her camera, and Rebecca helped her carry the dress box and a few more props out to the cab, where Mary and Marie now waited.

"This is so exciting!" Marie sang out as Jessie slid onto the leather seat. "My first dance ever!"

"You've been to them before," her mother corrected. "Remember that time we were with—"

"But this time I have a dance card. I'll be meeting boys—I mean gentlemen—there," Marie said.

Jessie remembered being that excited once, but not about a dance.

At the Traub Bank building, Marie grabbed the dress box while Henry paid the cab, then took his wife's arm to assist her up the stairs. Jessie managed the camera and the props on her own. Jessie had taken a single chair the Harmses had loaned her to the dance hall the day before. Many of the social and sporting dance halls were open every night except Monday, but the Traub building, housing respectable businesses by day, only opened for weekend dances and only during the season. The wide marble steps took people right past the oak doors of the bank and doctors' offices, up to the third floor, where the smooth oak would be covered with cornmeal to make the dancers' feet slip more easily across the floor.

"Wait until you see how they've decorated," Marie said.

"I was here yesterday, remember?" Jessie said.

"Oh, but they always do amazing things the last day. Don't they, Mama?"

Mrs. Harms concentrated on the stairs but nodded.

"We can take the lift," Jessie said.

"I wouldn't step foot in that Otis thing," Mary Harms said. "Can't imagine riding in a room held up by cables and such."

Jessie had no such reservations. Marie asked if she could go with Jessie, and Mr. Harms concurred, looking wistful as he held his wife's elbow to steady her up the stairs. The girls walked to the end of a narrow hall, where an operator wearing white gloves opened the sliding iron-grill door. They stepped inside.

A jolt as it started caused Jessie to gasp, and Marie squealed. Jessie felt her stomach jump, but the excitement of the entire evening ahead caused this as much as the Otis lift, of that she was certain.

At the third floor, the elevator stopped. Jessie stepped out with her case and the props, and Marie ran ahead with the dress box. Jessie lugged her items down the hall, then went through a door into the dance pavilion, where Marie waited.

"Isn't it swell?"

Jessie stood in awe at the overnight transformation. The room was decorated like a Christmas gift with bows and glitter, including two fifteen-foot trees in each far corner, both with tiny gaslights, silver tinsel, and red bows taking one's eye to the ceiling and the angels on top. Red and white bunting lined with pine boughs looped across the tops of tall windows. The pine scent swept through the room. Candles, not yet lit, sat at every windowsill and on the long tables being loaded with food. Holly abounded. So did mistletoe, on great red ribbons that hung from the dozen bright chandeliers. Jessie twirled around slowly. She hadn't seen anything as lovely.

An orchestra warmed up on the far side as the Harms adults huffed through the door. "I'll take the Otis down with you," Mary said, puffing to catch her breath.

"Its advantage is in the going up," Henry said.

Jessie looked for the chair and backdrops she'd arranged earlier. They'd been set aside as the musicians apparently needed the additional space. She scanned the room and headed for the end of the refreshment table. It was not too close to any mistletoe, but closer to the punch bowl and tree than she wanted. She had hoped for an uncluttered area to hang her backdrop. At least social dances didn't allow liquor. She could be grateful for that.

She'd brought an extra roll of film in the side pockets of her Graflex, but she hoped she wouldn't need it. Finding a place dark enough in which to take the film out and put another roll in could be difficult.

She set to work rehanging her backdrop, aware of the time. She wanted to look calm and professional when she greeted people, to put them at ease. The musicians played a waltz. She tried not to think of the elegance she was so unfamiliar with. A professional presented herself as though she knew just what to expect, as though she did this sort of thing every day. If only she could get the backdrop hung! She was taking too long and noticed a few impatient glances from those organizing the refreshment table. She stepped up on her chair, hoping to reach the top and get the adhesive better situated. She was using a glue ball to press the backdrop against the plaster walls, but the cold air made the adhesive brittle, and the backdrop, heavy as it was, kept slipping.

"Maybe I could be of assistance."

The voice came from behind her, a Yankee accent. With the orchestra playing real music now, no longer warming up, she knew people would be arriving soon. She had yet to change into the Madeleine dress.

"I should be finished in a moment," she said. "I came earlier to get set up, but I chose the wrong place, apparently."

"If I might make a suggestion..."

Out of frustration with the backdrop, she wanted to say, *No, you might not make a suggestion,* but instead she turned.

She looked down on him from her chair perch. "I know you," she said. "You're Joshua Behrens."

He looked surprised. "And you are?"

"In a better mood."

He looked confused, his slicked-down hair parted to one side. He wore a cream-colored wool evening jacket with a black cummerbund, just as Henry was dressed. But he was much younger and thinner than Henry Harms.

"Jessie Ann Gaebele." She allowed him to help her down, and then she shook his hand when on two steady feet. "We met on the streetcar last summer," she told him. "I wasn't very sociable."

"Ah. Yes," he said. "I remember. I haven't seen you all winter. I thought you'd moved. Did you?"

"I like the walk. I don't take the streetcar unless I have lots of time."

"Lots of time?"

Jessie smiled. "I like to ride to the end of the route and back when I've a bit of thinking to do. I could use help getting this thing hung," she said, turning the conversation away from anything personal.

"I assume you're going to photograph guests." He looked at her camera set up on the three-legged stand. "Not necessarily while they're dancing. Might I suggest you move your studio to the front area, in the wide hallway?"

His idea annoyed her, and her face must have shown it.

"Perhaps leave one of those framed photographs here to remind people, with your listings on the refreshment table. But in the corridor, they'll see you when they come in, before they enter, and they might decide to have their portraits made right then and there, just after they've checked their coats."

And if they didn't, they'd never think about having a photograph made once they entered the ballroom. She'd be out of their sight and out of their interest as they took in the glittering trees and the music. She'd never get them back outside until they were ready to leave, and then they'd be in too much of a rush to want their portraits made.

"I don't think that will work," she said.

"Besides," he continued, "there are hooks along the one wall where you could hang your curtain." He pointed to the backdrop now dangling from one side.

"But I need the lighting." She pointed to the chandeliers. "That's far more important than the hooks on the wall."

He paused. "Then I'll do my best to help you hang your curtain."

"It's a backdrop," Jessie told him as the final adhesive let loose and the material fell to the floor.

"Perhaps if we moved your chair to that corner over there, you wouldn't need it—the curtain. The backdrop."

Jessie let her eyes move to where he pointed. This idea had merit. "Let's try it," she said. She picked up the camera on its stand and carried it to the corner he'd suggested. It wasn't perfect, but he was right about not needing anything behind the subjects. The white wall would reflect the light, and the corner was one of the few places without a window breaking up the long walls. Maybe she could drape the backdrop over the back of a tall chair to have as contrast. Or maybe not.

While Jessie considered, Joshua removed the framed portrait hanging on the wall closest to the corner. "An old ancestor," he explained. "I'm sure he won't mind being unhung for an evening. It's fortunate he wasn't hung when he was alive." He grinned.

"I can't imagine anyone with his portrait in a bank building having to worry about being hung," she said.

He laughed. "You'd be surprised."

"I think this might work. If you'd be so kind as to retrieve my chair for me, I'll bring the props and be ready." From across the room, Marie pointed and mimed slipping a dress over her head. "I promised my hosts that I'd change into more formal wear." He nodded and motioned for Jessie to precede him so they could collect the last of her belongings.

She was aware of his presence behind her as they walked across the floor. That surprised her. She usually didn't notice young men, except as potential portrait subjects, and she'd been so busy getting settled that asking to take his picture hadn't occurred to her. She would do it later. He had fine features: a patrician nose not unlike Fred's. Joshua was much closer to her own age, unlike Fred, who had twenty-six more years of living than Jessie. She wondered for just a moment what Mr. Behrens might be thinking as he followed her slender frame. She shook her head.

"Is something wrong?" Mr. Behrens asked her.

"No. I'm fine," Jessie told him. It might have been a lie, because for the first time since Fred, she felt her heart beating a little faster, and it wasn't because she was frightened or riding on an elevator. She'd have to ask Henry what he knew about Joshua Behrens. She didn't need another "episode."

Marie Harms, first dance
December 1910, Milwaukee
5 x 7 Graflex

Intuition

I wish I could tell you how much Marie enjoyed herself. She talked about the cotillion for weeks afterward, and I have to say that her enthusiasm wore well on the other guests. She insisted I take her photograph first and made a fuss about it in a positive way. She wanted people to notice me so they'd have their portraits made. She wore a bighearted spirit that night—and always, truly—but I wonder how many others would have stepped forward if dear Marie hadn't made such a joy of the activity.

She danced often. But if she noticed I was standing alone in my cream-colored dress, she'd bring her partner over, and after introductions she'd suggest he have his portrait made. The men mostly refused, and then she'd say, "Well, I'm not afraid of a camera," and she'd sit down on the wicker chair or stand behind it looking regal and say, "Shoot me, Miss Gaebele." The boys would laugh, and I would bend to focus the lens. I wondered if I wasted material that night, but a good reputation begins in many forms, and like sourdough starter, one needs to put in a little flour to take more out.

When I look at this portrait, it's the shadows I see first, how they heighten certain parts of the image: her neck and back, the side of her face. Shadows tend to make what is not in them more interesting, illuminate in a revealing way. My time in Milwaukee was like that: I lived in Fred's shadow even though he was far away, and yet in that separation, things became clearer. The props, for example.

The palm fan had been a whim. At the Bauer Studio I would have grabbed peacock feathers or a basket filled with pine boughs to set beside the wicker chair. But the palm fan beckoned because it was so different. I wondered if Suzanne and Harold had gone to Tampa once, if that's where Suzanne had gotten it. Lots of people from Winona traveled to

Florida in the winter, and I imagined people from Milwaukee taking the train out of snowstorms to wade in Tampa's tepid bay. Or maybe a client had given it as a gift, as such frivolities often seem critical in one place and time but are of no use when one returns home. It's an advantage to a photographer that seemingly needless things like palm fans can be turned into practical applications for a portrait. Even the shadows on the fan give interest, as though the tips of the fronds are reaching for light.

Marie wanted one of her dance partners to be in the photograph with her, but none were willing. She didn't seem to take that poorly. Instead she told them they could purchase a print of her alone to help them remember their evening. Several of the fellows standing around watching me pose Marie chuckled at that. But she turned her card over for them to write on, and to my surprise, four gave me their addresses and paid my price of fifteen cents so I could send them a print.

Several dance couples had their portraits made. From the way they talked to each other during the pose, I assumed that most of them were married or engaged. Who would want a portrait made together without an understanding of a shared future? What would a person do with an old portrait if the relationship ended? One wouldn't want to keep the print, surely a painful reminder of a broken promise or abandoned love. On the other hand, if something happened to a loved one—if they were still the dear one when disaster struck—then a photograph would be a treasure without price.

One couple that I could tell were newly courting smiled as I stood them together rather than have the man sit and the woman stand behind him. I posed the beaded purse she carried in front of her, occupying both hands, and had him place one arm loosely around her shoulder. He tugged her to him momentarily but then returned his arm to a position of decorum. She turned to look at him; he gazed at her, and I could see new love in the exchange. They risked a permanent record of this evening and carried a hopeful future with them.

Marie looks younger than her seventeen years here. I'd pulled the sleeves just off her shoulders, then used the fan to cast a shadow on her back so her mother wouldn't worry over how exposed she was.

The palm fan turned out to be the hit of the evening. Several girls asked to be posed with it. That surprised me. I suppose there ought to be room in life for spontaneity, for having things happen as they might, without always organizing and arranging. Still, the one time I'd jumped into momentary desires, I'd paid a price. I was still learning how to distinguish an instinctive move that advanced my art (like using the palm fan) from an impulsive one (like allowing Joshua Behrens to kiss me beneath the mistletoe without protest). I still had much to learn.

EIGHT

Prone to Wander

THE MISTLETOE KISS ENLIGHTENED JESSIE. Aside from affectionate pecks from her family, the only time she'd been kissed by a man had been by Fred. His kisses, passionate and consuming, had been tainted with all the colors of the rainbow, including the deep violet shade of guilt. Still, it was the memory of those kisses that preoccupied her. She longed to repeat them despite the path they'd taken her down. She supposed allowing the kiss at the dance spoke the wrong words to Mr. Behrens and she ought to have acted offended. But she'd noticed a few other couples chastely touching puckered lips, their bodies wide apart as they arched beneath the mistletoe. People around them applauded, their gloved hands making sounds as soft as summer raindrops on rooftops. She and Mr. Behrens weren't a couple, of course, but he had been attentive through the evening, filling it with mindless chatter several times when they stood alone in that corner.

"Isn't your name on any dance cards?" Jessie had asked him when the music started and he didn't leave to select a dance partner.

"I came to make my parents happy," he said. He pointed to a matronly couple that might have been his grandparents given their age. "They rather indulge me, so this is a small return I can give them."

"Are you spoiled?" Jessie teased.

"Ruined. Just like a puppy given its way every day." He grinned at her, and she noticed then the dimples that reminded her of her younger brother, Roy. "And what about you? Don't you have a dance card? I'd put my name on yours."

Jessie shook her head. "I'm working."

"Yet you're dressed for dancing," he said. "And beautifully so."

"My wearing this made the Harms family happy," she told him.

"Ah. So you return their indulgence now and then too. Spoiled, like me."

"Ruined," she concurred. It was closer to the truth than he could know.

He didn't press her to dance, and often they stood in comfortable silence, not unlike the way she and Fred had when they worked together, before everything changed. She kept making observations that reflected positively on Mr. Behrens—Joshua, he insisted she call him—how he reminded her of her family, that his help was reminiscent of a friend's in Winona. She had meant Voe, yet his dapper looks brought Fred to mind.

So when she turned from putting away her camera at evening's end and saw him holding the mistletoe high over their heads, a bashful grin on his face, she didn't back away. He bent, hesitating just a moment to see if she'd object. She was eighteen, nearly nineteen, a woman working on her own. There was nothing wrong with one small kiss to mark an evening's labor.

Kissing Joshua had been like bussing a cantaloupe: interesting, with a new texture to remember, but no desire to repeat it.

Each pulled away. "Merry Christmas," he said to her.

"Good greetings of the season," she told him. She dropped her gaze to her shoes.

Jessie assumed she'd never see Joshua Behrens again except in passing. He'd planted no relationship with that mistletoe kiss.

Weeks later she regretted the kiss and wanted to avoid Mr. Behrens, who had jumped off the streetcar more than once since the cotillion when he saw her tramping through the snow. She really didn't want to run into him again. Still, the first time he leapt off the streetcar to join her, she found that she enjoyed his company again as they trudged along. She learned that his father was the chief cashier at the Traub Bank building where the cotillion had been held (that really was his ancestor's portrait on the wall) and that he attended Marquette University's newly opened business school. Mr. Behrens didn't seem the least threatened by her occupation or her independence and told her with pride that Marquette permitted women to attend starting in 1907, the first Catholic university in the country to do that.

"That's the year I started my own training in photography," Jessie told him. She shared little of her personal history but did tell him of her wish to one day have her own studio. They spoke of politics. The politician Woodrow Wilson planned a trip to the Cream City. The butter-colored bricks from which so many of Milwaukee's buildings were made gave the city its nickname. Jessie didn't keep up much with political things but found Mr. Behrens's observations interesting, just as Fred's had opened her eyes to events beyond Winona's streets.

When he tried to find out more about her, though, asked questions beyond photography, or wished to expose the reasons why she'd left Winona and how long she planned to stay, she colored her answers in pale shades. She felt herself closing the way a morning glory did at night, protecting, showing its finery only with the invitation of true light. When she reached her destination, he had caught the next streetcar and continued on his way, and she hoped her reluctance to reveal herself served as wind to any seed he thought that kiss might have planted.

Then, in mid-February, Joshua knocked on the Harmses' door and asked to see her. Marie carried the message up the stairs to the darkroom, where Jessie worked to develop the portraits from her most recent dance. Henry Harms had arranged for Jessie to attend and photograph a few other dances through the winter, and she was grateful for his efforts. She'd just placed the canister holding the film into the stop bath solution, then recited psalms that took her two minutes, the amount of time she needed before checking the status of the film.

"He's downstairs, right now!" Marie shouted through the closed door, respecting Jessie's rules about not letting light in. Jessie had admonished her about never entering if the sign "Working!" was on that attic door. "Papa wouldn't mind your seeing him, I know."

"Your father doesn't have say over me," Jessie said. She hadn't meant to sound upset. Her head throbbed. Maybe it was the smell of the chemicals. She was shorter with people than intended.

"I only meant he's a nice man. Your own papa would approve."

Marie was too young to understand. "Please tell him that I'm busy, working in my darkroom."

"I'll bring him up, and he can talk to you through the door. Is that all right?"

"No! He'd see my bedroom, Marie. Just ask him to leave his card. I don't know why he thought he could come calling anyway."

She would have to put him off more firmly, just as she had the other men from the cotillion who had given her their addresses on the back of Marie's dance card. When the prints were ready, she'd arranged for a time when the men could come to the Harms home and pick them up. They came, collected, and if they tried to linger, she made herself as unapproachable as Winona in a snowstorm and sent them on their way. Apparently, she'd have to create a blizzard to keep Joshua away.

Marie left but returned in a few minutes. "He says he'll wait."

"Confound it," Jessie said to herself.

"I'll entertain him in the parlor," Marie said. "With the chessboard."

"Surely he won't stay that long," Jessie said through the door.

She heard no answer so went about finishing her work, annoyed now that the time she liked to take felt rushed. It wasn't Joshua's doing, but she couldn't calmly go about her work knowing that people waited. She carried the film downstairs to wash it, then back up to hang it to dry. To make prints, she had to carry the film to Suzanne's. She finished, wiped her hands on a towel, then headed down the three flights of stairs to the receiving room.

"It's really not a convenient time for you to call," Jessie told him when she entered the well-lit room. Might as well make everything clear before he clouded it with courtship.

"He's a good chess player, Jessie," Marie chirped.

"I'm sure he is." She wished Marie would leave but didn't want to suggest that she go ask Rebecca to bring tea, as that would make him linger. He said nothing, so she greeted him more civilly. "Mr. Behrens." She nodded to him, her hands clasped in front of her. "What can I do for you?"

"My classes have resumed, so I've missed you these last weeks."

"So you have."

"I'll ask Rebecca to bring us coffee or tea," Marie said.

"No! I mean, I'm sure Mr. Behrens can't stay."

He stood now, hat in his hand. "You're right, Miss Gaebele. I can't. But before you toss me out, I've a business proposition I thought might interest you, and negotiations always go better with tea."

"I'll speak quickly," Joshua said when Marie left. "May I sit?"

"Of course." She took the chair angled across from the settee, intrigued by his comments but on guard. He moved the chess table aside so he could sit down again and leaned forward, elbows on his knees.

"It's risqué, this idea, but an independent woman as you are might see the possibilities," he said. "I remembered your saying that you hope to have your own studio one day, and I see this as a way toward that."

Had he found a studio for her? What good would that do though? She didn't have the money. Her photographing of cotillion participants did appear to have a future, though the income was limited for now. Once people saw the prints, then others would want copies or their own pictures made, and that's where her investment of time and effort could pay off. Reprints. Fred had always said that was where photographers made their way.

"Something daring, is it?"

He couldn't know about that streak in her; she'd never told him anything of that.

"Nothing bawdy or vulgar, but yes, a bit provocative, for a woman." He cleared his throat. "I attended a sporting dance the other evening. They meet nightly at the halls, except for Monday, attracting people from throughout the city. Mostly our age or younger. Always good music, from a local band or two, and they play the newer dances like the Texas Tommy and the Grizzly Bear. The Turkey Trot. Quite a show. There are saloons attached to these. Women aren't allowed in the saloons, of course."

Saloons and dance halls together, the perfect mix for trouble. She could just hear her mother's voice.

"Aren't they the places where women charge a dime for a dance? Maybe for...other favors?" Jessie asked.

"Not these. At least I didn't see that happening. What I noticed is that when the men headed to the saloons, the girls just sat around talking. Sometimes the band lured devoted couples to remain. A few girls danced with one another. Others headed outside, and I suspect they might have been smoking. But the majority stayed inside. Exuberant," he said.

"Excuse me?"

"It was written all over their faces, Jessie. The girls were, well, beautiful." He hesitated. "Not in the way you are. But in that way of girls who have worked hard all day emptying other people's slop jars or sweating in the candy factory, then get to blow off steam moving their bodies to music."

Jessie knew something about the fatigue of a day's labor. She'd worked for a printing company in Winona, and her younger sister had worked as a domestic and now as a milliner. Her older sister, Lilly, held a supervisory position in the glove factory. They hadn't "blown off steam" by going to dances, but she could understand why many would. They'd had to find other ways to "wash the soul of the dirt of daily living." Jessie had embroidered a punch kit written in German that her mother had translated as *Music washes the soul of the dirt of daily living.* She was certain her mother had meant the music from her favorite hymn, "Come, Thou Fount of Every Blessing," and not the tones of the Turkey Trot.

"Here we are," Marie said. "Set it right there, Rebecca. Have you been to any of those halls?" Marie asked the housemaid then.

The color on the maid's round face paled to cream. "I…I…"

"Marie, it's none of our business what Rebecca chooses to do with her own time."

"I didn't mean to be rude. I just thought she might have."

"You were eavesdropping," Jessie said.

"I was, but it's so interesting. I'll never get to go to such places." She pouted, folding her arms over the bodice of the sailor dress she wore. The wide collar in the back bounced with her movement of chagrin.

"Will that be all, miss?" Rebecca set the tray on a side table. Faint color had returned to her face.

"Marie…," Jessie prodded.

"I'm sorry if I offended you," Marie said.

"It's fine, miss," the maid said as she curtsied. "Fact is, miss, I have been to such a dance. Once or twice."

"Would you mind giving us your opinion of it?" Joshua asked.

"I don't know nothin' about music, sir," she said.

"But when you were there, would you have been interested in having your picture made?"

"Oh, sir, I wouldn't want no one to know I'd been there."

"What if it was just your face? Not the background at all. No one would know where the picture was made. What then?"

Rebecca blushed now, lowered her eyes. "Girls like me don't have coins to do such as that. And it's not the sort of thing a girl like me should want… I've work to do in the kitchen, so if that's all?" She turned to the door, and when no one stopped her, she left.

The girl's slight of herself caused Jessie to say, "Why shouldn't girls like Rebecca have their pictures made? They're just as deserving as anyone else."

"I agree. There's a certain stigma attached to the dance halls of working people like your maid, but except for the saloons, there's really nothing to separate those dances from cotillions," Joshua said.

There's nothing separating me from Rebecca either, Jessie thought. We're both working girls who couldn't aspire to cotillions without the interest of a wealthy beau. In a wash of emotion, she felt grateful. Grateful that she'd been given a talent, a passion, and someone to nurture it in her. She was equally grateful that she hadn't eclipsed all that good by succumbing any more than she had to temptations. She'd found a way out by coming to Milwaukee. That's all those girls were doing: finding ways out, seeking pleasure after a long day of labor. If she could help them do that, give them a little joy through her own talent, what would be wrong with that?

"I've heard that the punch bowl can get sparked at cotillions," Marie said.

"I believe the word is *spiked,*" Joshua corrected.

"Looks like Marie knows as much about this saloon business as I do." Jessie laughed.

"What I'm proposing," Joshua said, "is that you take your camera business to the sporting dances. You might not be able to charge as much as at the cotillions, but you could photograph six evenings a week if you wanted to. So there'd be volume."

"Few reprints though," Jessie said after a minute of thinking. "Six evenings…when would I ever find time to develop and print? After I got back home, I suppose." She could give up sleep or print the film during her lunch breaks.

She'd also have to find a way to get the prints to the working girls, which wouldn't be easy. Many of them only got one day off a week, and it wasn't always Sunday. She didn't want to work on Sunday anyway, though she'd proposed doing just that to Suzanne. *But maybe for something like this.*

"I wouldn't see many referrals for more portrait shots. Besides, these girls send most of their money back home. They haven't much to spare. You heard Rebecca."

"That's why you'd have to charge them less. Maybe make postcard-size prints instead of the larger ones to save paper costs."

Jessie nodded. "Then there's the lighting," she said. "Those dance halls won't have much light, will they? And it'll be at night. "

He sat back. "I hadn't thought of that."

"If you stay at the same dance hall each night, if you find just the right one," Marie said, "maybe you could bring your flash-light equipment and leave it there, have your own corner like you did at my dance. You wouldn't have to take things back and forth. Except your camera, of course. Maybe photograph just three nights in a row and leave a fourth night for the social dances."

"Swell," Joshua said clapping his hands. "That's a great idea, Marie."

She beamed.

"It would provide a way to get the final prints to their owners," Jessie said. "When they come back. But then there's the issue of, well, my being a woman alone there. I mean, there are other girls present, of course, but they're chums with each other. I'd be off to the side and—"

"That's where I come in," Joshua said. "I'll be your assistant."

"You? I can't afford that," Jessie said.

"Won't cost a dime."

It could cost her much more than that if she allowed it.

"Why would you do this? Just to spend time with me?"

"Ah, that too," he said. "But I have an ulterior motive. I've proposed this as a business idea for one of my classes. I'd ask only that you share information about your costs and expenses with me so I could write about it. And maybe use a few of the photographs to illustrate my report. I'd earn top grades while you earn money for your studio, and together we'd bring cheer into the lives of those working girls. A perfect proposition." He rubbed his hands together.

It just might be. Jessie felt new energy surging through her.

But what would her parents think about her participating in such dances—if they ever found out? Not only were men and women dancing closely together, but they had no chaperones the way the cotillions and social halls did, and liquor loomed close by. Despite what Joshua said, there might well be dance-for-dime activities going on there too, maybe even more. The mixture of freedom, alcohol, music, and pent-up men and women together for an evening was a temptation cocktail.

Don't do it.

But why shouldn't girls like Rebecca have their portraits made? The Bauer Studio often had clients who made their money in the lumber camps or flour mills. They'd schedule sittings. They'd be awkward at first, but like so many patrons, when put at ease, they made wonderful subjects. Jessie loved seeing their expressions when they picked up the final prints. Warmth spread inside her when they responded with delight at their own images, and she wondered then if giving to others might actually mean receiving more in return. She thought of Minnie Raymond's cheerful face.

There'd be good challenge in taking such photographs, at night, in a hall. She'd have to work quickly, make easy arrangements to contact them to let them know their prints were ready. Or maybe they'd have to follow up with her. If they paid her there, she wouldn't really need to know where they lived. But if she knew, she could send out notices at Christmastime, encourage them to come in for a more formal sitting and remind their friends that they could have their pictures made too.

She imagined herself at the dance hall, pictured wet curls stuck to the sides of a girl's cheeks, the tightly woven hair bobs loosening as she danced. Jessie could almost smell the ale and cigarettes and young bodies hot with sweat. Most of all she envisioned the smiles. It was one of the surprises at the cotillion, the smiles. People acted happy at the dance, as though the music really did wash away the cares of the day. She knew music could do that. How many hours had she spent listening to piano and organ sounds? Selma, her younger sister, had a singing voice, and Jessie remembered fondly how soothing her songs could be.

Maybe dancing didn't have to be a bad thing, Jessie thought. Maybe, just like a young woman moving into a man's world, the new decade offered a change in the way to view things that wasn't sinful. Her parents might not approve, but she wouldn't be dancing herself. She would be watching, standing off to the side, waiting for the intermission so she could get engaged, take a picture. There couldn't be anything wrong with that, so long as she held true to her own virtue.

"Let's work out final details," Jessie said. "You find the perfect hall, Mr. Behrens, and we'll visit the manager together with our business venture. I just hope he won't want a part of the profits."

"He'll be happy the girls have a reason to come back, to pick up their prints. Deal?"

"Deal," Jessie said as Joshua shook her hand.

Jessie's stomach hurt a little as she headed back up to her room. People were always anxious when they did something unfamiliar, weren't they? It didn't mean she was doing something bad. Nervousness was part of human nature, not necessarily a warning. She hummed her way back up to her darkroom, vaguely aware of the lyrics from her mother's favorite hymn: "Prone to wander...prone to leave the God I love." Whatever could that mean?

NINE

Adding Light

MUSIC THROBBED AS DANCERS STOMPED the pine floors at the Prospect Avenue dance hall. They danced the Grizzly Bear, looking more like ducks waddling with their derrières stuck out and their feet stomping as they shouted, "It's a bear!" in unison. Jessie startled every time they yelled. An energy Jessie was unfamiliar with filled the room but also heightened her own senses. People laughed and talked loudly, their eyes wide, perspiration dripping at their temples as they wiped their faces and necks. The yeasty smell of ale from the saloon next door made Jessie sneeze.

This was another world, a wildly exotic one where limbs and emotions intermixed in unpredictable ways. The fiddlers bowed and stomped along with the dancers at a frenzied pace that gathered volume as more young people made their way into the already crowded hall, shouting to friends, laughingly calling attention to themselves. The closest Jessie had ever come to this energy was at the church hayrides, and even those were subdued by the presence of adults riding along in the back of the wagon.

What surprised her most was that she had no desire to join them. She didn't want to dance, didn't want to be out in the mix of the throng. Just as she'd endured the hayrides because of her sisters, she was here because it was part of her larger plan to put herself into a respectable studio of her own. This was her kindergarten, she smiled to herself, a place to learn.

Joshua helped her set up the camera, challenged with leveling the tripod on the uneven wooden floor. Twice they moved it, hoping to find a better place. Lighting was terrible, and the hall's gaslamps appeared to be set low so people could disappear into the darkness off the dance floor doing who knew what. She'd have to use a flash light each time to get any image at all.

One interested girl, a foot taller than Jessie, came over and asked questions about how the camera worked but declined when Jessie suggested she have her portrait made. The girl had stood along the wall for quite a while without a dance invitation and only hobbled around doing the Grizzly Bear with other girls when the men moved into the saloon. Revelers returning from tipping up their pints laughed louder, danced even more bawdily. One or two came by calling her "girlie" and asking if she wanted to experience their wonderful talents on the dance floor.

Her uneasiness grew when Joshua's attention was diverted. At the cotillion, she hadn't really needed him, but he'd remained close. At the sporting dance, she could have used his help. Still, she was an independent woman, so she ought to take care of herself and not worry about Joshua's neglect.

Then, as she held that uncharitable thought, Joshua walked toward her with a potential client. When it appeared that even curiosity wouldn't lure the dancers from their stomping to her camera, Joshua worked the crowd, bringing people over. Jessie clicked the shutter and got the person's name, quick as a flash to send them back out to the floor, Joshua escorting. Now he led a girl who worked in the candy factory. Jessie made a note in the ledger book, swallowing a sigh as she did. She was tired; she'd worked a long day, and it wasn't over yet.

As the night wore on, she photographed several young women, talking fast to get them to settle while she lit the flash-light powder and pulled the shutter. The puff of light and smoke brought her a few more customers, and she was busy most of the evening. When Jessie noticed young girls and boys pairing off, looking for dark corners, she glanced at her lapel watch. Midnight. Her best business hours appeared to be between 10 p.m. and the bewitching hour. She'd have to decide if two hours of action were worth the preparation and developing hours required.

Joshua took longer and longer checking back with her, and by the time she'd brushed off the third ale-influenced male, she affirmed her mistake in staying longer than she ought, let alone in coming to begin with.

Then a fight broke out in the alley. She could hear it because the owner had opened the door to let cold air inside, but snow, cigarette smoke, and apprehension rode in with it. Men streamed out from the saloon forming a circle around the two pushing and shoving each other. Girls clustered at the door, and Jessie found herself shoved up against the wall with the camera pushed into her chest. Where was Joshua?

What was she doing here?

What else could I have expected? she thought. She was in a place she shouldn't be, and her presence had spoken in ways she didn't want. Had she learned nothing from her motorcycle episode? Apparently not. The idea of making additional income had lured her here; that and Joshua's persuasion and her own desire to see how other people did things. She wanted to help Joshua with his business coursework, and she did think young working women ought to have their photographs made. But not here, not in this place. She shouldn't be here, working or not.

"Let's go," Jessie said when Joshua finally pushed his way through the crowd toward her. The fight gawkers thinned out; the men in the circle hugged each other over slurred words and bruised faces; and people moved back into the hall. Cigarette smoke clung to their clothes as they passed. Jessie coughed. "I've had enough. Let's pack up."

"It's early," Joshua told her, genuine surprise in his eyes. "You have to be patient. Business ventures take time."

"Not my time," Jessie said. She began folding up the camera, putting it into its case. She picked up the flash tray and tripod.

He grabbed her hand, gently but firmly. "We've barely been here three hours," he said. "Lots of the girls won't even get here until later."

"They won't arrive until after midnight? I can't imagine that. And how is it that you know the routines of working girls?" Jessie said. For the first time she questioned Joshua's real motives for being here. "Is this your slumming time?"

He frowned as he dropped her hand. "I only wanted to help," he said.

"Help yourself," she said.

Still, there was no reason to be angry with him; she'd come here of her own free will. "I'm sorry. That wasn't called for. Coming here was a mistake, for me at least. You can stay." She said that last lightly so he'd know she wasn't upset, but also to hide how much she wanted him to leave with her. She'd have a difficult time getting back to the Harmses' at this hour. She'd have to get a cab, and she wasn't sure she had enough coins with her to pay for it. Or she'd have to walk the several long, dark blocks back home carrying her equipment. She hadn't planned ahead at all.

"I'll go with you," he said, but she could tell he didn't want to leave. "I just wish you'd stay. Until two o'clock. Everything is over by then."

She'd have to develop the film when she got home, then print it the next day in order to bring the images back the following night. She'd need him even more then to help her not only take new pictures but also find the girls and give them their prints. And if she didn't find them, she'd have to locate them at their places of employment. She didn't have the time for any of that. She just hadn't thought this through.

"This is embarrassing," Jessie said, "but I'm not sure I have the money for a cab. If you could loan me the fare, I'll return it. That's all I'd need, and really, you could stay."

He hesitated, and she almost suggested he take her home and then come back. But before she could, he said, "Thanks, Jess," using a nickname for her that she hated. "I'll get a cab for you and pay him." He hiccupped. *He's been drinking.* "Thanks for understanding."

He left to find a cab while Jessie finished packing up. Her face burned with humiliation, from her own poor choices, the failure of the entire idea. The evening had cost her cab fare, lost time, and dignity, and she still had to come back the next night to give the prints to those who had already paid.

Water under the bridge. She'd have to do finish what she had started. She straightened her shoulders. Another lesson learned, she hoped.

Joshua hailed the cab and paid the fare, then leaned down before he closed the door. He'd been interested in his coursework and not her, which ought to have pleased her. At least she didn't have a sticky, maudlin good-bye to say.

"I wish you'd stay longer," he said. "Things are just getting started."

"Not for me," she told him. "I'll pay back the fare."

"Don't bother," he told her. "It's a business expense." And he closed the cab door.

When the cab broke down, Jessie got out to walk. She wasn't that far from the dance hall on Prospect Avenue, and she considered going back and waiting until Joshua was ready to leave. But returning would only prolong the humiliation.

"If you w-w-wait, I'll get it fixed," the cabby told her. "It's a c-c-cold one. You don't want to be walking in this."

"You… Your speech," Jessie said.

The driver bowed his head. "S-s-sorry, miss."

"No, please. My brother stammers."

"Used to b-b-be worse," he told her. "Th-there's a school here. On First."

"There is? I'll look for it."

"Wish I could t-t-take you by there. If you wait…"

Waiting. Why did everyone expect her to wait tonight? But waiting in the cold was worse than walking. "Thanks," she told him. "But it'll be better for me to keep moving."

Jessie headed out. Fortunately, she hadn't brought the props along, only her camera and tripod and the flash pan. She juggled the pan and her tripod in one hand, carried the camera case in the other, and began to trudge past walkways, some shoveled, others thick with icy snow. In places, she stepped out into the street, where the cabs and drayage carts had packed the snow as hard as concrete, avoiding the deeper drifts in front of houses. The cold air hurt her lungs. It was easier walking in the street, but when she met a horse-drawn sleigh near St. Mary's Hospital, she stepped back onto the sidewalk. A new moon slivered the sky, casting pale light. She tried to remember just how far it was, how long the drive to the hall had taken. A couple of miles at least. No use complaining. At least she had a warm coat and wool muffler wrapped around her head and throat. She wore mittens instead of carrying a muff. That had been wise. The lake winds stung her nose and cheeks, exposed to the night. Her eyes adjusted to the darkness. She could see pale lights from houses.

Perhaps, as Joshua said, the maids were just now heading to the dance, having put the households to bed. That was why they didn't arrive early, Jessie thought. Early arrivals were those who got off work from the candy or sewing factories. Domestics had to keep working until all went to sleep and then slip out of the households to dance and chatter. They'd grab a few hours of sleep, then rise early to tend to the pampered girls like Marie. And like her, Jessie thought. She was being pampered by the Harms family. And by Fred. She put him from her mind and thought of Roy.

A school for stammerers! She'd not heard of such a thing, but then, she hadn't been paying attention to resources that might help her brother. She'd ask about the school tomorrow and see what she could find out.

She thought about Rebecca, the Harmses' maid, and wondered if she would go out dancing tonight. Surely not to the club Joshua had picked; it was too far to walk. There must be halls closer, but Jessie hadn't paid any attention to where they might be, letting Joshua make the choice.

She slipped and stepped into a drift. Snow filled her boots, chafing her ankles despite the woolen stockings. "Confound it!" she said, the words making her think of Fred yet again. It was his exclamation of frustration. She brushed away the snow, picked up the tripod, and told herself that if she took photographs away from the studio again, she'd leave the tripod and flash lights at home. She was steady enough to hold the Graflex, or she'd learn to be, to save her time and effort.

Her walk forced new goals: become more proficient and see about that school for Roy.

Try as she might, Jessie could not get the camera through the teller's window. "Just take it. It's enough, I promise," she said. "You can believe me."

"We don't accept such d-d-deposits," the teller said. He looked like Jessie's father but had her brother's dimples, and he wore a hat similar to the one Joshua Behrens wore. His mustache belonged to Fred. "If you w-w-want credit, we must b-b-believe you. Do you have anything else to s-s-secure the loan?"

Jessie shook her head. "I'm prone to wander," she told him.

"What about your s-s-soul? How have you invested it?" The teller reached his hand as though to grab her, and she fell back, the camera slipping slowly to the floor while he wrenched her heart—or maybe it was her soul—from within her. Blood dripped, wet and red all over the cream beaded dress. However would she explain it to Mary Harms?

"No! No!" she screamed, waking herself up.

Her heart pounded like a racehorse running, and her entire body felt wet. She threw the covers back and shivered as the cold air hit her. She pulled a paisley shawl from the corner bedpost, one she often wrapped herself in while she read at night. But last night she'd fallen quickly into a dead sleep. She looked at the clock: four in the morning. She'd barely been in bed an hour.

Wide awake now, she padded to the window to watch the full moon. It looked so serene reflecting off the snow-covered city. Everything appeared still and separate, as though each household went about its business alone. She didn't often dream. This nightmare made her shiver. A gulping cry escaped her chest, and she felt the waves of despair move through her as she allowed herself to weep. It was pitiful to feel sorry for herself, she knew that, and yet her chest ached as though she had lost her soul. That teller in her dream had taken it, or maybe she'd left it behind at the dance hall or in Winona. All the months of separation, of writing home and saying how fine things were, of reading and rereading the letters from her family, of longing just to go back, to go home...all the ache of absence weighed on her as she looked out at the cold, sterile moon.

Jessie prayed then. She prayed she'd settle what she was supposed to learn while in this distant place. It had been her idea to come, to begin a life that had more future than longing after what could never be. Wasn't the wish to own a studio worth pursuing? She was certain that leaving home, with all its reminders of past waywardness, would put her on the right path.

"Please, please, please," she whispered, not even certain what she so desperately needed. "Don't let me wander."

A sound in the hall startled her. She wiped at her face with the edge of the shawl, pulled it tighter around her flannel gown. Rebecca's room was also on this third floor, across the hall. She hoped she hadn't awakened the girl. *Maybe she went to a sporting dance too.* Jessie eased open the door.

Rebecca stood in the hall holding a candle, a nightcap on her head.

"Are you all right, miss?" she asked.

"I'm sorry to wake you."

"Nothing you did," Rebecca said. She pressed her fingers against her eyes, rubbing sleep from them. "I weren't sleeping well."

"Me neither."

Aside from the day in the receiving room when they'd briefly discussed the sporting dances, Jessie'd rarely conversed with the girl except for discussing daily tasks. She felt ashamed that she'd never noticed the girl's large eyes or the way she chewed at her fingernails as she did now.

"Did you take pictures, then?" Rebecca asked. "At Mr. Behrens's dance?"

"Just a few," Jessie said.

"That's too bad. I guess I were wrong then."

"The lighting was poor, and people came to dance, not to be photographed."

"You was there a long time."

"I left at midnight, but the cab I took broke down and I had to walk. Miles."

"Oh, miss, let me heat water for the rubber bottle for you. Mrs. Harms loves one at her feet."

"You've done a day's work already, Rebecca. Go back to bed."

"It's no trouble." Jessie shook her head. "Thank you then, miss," Rebecca said. She turned, then stopped. "And, miss? Girls do like their portraits made. I know a lot of girls who'd like a picture."

"Just not when they've been dancing," Jessie sighed.

"Someplace nice instead," Rebecca said. "If you don't mind my mentioning it, a place like the Harmses' parlor."

Why hadn't she thought of that?

TEN

The Present

THE ARTICLE ANNOUNCED "the opening of the third class for stammerers now available in the Milwaukee Public Schools." It was funny how when one paid attention to a topic, pebbles along the path appeared out of nowhere, leading one closer to it. At Jessie's query, Henry Harms told her that there'd been a special school in Milwaukee since 1909 for children and adults with speech impairments, and now children received instruction in public schools too. "A few instructors at Detroit's stammer school don't like having public teachers trained. They want the business," Henry told her. "But our schools want to reach whoever needs it, same with the stammer-school people here." He'd shown pride in the community's efforts, with no embarrassment at all that there were children who needed such extras.

Maybe Roy could come and live with her here in Milwaukee! She wouldn't be alone then, and he could receive special instruction just by attending the public school. Or maybe she could afford extra help for Roy at the stammer school.

She took the streetcar, then paced back and forth in front of the North-Western School for Stammerers, gathering her courage. Eventually, she ascended the stone steps with plans to introduce herself to the director. While she waited she noticed the Winter Term Announcement with its bright poinsettia on the front cover wishing "Merry Christmas and Happy New Year" in a big ribbon. Inside, a message from director Lee Wells Millard listed twelve reasons why one should choose his North-Western School. Jessie liked number four: "Our method is void of all singsonging, time-beating with the arm or hand, nodding the head, heel and toe movement, monotone drawling, sniffling, and of substitutes and subterfuges of all kinds." She smiled, recalling some of the activities suggested to Roy by the Mayo brothers' hospital, where he'd had to try to speak while swinging his arm in a figure eight. She knew he hated that practice. "Th-th-they l-l-laugh," he told her, speaking of his schoolmates. "I l-l-look like a sc-sc-scarecrow."

"And you feel like you'd like to fly away," she told him. At least she made him laugh.

"He'll be with you shortly," Mr. Millard's secretary, a skinny man with round glasses, told Jessie as he sat behind his desk.

Jessie thumbed through the Winter Term Announcement until she found the tuition page. The cost was beyond anything she could imagine raising for Roy! She stood to leave.

"May I help you?" The baritone words were spoken by a man wearing a three-piece suit with a red handkerchief in his coat pocket.

"I don't know," Jessie told him. "I, that is, I...have a brother who, well, he stammers. He had a fall as a child, and—"

"Our method deals with both the science of speech and the psychology. We're familiar with such issues. Won't you come into my office? We can talk about your brother there."

"I'm afraid I'll be wasting your time," Jessie said. "I have no way of paying up front for any kind of tuition; my brother doesn't even live here. And I don't imagine you accept credit."

"Some of our students come from thousands of miles away," he assured her as he stepped back and pointed toward his office. "We have people who pay on credit, over time. Our dormitories and staff provide all that anyone needs."

All that anyone needs. Wouldn't that be heaven? Jessie thought as she walked through the man's door. All she had to do was convince him to believe in her ability to pay. Oh, and convince her parents to let Roy come and live with her in faraway Milwaukee.

Jessie's birthday arrived on a sunny day in February, the same day as the fallen President Lincoln's birthday. She was nineteen. She said nothing to the Harmses about the day and expected nothing special. Melancholy settled onto her shoulders as she planned to spend her first birthday away from Winona, separated from her family. Milwaukee was full of separating firsts: Thanksgiving, Christmas, and now her birthday. The day did bring back memories of birthdays past, including the jokes of her uncle August and the affection of her grandparents and family. She recalled the pillow fights with her sisters in the bed they all shared and her father shouting up through the heating grate in the floor, telling them to "settle down or you'll bring the bed down on the kitchen table and your mother never will get the birthday cake baked." She remembered the gift of her camera case and the photograph Fred had taken of her tucked within it, and the camera he'd given her another year.

"Put him from your mind, Jessie Gaebele," she told herself.

Her parents sent her a card that held a small coin purse with a dollar inside. Her mother told her to buy herself a bauble. Her bauble, bought with a tincture of guilt, was film she needed to photograph the Saturday cotillion dances.

But when she arrived home from work that February 12, Marie Harms greeted her by saying they had a surprise she would never, ever guess and that would make her so happy. Marie clasped her hands and unclasped them with a wry smile that lit her face. Jessie wondered if her parents might be waiting in the parlor. Her heartbeat quickened. "Close your eyes," Marie sang as Jessie let herself be led into the room.

But it wasn't her parents; it was a cake. A lovely cake with Jessie's name written in lavender-colored frosting.

"How did you know?" she said as she pulled off her gloves. "Happy Birthday" spread in yellow just below her name.

"Oh, Gottlieb told us," Mary said. "His Winnie has the same birthday as yours. Did you know that? He wrote and mentioned the plans for Winnie's party and said that brought you to mind, and he thought he'd send a note along with his...ah..."

"Payment for my room and board," Jessie finished for her.

"So I had Rebecca bake the cake. Henry will love the dessert, so don't say we shouldn't have."

She wouldn't say that to them, but she thought it in reference to Fred. He shouldn't have told them, and he shouldn't be paying for her stay here. Her need to repay him was an increasing weight of guilt. She'd have to unload it in the future and would consider how to do that more carefully than she'd considered Joshua's business proposition.

"We have a present for you too," Marie said.

"Now that you shouldn't have done," Jessie said.

"It's something we already had," Mary told her, touching Jessie's elbow. "Come see."

Henry Harms had apparently decided that Jessie could use a room in their home as a studio—but not the parlor. And while the third floor held an unoccupied servant's room, Mary didn't want strangers moving through the house. All this was told as part of the story while Marie repeated, "Keep your eyes closed," and they led Jessie into a downstairs room that had once served as a sewing room.

"It has good lighting, especially in the morning," Marie pointed out. "I know you said that matters." Windows frosted with ice let sun spill into a room more than large enough for backdrops and chairs. Its location in the house meant running up the stairs to develop film, but that was a small price to pay to walk through this door to her future.

"But how did you—"

"Rebecca said, 'Wouldn't it be nice if Miss Gaebele could take pictures in the parlor?' and I said that was a keen idea and told Mama, and she talked to Papa, and here you are."

They'd actually listened to their maid! Jessie would make certain that Rebecca's portrait was the first she took in her new "studio."

Jessie considered letting Joshua know that he might have another subject for his business paper, but she'd not heard from him since she repaid the cab money. "You didn't need to," he'd said the day she rode the streetcar hoping to find him. He was right: she didn't need to repay him since the cab hadn't taken her home, but she didn't tell him that. She'd given him her promise and she kept it. Beyond that, they had little to say, and she was relieved that she wouldn't be seeing him again except in passing. There'd been little flickering light inside her heart when she'd met him, just a notice that he was a fine-looking man. But she hadn't convinced herself there was anything more. She'd been truthful at least about that.

So Jessie's studio began not in the way she'd hoped: it wasn't where she wanted it to be, but she would take what came her way, believing that each photograph she took put her closer to a real studio in Winona, closer to paying for Roy's treatments, and closer to home.

She had sent the information about the stammerers' school to her parents. She talked to the school's owner several times over the next weeks and convinced him that she ought to photograph the students at the school come spring. Mr. Millard thought that a fine idea once he'd seen her samples, and Jessie left that meeting with her stomach in knots. She could convince people of her abilities but wasn't sure she believed in them herself. However was she going to photograph the students, follow up with the dance cotillion patrons, and still be a good employee for Suzanne Johnson? Had she taken on more than she could do?

Jessie couldn't imagine Roy living in a boarding school even if everyone there suffered from the same speech problems as he did. No, she hoped to have him come for the summer session and share her room at the Harms household. If he liked it and if he did well, they'd explore his staying in Milwaukee and maybe finding their own apartment together. If she could make that come about, her exile in Milwaukee would at last have been for something truly good.

Into separate envelopes Jessie began putting her savings. The first held payments for the cost of her stay with the Harms family. She'd decide when she left whether to give it to them or to "Gottlieb" himself. And when the time was right, she'd confront Fred about his taking care of her.

A second envelope kept the portion she sent to her parents once a month with a sum added for Roy. A third held money for personal needs and for her own gifts to charity, and the fourth held coins saved toward the purchase of a studio, ideally one in Winona. Her family's absence from her daily life wore a dark color; she wanted to replace it with bright light.

As spring approached, Rebecca brought her friends who wanted their photographs taken in a nice place. The matrons of the households where the girls worked took notice of the quality of Jessie's photography. Upon learning that her studio, such as it was, operated in a well-respected district, they made appointments, and Jessie's business began to grow.

"I can help with phone calls," Marie suggested one day after she arrived home from school. "You could also show me how to keep records of the prints. I can work for you after class."

Jessie still had to repay Suzanne for the paper, but her employer had allowed Jessie to purchase an enlarger on credit so she could print the film at the Harms household. Keeping track of everything did take time.

"I can't pay you very much, Marie. It wouldn't be right for you to—"

"It would be good for me to learn a trade. Papa started out as a bookkeeper."

"There's still the matter of payment."

"Show me how to develop my film, the way you do it, in the

darkroom. That would be payment enough. Besides, what respectable business doesn't have a receptionist?"

"It would help," Jessie said. "But next fall, you'll be off to college. Don't even think about making this kind of work your future."

"Mama wouldn't let me," she said. "But until then, I'm yours, Miss Gaebele." Marie curtsied. "When I'm not visiting my friends or sledding or skating. I have such a busy life."

When Marie headed off for a skating party while Jessie developed film, it crossed her mind that maybe she spent too much time in photographic pursuits. She didn't have conversation to share with the Harmses over Sunday suppers unless they spoke about photography or sermons. Marie stopped asking her if she had any beaus when Marie began to be courted by her own peers. But Jessie had her goals; those consumed her, giving her scant time for pleasure.

Her future success required vigilance. Jessie knew that like a kite she could be riding high one day but be swooped down in a flash by a change in the wind. She would put in as many hours as she could in the event that Suzanne decided to sell. If that happened, she'd need an alternate plan. She didn't want to stay in Milwaukee all her life, so buying the studio wasn't an option. Her "Harmses' studio" wasn't enough to survive on. She needed to consider work elsewhere—not Winona. She wasn't ready to go back there. But she must not be caught without a plan. She would order a photographic magazine that listed assistant positions. They might be in faraway places like New York or Seattle. She'd keep watching. Meanwhile, she'd save and one day enter a bank and show them that she was good for the payments, that they could give her credit to buy a studio when she found just the right one. Hopefully one day in Winona—when she deserved it.

In March, Suzanne asked Jessie if she had any hobbies. Jessie was startled both by the personal nature of the question and that she didn't really have an answer. "I like music," she said. "I wish I played the piano."

"Every woman should have a hobby," Suzanne said. "Piecing or sewing or gardening. Something she can lose herself in. Maybe even fall back on to earn money."

"I get lost in photography," Jessie said. "It's my hobby and my work. What about you?"

"Harold and I used to like to travel. We spent a week in Florida once, when the weather here was ghastly cold. But Harold liked Wisconsin winters. I think he enjoyed telling people how cold it was here or how much snow he had to shovel, to demonstrate his hardiness. Especially when we traveled south. We played tennis then. And Harold was going to take up golf, President Roosevelt's game." Suzanne was thoughtful, and Jessie wished she had a hobby if for no other reason than to keep this kind of conversation going. "Such pursuits help a person during a challenging time I think."

"I'm sure they do," Jessie said. "I like to skate," she remembered. The two worked in silence while Jessie wondered what had initiated Suzanne's interest in hobbies.

"Me too," Suzanne said then, surprise in her voice. "Or did. I just haven't had the energy for skating since Harold's death."

"The Menomonee River is still frozen over, and there are ponds."

Suzanne frowned. "Oh, I wasn't thinking of now. These headaches…"

"You said yourself that hobbies help in times of trial. I'll see if Marie has an extra pair of skates," Jessie said. "Maybe doing something you like would make the headaches go away. My sisters and I used to skate on Lake Winona. And we tobogganed down the hill from the cemetery too." She wished she hadn't mentioned the cemetery.

"I doubt that skating will address my headaches," Suzanne said. "More likely it'll bring up bad memories."

"Memories aren't supposed to hold us hostage," Jessie told her.

"They're meant to transform us, make us different, but in a good way. When someone is missing from our lives, I think the memories of them ought to bring us comfort, a hopefulness that even though they're gone, we have them here." She touched her heart. "We still know them in ways no one else ever will, so they stay a part of our lives."

Suzanne started to speak, then halted, but she didn't retreat to her apartment the way she usually did. Jessie hadn't known she possessed that bit of wisdom, but the saying of it comforted. She didn't feel so alone when she thought of the happy times with her family before things got complicated. She needed to bring the memories into this place so that she could have confidence instead of concern. Separations could color a soul with good shades, she decided, and not only be reminders of loss.

Marie's skates did not fit Jessie well, not even with stockings stuffed into the toes, but Jessie didn't plan to make any quick moves. Her skates were back in Winona, and it hadn't occurred to her to bring them. Chilly March winds brushed against their faces as she and Suzanne held hands and poked their skates out onto the frozen river.

"I can't believe I let you talk me into this, Jessie," Suzanne said. Jessie didn't correct her. Suzanne had been the one to follow up on their conversation. The next day she had told Jessie that Saturday would be fine for skating. Jessie had to scramble to rearrange a portrait sitting so she could go and chastised herself for making commitments that caused her complications. But it was worth it, because she was so pleased that Suzanne wanted to do this with her.

"Do you have a headache?" Jessie said as they sat at the warming house putting on their skates.

"Only from the cold," Suzanne told her after a moment of thought. "This is how Harold and I met," she said. "I'd come here with our youth group, and I guess my lanky body must have stood out above the other younger heads. Anyway, he sought me out, introduced himself, and his smile nearly melted the ice beneath my skates." She laughed, and the tiny mole on her cheek disappeared inside pleasant wrinkles. Jessie watched closely for signs of sadness as Suzanne told her tale, but there were none on this day. Her own spirits stayed kite high.

It took Jessie a bit of time to get her skating legs, her twists and turns making her think of the wild dances of the sporting hall. Suzanne looked like a flailing scarecrow, arms straight out, legs threatening to slide into splits. She found herself laughing, hard, and Suzanne did too. They both took spills, once while trying to help the other up. Their laughter kept them a puddle of wool coats and skirts and mufflers on the ice until a couple skated by and the man offered his hand to both of them. They stood, supporting each other, and shouted thanks as he and his partner glided off. The laughter filled Jessie, both Suzanne's and her own. The cold wind froze her mouth so she mumbled her words, which caused even more laughter.

They skated for more than an hour, mostly going around and around the swept area near the warming house. Dark tree branches etched the sky lining the river. Speed skaters raced low past them and around the bend out of sight, leaving Jessie and Suzanne with the children and couples swirling.

"I've had enough," Suzanne said then. Jessie nodded, and they skated without hanging on to each other toward the warming house. No one else was in the hut, but they could expect company soon enough. March promised spring, but the low sun in the opaque sky still spoke of winter, and the popularity of the warming house with its scents of wet wool and burning wood wouldn't allow them to stay alone for long.

"It is a coupling world, isn't it?" Suzanne said as they sat by the stove to remove their skates.

"You noticed that too," Jessie said.

"When you're widowed, that's all you notice, how everything is in twos. You remember what you don't have anymore, all the things you have to do alone."

What Jessie missed had been part of an awkward trio. Shame kept her from mentioning it. She wondered if Harold had known Fred, or maybe Suzanne had met him at photographic association meetings. "How long were you and Harold married?" Jessie asked.

"Three years, two months, and five days. I was a few years older than he, but it didn't seem to matter to him. It mattered to his mother, however." Suzanne sighed. "Neither of our families was very happy about it I guess. And soon after we married, his mother passed away. I always wondered if Harold thought our decision to marry had hastened her death, but we never talked about it. Eventually we would have. We didn't have much time together to talk about all those deeper things."

"It's good that you didn't let your mother-in-law's opinion keep you from those happy years," Jessie said.

Suzanne nodded. "They *were* happy years, and my family came around before he died. I've been thinking about what you said the other day, about memories keeping a loved one alive. I'm planning on seeing Harold again one day, and when I do, I don't want to have to explain why I spent so much time being sad when he came to mind. He'd be pleased I went skating. I'm going to do a few more things that I've been putting off too."

"Good. Don't be sad when you look at the bruises from all the falls we took either. 'Bottoms up' has new meaning for me!"

Suzanne laughed out loud at that. "At least my headache is gone. You're good to have around, Jessie. I'm going to miss you."

"I'm not going anywhere," Jessie said as she bent to hook her shoes.

"No, but I will be. I was going to wait to tell you, but now is as good a time as any." She pulled her mittens back on, stood. "I've sold the studio, Jessie. I'm going to begin again with Harold's memory with me, but making new memories too. The new people take over in June. It's a couple, and they've decided they don't need any hired help." She hesitated, then added, "I won't need you after the fifteenth."

⟡

April 4, 1911

Dear Sister,

How are you? I am fine.

How did you spend your birthday? I thought of you and wondered. You never mentioned it in your last letter. Did I tell you that Mr. and Mrs. Bauer came in to Lottie's and bought a round muff for Winnie? Her birthday is the same day as yours. The one they chose had a satin lining with curled hair for the stuffing. I told them they ought to purchase gloves as well and I quoted from a valentine I'd seen: "If that from Glove, you take the letter G, then Glove is love and that I send to thee." Mr. Bauer said he'd remember that, and they bought a one-button glove that I guessed would fit Winnie to her wrist, which is what a one-button size is designed to do. You probably know that, but it's what I'm learning at Lottie's. Mr. Bauer then told me stories of gloves and how in ancient times a glove was like a name, a signature on a piece of paper, and that a king was given authority by the delivery of a glove. I can't believe that last is true, but Mrs. Bauer said she was sure I wasn't interested in his history facts, so I guess it must be so.

Spring has come to Winona at last, and I'm happy about that even if it does mean that preparing the garden ruins my fingernails. Oh, did I tell you that a professor at the normal school made a special photograph of scenery east of Sugar Loaf? His new lens was written about in the paper. Did you know about that new lens? You probably did.

What are you taking pictures of in Milwaukee? Does it have a Sugar Loaf you can drive to the top of to see the whole city?

Lilly's sewing many dresses but not enough that she can leave her job at Stott's. She was elected treasurer for their laboring group, so now she arranges for gifts when someone has a baby or when there's an accident and a person can't make gloves there anymore. She said she got more referrals for new gowns when you worked at Mr. Bauer's and maybe she'll take her Fine Stitching as YOU Like It cards back to the Bauer Art Studio, as they are probably all gone. Did you know that Mr. Bauer had a new sign put up that added the "Art"? Anyway, Lilly wrinkles her nose and says maybe she won't, because making money from that studio after all that happened there isn't "a Christian thing to do."

Yesterday we went fishing along the Mississippi River. Papa put the worms on Mama's line, and she got the first, the biggest, and the most.

We saw the Bauers there, all of them. Mrs. Bauer and Russell did most of the fishing while Mr. Bauer walked with his hands folded behind his back and watched Robert and Winnie wade, chasing polliwogs. I guess they have a cottage there because the children ran up to this house every now and then and brought out apples they shared with Roy. Winnie brought Mr. Bauer a straw boater from there when the sun started beating on his head.

The oddest thing happened there. I wish you'd seen it so you could explain it to me. You're good at observing things. Papa failed to put his hand out when Mr. Bauer did, to shake it when they recognized each other along the shore. Maybe Mr. Bauer's hand had fish goop on it, but that's never stopped Papa from taking a man's hand before. He didn't even tip his hat. They had words, too, but I couldn't hear them. As silly as it sounds, I wish they'd had fans to hold so I could have seen what they said, or exchanged a glove. What do you think that means? I didn't want to ask Papa why he was rude because his jaw gripped tight when he turned his back and walked away. Mr. Bauer's hand looked like a stick adrift as he dropped it to his side.

That's all I have to say for now. I still wonder how you are. I'm fine.

Your little sister,

Selma

The girls of Marquette
May 30, 1911, Marquette University, Milwaukee
3A Graflex

Homesickness

What were these young ladies of Marquette University pointing at? It wasn't me, though I fell into that photograph too. There I was, big as life with my manlike hat atop a shadow pointing toward them. Detail and balance required that I block out that shadow and a section at the top when I enlarged it from postcard size.

Joshua arranged for the picture. Yes, he found his way back to me, so I was able to at least thank him for what he'd started, my studio in the Harms home. He saw me one day on the way to the postal building as I carried a box of packed items. I told him I'd be leaving soon, and he said he was sorry to see me go. I didn't say that my leaving wouldn't be much different for him than my being in Milwaukee, as I hadn't encountered him here all that much. That would have been rude. And who knows, maybe if I'd stayed I might have found reasons to cross his path. I could have done worse in my life. In truth, what separated us was my annoyance at going along with something I knew was wrong and my assumption that he didn't regret not having taken me home that evening as a gentlemen should have. Or maybe it was that we came from different worlds, though our dreams were tinted with the same shade of hope.

So when I trudged up the marble steps of the postal building with my box, addressed to my father, I accepted his offer of help. I planned to send the heavier items I'd accumulated by rail. One trunk would go to Winona, storing winter things I wouldn't need, and the other I'd ship to Eau Claire, Wisconsin, where I'd secured employment. I'd only be visiting Winona.

Joshua and I went for sandwiches afterward, and he told me how his classes had gone and that he planned to work for the bank through the summer months. I told him about my making portraits of domestics and their matrons and shared with him how much I loved to see the faces of the girls when they picked up their prints. I didn't retouch much on those prints, but the matrons, they needed more work to wipe away a wrinkle here, a thickening chin there.

"I'm going home for a visit," I told him, "before heading on to a studio in Eau Claire. I've been separated from my family for too long."

He talked about homesickness then, a term I'd never heard before, about how people can actually get ill from separation, have stomach pains, headaches, or worse.

I had not been ill, unless such a homesickness was the cause for my waking in the night, sleep vanished in an instant, when I punched my pillow, knowing I must go back to sleep or not be alert for tasks daylight demanded. I'd lie for hours aware of an emptiness of spirit. I wished for someone with whom I could share my longings and regrets. Sometimes I ruminated in the darkness, adding up the funds I'd saved, thinking about Fred's kindnesses while sorting those acts from knots he put into the thread of our connection, knots that kept me from truly untying our bond. Loneliness marked my time in Milwaukee, but maybe homesickness described it better, could fill the hole devoid of family, house, and community. I wondered if having a new name for the feelings would lessen their impact. No one had claimed my heart here in Milwaukee except the Harms family. Would I be homesick for them? Probably not. I wondered if that made me hardhearted or just pragmatic.

Joshua and I said good-bye. Then, a few days later, he called and asked if I'd like to come to Marquette, where the girls were planning a picnic before leaving for the summer. They wanted a photograph made. I said I'd be pleased, and when he offered to pick me up, I said it wasn't necessary. I would only bring the camera, since I'd cultivated a steady hand and wouldn't need the tripod. But he insisted, saying that finding the place on campus might be difficult and it was no bother at all for him to come by.

From my first encounter with the Marquette women I could see that they'd one day be professionals with their college degrees: teachers, I guessed. But when they talked about their coursework, I heard words like telescope and laboratory and physics, the latter a word totally unfamiliar to me. Women were moving into many fields, which I should have realized, my being an uncommon woman with a camera in her hands.

A couple of the girls were older than I imagined a student might be, and I wondered about their stories, making them up as I watched. Maybe one was widowed like Suzanne and had the means to pursue an occupation rather than sell her business and move in with her sister in Chicago. One girl with perfect olive skin made me wonder if she might be an Indian, for her speech had a rhythm different from the rest. Later, when she described where she'd spend the summer, she mentioned Winnipeg, so I knew she was Canadian, but maybe from a First Nation too.

I felt shy around them all with only my grammar school graduation certificate. But they expressed interest in a woman making her livelihood as a photographer. I told them there were a few of us, though most were in large cities and did studio work, while I liked taking outdoor shots or making photographs of people who might not think of having their pictures made.

They began to pose themselves—the tallest stood at the ends and the shorter ones in front. I often allow families to arrange themselves because it speaks to their relationships with each other. Who directs the setting? Who moves back? Who sits, who stands, what might it mean where they place their hands (in pockets, close enough to touch a shoulder)? I look to see who crowds, who doesn't, and who might be annoyed with whom, or who is considered the outsider of the group, posed at a spacing wide enough to ride a bicycle through. Most of the time I never get to know if I'm right with my musings, though looking at photographs of people I've come to know and spend time with often bears out my guesses.

Once, I looked at a photograph taken of my brother and sisters and me and realized my place within that pose: behind the other three, in a row alone, touching no one while they leaned into each other, Roy in the center. I was separated from them; the photograph didn't lie.

But with the Marquette girls, I liked their arrangement. Rather than a graduation shot where each looks no more distinct than a single kernel on a cob, I suggested that those in the front row squat down. That caused giggling, as they weren't all accustomed to such positioning on grass and said things like, "Don't take too long or I won't be able to get back up." They'd been chattering about their travel plans, reminding each to write through the summer, and spoke of coming back again next fall. So I suggested that they point to that place where they'd all meet come September. They laughed but liked the idea apparently, as they all pointed.

All but one, I noticed when I developed the film. She didn't smile either, looked sad almost. She also wore the only visible skirt that wasn't a dark color. Another checkered skirt was well hidden by the front row, but this woman stood out for her fashion and for the fact that no one knelt in front of her. Maybe she felt self-conscious. I didn't think she looked old enough to be the instructor, setting herself apart by not pointing, but the difference in her expression made her distinctive too. Still, the causes of an expression aren't revealed in a photograph, only the result.

"Right here," they told each other, aiming at the trampled grass. "We'll remember to return right here next fall." I clicked the shutter and held their promises on film.

I collected addresses. Joshua gathered payments, which he put into an envelope for me. He assured me there was more than enough to cover postage, even to faraway places, when I was ready to mail them. I gave them each my card, on which I'd written down my parents' address in Winona, and told them that if they didn't have a print from me within the month to write and tell me.

They dispersed for their picnic then, and I watched Joshua walk closely beside the girl wearing the white blouse who had posed in the middle of the photograph. She leaned her head toward his as they spoke, and she laughed. A slight touch of their hands told me that this one was special, this girl from Marquette. I was certain he hadn't met her at a sporting dance.

But the unsmiling girl in the checkered skirt with the gold chain around her neck stayed behind. I thought maybe she wanted to watch me push back the camera bellows and drop it into its case. "I won't be coming back next year," she told me softly as she slipped a coin into the envelope I held. "So I'll really appreciate having this photograph to remember my time here, as hard as the lessons were to learn. Marquette's a good school."

I thanked her as Joshua approached alone, and she sauntered off toward the others already clustered around baskets of food. A part of me wondered if maybe homesickness—that new word I'd learned—might have afflicted her too. Or maybe she recognized that she'd taken a wrong path that now left her both lonely and wise.

It was what I thought about as Joshua sat beside me silent in the cab, a friend riding with me, making sure that this time I arrived safely home.

PART 2

PROPS

ELEVEN

Lament

F. J. BAUER, FRED TO HIS FRIENDS, Mr. Bauer to his wife, waited at the Second Congregational Church to pick up his only daughter, Winnie, who was growing up. He could tell by the length of Winnie's dress, which showed flesh above the white stockings when she stepped outside and squinted into the sunlight. When had that happened? The last year had been a blur. Perhaps it was better to mark the passing of time by noticing changes in his children rather than in the thinning of his own hair. He watched Winnie skip down the stone steps, swinging her tin lunch pail while chatting with one of her friends. He didn't know the child's name, but she was the daughter of one of his lodge members. He should know the names of the children who influenced his. He'd have to find out.

Winnie stopped to talk to another child and turned her back to him. "Winifred." He raised his voice. "We need to go."

Winnie turned and saw him. Her face lit up with a smile that could melt steel. "Coming, Papa," she called back, taking but a moment to say good-bye to her friends, then racing toward him, her gait wide but agile. Her running made him think of Donald. She was now two years older than Donald had been when he died. She'd never known her older brother. The photographs Fred had taken of Donald kept his middle son frozen as a four-year-old. But every now and then he came alive in a certain smile on Russell's face, or in the way

Robert brushed off his pudgy palms by slapping them together, or in Winnie's gait.

"Did you have a good day, Papa?"

"I did," he said as he closed her door on the touring car. He drove the car more often now, and even Mrs. Bauer tolerated with minimal complaint the wind whipping the feathers on her hat. He stepped into the car, having already cranked the engine.

He asked for the name of her little friend, and then Winnie quizzed him. "What did you learn today, Papa?" she said, settling her hands in her lap. She looked like he did, he thought, when he was about to interrogate Russell regarding his lessons.

"A father is supposed to ask that question," he told her.

"I'm faster," she said. "I give you my turn."

He smiled. "What did I learn? Let me think. Well, I learned that Miss Gaebele is returning to Winona."

"Do I remember her?"

"You might. She's Selma's sister. You remember Selma? Yes, well, Miss Gaebele worked with me at the studio, along with Mrs. Henderson. She has a birthday the same day as yours, yes?"

"Jessie!" Recognition brightened Winnie's blue eyes. "Jessie, Jessie, Jessie. Why did she move away?"

"Now it's your turn. What did you learn today?"

She took a deep breath. "God made a big boat, and He took all the animals along so everyone could go fishing."

Her summer Bible-school teacher would chuckle to know how that story had been remembered. "That's why God had Noah build the boat, for fishing?" he teased.

Winnie stayed serious. "Yes sir. But it rained so much they couldn't go. Then a bird found a dry place so they could fish from the shore, and God sent a rainbow so they could find the dry place where the pot of gold sat, and they never had to worry about being wet again because God said so, and they were all very rich because they fished on a certain side of the boat, and God is so good."

"You've gotten the last part exactly right," he told her. He turned the corner and slowed down to cross the railroad tracks close to their home.

"Is Jessie coming to visit us?"

He shook his head, wishing he hadn't mentioned Jessie's return. Winnie might blurt that out at home, and he wasn't sure how the news would be received. In the past year his wife had not mentioned the girl who had run the studio and kept them solvent on two occasions due to his illnesses, but she'd found other things to chide him about. Their trips to Rochester to "talk out their problems" brought improvement, but he knew she wasn't happy, and he didn't always know what subjects might trigger her telling him about it. Still, he was quite certain he noted a flicker of annoyance whenever Miss Gaebele came into a conversation. He'd never confessed his indiscretions to his wife. What would have been the point? He wasn't ever going to pursue it, repeat it, make the same mistake. He'd recommitted to his wife and family. Telling her of a time when he'd wandered, if mostly with his emotions, could only hurt his wife and the best chance they had at keeping their marriage together.

"We might see her around, right, Papa?" Winnie said, and he smiled. One minute she was a child chattering about fishing, and the next she sounded like an adult putting the future into perspective.

At their South Baker Street home, he let Winnie out, and she ran into the house while he backed the car into the garage. Before closing the shed door, he wiped the fenders down with his rag, checked the tires and the fuel tank so the car would be ready the next time he drove it. He took the rug out from where he placed his feet and shook it. Then with a brush he kept for the car, he swept the area before putting the rugs back. *Killing time,* he told himself. *I'm killing time.* He picked up his cane and walked into the house just as Winnie told her mother, "Jessie's back in town."

"The Gaebele girl?" Mrs. Bauer said. "Who told you that?" Mrs. Bauer was having a good day. She wore a new apron with strawberries printed on green fabric. It made her think of summer and the garden, and she planned to whip cream to serve with the small crop of strawberries she'd picked in the backyard. Now she felt annoyed, though she didn't know why.

"I did." Her husband removed his hat, and she noticed he wore a pinched look on his face. He hung up his jacket and tugged on his suspenders as though they weren't straight, which of course they were. Her husband was quite tidy about his person, expected the same of her. "We played, 'What did you learn today?' and that was my news. I thought she'd remember the girl, but she didn't at first. And I'm not certain that Miss Gaebele is back, just that she might be coming back."

"She's Selma's sister, isn't she, Mama?"

"Yes. Go change your dress now, Winnie. There's time for you to play before supper, but not in your Bible-school clothes. Your father wouldn't want you to get dirty."

"She needs a new dress or two," Mr. Bauer said as Winnie left the room. "Her knees will be showing soon."

"Heaven knows I haven't had time or energy to sew," Mrs. Bauer said. He was always so critical of her and everything she did. "I have Robert to look after and the garden and—"

"It wasn't a criticism, just an observation. Perhaps we could have Lilly Gaebele sew a frock for her. Save you the trouble."

"Why would you say such a thing? It's no trouble to sew for my own child." How could he think that doing for her children proved a burden? She loved her children. They meant everything to her. Those two occasions when she'd gone home to her mother's hadn't been to avoid her children but to find a place of peace, to separate herself from the demands of the day-to-dayness that being a wife required. She could feel weight settle on her shoulders like the heavy fur cape she wore in winter. She had to stop the downward pressure.

What had Reverend Carleton said? Could her husband's words hold a different meaning? She must think of other ways her husband's words could be construed, not always go with her first impression, which was that he criticized. Maybe it was just an innocent comment about the children's needing new clothing.

"I happened to notice that the dress looked short, and I thought of the Gaebele girl's sewing business, that's all." *Jessie Gaebele.* That's why she was irritated. It wasn't her recent lack of sewing that had given her pause. It was the mention of that girl. Mrs. Bauer had no idea why that should upset her. The girl had done nothing but assist them during difficult times, yet whenever he mentioned her, she found herself defensive, comparing herself to the pretty young woman with photographic talent that rivaled her own. Mrs. Bauer always fell short. Reverend Carleton had said she ought to talk with her husband about such reactions—not that she'd mentioned to him about the Gaebele girl. Heavens, no. She couldn't imagine doing that, speaking about a person or an issue that she couldn't frame in her own mind. Her husband's nimble words would snarl hers, and she'd end up feeling worse than if she'd never brought up the difficult subject.

"What? Were you speaking to me?" She turned to him.

"Yes, I was. You were drifting. I think I hear Robert up from his nap." Her husband sighed. "I'll go get him. Where's Russell?"

"Melba will get Robert, and I didn't drift off. I was thinking," she told her husband. *Is he changing the subject on purpose?* Good. They were supposed to find ways to step over little annoyances until they'd had a chance to clarify what was so upsetting and talk about it later, when they were both calm. "But I'm sure Robert would be pleased to see you." She spoke the words as though introducing a new member of her Ladies Aid Society.

"Good. I'll have him help me read the paper," he said.

Mrs. Bauer let him go. Strange how she'd gone from a happy day to one where she wondered if she'd have the courage to talk with her husband about how he knew that Jessie Gaebele was back in town.

TWELVE

Reunion

THE TRAIN RIDE BACK FROM MILWAUKEE felt very different than when Jessie had headed southeast the year before. Fields of corn rose up, far from harvest. No migrating geese clustered in the wetlands. All around her the world did the work of maturing, and she did that too.

She'd met a few of her goals, she decided. She'd eked out a payment to Marie for her receptionist help, paid Suzanne for the chemicals, sent small amounts home, and saved the rest for her debt.

Suzanne's surprise envelope, given just before Jessie left, made being debt-free possible. "It seemed only fair for you to share in the profit from the sale of the business," Suzanne had told her. "Without you, I wouldn't have had a business to sell."

Funny how Suzanne's money held no obligation; Jessie received it as a gift.

On the other hand, she fully intended to return the money Fred had paid the Harmses for her room and board. She'd give him a piece of her mind as well. He'd had no right to impose that kind of obligation on her, or on the Harms family either. She'd found out the amount he sent, and saving to pay it back had been her highest priority.

Jessie wondered about her family's reception of her on this visit home. There was still history—the weight of Roy's stammering and how her relationship with Fred had disappointed her parents and her sisters. Lilly had never written to her in Milwaukee, not once, and

Jessie wondered how she took the reading of Jessie's letters out loud after supper. She probably retired early so she didn't have to hear them.

Jessie stood up on the train, just to change her thinking. *Finally, brethren, whatsoever things are true, whatsoever things are honest, whatsoever things are just, whatsoever things are pure, whatsoever things are lovely, whatsoever things are of good report; if there be any virtue, and if there be any praise, think on these things.* She remembered the verse from Philippians and found herself smiling as she shifted her weight from foot to foot. Memorizing scriptures and poems, her mother had said, was like filling a pool from which one could later draw nourishment. Jessie hadn't deserved that pool from which she might easily draw courage or confidence; she'd put a cover over the cistern of her soul.

So the arrival of the verse as though from nowhere lifted Jessie's thoughts away from Lilly's disapproval. True, just, pure things she contemplated as the Chicago and Northwestern chugged through Wisconsin, crossed the mighty Mississippi River, slowed and screeched into the Winona station house.

Jessie knew there would be no one to meet her, as she hadn't told them the exact date she'd be leaving Milwaukee, so she wasn't expecting to see her father standing on the platform, his eyes searching the windows as the steam billowed its way back across the train, clouding her sight.

"Papa!" she shouted, though he couldn't possibly hear her through the steam and the clanking. She waved her gloved hand, grabbed her camera case, and began running through the car toward the door. The porter held up his palm, his dark face holding a smile as she told him, "That's my papa out there. He's waiting for me!"

"In a minute, miss. In a minute."

She nearly lost her balance when the train finally stopped. The porter reached for her elbow to steady her, then stepped aside as he pulled open the door. Jessie jumped off, and with one hand holding her hat and the other swinging her camera case, she raced back toward the spot where she'd seen her father standing.

"I'm here," she shouted, and he turned and opened his arms to her. It was the best homecoming present she could have. "But what are you doing here?" she said when he set her back on her feet. "I didn't tell you when I was coming. Oh, wait. I've left my bag on the train." She raced back to where she'd been sitting, pushing through the passengers heading out, grabbed the carpetbag, and surged back with the crowd to link arms with her father.

"A little flummoxed?" he teased.

"Just tell me how you knew."

"Only one Chicago and Northwestern brings people from Milwaukee each day," he said. "Five o'clock." He looked at his watch. "On the dot."

"You've come here every day?" she asked. "Since I wrote?"

"Just since last week. When your trunk arrived. Stationmaster called me to say they had a trunk to be sent to our address. It sat all weekend before they notified us."

"I'd planned to pick it up when I got here," she said.

"Already at home. Hauled it there myself. Roy could hardly keep from opening it, said he wanted the surprise you promised to him."

"I do have a few small things for everyone," she said as they approached her father's drayage wagon. "But Roy's surprise isn't in there. I'll take care of that before I leave for Eau Claire."

Her father stopped. "You didn't say anything about visiting Eau Claire," he said. "Not right away, I hope."

"I'm not exactly…visiting," she said. She decided she'd tell him now, even though the tone of his voice indicated that he might not like hearing it. "I've taken a position there."

"In photography?" Jessie nodded. "Your mother hoped maybe you'd given up those pursuits. Milwaukee didn't discourage you then?"

If anything, Milwaukee had given her new hope, after a few stumbles. But even then, she hadn't fallen. "I thought you'd be happy I've found another job," she said. "So I won't be a burden on you and Mama." At least the episode with Fred hadn't spilled into the public like the affair of that architect Frank Lloyd Wright and his paramour,

Mamah Borthwick Cheney. What stings and assaults their families must've been enduring, having their relationship discussed daily in the newspaper. Mrs. Cheney had gotten a divorce, but Mr. Wright had not. It was a scandal.

Not that she and Fred had participated in an affair anything like theirs. Just an episode. But she knew her family carried grief for her actions. Lilly had added to Jessie's guilt by telling her before she left that her parents blamed themselves for not giving Jessie more upstanding morals.

"You're not a burden," her father said. "I'm just disheartened that you didn't look for work in Winona, maybe see if Reverend Carleton might be in need of a receptionist. I believe your mother and I, and your sisters, are willing to let bygones be bygones."

She was tempted to ask him what had transpired between him and Fred at the river when they'd been fishing. Had he let bygones be gone and had Selma just misunderstood?

Think on these things...

She patted his large hand as he bent to lift the reins. "I'm a businesswoman now, Papa. And we professional women need to go where there's work. The Everson Studio in Eau Claire needs an assistant, and Suzanne Johnson gave me a solid recommendation."

"Don't be too prideful now, Jessie," he cautioned.

"I wasn't... I... She let me read her letter. It was nice of her to recommend me, that's all. She's the one who told me about the opening anyway. There'd been a notice that her studio had changed hands, and Mrs. Everson guessed that Suzanne had an assistant who might be needing work. At least Eau Claire is closer to Winona," she said. "I'll visit. Maybe you could visit me there too."

"I thought we'd stop on the way home, just to see Reverend Carleton," her father said. "Maybe he'd offer you better pay than you'll get in Eau Claire."

She didn't look at him, brushed at a smudge on her glove. "Papa, I'm already committed to Eau Claire, for at least six months. You wouldn't want me to go back on my word, would you?"

"Well, let's not tell your mother just yet," he said.

As the wagon rattled along, Jessie breathed in the familiarity of home: the majesty of the bluffs, the clatter of horse-drawn carriages and autos crossing over the streetcar tracks. The rough weave of her father's shirt rubbed against her arms. She slipped her elbow through his arm and pushed back her father's disappointment—threatening to stick its nosy head into this precious reunion.

Fred had seen the trunk with the Gaebele name on it when he'd gone to the train station to pick up an order of his own photographic supplies. Voe Henderson, his assistant, often did that for him, but she'd been "feeling poorly" as the women often said, and her husband had called in to say she couldn't pick up the supplies that day because she'd be late. It was one of the difficulties of having hired a married woman who was expecting her first child. He wondered how long it would be before she told him she couldn't continue her employment, forcing him to train another assistant yet again. Voe had worked with him for several years now, hired when Jessie was. Voe wasn't nearly as artistic or as efficient as Jessie, but neither did she cause distractions. She did her job, made him laugh occasionally, then went home to her husband, at least on days when she came to work. When she didn't, he had to handle her jobs too.

His wife had once done a great deal of photographic work with him. She'd managed most of the retouching and tinting, which Voe didn't like to do. Mrs. Bauer had otherwise helped out at the studio too, but that was long ago. Now Voe managed the appointments and made patrons feel comfortable. Voe also did most of the developing, as he'd twice been affected by the mercury poisoning and avoided the chemicals now as much as possible. So he assumed the duties of the portrait taking, printing, tinting, and retouching.

Mrs. Bauer was a skilled retoucher, but with young children to care for, she'd insisted he manage those things by himself. Fred believed that during the school year, when only Robert was at home,

Melba could easily look after him for an hour or two so his wife could work with him at the studio. But Mrs. Bauer resisted. Anything having to do with photography distressed her. But then, most things did distress her, even with her following the doctor's suggestions.

Maybe she'd reconsider if Voe Henderson left to have her child and did not return. Maybe his wife would see then that she had a role to play in his life beyond that of keeping his house and looking after his children. Their house, their children. If he could engage her in his life in a meaningful way, perhaps old sparks that fired when he'd met her would return.

That's what he'd been thinking about when he happened to look down at the train station and saw the trunk with Jessie's name on it, addressed to her father, sent from Milwaukee. He'd heard himself gasp. Maybe it held a few items the girl didn't want to store in that city. Or maybe it preceded her and she'd be arriving on a later train. His heart beat a bit faster with that thought, and then he shook his head as though talking to himself. What was wrong with him? It would be best if their paths never crossed again. His arriving in Milwaukee for the convention last year had clearly been upsetting to her.

Yet, the day he'd seen her trunk passed quickly, and he'd felt a lift to his steps. When his last appointment of the day asked that the sitting be redone as none of the contact prints were pleasing, he wasn't even frustrated. He simply rescheduled her. After that patron left, he found himself driving toward the train station around the time the Chicago and Northwestern usually pulled in. The train already looked cavernous beside the platform, all passengers having disembarked. He got out and walked back toward the docking area just to see if perhaps more boxes with the studio name on them had arrived, giving himself a reason to be there. Jessie's trunk still sat in the storage area.

"Forget something, Mr. Bauer?" the clerk asked. "Thought you picked up your supplies this mornin'."

"I did, William, I did. I just thought I'd see if I had any more shipments."

"Nope, not a thing."

"Uh-huh." He looked around, then pointed casually. "I noticed this trunk here this morning. Have you called for it to be picked up? Shouldn't let it sit through the night."

"Thought maybe the owner of it would be getting off the train soon. It's been here a few days."

"Definitely should call the addressee, then," he encouraged.

"I'll do it now," the clerk said. Fred took his hat off, brushed it against his thigh, followed the clerk into the station house. He surveyed the high ceilings. Maybe he'd photograph the interior with its marble and gilding. Yes, it would make a fine subject, though he didn't like shots taken away from the organized setting of the studio. He eavesdropped as he evaluated the lighting and the shadows on the gilded trim.

"That was good," the clerk said as he hung up the black telephone receiver on its hook. "They didn't realize it was here, thought their daughter would have brought it with her. Guess she's coming in a few days."

"Always good to follow up," Fred said. "Good business practice."

"That it is, sir."

He let himself peruse the room, considered how the marble would photograph, whether there'd be too much light reflected from it, then walked to his car. He told himself he'd only done what he hoped someone would do for him if he sent photographic supplies on ahead to an address. A call ought to go out immediately saying the item had arrived and needed to be picked up. Just caring for his fellow man. Doing a good deed gave reason to smile, which was how he felt when he picked up Winnie from her Bible school that day. That's probably why he mentioned Jessie's name when Winnie surprised him by asking what he'd learned.

That had been a week ago. Since then, he'd found himself thinking often of Jessie Gaebele as he worked in the print room or while he pulled weeds from the studio's back garden. Today, as he prepared for his first sitting, gathered the props necessary for the children he expected in this family pose, he wondered about Jessie's time in Milwaukee. What shots had she taken? How she'd distanced herself from him at his unexpected visit to Milwaukee. Was she coming back to stay?

Several months earlier, an ad in the photographic journal told him that Suzanne Johnson planned to sell her studio, and he wondered if Jessie could remain working with the new owners, assuming the Widow Johnson could get her business sold. He knew Jessie wanted to buy her own studio one day, and he'd considered writing to her to see if he might loan her money to purchase the Johnson business. He'd written, but it was a frilly letter, just telling her he'd seen a story that had been written up about the portrait she'd taken of a child. He hadn't mentioned a word about the studio, and since she hadn't responded, he hadn't written to her again. She'd moved on, he decided. Besides, if she purchased the Johnson Studio, he might never see her again except at a photographic conference.

That was the truth of it. And the thought of that—the thought he might never again encounter her small frame stepping across his path in Winona—made his heart ache almost as much as the absence of Donald. Guilt wrapped itself up with both pains.

"Mr. B.? Did you hear me?" Voe asked.

"I'm sorry, I didn't," he told his assistant.

"Your head was in Germany or somewhere far from here," she said. He agreed, laid the peacock feathers on the settee in case he needed them. "I thought I'd best tell you that, well, you know Mr. Henderson and me are waiting on our child, and we've been thinking about me working here and all after that happens."

"I've been expecting this conversation, yes?" He folded his hands in front of him the way he did when he taught his photographic classes, looking professorial, patient, in charge. "When do you think you would be leaving? I hope you'll give me ample time to replace you."

Voe frowned. "Who said anything about leaving? At least not permanent-like."

"Oh, I just assumed."

"You assumed wrong, Mr. B." She shook her finger at him. The girl took liberties, but he tolerated it because of her good nature. "Daniel thinks I can keep working here, and we'll get ourselves a girl, the way you and Mrs. B. have. He's on with the railroad permanent now and says we can afford it. But I'd like a month away when the child arrives."

Voe wasn't going to retire from her photographic work. He wouldn't need to hire a replacement. Disappointment surprised him. "You'd want only a month? Well, I'm sure I can get an assistant for that amount of time. Fairly soon, from the look of things." Voe blushed. He hadn't meant to embarrass the woman. "Maybe Miss Gaebele would be available," he said, the words slipping out as though he proposed a cup of coffee to replace the tea he usually drank. "I think she might be coming back to Winona."

"I haven't heard that," Voe said. "But then she didn't write me much, and I don't write letters so good myself."

"Well, just rumor then," he said. "The studio she worked at in Milwaukee has sold. But not to worry. I'll make a temporary arrangement while you're off with your baby."

"I'm looking forward to this child playing on the outside of me instead of banging me around from the inside," she said, rubbing her belly. "Another month and I'm home free, as they say in baseball."

" 'Home free' takes on new meaning with children around, Mrs. Henderson. It seems nothing children need is ever really free." He thought of his sons, his daughter, the absent Donald, and how much he loved them all, and how he belonged to them in ways his own parents had never remained connected to him. His parents had set him free from Kirchheim unter Teck at the age of fifteen, just three years older than Russell was now. By that time, he was already a skilled carpenter, so they'd sent him sailing across the ocean and let him lead his life far away from the vineyard and farmland of his family. His father had died eight years ago, and he hadn't seen his mother now for thirty years. He couldn't fathom not seeing his children for that long, couldn't imagine setting Russell adrift at the age of fifteen. His children, living and deceased, wound themselves like a ball of thread into the full place in his heart. They were really the only tether to their mother he still had. The realization startled him.

"Love is free, Mr. B. I think so," Voe told him.

He didn't correct her, but he knew that even love came with costs. Grief was the tax one paid for that luxury.

THIRTEEN

Gifts Given and Received

"OH MY, OH MY! We didn't know you'd come today," Jessie's mother said. Ida Gaebele hugged her daughter tightly, then held her at arm's length. "Your eyes look strange, more blue than gray. You've lost weight. Didn't you eat properly? What kind of board did you have in Milwaukee anyway?"

"My eyes are fine." Jessie laughed. "It's the light here that makes them look different to you. And I had fine food, Mama. I kept busy working and running my own photographic business, so I ran off whatever I ate." Jessie thought of the rich meals the Harms family served and noted to herself that she was fortunate not to come away from Milwaukee having to ask Lilly to let out all her clothes. Instead, she'd be taking them in. Selma hugged her then, still holding a book in one hand as she twirled her around. They almost danced. Lilly wasn't home from Stott's yet, and Jessie wondered if her sisters ever considered going to a sporting dance. She guessed not.

"Little Women," Selma said when Jessie eyed the book she held. "It's about four sisters. You ought to read it."

"M-m-mama will f-f-fatten you up like a r-r-rooster," Roy said. He stuttered nearly as much as he always did, Jessie thought, but he was more courageous trying out this longer sentence, and no one finished it for him. She squatted to be eye to eye with him.

"You think so, do you?" He nodded, and she kissed his cheek as he pulled her to him. They tumbled backward, putting Jessie into a sprawl that twisted her skirt.

"Ach," their mother said. "Stop that now, Frog. Jessie. Someone will get hurt."

But Jessie laughed and Roy laughed too, his eyes sparkling as he brushed bowl-cut hair from his forehead. The joy she felt at being able to tumble like a puppy with her own littermates was unequal to anything she'd felt in Milwaukee. She loved these people and hoped she'd never have to be so far away from them for so long again.

At Roy's insistence, Jessie opened her trunk, which Roy hauled in from the porch. "Though I think we should wait for Lilly before I give you your gifts," Jessie said. "Roy, one of yours you'll have to wait for anyway. But I'll show you a few pictures." She brought up a print of the Marquette girls and explained as Roy frowned over what the girls were pointing at. Selma wondered if the women were her friends, and Jessie said no, just patrons. She showed them a print of Mary and Marie Harms in their living room along with a shot of a rose from the Harmses' garden and a lake scene or two. "I think this is the tallest structure in all of Milwaukee," Jessie said, pointing to a picture of a flour mill stack that seemed to scratch the sky.

"Wh-wh-who's this?" Roy asked, pulling several other prints out on his own. "A M-M-Marq-q-quette g-g-girl?"

"No, a girl who worked for a Milwaukee family," Jessie told him. "There are several photographs there, of domestics and young women who make their living in the candy and sewing factories."

"Did you go to the factories to take these?" Selma asked. "It doesn't look like a studio pose." She held one of the small prints in her hand.

"They were…ah…"

"I'd love to work in a candy factory," Selma continued, rescuing Jessie from more detail. "Imagine breathing in chocolate all day long." She swooned as she said it.

"And these are students at a school for stammerers." She looked at Roy. "I had this idea that you'd go to Milwaukee and attend it one day and—"

"He's not going away from home," her mother said. "Goodness. What are you thinking putting such a thought into his head, Jessie?"

"I-I-I might like to g-go t-t-to M-M-Milwaukee."

"Don't be ridiculous," Jessie's mother said. "You're much too young to be away from home, whether with your big sister or not."

"These are of friends of Mrs. Harms," Jessie said. "And a few of their daughters." She brought out other prints, careful not to show any more of those taken at the dances, cotillions, or sporting hall.

"They look like Roman goddesses," Selma said, "in those long dresses."

"It's all the rage in Milwaukee," Jessie said. "I hope to introduce it to Eau Claire."

"Eau Claire?" her mother said. "When are you visiting Eau Claire?"

Jessie bit her tongue as she looked at her father, who frowned now.

"I have work there, Mama. I start next week. I planned to wait until after supper to tell you, but it just slipped out."

"But I thought… We all thought you'd be moving back home," her mother said. "Reverend Carleton was hoping you'd come by. He might have work for you right here. At home."

"I have work in Eau Claire, Mama," Jessie affirmed.

Lilly arrived then, and the sisters gave measured embraces while Roy fluttered about the presents and Selma mentioned Jessie's new job.

"In a photographic studio," Jessie said. "Mr. Everson has mercury poisoning. I'll run the studio with his wife just as I did for Mr. Bauer when he was ill."

"Funny you'd mention him," Lilly said, removing pins from her hat. "His wife called today and asked if I'd sew up dresses for Winnie. You remember Winnie, don't you, Jessie? Their youngest child?"

"We share a birthday," Jessie reminded her. She wondered why Lilly goaded her, or maybe Jessie read emotion that wasn't there.

"Ah, yes, that's right. You share a birthday."

"Pr-pr-presents," Roy said.

"I wonder what Jessie's done that she needs to bribe us with gifts," Lilly said, a smile lifting the corner of her lips.

"Presents can wait," her mother cautioned. "And Lilly, that's no way to greet your sister."

"I brought this handkerchief for you, Lil. It has fine embroidery that made me think of you when I was far from home." They'd finished supper and sat now outside on the porch trying to cool themselves in the sultry June evening. Black bugs the size of her thumb dotted the grass—June bugs, named for the month they most often appeared. Crickets chirped. Jessie hadn't sat on a porch for months. She'd always had tasks to attend to in Milwaukee, tasks meant to take her closer to her own studio. While the Harms family wanted to treat her as family, she knew she wasn't.

"It looks…foreign," Lilly said, holding the handkerchief. Lilly's natural waves framed her face, and Jessie thought how beautiful her sister was even in her most judgmental moments.

"It is. From Poland. A woman paid me with it. I never used it. It was too beautiful and the work so intricate. I thought of you whenever I looked at it."

"Thank you," Lilly said. Her eyes softened, and for the first time since Lilly had entered the house, Jessie felt a thawing.

"What did you bring me?" Selma sang. "Something pretty I hope."

"Something practical. I know you might have one of these to use at Lottie's, but I thought you'd like one of your own." She handed her younger sister a rectangular carton bigger than a hat box.

"A glove press!" Selma said as she pulled the contraption out. "I can press my own gloves now and yours and Lilly's and Mama's too. I love it!" Selma hugged her and handed the metal hand-shaped object to Roy, showing him how it would be set upon the box and the gloves stretched down over it. "It's electric," Selma continued when she noticed the cord. "It must have cost a fortune."

"One of the Harmses' friends got a new one, and she gave it to

Mary Harms, who gave it to me. I thought you'd be the perfect person to have it and you wouldn't mind a used one."

"Don't leave it plugged in," Lilly said. "You could burn the house down."

"Won't you need it to press your own gloves?" Selma asked.

"I still have the one I heat on the stove," Jessie said. "You're the modern girl." She almost said "modern Gibson girl," but her mother would have fainted if she'd compared innocent Selma Selena to one of those provocative cartoon drawings of curvaceous women. Jessie had seen a Gibson drawing on fans used for advertising St. Paul city's Hamm's beer. She hoped one day she'd take a photograph that might be used in an advertisement that would bring new customers to her studio. Her fantasy studio at the moment.

Jessie presented her mother with a half apron in a windowpane cotton weave with rows of rickrack and lace trim. "I'll keep this one for good," her mother told her as she stood and tied it on around her waist. She lifted the ecru cotton, sending a small breeze through the otherwise still evening.

"For my birthday," Selma said. "Wear it then."

"For you, Papa, I brought a packet of herbs. My former employer, Mrs. Johnson, said her husband had problems like yours with his stomach, and these packets helped."

"I thank you for thinking of me," her father said as he turned the packet over and over between his fingers.

"She got them from a gypsy," Jessie said. "But Mama, before you protest, Mr. Johnson used them all along, and they did help his side without having any other effects. Suzanne wouldn't tell me that if it wasn't true. It's just herbs. Things you grow in gardens, she told me, gardens in faraway places."

"M-m-mine?" Roy said.

"This one will have to do until you get your real gift," Jessie said. She handed him the small whistle. "It's made from the bone of a bird," Jessie told him. "I got it at a market. Milwaukee has all kinds of markets in the open air."

"Where's it from?" Selma asked.

"Wisconsin. It was made by a Chippewa Indian. Blow on it, Roy."

Her brother blew on the tiny whistle, and the haunting sound reminded Jessie once again of hawks that dipped below the bluffs. In an effort to help Roy slow his stutter, she'd once told him to imagine wind slowly sifting over his words. Roy grinned up at her. "The bird whistle is related to the present we'll get in a couple of days," Jessie said. "But for now, this will have to do."

Roy jumped off the porch and marched in circles on the walk, tooting his new toy.

"You'll have to do more discussing tomorrow too," her mother said after a time. "To bed, all of you."

"Mother," Lilly said, "we agreed you wouldn't treat me like a child."

"Oh, you may remain up, Lilly. But Roy and Selma, tomorrow is another workday, and a good night's sleep is just what you need."

Roy groaned, but he joined Selma as they kissed their parents. "Save my place in the middle of the bed," Jessie told Selma.

"It's so nice to have all my children clucked around me," her mother said. "Safe and secure. I don't like all this talk about doing things on your own. It's not good for a woman's mind, Jessie. I've read about brain poisonings for girls who went on to college. The *Republican-Herald* had an article about that. We women just can't handle that much knowledge."

"You better not let Selma read any more of her book then," Lilly said. "Louisa May Alcott thinks it's as much a right and duty for women to make good of their lives as it is for men."

"That does sound like a good book," Jessie agreed. She and Lilly exchanged a knowing look.

Mrs. Bauer felt strong enough now to do it. Melba had put Robert to bed, Fred had read a bit to Winnie before she slipped off to sleep, and Mrs. Bauer had looked in on Russell sitting at his desk, studying an old camera his father had given him. Her oldest son had a talent for picture taking, and Mrs. Bauer thought one day he might take over the business or perhaps begin working beside his father before long. After he'd finished school of course. She wanted him to go on to college. They'd have to save money for that, but they could afford it. Surely they could.

She approached her husband reading in the living room, catching a glimpse of herself in the hall mirror. Her mink-colored hair had few gray streaks, but her deep blue eyes looked cold as Lake Winona, even to herself. She closed her eyes and imagined warmth, wanting to be compassionate, not critical, as she brought up the issue. Still, it was now or never. She opened her eyes and joined her husband. "Could we talk about what happened last week, when you first arrived home with Winnie?"

FJ raised his eyes from the *American Magazine.* "I'd like to finish this article on efficiency, yes? I didn't get to it last month. It's the final installment. Quite informative, all about management. Requires sound goals to begin with, then time can be distributed accordingly, led by scientific principles."

His level of detail about something of limited interest to her while she exposed her emotions nearly caused her to snap at him, but she didn't. Reverend Carleton would be proud of her. She was glad she'd decided to speak with the evangelist rather than her own pastor, who might share what she said to him with her husband, and she didn't want that. FJ thought it was the Mayo hospital doctors who directed her, but she'd found their assistance less useful than the reverend's. The doctors focused on what she ate and on exercise and such, while the pastor knew it was her heart and soul that needed healing.

"When might that be, when you've finished your article on such important, sound goals?" She heard the thread of sarcasm in her voice. She needed to counter that. No sense bringing fuel to a fire she wanted to put out. "Maybe I could prepare us tea while I wait."

He put the magazine down. "I'd like that," he said. "I'd like that very much. Good." He smiled warmly at her, and she turned and headed to the kitchen, hoping he wasn't watching her walk away. She didn't want him ogling her, and she couldn't trust that smile. Where might it lead?

She set the teakettle on the Monarch, turned the knob. She heard the pilot light *pusch* as it caught the flame. She only wished to talk about her irritation and propose a way through it. She needed to see if they could have a civil conversation that wouldn't end up with fury rushing through them by the end. That smile, though. She didn't want anything intimate, anything passionate, to result from this upcoming conversation. When she let her guard down, attempted pleasantries, he assumed she offered more. Reverend Carleton didn't understand that. He'd said she must be submissive, which didn't mean she had to take whatever her husband gave her, only that at times she might not get her own way. There was wifely duty to consider, but a husband's duty as well, he'd assured her. She couldn't remember when her husband hadn't gotten what he wanted. Well, she supposed he didn't like having separate bedrooms with locks. But when it came to intimacy, she had to have her own way or she'd suffocate.

The teakettle whistled. She poured the hot water through the leaves and inhaled the sweet scent. She could feel the steam above her lip as she placed the cups on a tray. Cookies. Should she put cookies on a plate? No, that would suggest ordinary, and she didn't feel ordinary. Besides, he might not like the ones she chose. He didn't like sugar cookies, as they crumbled and he had to brush his suit. She didn't have oatmeal, the ones he preferred. Better to leave cookies behind. She headed into the living room.

"There you are, Mrs. Bauer," he said, walking toward her. "I thought I heard the kettle whistle. You turned the stove off, yes?" His eyes looked past her. *Had she?* He clucked his tongue. "I'll do it. No sense wasting gas, and it's dangerous I'm sure you know."

That tone again, the one that made her feel like a child. "I intended to come back and take care of it after I took care of you," she said. *No!* This wasn't what she wanted. *Think. Think.*

He took the tray from her and set it on the sideboard. "This is very pleasant," he said. "Very pleasant. Just the two of us, having tea. No cookies?" She shook her head. "I don't need them anyway," he said and patted his stomach, which was flatter than a glove press. *Was that a veiled reference to my widening hips?* She smoothed the linen over her burgeoning waist. "Now, what was it you wished to discuss, Mrs. Bauer?"

"Call me Jessie," she said. "I think it's time I had you call me by my given name."

He sat back on the settee. "You've always insisted on Mrs. Bauer."

"I know. And it's how I think of myself, as your wife, now and forevermore. But I need to be my own person too."

"This is from the doctors?"

"It's my own thinking," she snapped. "I let you think too much for me. I believe I waste my time trying to imagine what you want. I've forgotten what it was like to know what I want."

"The very point of my efficiency article," he said. "One has to know precisely what the goal is, and then all can be worked toward accomplishing it. If you wish me to call you Jessie, I'll certainly comply." He picked up his spoon and blew across the tea, then swallowed. He'd drink the entire cup that way, one teaspoon at a time. "But what is the goal you're attempting to attain by having me do so?"

She frowned. She hadn't sorted out any real plan. "I thought that if I heard you call me by my name that I'd be less...upset whenever I heard Miss Gaebele's name, Jessie Gaebele's name."

She thought his hand shook when he lifted the spoon to his mouth. "The Gaebeles have been more than helpful to our family. Selma took good care of the children. You like the tailoring of Lilly, yes?"

"Yes, of course. But when you mentioned having her sew for Winnie, I felt, well, that you were being critical of me."

"Nonsense," he said. "You're imagining things."

"I thought you were finding fault."

"You were wrong."

Her chest tightened. This wasn't what she'd wanted to say.

"I'm not certain why hearing Miss Gaebele's name upset me, but it did."

"Nothing there to worry over," he said. "Maybe you're...envious that Winnie spoke of her with such exuberance."

Envy was not a word she would have used to describe how she'd felt. It was more like...fear. Could she tell him that? He'd say it was senseless.

"Her coming back to Winona causes me to feel, oh, a bit alarmed I guess, though I can't imagine why." She felt hot. Why didn't she serve him iced tea instead of hot tea? What was she thinking, with this sultry weather bearing down on them?

"I can't imagine why either," he said. "Maybe it reminds you of my illness and how the girl had to run our studio that year. That's likely it. But I'm healthy now."

"I'm not so certain," she said. "It...frightens me that I feel these things but can't explain why. You or Winnie speak, and I skip right over what you might have meant and find myself falling into a frightened place." She could hear her heart pounding as she talked to him, exposed a portion of her darkness.

"Well any worry over the Gaebeles is wasted time, won't get you nearer to your goal, which was what again?"

"Yes, but I thought I saw Mr. Gaebele, at the shore last year, refuse the offer of your hand," she said. Where had that memory come from? "Maybe it's good that I bear reluctance toward them if there's contention between the two of you."

"Oh, I doubt that," he said. "Something you misinterpreted I'm sure...Jessie." He smiled again. "Sounds good. There, you see. You've accomplished your goal, Jessie."

Had she? A portion perhaps, but she couldn't be sure. Still she said, "Yes. Yes, I believe I have." Maybe it was the tea that soothed her.

Roy and his chickens
July 1, 1911, Gaebele parlor on Broadway, Winona

Relief

I love this photograph because my only brother got the chickens calmed, and yet his hands are blurred a bit, fingers in motion as they are in life. When he comes to mind, it's always in the presence of an object: he carries a hoe for his garden patch or a small screwdriver to repair Selma's glasses. His long fingers strum his banjo, which he plays quite well now, and he sings sometimes when he thinks no one is listening, the words tripping off his tongue as smooth as any of ours. He just can't translate that pacing into speech. The photograph shows his closed mouth and fingers always busy when his tongue can't be. Here he looks a typical boy even though he isn't. What typical boy would choose to put his suit on in July when he didn't have to? "L-l-look prof-f-fessional," he said. "L-l-like you, J-J-Jessie."

"Men can be professional even when they have dirt on their pants," I told him. "Papa is professional. He works hard, is good at what he does. A professional is someone well schooled in their work, their profession," I told him. "It's not about how they dress. That goes for women too."

"I look af-af-after ch-ch-chickens."

"You're right. That's your profession today. I'm sure they won't mind you dressing up for them."

The heavy drape in the parlor formed the backdrop. It kept the light from fading Mama's finest furniture and on a hot day kept the room the coolest place in the house, except for the root cellar underneath.

After printing the photograph, I noticed the scratch. We'd removed the runner on that library table so the chickens wouldn't slip and slide as much, but I honestly don't know if the gouge in the finish was there beforehand or if we made it. The scratch was so large I wondered why I hadn't seen it when I clicked the shutter. Maybe I didn't want to see it so I didn't have to explain it to Mama. That German doctor, Mr. Freud, in his new book about our minds, says there are no mistakes. We do and say things that might get us into trouble, but we do them for a reason even when we claim we don't. I wondered if that explained why I slip and say things that stumble me. Maybe I just want my path out in the open, where those who love me can warn me of the cliff ahead.

I retouched this print and took the scratches out before I sent it to Roy. It's one of the benefits of the art: one doesn't always have to live forever with one's mistakes.

It may be my imagination, but now that I look at the photograph more closely, Roy's eyes look sad to me. They're kind eyes. He wore gentleness and generosity all the days of his life, and yet I see no sparkle here. I know he enjoyed the chickens I gave him as his special gift. He named them Pancho, Madero, and Díaz, the principals of the Mexican war going on. Roy kept in tune with what happened in the larger world. I think the people in newspaper stories and books became his companions, when so many children his age avoided him for his lack of conversation.

Selma distracted the birds, so they looked at her off to Roy's left rather than at the camera, and while I wanted Roy to be the subject of this shot, the chickens stole the show. I had good intentions; but then I always did.

My mother wasn't pleased that we brought the poultry into the house in the first place. She put up a fuss about it. She'd have been even more troubled if she'd known what had happened earlier that day.

As a courtesy to my parents' wishes, I'd stopped at Ralph Carleton's offices, and he was in. He wore his usual white suit, but he'd taken the jacket off in the ghastly heat and placed it around the back of a chair. His blue vest hung unbuttoned. His receptionist was out—it was lunchtime—and he welcomed me warmly, rising from behind his oak desk. Jovial and kind, he'd be a good man to work for, but I didn't want that now. Before he could raise the issue that I was sure my mother had primed him for, Mrs. Bauer came through the door.

My heart leapt, I confess. I looked immediately past her to see if her husband came behind her, hoping that he wasn't—hoping that he was. Of two minds I am, always needing retouching.

"You know Mrs. Bauer?" Ralph Carleton asked, preparing to introduce us. I guess I must have gasped. I nodded. She wore a large straw hat over thick brown hair that showed just a trace of gray. Her dress had a scoop neckline revealing ivory skin. The pale blue skirt skimmed the tops of her white kid shoes. She carried a parasol against the sun and gloves with tiny embroidered flowers on the back.

"Miss Gaebele." She nodded. "We're acquainted, though I haven't seen you for a time. I heard you were back. Are you home for good then?" She swirled the closed parasol at its point, both hands resting on the handle. Her blue eyes bore into me.

"If we can talk her into it," Ralph Carleton said cheerfully. My mother obviously hadn't told him everything she knew.

The blue of her eyes faded, or maybe the effect was from their narrowing. I hoped I could restore their color with my own response. "No ma'am," I said. "I have employment in Eau Claire."

"Do you now?" I thought I saw relief flicker in her eyes. I wondered what Fred might have told her. But if he had confessed, surely she would not have stood so civilly before me, nor dismissed me so easily. "Well, I wish you well." She turned to Ralph and asked, "Shall I come back later?"

"No, no. This is your time, dear lady." To me he said, "The offer is always open."

I didn't remind him that he'd made no offer, but we both knew of my mother's intent. I walked back to Broadway with time to think of Mrs. Bauer, what her business with Reverend Carleton might be. I knew she attended the Second Congregational Church, and Ralph was an evangelist, not a pastor with his own church. Maybe he served on a committee with her, because he had said it was "her time" there. Yes, that was probably it.

The look in her blue eyes when she thought I might be remaining in Winona stayed with me. I tried to find the words to describe it. Caution? No, fear.

Curiosity pricked at how Mrs. Bauer might have heard of my being home. Maybe Lilly mentioned it when she sewed for Mrs. Bauer. A part of me was pleased that I might have been a topic of conversation within the Bauer family, and then I felt shamed for such a thought. I had no place within that family conversation, no place at all.

I reached home, and Roy and I headed off for our chicken buying. We carried one cage, as I was planning on purchasing only one bird. Roy and I cheered each other with our musings about which chicken to buy, and then when we found the rooster, he said, "H-h-he'll be l-l-lonely," so when the farmer added that the three had been together a long time and it was a shame to split them up, I said all right, we'll buy three. I told Roy he was a professional salesman. "S-s-salesmen t-t-talk." Indeed they do, I assured him, which made him smile and show his even white teeth.

We settled on the Barred Rock rooster and a white Plymouth Rock and a single hen. Only the roosters remained on the table for photos. The hen hopped off, heading toward Selma and the parlor's horsehair couch.

After the photograph was taken, we prepared to introduce Roy's chickens to the others in my mother's flock. "You'll have to wait to put the new ones in with the other hens Mama has," I reminded Roy.

"W-w-why?"

"Because otherwise they'll argue with each other. Grandma Gaebele told me that if you wait until it's dark and the old chickens are roosting, and then slip these new chickens into the pens, when the others wake in the morning, they'll see them and think to themselves, Oh, they must have been here all along and I just didn't notice them before. They won't peck at them as intruders that way."

"Ch-ch-chickens can be t-t-tricked?"

"Like most of us," I said. "We even trick ourselves sometimes," I told him.

I made a point of going to the Bauer Studio early the next morning, slipping out so I could be there when he opened. If Voe arrived first, it would be fine. I wanted to see her too, but there wasn't much time before heading to Eau Claire, so I hoped Fred would come first.

My last visit to the studio had been filled with drama. He'd surprised me at that encounter, where my thoughts jumbled like a cat caught up in yarn. This time I was prepared, all business, professional. Yet my resolve almost wavered when I saw him drive up and back the car into the shed.

Be strong.

"Jessie," he said, stopping at the bottom of the steps. He removed his hat.

"Mr. Bauer," I said. I stood.

"What a... It's... Here, come inside. I'll fix us hot chocolate, or would you like a glass of tea? Voe still brings tea. I don't believe she's here yet."

"How is she?"

"Good, good. Plans to take time off when the baby comes." He hesitated. "You're not looking for work, are you?"

"Not ever," I said. "I've a job in Eau Claire. The Everson Studio."

"Ah. Yes. I heard he was ill. What can I do for you?"

I put my hand to my throat, calmed my throbbing heart. "It's what I want to do for you," I said. "And for myself." I handed him an envelope.

He pulled a small knife from his pocket and slit the top. He peered inside at the cash I'd placed there. "What's this?" he said, frowning. "I'm not aware of any debt you owe me."

"The money you gave the Harmses," I said. His cheeks flamed. "You had no right to do that, to suggest that I couldn't make it on my own."

"I wasn't... I merely—"

"Asking them to keep a secret wasn't right either." I hadn't arrived annoyed, but I was now, old outrage steaming back.

"They told you," he said, his eyes on the envelope. "Confound it, I asked them not to."

"It slipped out. It wasn't their fault, so don't you blame them," I said. "As it happens, I did quite well in Milwaukee until Suzanne decided to sell the studio. I had my own small business of sorts in the Harms home, but it wasn't enough to sustain me...and still pay you back, or I'd have remained there. But now I've paid you."

"It isn't necessary, Jessie. I only wanted to help you out."

"But it was a gift with obligation," I said.

"It wasn't meant that way." His words were soft as butterfly wings.

"Then why make it a secret? Because you knew I'd decline it. You knew and you did it anyway. You...stepped over a fence, Fred Bauer, one you had no right to cross."

He hung his head.

"I owe you nothing now, not for your training of me, for the boarding of me, not for...anything. In time, I hope to own a studio, maybe right here in Winona, but I'll do it on my own, in my way. I'll be your competition one day, and I want nothing to get in the way of that development."

He looked up at me, smiled a wistful grin. "You've made a pun, yes?"

"If you get more than one meaning from what I've just said, then enjoy," I told him. "As I'll enjoy being free of my debt to you."

I turned into the wind, all uncertainty shaken loose and gone. I expected smooth sailing ahead.

FOURTEEN

New Exposures

THE TRAIN ROLLED INTO EAU CLAIRE midmorning on a bright July day. Robins and pigeons vied for space atop the turrets of the train station. A few passengers were disgorged along with Jessie, but most remained on board, traveling toward Green Bay, a city growing more quickly than this town named by a Frenchman. *Oh, Claire!* Jessie thought to herself. Her new home until she had enough money for her studio. The town was named either for the sparkling river that ran through it or for the beauty of a Chippewa Indian maiden, depending on which story one believed. Independence Day celebrations loomed, and Jessie hoped there'd be a street fair or Mr. Ferris's wheel to entertain them. She always loved the circus, too, and had even tried to convince Lilly she should become a costumer for Ringling Brothers, work in Baraboo in the off season. Lilly had scoffed.

"Here begins my next adventure, Lilly," Jessie said out loud as she disembarked. She was on her own, clear of debts and with a new, sound plan. The sense of freedom made her step lightly and inhale the warm morning air in one long breath of delight.

Elm trees offered shade. Perspiration dripped inside her whalebone corset, wilting her linen. She ought to have taken a cab, she thought. The Eversons would greet a perspiration-drenched photographer. She hoped Roy wasn't right about clothing's defining professional.

Carl G. Everson made no indication that he was offended by

Jessie's rumpled state when she arrived just before noon at the Everson Studio and apartment on busy Barstow Street. Perhaps his illness was greater than his offense. Dark mercury spots dotted his jaundiced skin, thin as vellum. The sight of them brought back hard memories for Jessie of Fred's suffering. The yellow surrounding his eyes couldn't mask the fear. She didn't stay long in this sickroom in the back of the studio.

Hilda Everson, his wife, pulled the door shut behind them as they walked the narrow hall to the kitchen. Jessie had entered from the back alley, as directed by Hilda Everson's letter, so she had yet to see the operating part of the studio.

"I welcome you," Mrs. Everson said. "Sit. We have tea." She appeared to wear one of the older S-curve corsets. Her torso lurched forward and her derrière curved well out to finish the *S* that her body formed. Jessie's corset was much less taxing, and in the stifling heat of the room, she was glad. "Now then. You seem small for one to carry on a big business." Mrs. Everson set glasses of amber liquid before Jessie.

"Didn't Mrs. Johnson's letter speak of my qualifications?"

"*Ja,* it did, but I expected someone older, with more experience and"—she squinted—"with a little more meat on her bones."

"I'm small but hardy," Jessie said. "You give me a task to do, and I can do it."

"*Ja,* well, we'll be glad for that, my Carl and I. You can do all the parts? Portraits, developing, proofs and correspondence, prints?"

"I need to learn your system," she said. "But, yes. All of it."

"I help as I can, but it's Carl's studio. The system, as you say..." She raised her palms and shrugged. "I try to show you. You can see how weak he is. I take care of him. My first duty."

"I understand," Jessie said. The way Hilda spoke of her "duty" didn't sound like obligation at all. Jessie read worry in the woman's face and in the pudgy hands void of rings. Running this studio would require full effort. She would be more than a mere assistant. The weight of Jessie's responsibility settled onto her shoulders. "You take care of Mr. Everson," she said. "Do what the doctor tells you." Hilda Everson frowned at that. Jessie continued: "I've had experience, before I worked for Suzanne Johnson, when I operated the Bauer Studio in Winona. Mr. Bauer took the mercury poisoning too."

"And is he...well?"

"Very well," Jessie said. "Even after having the poisoning twice." Jessie sipped her cool tea. "Your husband must have been in business a long time?" Hilda nodded. "But this is his first time contracting the poison?" Another nod yes. "Then things look good," Jessie said, her voice light. "I never saw Mr. Bauer at his worst, only when he first got ill and once during a later part of the recovery, but he came through it. We'll pray Mr. Everson does too."

"*Ja,* well, it is good to know someone else became well. Mrs. Johnson's husband—"

"Died of an accident," Jessie said. "It wasn't related to the poisoning at all."

"Ah, that is good to know. Not that her husband died, but the how of it. We welcome your prayers. Carl and me, we rely on prayer only, no doctors. Prayer heals all. I show you the newspaper, *Christian Science Monitor.* You've heard of this?" Jessie shook her head. "Well, I show you. The Bible instructs all healing paths. You join our readings on Sunday. Now, I show your room. Very small but you spend little time there, *ja*?"

Jessie followed Hilda to a room just large enough for a narrow bed and small stand holding a pitcher and bowl. She'd have difficulty with her rolling exercises here. Three pegs hung on the wall for her clothes. Jessie felt the warm breeze flowing in through the single window, up high in the wall so she couldn't really see out. The room must have been a linen closet once. Sounds of traffic and streetcars, horses clopping along the back alley, all rose up and slipped in with the breeze.

"We share the water closet," Hilda said. "Go ahead. Put your bags below the bed there," Hilda pointed. "Come. We have lunch. I shut the windows for you at night so the noise won't be so bad."

"I like a breeze in the evening," Jessie said.

"Not here. The night brings in disease. Lights must be out by 9 p.m. so you get enough rest. I show you our newspaper. We read it together. But now, I start to fatten you up. Your mother would not be pleased if you return home looking so pencil thin. Go, to the kitchen."

As she walked, herded by this sturdy woman, Jessie wondered if her feet had suddenly taken a turn off her very independent path.

Jessie finished enlarging the postcard-size photograph for Hilda Everson's patron. It was late Saturday of a January evening, and while Jessie liked the work she'd done these past seven months and could lose herself in it for hours, she wished she could have even a little time to herself, especially today, when her heart raced with hopeful possibilities. She had a letter waiting for her reply that she'd put off reading until she could devote her whole self to it, uninterrupted. It nearly burned a hole in her apron pocket, she expected it to hold such hope.

She pulled the last print from the wash solution, looked at it carefully. She'd dodged the light to get the effect she wanted. She wasn't always certain she was doing her best work here, as she had few breaks in her routine, and an artist needed that, to maintain her enthusiasm if not her craft. Even the weekends hardly marked a time of rest, but rather the beginning of the next hard days. The youth group at the evangelical church met on Saturday evenings, and she'd gone once after she'd first arrived in Eau Claire, but Mrs. Everson met her at the door when she came in at ten o'clock and suggested that her "late hours" were upsetting to her husband.

"Late hours?" Jessie had said. "It's still light outside." A dusky light, but one could easily see the neighbor's beagle lying on the lawn across the street.

"Nevertheless, Mr. Everson has need of his sleep. It's best you pray with us in the morning and take your own time on Sunday afternoons."

The people who gathered in the Everson parlor on Sunday mornings were friendly and kind, and their prayers sounded very much like the prayers of Jessie's experience, but it seemed to Jessie that they read more essays out of the *Monitor* and talked about their healings without benefit of physicians more than they relied on Scripture for encouragement. Essays were all well and good, but Jessie felt constricted by not being able to be where she wanted to be, *when* she wanted to be there. She longed for organ and piano music and the insights that sliced through her loneliness, words of hymns that reached directly to her soul. Her mind wandered during readings in the Everson parlor just as they did during sermons at church. But music and the lyrics always took her "into the Presence," as she thought of it, music drawing her away from homesickness and toward the comfort of an eternal home.

She'd especially missed going home for Christmas and hearing Selma sing. They'd had more snow than usual just days before she'd planned to leave, and Jessie felt it better not to risk the trip. She remembered that terrible train accident in the winter of 1910 near Seattle, when a hundred and eighteen people had died. After being stranded for days on a train, an avalanche pushed the cars from the tracks over a cliff just before the rescuers could reach them. Caution was a good lesson she'd learned the hard way, a Milwaukee motorcycle shop's being the best teacher.

She'd celebrated with the Eversons instead of going home. They did enjoy Christmas, so that was a relief. By then, Mr. Everson was much improved, and Jessie hoped that their need of her would come to an end by late spring or early summer. They paid her well. Her room and board were included, so she'd been able to save almost everything she earned. She'd spent nothing on new dresses or hats. Slowly, she met the criteria that kept her from Winona: she'd repaid Fred, she'd not made any bad mistakes in the studio or in her personal life, and she'd sent money home to her parents. Most of all, she'd built that nest egg for her own studio purchase.

January was always a dreary month, with little sun and air so cold it hurt to breathe when she took her quick walks around the block to clear her head of Mrs. Everson's constant chatter. Barstow Street proved noisy, and the Everson Studio opened right onto a boardwalk. Store awnings rolled up for the winter still flapped in the wind, and sometimes in the late afternoon the skies would be so dark the gaslights came on as though it were night. A big bank clock across the street clanged the hours.

In Milwaukee, Jessie'd wished Suzanne Johnson would've spent more time talking with her, becoming her friend, but here she longed for silence and time on her own. Sunday afternoons—her only free time—raced away like the skaters disappearing out of sight on the frozen Chippewa River.

Fred had written to her, but that was not the letter she held. Fred's letter had arrived in December. She'd waited all day before opening it too, taking a good deep breath of cold December air before she did. It was a cordial letter telling her of George Haas's plan to sell the Polonia Studio and the building. *I remember your interest in one day owning your own studio,* he'd written. *So I pass this along to you as a colleague, thinking you might wish to pursue it.* Her heart beat faster at the very idea of owning the Polonia. Her wet palms had to do with the nearness of her dream and not with the idea that Fred Bauer had actually written the words on the thin paper of his personal stationery. The Polonia had a good reputation, and its name suggested a steady clientele from the Polish immigrants of the region. She expected they'd remain with whoever purchased the studio. It apparently hadn't been put up publicly yet, so Jessie felt a bit of pressure to follow up, which she'd done.

She'd written to George Haas immediately. And now he'd replied.

Jessie finished the final bath and hung the prints to dry. When she owned her own studio, she'd arrange it differently than this one, with easier access to water so she didn't have to carry the tubs through the house. She'd want a room with better ventilation too, so when she was finished, she could let fresh air move out the acrid chemical smells. Sometimes she wondered if what photographers breathed in through their lungs might not be worse than the mercury that seeped in through their skin. She had plans for the reception room too, without all the heavy drapes, frilly tablecloths, and bric-a-brac collecting dust, the cleaning of which was also a part of Jessie's work. The lighting was good though, better than in the Johnson Studio but not as good as the Bauer Studio. Fred had built that studio from the foundation up. He didn't have to adapt a building meant for family living or a grocery. In all these experiences, she acquired wisdom for her own business. She hoped that thinking of herself as wiser wasn't a grievous sin.

She tiptoed past the Eversons' door and stepped outside. She leaned against the wooden rail bordering the steps to the alley. The air bit at her face as she took several deep breaths and raised her arms up over her head several times. While the Eversons didn't subscribe to the latest photographic journals, they did take papers related to health, and Jessie read them and concurred with the view that fresh air helped one think more clearly. She put her hands in her pocket and pulled out the letter.

She anticipated details of the costs of the business and all the rest that she'd asked for.

Jessie sent her savings each month to the Winona Savings Bank, even though there'd been problems with banks just a few years before. They said they'd pay her a small amount of interest for being able to use her money in loans to others, but that whenever she needed it, she could have it. Her father had said he wasn't so confident in their promise, and he kept his money in a box under the bed. Jessie told him they ought to get a cat, or the mice might pay interest to his money. Jessie knew that Fred had a banking account, and it seemed to her that all professional people did. She didn't want to dispute her father's point of view, but she took responsibility for her own choice. That she had a "meaningful deposit relationship"—as the bank manager called it—meant she might be able to borrow money from them one day. At least Jessie thought that was what his remark had suggested.

She didn't want to write to the bank about seeking a loan; she wanted to talk in person to the bank manager about borrowing the remainder of what she'd need for the purchase of the studio. She knew the building that housed the Polonia on East Fourth, and she was certain that a small apartment either at the back of the property or within the building itself would be part of the purchase. Tenants rented the second floor. It would be perfect. Because Fred had mentioned it to her, he must have thought she'd be up to the challenge too.

Holding the envelope, she went back inside to sit on her narrow bed. The old proverb came to her as she did, and she thought of it as a kind of prayer. *Desire accomplished is sweet to the soul.* To own her own business, to have everything she ever dreamed about, and in her own town where she could be near family, even Lilly, would be such a gift. And in these words lay her future. She carefully lifted the letter and read:

> *While I appreciate your interest in my studio, I fail to see how a young woman such as yourself would be able to afford the sale, let alone operate the studio alone. It is my professional opinion that young women should work only to support their husbands or families, and then under the direction of a competent man. I have other offers to consider. Thank you for your inquiry. Signed, George Haas*

His words brought heat to her cheeks. How dare he decide *for* her what she was capable of! Hadn't he read what she'd told him of her experience running other people's studios? Did he think she'd exaggerated her professional abilities? Most photographers hired help, and she would too, assuming his books showed that the income was sufficient. Even if it wasn't, she knew how to expand a business, bring in clientele that might not otherwise take the time to have their pictures made. He hadn't even answered her questions about how many glass plates he had available for reprint and how much of his annual income came from reprints, postcards, and the like. Why, he treated her as though she were a schoolgirl asking a busy man if she could visit his business just to admire his work. She wondered if Jessie Tarbox Beals had to put up with such nonsense as this! No wonder that woman had gone out on her own. *Young women should work only to support their husbands or families.* She seethed. Women weren't supposed to have any desires of their own, she supposed. *I have other offers.* Then why did he continue to advertise?

Jessie crumpled the letter in her hand. She paced her narrow room.

She would go to see him, as well as the bank, face to face. Both of these men would recognize her determination and her abilities. She would convince them. She knocked on the Eversons' bedroom door. They'd have to give her a few days off, or she'd terminate her employment early. Nothing was going to keep her from owning the Polonia!

January 15, 1912

Dear Sister,

How are you? I am fine.

Thank you for the Christmas gifts. The locket is beautiful. I see why you bought it. I wish you were still here so Lilly would have someone else to watch. She acts like I'm going to do awful things with Art Roeling, my new beau, though we're never alone, not ever. What Lilly needs is her own beau to worry about instead of mine.

I'll be glad when you meet Art. I'm glad Mama didn't

know that he was special, because she might not have let him come to the Christmas party with the other boys, because he doesn't go to our church. It was a good idea to invite boys from the youth group too. Thank you for suggesting that. Art is in high school, but he works at the printers where you worked once. When he stops by Lottie's on his way home, I can smell the ink on him and see it on his fingertips.

I'm sorry that where you're working in Eau Claire isn't an easy place to be. I hope it gets better. You have to make the best of what is. That's what I'm doing with Lilly, who tells me what to do and what to wear just like Mama does! Did they do that to you? No wonder you left Winona.

Mama lets Roy's chickens come into the house, which surprises even Papa. They're good chickens and will sit on your lap and let you stroke them just like a cat. Not that we have a cat in the house, but I think we should. I hear scratching in the walls at night and I think the sound comes from mice.

Is the weather changing where you are? It's so cold here! I'll be glad for spring, when trumpeter swans stop by the lake's edges and pluck at rice, and the geese come back to peck at grass. Papa says I can go ice fishing with him and Uncle August and Roy if I want to next week. Why would I want to? It's always so cold! I didn't say that to him. He enjoys it. At least when we ice skate we stay moving and warm.

I know I'm not supposed to talk about Mr. Bauer with you, that's what Lilly told me, but I will tell you that he came by Lottie's today and asked about you. He was buying a gift for his wife. He wanted to know how you were, and I told him you were fine but that you didn't like Eau Claire much, or at least the Everson Studio where you work. Was that all right, that I told him that? I just wonder. He bought Mrs. Bauer a fur neck muffler and matching fur muff. He has "fine taste," as Lottie said, and likes the more expensive things. Which is nice for Lottie and for Mrs. Bauer.

When are you coming back to Winona? I just wonder.

Write to me soon. I'm fine.

Your loving sister,

Selma

FIFTEEN

Intrusions

IT WAS PURE CHANCE THAT THE TRAIN pulled in when Fred had stopped by to pick up supplies. He'd taken over that task from Voe and told himself it was simply more practical for him to do it with the car or a cab if the weather turned sour. But he did notice the other deliveries when he picked up his own and then chastised himself for wanting a connection to Jessie, despite how faded that attachment might be. As the train eased by, chugging and belching, his eyes followed the windows. He swallowed when he thought he saw her profile and decided to wait until passengers unloaded. He was being silly. He couldn't imagine any reason why she'd be coming to Winona. He hadn't seen her over the holidays, and she hadn't answered his cordial letter about Mr. Haas's wish to sell.

Yet there she was, standing a distance in front of him, staring at the street. He waved as though he'd meant to be the one to pick her up all along, and when he got her attention, she tilted her head before indicating she recognized him. She waved her fur muff as he approached her. He thought tears would fill his eyes and reveal the pain of her absence and the depth of his relief when she walked toward him, slowly, the way a photograph formed onto the paper.

"It seems our paths cross," Fred said.

"So they do." She looked beyond him, seeking the streetcar, he imagined.

"I have the car. I'd be pleased to offer you a ride home."

She hesitated, and yet he was certain he'd seen a look in her eyes, a flicker of interest as he put out his gloved hand and reached for her tapestry bag. Paying her debt had put them on equal footing. At least he imagined she might see it that way. She nodded and moved toward the car.

He cared for her, longed to be someone who helped her advance her talent, would do almost anything just to know he could have a conversation with her now and then. He'd keep his distance, he would; but if he didn't have to, if they could be friends again, it would bring such joy to his life.

"How nice to see you back, Miss Gaebele," Fred said. He wasn't sure how to address her. She was Jessie in his mind and always would be, but now saying that felt like a betrayal to both of the women in his life. They both bore that name, and his wife's request that he use it for her made the confusion in his heart even greater.

Both of the women in my life.

The woman before him, spare and splendid, was not a woman in his life, could never be. And yet his breathing quickened, and when his glove touched hers, he felt a spark. *Probably the dry air crackling in the cold weather.*

"It's nice to be home," she said as she stepped into the car.

"Staying long?"

"That depends."

He loaded her bag into the backseat and wondered if she remembered that the last time she'd ridden in this touring car, she'd left her blue hat there. It seemed years before. He smiled to himself as he walked to the front and cranked the car. It *had* been years before, nearly two. The hat she wore today was a midnight blue velvet trimmed with black ostrich plumes that shaded her eyes. She didn't look at him as she held onto a large portfolio case. Her small ears were pink from the cold.

"On what does your stay depend, Miss Gaebele? Your family is well, I trust," he said as he opened the driver's side door. "You haven't come home because of illness or—"

"No," she said. "Everyone is fine." She started to speak, cleared her throat only to take in a deep breath. "I've come to buy Polonia Studio."

He slapped the steering wheel. "Good for you!" He knew he beamed like a father watching his daughter stand up in front of the school to make a recitation. "I hoped that would come about. I told George you'd be a fine candidate. Skilled, reliable, good with patrons, inventive. I gave him all your greatest attributes."

"Apparently your glowing recommendation was insufficient," she said.

"What?" He turned to look at her, but his eyes were wrenched back to the road by the car tires hitting the streetcar track. "What do you mean?"

"George Haas has decided that a young woman should only work to support her husband or her family and shouldn't even think about owning her own business. Apparently he doesn't agree that I could run a studio. I plan to show him copies of *Camera Notes* and educate him about the contributions being made by female photographers, including those who aren't married. The very idea," she said. "What's a girl to do if she needs to work? Men." She spoke the last under her breath.

"Perhaps I could talk with him, on your behalf," Fred said. "I'd be honored. Maybe I didn't make as strong a case as I might have. I could provide detail about your retouching work." His voice cracked, and again he looked at her to see if she remembered, if that day they'd worked in the retouching room so close, so very close, still resonated with her as it did with him, the memory a bow drawn slowly across his heartstrings.

She glanced at him, then turned away. "You did speak to him, and I thank you, but it had no effect. I'll do this on my own. I'm going to go to the bank and get a loan. If I can convince those bankers that a woman has capabilities, then perhaps they can convince Mr. Haas with me. It's so…frustrating," she added, plumping her muff as she shoved her hands into it.

"You have copies of your work?" Fred nodded toward the folio bag that leaned against her knees. It acted as a shield between them. He hoped she wasn't afraid of him, wasn't thinking he'd do anything to reignite the fires that had rushed through their lives, burning them both. "I'd be pleased to see them."

She hesitated. "I am rather fond of the sample I made. This woman, she had such a fine look about her, a natural beauty. She didn't think so, of course. It never ceases to amaze me that women who I think have so much character in their faces often discount it. I think a photographer must become like one of those mind doctors who reads the heart and soul and draws out the secrets in the subject."

"I hadn't thought of it as mind doctoring, but you have a point," he said. He laughed. "Might be a new kind of attraction for a studio: 'Minds developed while you wait.' "

She looked shyly at him, grinned. "You don't really think that."

"One never knows about the mind," he said. "Photography might be as effective as, say, doctoring at Mayo."

"Oh, I doubt that. But I do find it fascinating to let people pose themselves. Have you noticed how they act out annoyances that might be shown in the reception room or even when they made the appointment? Whether they're demanding of a certain time or timid or show up late or early? That all appears in the sitting."

"I confess I hadn't noticed," Fred said. "But now that you say it, yes, there are times that the props they select reflect their personalities. Flamboyant or shy. And the way another family member chastises them for their choice can show up in their faces too."

"Of course, I never tell them what I've seen."

"One shouldn't."

"I just find it...interesting. It's as though how they behave in the studio allows me to enter their thoughts, and the experience keeps them with me long after they've gone."

He could feel her enthusiasm for her talent and profession fill the car, and it pleased him. Who else could he have such a conversation with?

She continued. "Maybe it shows in the photograph whether I've captured special qualities in them, whether the person behind the lens contributes as much as the subject." She turned to face him. He could see her stare from the corner of his eye as he kept focused straight ahead.

"Yes. The person behind the lens does express a part of themselves in the final result." His hands grew damp inside his gloves as he remembered the photograph he'd made of Jessie, had given her as a birthday gift so long ago. Could she be thinking of that?

He turned the car toward her parents' home, but she redirected him. "I planned to go by the Polonia," she said. "I'd better see for certain what I'm buying. I can make my way home from there."

"I'm more than happy to wait," he said. "My presence might lend credibility to your negotiations with Haas."

She seemed to think about that and then said, "All right. But let me do the talking."

It was their usual time together in the evangelist's small back office. Mrs. Bauer's eyes focused on photographs that her husband likely had taken: portraits of the evangelist's family, Reverend Carleton's boys and girls. The cross on the shelf behind him was made of tiny seashells, and often when her mind refused to let her listen or absorb what he said, it was because she counted them, those shells, over and over again.

Mrs. Bauer had told Reverend Carleton everything she could think to say, and yet each time she came to visit, more thoughts poured out. Through tears that wouldn't stop, she told him about Donald's death and how it had been her favorite horse they'd had put down afterward, which was only right. And yet, if her husband hadn't insisted on letting Donald stand up in the wagon, the child would still be here today, not a victim of a freak accident. She told the reverend of her grief and how she never wanted to see North Dakota again, though she missed having horses. "I cannot forgive him," she whispered.

" 'For if we sin willfully after that we have received the knowledge of the truth, there remaineth no more sacrifice for sins,' " Reverend Carleton told her.

"Yes, yes, I know I'm a sinful person to not forgive him, but I just can't seem to. And that adds to my weariness. I don't have enough of what I need to get through this."

" 'My grace is sufficient for thee.' "

"But you see, God's grace doesn't seem to be. That's another of my failures." She dabbed at her eyes with her handkerchief.

She told him then about FJ's temper, how he'd smashed in her bedroom door when she'd locked herself inside and told him she'd had enough, didn't want to keep going on this way. Reverend Carleton said perhaps he was worried about her, didn't want her to harm herself, and she'd thought about that as the evangelist handed her a fresh handkerchief. Hers, embroidered with daisies, was so wet it could no longer hold her drenching tears. She twisted it in her hands. "I know, I know. He's a good man, though impatient. He barks at the children, at me. I feel as though I can do nothing to please him."

Was that the same look of exasperation in Reverend Carleton's face as in her husband's? On days she thought she saw such a thing, she could say no more, would sit in silence while he spoke scriptures that she tried to remember, hoping they'd wash over her when she was in the safety of her home. She'd never had the courage to tell Reverend Carleton that there were times when she simply felt relieved that Fred wasn't home.

Their marriage mixed confusion and regret with uncertainty and disdain. How could they reestablish a marriage on such a basis? She'd forgotten the last time she laughed with FJ. Maybe it was the day they'd gone fishing together, though she'd laughed more at her success catching fish and the children's delight than at anything that transpired between her and her husband.

Her prayers had encouraged her to speak more openly to Reverend Carleton, and lately she'd begun to tell him more of how she felt, of those inner thoughts that intruded. She often refused to let them come to the surface for fear they'd overtake her, the way rice boiled over when it should simply absorb. She wasn't certain she was ready to deal with all the hidden things, the feelings she kept cloaked, but when she was with this man, this kind and predictable man, she came closer to facing the truths of her life.

An odd thing also occurred before her visits: she noticed that when she prepared for her appointments with the reverend, she dressed more consciously. She put lavender scent behind her ears and primped to be certain that the dress she chose didn't pull at her thickening waist. She'd purchased extra face powder at Choate's, but she used it lightly because she almost always cried during their meetings and she didn't want her tears to cake ridges on her face. In a mirror, she'd once seen herself crying and was horrified at the image. Who would want to look at a face resembling the contortions of the fat lady in the circus, made worse because of tears?

One, two, three, four shells on that row of the cross.

She hoped that how she felt about Reverend Carleton wasn't wrong, even though she did think about him when she was at home peeling potatoes or pumping water into the pitchers. She hadn't told him any of this. She didn't want him knowing, and she feared that if she told him he would tell her she was sinning and perhaps suggest she not come back until she ceased her ways. She had to let him know that he helped her, that she made progress. She had to tell him of more…intimate things so he wouldn't feel he was wasting his time.

Five, six, seven.

"Mrs. Bauer?"

"I think he might be interested in…other women," she told the reverend. It was their first meeting after Christmas, and he'd told her that come spring he'd be traveling and would not be able to see her as frequently. She said she understood, but her chest had tightened, as though he'd told her there'd be less water to drink.

He leaned away from her. "Why would you say such a thing?"

She shouldn't have said it that way.

"It's… He's distracted with me. He used to, that is, we haven't been, intimate, that is, well, not for some time." She looked down, didn't want to see the judgment in his eyes. "He used to shout at me about that, complain when I didn't want him to touch me. I... We kept it from the children, of course. But then lately, maybe for the past year or more, he's not sought my...affection at all."

She wondered what kind of relationship Reverend Carleton had with his wife.

"Perhaps he's respecting your wishes," the reverend said. Had he sighed? He made notes on a pad as she talked. That was probably how he could pick up so quickly with what she'd said the last time. She hadn't thought of it, that he'd make notes. "Hasn't he agreed to call you Jessie, as you asked?"

She nodded. "Yes. Yes, he has. Maybe he's just doing what I want him to do, and then, you see, I make it terrible. How can he put up with me? A normal man would just—"

"A man who loves his wife would honor her wishes."

"Do you honor your wife's wishes?"

"We're not speaking of me and mine, Mrs. Bauer." He smoothed his slicked-back hair. "Let's stay to the point here."

Her face burned. How silly of her to cross the unwritten border of their relationship. Relationship! It wasn't a relationship at all.

"Though you should consider, Mrs. Bauer, your wifely duties to your husband."

She looked at him. What was he like to be married to? Did he sing "Let Me Call You Sweetheart" while he dressed in the morning? Did he help with the children? What would it be like to have him reach for her hand and stroke it? Would she jerk away as she did from FJ? Would she wish to have him breathe softly onto her neck while she cooked at the Monarch? Or would she find relief when he traveled as he so often did around the region, holding tent meetings? Maybe that was the way for women: having time without a man around offered relief, but they didn't ever dare say so, not even to themselves, for fear the thought violated heavenly law. "A Good Man Is Hard to Find." The song rolled through her head. *A good man may be hard to find, but he isn't hard to put behind other thoughts once in a while.* She suppressed a grin behind her gloved hand, made it look like she suppressed a cough. Good heavens, what was wrong with her?

"But his respecting your wishes, offering separation, is no reason to assume he is involved with any other woman, Mrs. Bauer. You mustn't let your imagination rule your thinking."

"No, no, I mustn't." He was annoyed with her, she could tell. She'd offer more. "But there is something...hard to describe."

He patted his wide belly as though seeking his watch, urged her on with his hand, the pencil bobbing. "Go ahead, tell me."

Do I detect impatience? What does he write down about me?

"Whenever FJ says my name, Jessie, there's a hesitation to it, as though his thoughts go first to...someone else."

"Who might that be? Do you know any other Jessies he encounters?"

"We had an employee for a time. The one who was in here last summer when I stopped by. Jessie Gaebele."

"She's moved away. Eau Claire now. She's not even in the city, Mrs. Bauer."

"I know. It's just that he—"

"If that's all you have to worry you, Mrs. Bauer, that he hesitates using your name after so many years of your asking him not to, you worry for naught."

"Do you think so?"

"He's simply making an adjustment, I'd say."

"So nothing to worry over."

"Nothing at all."

One, two, three, four, five, six shells on the left cross bar.

"I think our time is up, Mrs. Bauer." He pulled out his vest watch, clicked it open, then closed it.

How long had she been counting, not aware of where she was? She looked at him closely. His face was so firm, lips full, beard trimmed to a tiny point over his chin. Less tidy than her husband but fuller, rounder, a bigger man. Softer, with gentle hands. Deeply spiritual. Warm. She felt her throat tighten.

"Do you have scriptures to dwell on this next week, Mrs. Bauer? Received through prayer as I've encouraged?"

"First Corinthians 10:13," she offered up before even thinking.

He sat back. "Temptation? Whatever temptations do you struggle with, dear lady? Oh"—he checked his watch again—"it shall have to wait. I'll look forward to hearing more when next we meet."

"Until we meet again," she said.

Whatever would she tell him?

Patricia Benson, character study
January 11, 1912, Everson Studio, Eau Claire
4 x 5 Graflex

Desire

It is a favorite of mine, this character study of Patricia Benson. I love the looseness of her hair and the way the light filters through the gold-spun strands. I like how she looks to the camera, seeking. We all seek, are sent to the "limits of our longing" as the poet Rilke notes, sent by the very act of being a creative person, born to invent. In her eyes I see this cautious longing so common among women working in this world. When a man does well in a new business venture, everyone says how wise and wonderful he is, such a good planner. If he fails, well, it was a "poor market." Unforeseen circumstances caused his income to fall; nothing he did caused the trouble.

Yet a woman like Patricia Benson opens a bakery and it flourishes, but is she praised for her skill at starting something new, for her plans and implementation? No, her praise is that she picked a good time to open a bakery, the markets being good and people ready for such a thing. But if her revenues are insufficient because people have lost employment and no longer visit bakeries, those same sages nod their knowing heads and comment on her poor planning, how she didn't realize how complicated the world of business really is, and truly a woman's place is best spent baking in her home. They say this as they cluck their tongues.

It is the way of business, perhaps of the world.

This portrait is a sample I made while in Eau Claire. I noticed I misspelled sample on the back, reversing the l *and* e. *I do that often, which is why I'd copied my letter to George Haas several times to be certain I had all the spelling correct before I sent it.*

I colored this portrait myself. I thought it would demonstrate my versatility. I got the shadows right along her face and neck, tinted them not too dark, brought out the amber in her eyes so that she looks as though she's standing right before us. She wore a turquoise kimono that

Mrs. Everson had for props, and I allowed the right side of the photograph to bear a deeper tone and brushed the color on the other side. I took out all the background too. Nothing to distract the eye. And I asked her not to show her teeth, which, while perfectly straight, seemed large for her face. I asked her to think of something she longed for. She'd wiggled her nose at me and asked how I knew that speaking a desire was something difficult for her.

"It's difficult for all of us," I told her. "I can tell you what my sister wants, and my father, but when I'm asked to name it for myself, my mind becomes a blank glass plate. Or at least it did until I realized I wanted to have my own studio one day. After that, all my focus went there." Except for those distractions some years back. But I am past those distractions now.

I'll never know for certain, but I think the character study, as we photographers called such samples, gave me an extra step through the doorway that opened onto my dream. The day I met with George Haas, his eyebrow lifted in appreciation as I showed him this sample along with the Marquette girls and Misha, the Russian baby. But it was Patricia's portrait that he held the longest.

Still, he shook his head.

"I don't think you can do it," he said. "I don't want to be in Tampa next year and hear you've been consumed by the forces of finance. Or a fiancé," he added. His eyes twinkled and reminded me of my uncle August's teasing. But George Haas wasn't teasing.

"I've no intention of marriage anytime soon, and even if I did, I'd still be able to run my own studio. Any fiancé of mine would accept my business and either like it or skedaddle."

Both George and Fred laughed at that, but George seemed unmoved.

"She can do this, George," Fred told him then. I felt conflicted over his role in the conversation. "You can judge her considerable talent, and I've seen her with patrons. She's good."

"This isn't a woman's profession, FJ. You know that. It's dangerous. One's got to be aggressive. She likely can't do that with so many other studios in town. She can't join the lodges, can't teach the classes, all the things that make this business go."

I felt embarrassed by these men talking about me as though I were a mere prop in this picture. Their comments unsettled, made me wonder if perhaps I wasn't ready.

"I can give you the names of plenty of women photographers who are making it just fine," I insisted. "Frances Benjamin Johnston. Mary Carnell. Evelyn Cameron of Montana, for heaven's sake. Myra Albert Wiggins. Mary McGarvey. Why, Miss Belle Johnson makes her way taking photographs of kittens, and she does it in the burgeoning metropolis of Monroe City, Missouri!" I was no longer embarrassed; I was mad. "If you gentlemen think I can't do this—"

"I never said—" Fred interrupted, turning to me.

"—then I'll open my own studio. Who needs yours, Mr. Haas? You can sell the Polonia to whomever you find who adequately meets your esteemed requirements, namely, that they wear pants."

I gathered up my folio then and stormed out. I'd already retrieved my bag from Fred's backseat when he hurried down the steps, his cane hooked over his arm. "Listen," he said. "Give me a little time with him. He can be melded into shape."

"I'll do it myself, Fred," I said. My use of his name seemed to fluster him. He stopped moving toward me. "Mr. Bauer."

"Jessie. Let me help. Please."

I shook my head. "I won't have you doing anything more for me, Mr. Bauer. This isn't something anyone can do for me. Do you understand? I'm going to the bank, and I'll take care of it myself or I won't own a studio. That's that."

When I looked at Patricia's portrait again later that evening, I remembered how I'd dodged it, used my hand to burn light into one place more than another.

Maybe I wasn't meant to have my own studio; maybe some other area of my life had yet to be exposed and I was too dense to receive it, dodging good light all on my own.

SIXTEEN

The Road to Readjustment

Jessie walked from Fourth Street home to Broadway. It was a good hike in the cold January air, her fur collar tucked up around her face, keeping all but her eyes warm against the wind. Walking helped her quell her outrage. "So what is it I'm supposed to do? Just how am I to proceed?" She'd been bold saying she could secure a loan. She could start her own studio. She didn't need Polonia. Of course, the issue of money remained. Maybe she could borrow what she needed from her uncle August. He understood her adventurous spirit. "Would he loan money to a woman?" Maybe she should just ask Fred for the money.

Don't do it.

She ought to have declined his offer of a ride in the first place. But his smile warmed her, and he looked so, oh, professional standing there with his cane draped across his arm and his collar turned up against the cold. He wore no hat, which he should have, given the temperature and the icicles clinging to the depot's roof. Maybe the weather had convinced her to take up his offer for a ride. But then why did she let him come with her to Polonia Studio?

He was supportive, that was why. He was encouraging, gentle, just as she'd remembered him. A woman ought to be able to have a professional relationship with a man, oughtn't she?

She reached the family home.

"J-J-Jessie!" Roy greeted her at the door. "Mama, i-i-it's J-J-Jessie!"

"Well, sugar my beets if it isn't. Come in, come in, you look frozen as Roy's snowman. Why didn't you call from the station? Goodness, get over by the stove there. Roy, put fresh coal in. Oh my."

"I'm fine, Mama," Jessie said, but it came out as "I'mb fine, Bamba" because her lips were numbed by the cold. Roy laughed. "All right for you, Frog," she said, and he laughed again at her effort to speak. She unhooked the collar and set it a distance from the stove so it would warm up slowly; the muff and gloves she set aside too, to dry.

"Tea. Here's hot tea. Your sisters will be home any time now. When did your train get in? Were you on the 12:05? Why, you've been out in the cold all that time? Your father will be upset you didn't call him."

"I had business to attend to," she said when her lips had taken in the hot tea and she'd pulled a tiny leaf of mint from her tongue. Her hands warmed around the cup.

"What business? Photographic business?" Her mother frowned. "You didn't go by the Bauer—"

"No, Mama, I did not go by the Bauer Studio."

She nodded. "Are you finished at Eau Claire? I thought they'd need you into summer."

"I return in two days. I came home because I thought I could buy Polonia Studio," she said. "But Mr. Haas doesn't want to sell to a woman. Doesn't think I'm up to the task." She sounded disgusted and she knew it.

"Such a big venture for one so young."

"I'm nearly twenty, Mama. I don't have enough saved up to buy it on my own. But I'm going to the bank tomorrow to see if I can get a loan to add to what I have and start my own business. Forget Polonia. Let George Haas sell it to someone with a mustache, and I'll compete with him and the Bauer Studio and all the rest of them!"

"Jessie, Jessie, best mind your tongue." Her mother turned back to the jar of canned peaches she'd been opening when Jessie came in. "Maybe you could talk to Ralph Carleton to earn extra for your venture."

Jessie rolled her eyes toward Roy. "Mother, please. Don't. I'm sorry I brought it up." She picked up her portfolio and muff, put the bag in the other hand. "I'll take these upstairs and surprise my sisters, who I'm sure will be pleased to give up a third of their bed tonight."

"What will you do if you can't get a loan?"

"I'll...find work somewhere when the Eversons no longer need me." She'd counted on buying Polonia, having George carry the contract on credit. She hadn't thought much past that.

She considered writing to Joshua Behrens and seeking his business advice. But he was far removed from her now, and she didn't need advice; she needed cash. She needed someone with cash to believe in her.

When she came downstairs again, she helped her mother peel potatoes, picking off the eyes that grew through the fall and into the winter despite the cool storage they'd been in. She put the peels onto last week's *Republican-Herald.* An article beneath the pile of peels caught her eye. It was all about banks and what good shape they were in. It listed the First National and the Winona Savings Bank and all their officers and cashiers. The Winona Savings Bank would hold its meeting the next week, the article said. *How timely,* Jessie thought. She could meet with her own bank first, and if they turned her down, she'd make an appointment by name with the presidents of the other two banks. Surely one of the three would find a way to loan her what she needed.

Family chatter filled the kitchen as her sisters arrived home. Even Lilly appeared happy to see her, hugging her and letting Jessie be the first to let go. She caught up on family news about their Seattle aunt, the grandparents, her uncle "who is finally courting," her mother said with pride. Roy's hen, Madero, had assumed a special place in a pen on the porch, though she went back to the henhouse for the evenings. "He just loves that bird," Selma said when Roy got up from the table to bring the chicken in.

A warmth filled Jessie as she looked around the room. These were her people, and she needed—yes, needed—to be nearer to them, to find a way to see them daily and be a part of their lives. She posed them in a picture in her mind: Roy in the middle of her sisters, her parents standing behind them, but all of them close to one another. Bordering and protecting.

Exhaustion suddenly hit her. She'd had a train ride, an unexpected emotional encounter with Fred, a disastrous negotiation with George Haas, and a freezing walk home in the cold. She shouldn't have tried to see George immediately after arriving, and she shouldn't have let Fred join her at all. But that was water under the bridge. She'd rest, and then in the morning she'd go to the Winona Savings Bank and talk about that "meaningful deposit relationship," and if they wouldn't listen, she'd form a relationship with another bank.

Fred hadn't heard anything more from Jessie or about her. As he drove by Lottie's Millinery, he realized he could hardly ask her sister how Jessie's meeting with the bank had gone. For all he knew, she hadn't even done it, and he suspected now that she was back in Eau Claire. His sadness over the way she'd been treated by George, and his own regret over their talking around her while she stood there, hadn't gone away. He was supposed to keep quiet, and he hadn't. But he couldn't stand by and let George dismiss her, not when she had all the talent needed to be successful.

When she left he'd driven alongside her for a ways, leaning toward the passenger side, urging her to get in, but she'd refused. He didn't want to bring attention to them, so he'd pulled over and watched her walk away.

The rest of that week had passed without his seeing her, then another. His life had gone on, full of moments he imagined encountering her. These were innocent thoughts. Oh, sometimes when Russell brought his attention to a balsa airplane he'd glued together, Fred had to be called more than once because his mind wandered. When Robert waddled through the room and punched Fred's newspaper, showing his big smile even if Fred lowered the paper in annoyance, he'd realize he hadn't been reading anyway, merely thinking about Jessie Gaebele.

Now the early sap of the maples had darkened the crotch of trees, seeping black lines down the trunks, announcing spring. Daffodils and crocuses no longer had to push through old snow, leaned toward new grass instead. He'd written to her, just letting her know he was sorry if he'd offended her and offering whatever help he could if she'd let him assist her.

His daily pawing through the mail took on new interest, though she hadn't written back. Even in her absence she was more a part of his life than his wife, who had gone further and further away. One day a week she got herself up early, before he left for the studio, and she wore new perfume he thought, put on her most stylish dress. When he asked her what the occasion was, she said it was nothing special, that she was giving herself an "agreeable day" now and then.

"You look wonderful," he told her. "A sparkle in your eye."

When he'd said that, she seemed to disappear inside herself, her eyes taking on a dull look. She'd even stepped away from him.

"Please," he said. "I only meant to compliment you."

"Oh. Well. That's good then."

She'd stared at him as he donned his lighter suit coat, and she handed him his cane. "Have a good…agreeable day," he told her.

"Thank you," she said. "And you as well."

They were like people in a hospital waiting room, aware that this was not a place either wished to be, but here they were, making the best of it while they waited out whatever disastrous news had yet to come their way.

Then he'd seen the ad in the paper. That morning at the studio, he'd made up his mind. He had to let Jessie know that George still hadn't sold the studio and was now advertising for a retoucher. If Jessie came back and took that job, she'd surely be able to convince George of her abilities.

Maybe he shouldn't interfere. Well, he wasn't. He was simply being helpful. He'd be grateful if someone did the same for one of his children.

He could tell Selma about it and let her convey the message. But that was cowardly, using another child that way. No, he'd be a man about it. He'd be one colleague letting another know of an opportunity. That's all it was. He was certain.

He needed a break himself. He'd make a run to visit his sister Luise and her husband, Augie Staak, and his niece and nephew, near Cochrane, Wisconsin. It had been a while since he'd driven to their farm. She'd been the only one of his sisters to follow him to America and remain; another had come, married, and returned to Germany. He felt a special affinity for Luise. Like him, she'd endured great tragedy, when her first husband and two sons died of typhoid. Her oldest son had been the same age as Donald when he'd died, but her youngest, just a baby. And a husband. She'd come from Buffalo, New York, to visit him shortly after their deaths, and she'd met August Staak. She returned a year later to marry the farmer in 1900. They lived only fifteen or so miles away across the Mississippi.

He got out his map, unfolded it onto his desk. Voe came by. "Taking a trip, Mr. B.?" she asked as she leaned over his shoulder.

"No. Yes. To visit my sister," he said. "Taking Russell."

His eye fell on Eau Claire. It wasn't that far from Cochrane. Maybe what, fifty miles? Just a good day's jaunt. They could spend the night if things got late. Russell liked photography, and he could bring the camera along. Yes, that's what he'd do. Then he'd find the Everson Studio and let Jessie know in person about the job opening. It was the least he could do. He refolded the map perfectly, the creases lining up as they were meant to.

Jessie decided that missteps were fodder for better decisions. The one successful thing she'd done since returning to Eau Claire was to order the *Republican-Herald.* She read it diligently whenever it arrived.

She'd been remiss in not knowing more about the economics of a community. Since her failed visits with the bankers, she'd read with interest about the nature of work and banks and financial affairs. She rehearsed all the things she might have told the bankers to assuage their worries. If only she could have used their terms as well.

"The city has done well to overcome the closing of the lumber mills," Jessie should have said. She might have flattered and cajoled: "The Business Men's Association can take credit for their far-reaching thinking in preparing for their demise and working toward new industry in the region."

But she hadn't, because she didn't know about it, didn't know what to say when bank president Charles Horton asked her what assessment of the current business climate in Winona would warrant her belief that she could open and operate a successful studio. She supposed she should feel gratified that she'd finagled an appointment with the president and not just the chief cashier, but it did her little good. She wasn't ready. She hadn't prepared for the consequences of getting to meet that president, who knew nothing of her or her family and who was accustomed to loaning to his friends and acquaintances. Well, why not? Everyone wants to do business with those they trust. She had to find a way to become more than just another woman; rather, a woman with a good business sense, with whom a banker had knowledge.

It was just like the sporting dance escapade; she hadn't thought things through.

Sometimes she wondered if people ever learned from their mistakes. Maybe every trail wove through ravines and blackberry bushes, leaving a traveler torn and tired before arriving at the end. She was naive in thinking that if she just learned from her mistakes, she'd never be poked by brambles again.

Since returning to Eau Claire, she'd educated herself, insisting she have a few hours off on Saturday afternoons to go to the library. And she'd worked hard, printing and tinting photographs to place in her portfolio, convinced that she could manage a studio alone.

Mrs. Everson was not much involved in the business, so when Mr. Everson was improved, it was he who asked Jessie to consider staying on. She thanked him for his confidence but said she had other plans. She wasn't going to ask Mr. Everson for a recommendation either, fearing that once again a man's point of view might well be a mark against her rather than one in her favor.

At least she trusted that Fred had given George Haas a genuine "glowing recommendation," as he'd said. They'd so easily started talking about photography as they drove to Polonia that day. But it still annoyed her how the men had carried on in her presence. And then Fred had written to her apologizing. She didn't want to write back. Or rather, she did want to, but she didn't trust herself with the task. She'd begun to wonder about his having been at the station just when the train came in. Was that a coincidence, a divine gift to see if she could handle temptation? Or might he have waited there every day since he'd written the first time? Goodness, she hoped not. The man had a life to live that must not include her. Still, warmth filled her to think that he might have been waiting, that she'd been on his mind now and then all that time.

An ad in the paper told her of a retouching position at Polonia, and by post, Mr. Haas had agreed to interview her. Her library and newspaper research prepared her for it. When she returned to Winona for the interview, she'd also have time to tell Roy of the advantages of the stammer school. He didn't seem as excited about the possibility as she thought he would be—or should be—and that surprised her. She hoped to convince her parents of the merit of his going there, if Roy showed some enthusiasm.

She sorted through her clothing, deciding what she truly needed with her this trip. She planned to take the train from Eau Claire to Minneapolis, then transfer to Winona. She would stay a day or two at the most and then return…unless Mr. Haas offered her the job. Then she'd come back, give her notice, pack up her things, and start working on those bankers all over again. This time, she would be prepared.

"That's just fine," Mrs. Bauer told Fred. "It will be a nice outing for you and Russell."

"Yes. Yes, it will. We haven't done much together, have we, son?"

Russell nodded assent. At thirteen, the boy stood tall and lanky, easily edging out his father's five feet eight inches. Russell leaned forward as he stood, as though uncertain of his height for one so young. He had the kindest eyes, Fred thought. From the Otis side, warm, but brown instead of his mother's deep lake blue.

"Winnie and I and Robert will enjoy ourselves here at home. Tell Luise and the children that we'd love to have them visit here. Oh, you don't think they'll be offended if we don't all come?" his wife said. She tugged her apron strings. Then she sighed. "I guess we could all go. It's not that far."

"Now, no sense pushing yourself just to see my sister's family. She'll understand. They're busy with planting anyway since the fields are dry enough to be in them. We won't visit long. Might head on up north a bit. That would be all right, wouldn't it, Russ? Bring our cameras. We'll be camera boys."

"Swell, Dad," he said. "Me and my pals were going to shoot rabbits up toward cemetery road on Saturday. Maybe we could come back in time for that?"

Swell. The words kids use these days. "I thought we might leave early Friday after school, come home late Saturday night."

The boy didn't look too enthused, but then, did thirteen-year-olds ever act like they cared to join their fathers for the day? Fred apprenticed to a carpenter when he was thirteen and rarely saw his father after that. He wasn't exactly sure what a father did with a boy on his way to becoming a man.

"I guess," Russell said. He pulled at the striped socks beneath his knickers.

"That's settled, then. We'll go off to Cochrane after school and on to wherever after that. Maybe you could pack a supper...Jessie?"

he said. "That way we won't lose any time. I might even let you drive, Russell. Would you like that?"

Now the boy's eyes lit up. He stood straight.

"Out on those country roads, that's the best place to learn."

"Or maybe in Aunt Luise's pasture," Russell said. "We could spend the whole day doing that."

Fred nodded and became aware of the stone in his stomach. He thought of how little he wanted to spend the day driving in a pasture.

Fred and Russell arrived in Cochrane too late for pasture driving but with plenty of time for Luise and her family to gather them in like long-lost chicks. "Ah, Fritz," Luis said, kissing him on both cheeks and teasing Russell about how tall he'd gotten. She wondered aloud if they'd had enough to eat and pulled out apple pie as she talked. Whipping cream came next while Augie spoke of crop prices and their children, Violet and Freddie, his namesake, chattered on the porch. Luise made sandwiches, poured milk, and withdrew pickled watermelon rinds from the cabinet in between stories. Fred had missed this exuberance in a household. Russell seemed to like the attention, as the oldest of the three children present.

Fred slept well and ate an early breakfast fit for an army. The Staaks then headed out to the fields with their team of horses. His sister's family had been up for hours already. Freddie was only eleven, but he helped milk cows, and Vi and her mother slopped the pigs and gathered eggs, then headed to the large garden. All would be occupied throughout the day.

Russell and Fred drove to the pasture for Russell's "adventure" and circled around for what seemed to Fred like hours. The sun rose high in the sky. It was time to move on.

"You've had plenty of driving, Russell. You really can't go spinning around in the cow pasture turning up cow pies all day! We'll have to wash the car as it is before we can go further."

"You said we could drive all day." He slammed the door after he threw himself out of the car.

"No, *you* said you could; I didn't agree."

"You never do," Russell mumbled.

"What? What did you say?"

"I said you never do agree with me. Or with Mama or anyone else. It's always your way. You act like the only toy in the toy box." The boy clung to his elbows over his chest, holding himself inside.

"Watch your tongue, young man," Fred said. "Get in the car. We'll stop at the pump and wash off some of this mess, then head north."

"I'll walk," Russell said, and he stomped toward the pasture gate.

Fred drove slowly across the gopher mounds and through cow pies, glad that the bull was in a different pasture altogether. Russell opened the gate but kept walking. *Swell,* Fred thought as he drove through and got out to close the gate himself. At the pump, Fred lifted the handle up and down, filling the bucket. Russell sloshed the water against the car and tires, brushing at them with his hand. Fred thought to correct him. There was a much more systematic way to wash down the car—he'd brought rags—but he kept his tongue as he rubbed the vehicle, then rinsed his arms and shoes at the pump, serenaded by robins and a light breeze and the cooling shade of maples.

"Now, that wasn't so bad, was it?" Fred said.

"Why do we have to go north?" Russell asked when they finished. "Couldn't we just go back home and take pictures along the way back?"

"No. We're going north."

"Why?"

It was a father's prerogative to not give reasons or explanations.

SEVENTEEN

Truth Telling

THEY DROVE IN SILENCE, Russell hunched up against the door frame, his lanky legs like big knuckles finding their way inside a too small fist. Fred stopped once or twice, and they both got out to make a photograph of a well-laid-out hay field or to take closeups of the blooms on a chokecherry tree. Fred smiled to find himself making "tramp photographs," something he'd railed against when Jessie suggested that such shots could be as artistic as studio portraits. His son mellowed as they exchanged ideas about scenes and camera angles, whether there was sufficient light to capture the butterfly on the sumac branch, or if the finch would sit long enough for them to get the camera set the way they wished. It was all in all a good morning as they drove through farming towns like Mondovi before crossing the Chippewa River into Eau Claire proper, four hours from the farm. He knew the address of the Everson Studio because of its listing in his photographic association book and easily found the bustling street of Barstow.

"What are we doing here?" Russell asked, pulling up out of a nap. "Are we taking city photographs?"

"I have a friend here I want to tell about a position in Winona."

"You couldn't send him a letter?" Russell said. "Wouldn't that be more…efficient?"

"Don't be sarcastic, young man. I wasn't sure when her work here was finished. And since we were going this way—"

"Her?" Russell asked. He raised an eyebrow just the way his mother did when she questioned his explanations for spending time at his lodge.

"Yes, her. Jessie Gaebele. You remember Miss Gaebele, don't you?"

Russell frowned. "She worked for us, when Robert was a baby."

"No, that was Selma, her younger sister. Miss Gaebele worked for the studio when I was ill. She ran it with Mrs. Henderson for a time."

Russell said, "We oughta get home."

"Let's see if she's even here," Fred said, stepping out.

"I'll wait," Russell said. "I hate listening to old people talk."

"Watch that tongue, young man," Fred said, leaning back in across the seat. He wasn't certain if it was the tone of Russell's words or his reference to age that annoyed him.

"Why? Will you hit me?"

Blood rushed to Fred's face as he clenched his fists. He had slapped the boy once or twice. But it was rare, much rarer than his tongue-lashing, and he'd felt great guilt for having done both, vowed never to do it again. He took a deep breath. "You won't rile me today, Russell. We've had a nice outing. You took fine pictures, and you got to drive."

"Now you get what you want, I guess," Russell said. "To see your *friend.*"

"You have a visitor," Hilda Everson told Jessie as she knocked on Jessie's bedroom door.

"I do?" Jessie tried to think of the people she'd met when she attended the youth group that one time. None of them would visit. Maybe it was one of the patrons, the woman who sat for her sample. "Is it Patricia Benson?"

"A gentleman. Mr. Everson might know him, but I don't."

Jessie stepped out of her room and pulled the door shut behind her, then walked the narrow hallway, following Hilda's wide swaying hips.

Her breath caught in her throat when she saw Fred silhouetted by the reception room's back light. She knew him instantly: the cane, hatless. He smoothed his thinning hair back with his hand. "Miss Gaebele," he said, stepping forward, nodding his head toward her. "I'm so pleased to find you home and not off on a busy outing with your friends."

"Please, sit," she said and motioned toward a chair. Hilda Everson did as well, situating herself across from Fred. "Would you care for tea? This is Fred Bauer," she told Hilda. "I used to work for him at the Bauer Studio in Winona."

Hilda's shoulders relaxed. "That's good," she said. "So you know of him."

"Yes. We're colleagues. About that tea. I'll go—"

"No, you sit. I get tea. I'm sorry Mr. Everson isn't here. He would like to talk to a fellow photographer. He gets to do that so rarely."

I'm a fellow photographer, Jessie thought but did not say. "What brings you—"

"I hope you don't mind... Russell and I were out for a drive and—"

"Russell's with you?" She stood and looked out the window. "Well, have him come inside."

"You might get him to. I couldn't. Jessie, I don't have much time. It's a four-hour drive minimum back home. But I wanted you to know that George Haas is advertising for a retoucher. I thought if you applied he'd likely hire you, and maybe you could convince him of your abilities and he'd reconsider selling the studio to you."

"I'm going to ask Russell to come in," she said. "It's silly for him to sit out there by himself." She stepped outside, aware that Fred had risen too, but he remained as she skipped down the steps to Russell.

The boy, slouched in the front seat, looked nearly asleep as she approached. "Russell?" She touched his shoulder lightly. "Do you remember me? I'm Jessie Gaebele." He startled and sat up, pulled his cap straight on his head. "I'm sorry. I didn't mean to wake you. But we're having iced tea and cookies. Would you be interested?"

"Yes ma'am," he said. "I mean, no ma'am, I don't remember you, but the cookies sound swell."

"Come along then. Goodness, you've grown so much! I remember the day you came to tell us that your father was ill, when we sat on the back porch of the studio, Mrs. Henderson and I, and you'd made your way all by yourself from home. Do you remember that? You were almost as tall as me then, but now you've shot right past me."

"Taller than my dad," he said. "And most of my chums at school."

"I hope you're playing basketball. I see that the banks in Winona are sponsoring teams now, helping out with equipment."

"Yes ma'am, they are."

She led him into the reception room as Hilda Everson entered with tall glasses and a plate of cookies. "I get more for such a big one as you," she told Russell, and she scurried out.

"She'll bring you pie," Jessie said. "I've had all I can do not to end up as big as a cow with Hilda's cooking."

The boy sat down, and Fred sat back too, and then the room stilled with only the sounds of Russell's chewing cookies. "So did you tell her what you wanted to, Dad?" Russell asked at last.

"What? Oh yes. I told her." Fred stared at her. He cleared his throat. "I told her about that opening at the Polonia Studio."

"Will you take the job?" Russell asked.

"I have to apply first," she said. "But I read about the opening in the paper."

"You already knew? We didn't have to drive all this way." Russell groaned.

"Russell," Fred cautioned.

"Your father couldn't know that I knew," Jessie said. "It was very kind of you both to think of my welfare and to make such a long trip for nothing."

"Not for nothing," Fred said.

"Here's the pie," Hilda said. "So, you come to take our Miss Gaebele back with you to Winona?"

"No, no, we were just driving about and—"

"You could save her the train fare and our having to take her to the depot. Not that we want you to leave any sooner than planned, but you were only going for two nights anyway," Hilda told her. "Isn't that so?"

"You were coming to Winona?" Fred said.

"I have an interview," Jessie said.

"That's perfect then," Hilda confirmed. "Saves time and money."

"I'm sure Mr. Bauer and Russell have the rest of their weekend planned," Jessie said. "The train will be fine."

"Mrs. Everson does make sense, Miss Gaebele," Fred said. "No reason to take a train when you can have a car deliver you to your door. What do you think, Russell? Should we give Miss Gaebele a lift?"

"Can I drive a little on the way back?" Russell said.

"How quickly could you be ready?" Fred said to Jessie.

"Good idea, *ja,*" Hilda said.

Here they were again, everyone making decisions for her and acting like she didn't have a brain in her own head. On the other hand, why should she put out money for train fare when a perfectly good ride awaited? Returning with Fred now meant she'd be fresh and ready for her interviews with George Haas, the banks, and maybe even Ralph Carleton if she had to prove to everyone she had the drive and the means to make several things work. Best of all, Russell was along, a chaperone.

"It'll take me just a minute," she said. "I adapt quickly."

Fred directed Russell to the backseat.

"I thought I could drive," he protested.

"When we're out of the city," Fred told him. "I've no time to teach you the ins and outs of city driving, especially in a place I'm not familiar with myself."

The boy slouched into the back, cap pulled over his eyes, arms across his chest, as Fred placed Jessie's bag on the seat beside him. *The boy could have been a gentleman and helped,* Fred thought, but at least he hadn't protested to the idea of bringing Jessie back to Winona with them. And it hadn't even been Fred's idea! He settled Jessie in the front seat, and she tied her hat on even though he had the car top up. He wondered if she remembered: both the way the wind could whip a woman's hat in a car and that she'd lost one of hers on a certain day in June.

He pulled out his watch before bending to crank the car. He should have the boy crank it. The movement did get his heart pounding. They'd spent barely an hour in Eau Claire. They had a long drive and would be home well after the supper hour. Even later if he let Russell drive. But he'd have to do that or the boy would protest and maybe upset his mother. There would be enough to deal with, explaining why they went north instead of just coming back home after visiting his sister.

Once outside of Eau Claire, he asked Jessie to exchange places so Russell could drive. He was conscious of Jessie first beside him and then in the backseat, had inhaled the lavender water she wore when she moved past him. He had no indication from her that she shared his alertness. It seemed to him she deliberately avoided his touch, not even allowing him to help her step up on the running board of the car. He hoped she knew that his offer was simply a gesture of kindness. They could be friends; he'd show her that. And yet her behavior would make any explanation needed for his wife about this day all the truer. They were just colleagues.

Russell did fine driving, and Fred told him so. The boy kept the car in the dusty ruts and held the wheel as steady as he could when they reached intersections where cars and wagons crisscrossed, the bumps as discomforting as streetcar tracks. At least it hadn't rained, so mud didn't bog them down.

They'd have been fine, would have reached Winona by late dusk, but not far from Cochrane and his sister's farm, the car coughed and rolled to a stop in the middle of the road.

"What's wrong with it?" Jessie asked from the back. She leaned forward and put her hands over the backrest. *Such small, delicate hands.*

"Did you turn the ignition off, Russell? By mistake?"

"No. I didn't do nothing." The boy lifted his hands from the steering wheel as though it were hot. "Anything."

"I wasn't accusing," Fred said. "Let's see if we can get it restarted." As Fred walked to the front, his eye noticed the gas tank extended along the side. The gauge showed empty. "Confound it!" He'd meant to stop at an oil station in Eau Claire and refill both the tank and the reserve container they'd used up with all the racing around in the pasture. What had he been thinking!

Fred first walked alone to the nearest farm, hoping they'd have gasoline or a phone. He left Jessie and Russell talking about basketball and school, how well he'd driven the car. Fred returned with no good news.

"How far are we from Aunt Luise's?" Russell asked.

"You have family close?" Jessie asked. "I thought all your family still lived in Germany."

"Four or five miles. Maybe more."

"Someone will come along—"

"And we're in the middle of the road," Fred snapped at Russell.

"Maybe we can push the car out of the way," Jessie said. "And then I propose we start walking before it gets any later. Does your sister have a phone?"

Fred shook his head. "She doesn't. But there's a grocer not far beyond them where they make calls. Hopefully Augie will have fuel and can give us a ride back. Then we can be on our way, call home, and let them know we'll be pretty late so they won't worry."

The beauty of the sunset proved insufficient to ward off night, darkness fully cloaking them with no moon to mark their way. Jessie's eyes adjusted as the light waned, but now she was dependent on rubbing shoulders with Russell and Fred to keep heading in the right direction. Fireflies flickered their tiny lights.

They'd been walking a long time, and Jessie carried the portfolio and her camera bag. "I can't afford to have them carried off," she insisted. Russell and Fred left their cameras, and Jessie could tell they indulged her in helping with hers. Both men traded off hoisting the camera, but her shoulder still felt sore from the weight. At least her legs didn't hurt; all the walking she did, even short jaunts around the Eversons' block, kept them in good fit. The hard lumps of dried mud did press against the thin leather soles, though, causing her to wince.

Eventually, a pale light from a window shone through leafy maple trees, and Russell shouted, "There it is!" Drawing on youthful energy, he sprinted toward the driveway, leaving Fred carrying the case in one hand, his cane in the other.

"Let me take the case," Jessie said. "You carry my portfolio. It's lighter, and I might take your elbow so I don't fall flat on my face, if you wouldn't mind."

"No bother at all," he said and made the switch, his forearm warm where she held it. "I apologize for this...fiasco. I never should have let Russell drive around so much earlier. I should have remembered to get fuel. It's just... I do apologize."

"An honest happening," she said. "And Russell's being along keeps things...safe. I didn't mean to suggest that there was anything but...decorum in your offer. In the drive to Eau Claire. I mean it was Mrs. Everson who proposed you give me a ride back. That is, I didn't."

"I know what you meant," he said. "I know."

Augie and his son, she imagined, hustled out of the door and onto the porch, the boy racing down to lift Jessie's camera bag, his father pulling on suspenders, then reaching to shake Fred's hand. "Be really careful," she cautioned the child, "and thank you."

"Fred. What were you thinking, running out of gas? In your reserve too, Russell says. I tell you, you city boys just don't always think that far ahead, now, do you?"

Jessie could feel Fred's embarrassment as she let go of his arm.

"These things happen," she said. She thrust her now-free hand out to shake Augie Staak's. "I'm Jessie Gaebele," she said. He didn't seem to know what to do with a woman's handshake offer, and he nodded instead.

"Jessie, you say. That'll be easy to remember. Welcome." He took Jessie's hand to help her up the steps, then said to Fred, "Your sister's already putting on supper for you wandering souls."

"We don't really have the time," Fred said. "Would you run us to the grocer to make a phone call so Mrs. Bauer won't worry? And may I buy gasoline from you?"

"We use the horses still. We'll wait till morning when you can get fuel at the grocer, then I'll harness up the team and take you back to the car. He'll be closed already tonight. If he had a saloon attached, he'd be open, but he's dry. We can go to the neighbor to make the call home, but they're still farming with horses too. I'll harness the team."

Once inside the kitchen, Jessie introduced herself as "a photographer friend of Fred's. You must be Luise. May I help?"

"*Ja,* that would be good," the round woman said. "I'll fry up *Kartoffels* if you'll peel them. Fritz likes his—how you say it? potatoes?—all fried in lard and crispy brown. Violet's changing sheets on her bed so the two of you share the space to sleep."

Mrs. Bauer will be so worried, Jessie thought. It was good they could make the phone call, though she wished they could get fuel too. She had to get home tomorrow, get rested before the interview. Luise hummed as she worked. There was nothing to be done but stay.

Jessie didn't realize how hungry she was until she wiped her plate clean with the crust of brown bread that still crunched when she put the last of the bacon drippings into her mouth. It was more than she'd ever eaten at the Eversons at one sitting. Now they sat, and Jessie showed her camera to Freddie as shy Violet stood behind her mother's skirts watching the bellows slide out and back.

"Here's a pocket for extra film," Jessie showed him.

The kitchen smelled of berry pies. Crickets clicked in the night. The children were soon put to bed, with Russell sharing Freddie's quilts. Fred would bunk down on the kitchen cot, the place where Augie often took an after-dinner nap, Luise explained, or where a sick child could be kept close at hand while Luise cooked or canned.

Good-natured joking filled the evening as Luise told stories of Fritz, as she called him, when the two of them lived in Buffalo before Fred stepped out on his own. "I worked for another family," Luise said. "But even I heard about his Halloween prank."

"Now, don't go telling, Luise. Or I'll tell Augie a story on you."

"I've told him everything," Luise said, and her husband patted his wife at her waist when she bent to refill the coffee cups.

"I doubt that. Everyone keeps secrets," Fred said.

"You'd be surprised," Augie said. "Truth telling gets sympathy, especially when you tell them of the mistakes."

"Once," Luise said, talking to Jessie now, "he and his friends took apart a neighbor's buggy and, with ropes and pulleys, spent the whole night reassembling it on top of the carriage house of one of our great-uncle's friends. I wish I could have seen his face when he came out to see that buggy way up there!"

Fred shook his finger at his younger sister. "You don't know it was me."

"Ach, I do! It was carefully reassembled, and no one but you could have done that so quickly. Besides, you often commented on that buggy and how it could almost fly."

Fred laughed with the tips of his mustache bouncing. "Lucky we didn't do what my friend suggested: move the outhouse two feet back behind the pit."

"Ach, that would be terrible," Luise said.

"Only for those who didn't notice," Augie said.

"Those were fine times, fine times," Fred said, wiping at his eyes.

"You say it like there haven't been any since," Augie said.

Fred turned thoughtful. "There've been challenges, haven't there, Luise?" He looked at his sister with such tenderness. Luise nodded. He'd told Jessie Luise's tragic story as they'd walked the road toward Cochrane, and Jessie could see between the two of them that same expression of love that she felt in the presence of Roy and Selma and even Lilly. Sisters and brothers held a special bond. Luise had apparently always struggled with why she survived while the rest of her family perished to typhoid.

"Trials more easily forgiven than forgotten," Luise noted.

"Without those challenges, you wouldn't have come to Wisconsin," Augie told her. "And we wouldn't have two scamps snoring upstairs. There is always a bridge somewhere, even when the road appears washed away." He patted her hand, squeezed it, and she smiled at him with such devotion on her face that Jessie swallowed, blinked. She turned away only to see Fred staring into her tear-filled eyes.

They finished their evening with Jessie following Luise up the stairs to Violet's room, where she was shown the pitcher and bowl. "My *Bruder* is a *gut* man," she said in accented English. "I didn't mean differently, telling of the carriage."

"I know," Jessie said. "I worked for him for three years."

"Then you know, it is not always easy for him." She hesitated. "With his wife, *ja*? But he loves his children." She set the lantern down for Jessie to keep. "It is *gut* to see him laugh. I thank you."

Jessie slipped beneath the nine-patch quilt made without batting. Just the right weight for a cool spring evening. The coffee kept her awake, and she lay there staring up to the ceiling, listening to Violet's deep, steady breathing and the rustling of noises coming up through the heating grate over the kitchen. She'd done nothing to make Fred laugh, had she? And why had Luise said that about Fred's wife?

She heard the cot springs creak and let her mind take in that Fred lay there in the kitchen below. She wondered if he too lay awake thinking about a washed-out road that could never be bridged.

EIGHTEEN

A Second Exposure

JESSIE ASKED FRED TO LET HER OFF a block or so from her home.

"If that's what you'd like," Fred said. Russell slept in the backseat, and Jessie noted that the boy slept a lot. She tried to think if Roy slept that much, but he was younger than Russell. Growing tall probably took more rest. Maybe that was why she was so short, Jessie thought. She didn't seem to get much sleep. She certainly hadn't slept much the night before.

Few explanations were warranted when her family arrived to find her there. They assumed she came in on the train, and Jessie didn't correct them. And no one protested when she arose early the next morning, dressed, then made her way to the Polonia.

The interview went surprisingly well. She shared her portfolio, and this time George Haas actually examined her work, lingered over more than one of her samples. She was humble and didn't mention a word about trying to buy his studio. Maybe one day she'd be his competitor, but he didn't need to know that just yet.

"It's only a few hours a week," he told her as they were finishing up.

"But the ad—"

"I know. I hope to make it full time, but for now, it is half days, afternoon will be best. Morning hours are better for sittings, as you know."

At least he acknowledged that she had studio experience.

"I can begin in two weeks," she said. "I need to give my employer notice."

They shook hands, though George didn't seem to know what to do at first with Jessie's offered palm. She tightened her glove over each finger, lifted her portfolio, and said good-bye, walking fast to Reverend Ralph Carleton's offices.

Mrs. Bauer dressed carefully for her appointment. She chose a new corset designed to be worn under the new straight skirts. She had plenty to tell the reverend about today, how her husband had driven all the way to Eau Claire and picked up Jessie Gaebele to bring her back home, with their son along, for goodness' sake. What was the man thinking? Of course, he hadn't told her *that* when he'd called. Oh no. Then, he'd been placating and soothing, knowing she'd been worried sick that they hadn't returned. She'd imagined everything from the car getting stuck on the railroad track to Russell's getting lost while they were out taking pictures, or a bull or other raging animal on Luise's farm goring them both. The complexity of her imagination surprised her. She slipped the linen over her head and admired for just a moment her image in the mirror. The square neck flattered.

She'd stayed home, though, through it all, waiting for his return or his call. She hadn't escaped to her mother's, hadn't written him a note saying where she was and that when he got home he could just come and pick them all up, regardless of the time. No, she'd remained with her children. She'd read a few words now and then. She'd cut pieces for a log cabin quilt, one of the more complex patterns she'd challenged herself to do. Reverend Carleton had suggested that she explore things to occupy her time besides worry over waning emotions. He urged her to read Scripture but then allowed that other activities would be helpful too, to strengthen a woman's weak mind.

Relief flooded her when FJ called, not only to learn that he was fine but that he wasn't coming home that evening. That reaction surprised her. Once she knew where he was, that he and Russell were safe, she actually enjoyed herself for the rest of the night. Late as it was, she decided to heat up the irons and press the sheets and handkerchiefs that Melba hadn't gotten to. The girl even came to the kitchen with her nightcap on, asking if everything was all right.

"Splendid," Mrs. Bauer said. "Go back to bed."

This burst of energy consumed her until nearly two in the morning, when she'd tried on the newer style dress she now wore. That night, she'd gone to bed thinking how nice it was not to worry over whether she neglected wifely duties or what sort of argument she and FJ would get into over meaningless things. These thoughts were followed by guilt, of course, that she should like his being away, and deeper remorse over what she really wanted, which she realized more and more was to be free of the obligations of marriage while still holding tight to the treasures: safety in her home, financial security, her children around her.

The next morning, all that changed as she watched FJ back the car into the garage and noticed that Russell was in the backseat. She asked the boy about it when he came in. "Are you and your father not on speaking terms?"

"Huh?" Russell said as he tossed his cap onto the table.

"You should say, 'Excuse me,' if you don't understand my question," she corrected.

"Excuse me?"

"You were sitting in the backseat. Were you feuding with your father?"

"No. We dropped off Miss Gaebele, who'd been in the front seat, so I stayed where I was."

"Excuse me?"

"What did I say wrong this time?"

"You dropped off Miss Gaebele?"

"Dad drove to Eau Claire to tell her about a job. It turns out she knew all about it and was coming back on the train, so this old lady she works for said we should take her with us."

"What older woman are you referring to, Russell? And it's not polite to call someone an old lady."

"The lady who ran the studio, I guess. She said Miss Gaebele was packed up and taking the train back to Winona, and why didn't we drive her back since we were going to the same place. I drove partway." His face lit up with the story of his success.

"Did you...," Mrs. Bauer said. She could feel the heat rise on her neck. How dare he drive all the way to Eau Claire just to talk to that...that young woman. Why, she would have spent the night with Luise too! How dare FJ introduce Miss Gaebele to *her* relatives and then spend the night like that? If her friends learned of this incident, she'd be the subject of whispers and jokes.

"I'm hungry," Russell said, adding, "Aunt Luise fixed bacon and eggs and pancakes and fresh pie for breakfast before they hitched the team and drove us back to the car on their way to church. But that was hours ago."

She took cuts of cheese out of the Frigidaire, then sawed without much care the loaf of bread she'd baked the day before. "Here," she said. "Take it upstairs with you. I want to talk with your father alone."

FJ had come in unsuspecting, which suited Mrs. Bauer just fine. "So. You had car trouble, did you?"

"Ran out of gas. I let Russell drive around in the cow pasture and forgot completely to fill up in Cochrane."

"The side trip to Eau Claire had no part in your gas failure, I suppose."

He blinked and stepped back before saying, "I told you we were driving north and might go to Eau Claire."

"You failed to mention Eau Claire and didn't tell me the reason was to see Miss Gaebele."

"It was strictly photography business," he said. "It's always been that. You've nothing to worry over...Jessie."

"Nothing to worry over? You spend a night with a young woman in the presence of my son, and you think this is nothing to worry about? Where have your senses gone? Think of what people will say when they learn of this! What must Luise think? How…humiliating for me."

"For you? This has nothing to do with you. Nothing. Perfectly innocent. Perfectly innocent." He sat down on the chair and put his hand over his heart.

"Oh no. Don't tell me your poor heart is giving you fits now because I've caught you in a lie."

"I didn't lie to you, Mrs. Bauer. I told you we might go to Eau Claire, and you said—"

"You didn't say why! You kept that from me! That's a lie!"

"And what if I had said we were going there to tell Miss Gaebele that the Polonia had an opening? You'd have made an ocean out of nothing more than rain dripping from the eaves. It was a kindness, nothing more. Why, the girl is hardly older than Russell—"

"Hardly older than I was when you first met me," she said. "When I was young and beautiful and full of promise." She could feel the tears fall, and she hated their betrayal, hated that when she finally said what she felt, tears watered the way and drowned her words.

"Jessie," he said, rising to approach her, "it meant nothing. It was a kindness, and Luise and Augie were just being gracious. I hadn't planned to drive her back here. She was taking the train, she said, but her employer, Mrs. Everson, said why not ride back with us, and it seemed a neighborly thing to do. Nothing more. Please. Don't let this be a…silencing."

She turned from him then, went up to her room, and did not come back out until the evening, skipping her Sunday activities, unable to face her friends, who would know. They would know!

Monday morning, Fred left for work, and Melba got the children up and ready for breakfast and off to school. Now Mrs. Bauer was ready to go see Reverend Carleton, but remembering made her less angry. Russell hadn't seemed to be bothered by any of the encounter; FJ had assured her it was innocent. He hadn't seemed defensive, and he was right: if he had told her when he called, she would have been annoyed and thus robbed of the evening of respite she'd enjoyed. She'd tell the reverend of her progress.

She chose a small two-toned red felt hat lifted in the back with two simple feathers and a sloping brim toward the front. *Two-toned. To match my heart.* She would carry a fan today too and use it to cool her warm face as she told him of her double-mindedness. She tugged on summer gloves, then took one last look in the mirror: she felt dowdy and not at all as though this would be an agreeable day.

Jessie had been in Ralph Carleton's office several times through the years. She didn't consider herself the best typist or speller, but she worked hard and would perform well for him—if he'd have her. He'd almost hired her once, but she'd moved to Milwaukee. Now she hoped to use her photography to advance his work. He'd acknowledged her insight about the value of holding a women-only meeting, a suggestion she'd made once in passing when she met with him last year. Today she just wanted to see if he could use a clerk a few hours a day. She needed the equivalent of full-time work to impress the bankers.

"Miss Gaebele," he said, welcoming her with his booming voice. "Your mother told me you were returning."

"My mother's better than a newspaper," Jessie told him.

He laughed, his gray eyes sparkling. He wore a yellow and black vest stretched across his chest, wide as a streetcar bridge. He motioned for her to sit. "To what do I owe the pleasure?"

"Last year, you considered hiring me to organize your office and handle correspondence while you traveled," Jessie said. She looked around the room; quite tidy now. Chips of walnuts no longer surrounded the bowl on his desk. They had been replaced with a dish of penny candies sold in bulk called jelly beans. "It looks like you've become well organized," Jessie continued. "I wonder if you might consider having me make up your posters, to advertise your events."

"You draw?" He offered her the dish of candy. When she declined, he took a handful and popped one into his mouth. "I thought you were a photographer."

"I am. But I do draw. However, I think photographs would make good copy for a poster, let people see what they might expect when they enter one of your tents. Reduce the...uncertainties of a religious experience."

"A little fear goes a long way, Miss Gaebele," he said. "Maybe fear is necessary to bring about a change of heart. Fear of the consequences. If they know too much about what to expect, they might not enter that tent at all. Think of what they'd miss. Eternal life."

Jessie fidgeted in her chair. This had happened before when she'd interviewed with Ralph Carleton. "It's my experience," she said, "that people can't learn anything new unless they feel safe first."

Ralph frowned. "Jonah didn't exactly feel safe inside the whale. Yet he learned."

Jessie was at a loss arguing theological issues with a reverend and could only draw examples from her own life. "I notice this in my younger brother, who suffers from stammering," she said. "When he's being teased, how can he possibly learn anything? I just thought that photographs of you, or perhaps of people attending and being touched by your words, could be a good thing for your ministry. But perhaps I'm mistaken." She stood, resigned. "I'm sorry to have taken up your time."

"Let's not be hasty," Ralph said. "I'm sure—"

He was interrupted by the door opening, and both turned to look. There stood Fred.

"Mr. Bauer," Ralph boomed. "Are you looking for your wife?" He pulled out his pocket watch. "Not quite her time yet."

Fred blinked. Why would Ralph Carleton think he was looking for Mrs. Bauer? He'd come to talk about the studio portrait of the Carletons he'd taken a few weeks back. The proofs were ready, and since he was in the neighborhood, he planned to show them to Ralph. He had another objective too, but he felt his tongue thicken when he realized Jessie Gaebele stood before him.

"No, I brought your prints. I mean your proofs. They turned out well, I think. I…I hope you'll like them."

"You know Miss Gaebele, I believe?"

"We've met," Jessie said and nodded. "Good morning, Mr. Bauer."

"Of course. Miss Gaebele worked for your studio for a time, isn't that right?"

"Yes," both Fred and Jessie responded at the same time. Now Jessie looked down, and Fred thought he saw color rise to her cheeks as he looked away. Ralph cleared his throat.

What does he know?

"I also came by to speak to you about a business proposition," Fred said. "But I can see you're busy. I'll make an appointment and come back later."

"I'm leaving," Jessie said. "Please, stay."

"Miss Gaebele," Ralph said, "let me take your suggestion under advisement. Check back with me tomorrow, and we'll see what we can put together. Now then, Mr. Bauer, what can I do for you?"

Fred stepped back as Jessie slipped between the two men and reached for the door handle. Her lavender perfume wafted to him, and he caught Ralph Carleton's inquisitive eyes staring at him just before he took a deep breath. He wanted to make a good case for his business proposition. He didn't want to appear less confident just because the elegant Miss Gaebele seeped the air from the room.

He launched into his proposal and watched as Ralph shook his head. "Miss Gaebele proposed almost the same idea just moments ago," Ralph said. "Imagine that."

"She did?" Fred said. "But how—"

"Great minds appear to take photographs." Ralph smiled. "And I'd be remiss if I didn't take the first person who brought me the idea, wouldn't you say?"

Had Fred said something to her of his idea? No, he was sure he hadn't. He hadn't really thought of her as competition. He wanted Jessie to succeed, to accomplish her dream of owning her own business. That was why he'd driven to Eau Claire to tell her of the opening. That was the only reason. That he enjoyed the surprise of additional time with her had been like having a new horn for his car, a horn he'd put together himself with good solid materials that made his heart sing when he pressed the bulb and the horn blasted its joy.

"Of course," Fred said. "Well, let's take a look at these proofs, yes? So I won't have wasted your time."

Competition… She'd be competition. He hadn't really thought about that.

NINETEEN

Proving Up

JESSIE'S LIFE NOW CONSISTED OF her part-time retouching job at the Polonia and the side contract with Ralph Carleton. Her work wasn't unlike early settlers "proving" their property, doing necessary things until they could call the land their own. She wasn't meeting any Homestead Act requirements, only her own established list. Like those settlers, however, she took pleasure in the process, feeling fortunate that she wasn't making her way in a distant candy factory and that she was home at last, surrounded by the chaos and charm of family.

Occasionally, she traveled with Ralph, along with his musicians and "advance men," who spent the day of their arrival visiting with local ministers. These pastors had been contracted much earlier and served as hosts for Ralph's tent meetings. They'd inform Ralph about particular parishioners who might come, how they'd been advertising the event, what food would feed the masses. Ralph always asked about who would follow up after the tent troop left, who would assist those believers as they worked hard to follow their newly invigorated faith.

Jessie knew that charlatans roamed the countryside, where bringing in cash was more important than nurturing souls, but Ralph wasn't one of those. He genuinely cared for those he met. Jessie wondered out loud once what brought people who hadn't knelt at the altars of their local churches into his tent, and Ralph said it was often the outsider who brought the message that changed the heart.

"People can express their grief and misdeeds to those they don't know more easily than to those they might see on the street every day," he assured her. "Human nature. We just don't like to be faced with our truths in places where we'll have to wake up and face them again. It's why families struggle so when a secret indiscretion is revealed... Each day is a reminder of that infraction, and all must find a way to live with it."

Many of the tent meetings were held throughout the week for two weeks at a time. These travel arrangements worked out well because Jessie could do the retouching for the Polonia when she returned home. She'd go into the studio late in the evening or on a Saturday. For Jessie, the travels reassured her that she could be with men, working side by side, and not compromise her values or her virtue. She did more than make posters; she assisted and even encouraged women who appeared fragile and frightened as they came into the tents. She saw Fred rarely that summer and fall, and that was fine with her. She and Lilly also found a way around their previous tension by never mentioning Fred's name, neither of them. Lilly even confided to Jessie an interest in her own young man.

"That's wonderful, Lil," Jessie told her as the two girls washed dishes together. Most of the rest of the family had ended up on the porch outside, waving at strolling neighbors sauntering by.

"Not so wonderful. He...that is, I think he likes to...imbibe. Beer," Lilly whispered when Jessie stared. "He likes his beer."

"But how do you know?"

"I met him at the fair last summer. He was standing outside the beer tent, and I could smell it on him. At least I thought it was him, though that beer tent reeks like a hog farm for miles around."

"You never told me! Did you stop and talk to him?" Jessie couldn't imagine her sister talking to a perfect stranger at a fair.

"No, I... Well, I stumbled and nearly fell into the muck made by people tracking in front of the tent. It had rained. I was appalled. And this young man, Joseph O'Brien, stepped right over and helped me up. Well, he's not so young. He's twenty-eight, two years older than I."

"He wasn't so impaired by beer that he didn't see a woman in distress," Jessie noted.

"He was a perfect gentleman, but I could still smell the ale. He offered to buy me a sarsaparilla, at a very different tent, of course. I couldn't well refuse the man."

"Of course not."

"He'd saved my dignity, brushing off my skirt and rescuing my parasol. What was I to do?"

"Exactly what you did."

Lilly put the dried dishes into the cupboard while Jessie wiped the table, rinsed the rag, and hung it on the back porch to dry.

"He works for Watkins, in the warehouse, and helps on his father's farm too."

"Has he come courting you?"

"He wants to, but I haven't let him. He sent me a postcard of him and his brothers with their ox team, sledding logs. 'Compliments of your true friend,' he wrote, then signed it, 'Joseph 4 ever.' I couldn't believe my luck in getting the mail before Mama did that day! I wonder how people ever court, always being hovered over."

"You might consider moving out," Jessie said. "Now, before you protest, what about if you stayed at the YWCA?"

"I can't imagine leaving Mama and Papa," she said. "They need looking after, in case you haven't noticed."

"They seem pretty capable," Jessie said.

"Well, you don't see everything." Lilly's eyes expressed anguish, and she sank into a chair. "Papa would be appalled if he knew Joe was a drinker."

"I'm not sure that having a beer now and then makes a person 'a drinker,'" Jessie said. "Voe Henderson's husband sips beer, and even Voe does sometimes, or did before she had her baby. They're still good people."

"Don't let Mama hear you say that," Lilly said. "You're becoming worldly."

"If anything, my travels have made me aware that there is more than one way to see things. My way isn't always the only way. Why, in some countries in Europe, they drink wine because the water is so bad."

"I guess we should be glad Winona has good spring water," Lilly said.

"I'm not advocating beer or wine," Jessie said. "But if Joe is a good man, kind, responsible, a faithful man, then an occasional ale ought not to keep you from knowing him better."

"Maybe," Lilly agreed. "But Joe won't come to our church with me either. That's the ideal place to meet up with someone."

"Go with him to his."

"He's...Catholic," Lilly whispered.

"Oh. Well. You could learn about his faith. Maybe—"

"Mama would be flummoxed into her sickbed."

Lilly hung the towels, then began puttering, straightening the square salt and pepper shakers, wiping off the red caps. She appeared reluctant to join the others.

"Maybe he'd come to one of Ralph's tent meetings, and you could talk there about, well, faith matters and other things."

"I hadn't thought of that," Lilly said.

"In Eau Claire I didn't go to church much because of the Eversons' schedule, but they had church at home, and while I didn't agree with everything they said, I never felt that I was violating my faith by being there. Why, in places in rural North Dakota or Montana and farther west, they rarely see a minister, so they have to find ways to worship differently than the way they grew up."

"I suppose... But still, there's that ale."

"Ask him if he drinks."

"But I couldn't be sure of his answer."

"Oh, Lil. There's nothing sure. I'm sure of that." Jessie laughed, and so did Lilly. "It's just that life is made up of scraps of uncertainties that get quilted together in myriad ways. And people can change. It couldn't hurt to ask, then see how you feel about his answer. Who knows? Papa might even find he enjoys talking to Joe, even if he does drink a beer now and then or is a Catholic."

"Do you think so?"

"Papa sees people for who they are," Jessie told her, "and there's no perfect man. Or woman."

"That's true enough." Lilly picked at her fingernail, wouldn't look at her younger sister.

"Maybe you need to change how you think about Joseph O'Brien. Remind yourself he's a...gentleman. Let him prove it."

"Maybe I'll let him meet Papa. It would be a place to start. Thanks, Jessie. It's nice to have you home." Her sister kissed her on the cheek. The spontaneous gesture of affection left Jessie caressing her cheek as Lilly left the room.

Jessie thought of Ralph's saying that people preferred to confess things to listeners they didn't know. "True enough," as Lilly would say. On the other hand, maybe family served that purpose best, family who loved you no matter what you did.

Reverend Carleton told Mrs. Bauer not to think of things that distressed her. She'd poured out her outrage and the layers of betrayal she lived with. Perhaps she repeated herself; she couldn't be certain. Reverend Carleton appeared distracted, reaching for his candies more often than usual. She liked it better when he ate walnuts, though the crunching annoyed. Gertrude, his new secretary, must have found that candy required less tidying up.

Mrs. Bauer never told him about her relief the night FJ stayed with his sister. The reverend didn't ask how she managed the time after FJ had called either. Instead they'd dealt mostly with his having also spent the evening with Jessie Gaebele sharing the house. Maybe she should tell him that she'd felt strengthened in the days since, reminding herself how well she'd handled the evening alone. The confusion of emotion kept her unsettled, pushing the thoughts deep enough to grow roots. She'd finished the session wondering what she'd do when Reverend Carleton traveled more. Who would she talk to then? She asked him out loud.

"Stop by and see Gertrude," he said, as though what she had to talk about with him was nothing more than an exchange of recipes. Then, on the day of her next appointment, she forgot that he'd be traveling and arrived at her usual time. She didn't expect to see Gertrude, who came in only on Wednesdays and Thursdays. Maybe when Reverend Carleton traveled, she came in more often.

"Oh, Mrs. Bauer," Gertrude said. "Reverend Carleton began his tour this week. What arrangements did you make for your appointment times?"

That Gaebele girl sat across the desk from Gertrude as if she belonged, her hat hung on the coat rack, her fingers black with ink. Her presence violated. Even here the woman intruded.

"My appointment times? What are you talking about? You must be mistaken," Mrs. Bauer said. "I just stopped by to pick up"—her eyes darted around the room—"posters. I came by to pick up posters. To share with the Congregationalists. My church. Goodness, no appointment needed for that. No indeed. You must be mistaken, Gertrude."

The Gaebele girl stood up and reached for a stack of the fliers. The girl was as thin as French embroidery thread and just as smooth. "These are for Reverend Carleton's meetings near Rochester," she said, handing Mrs. Bauer the posters featuring a picture of the reverend with his arms open wide and a row of bowed heads before him. *Did FJ take that shot?* "There'll be events closer," the girl said. "If you'd rather have those, I could drop the posters off when I get them finished. I'd be happy to do that."

"No! I mean, I'll just stop by and pick them up. When might they be ready?"

"Early next week. But I'd be happy to deliver them to the church for you if you'd like."

"Did my husband take that photograph? He proposed doing that for Reverend Carleton."

"I...I took the picture," the Gaebele girl said. "I suggested it to Reverend Carleton myself. I... That is... It was my own idea."

"Harrumph," Mrs. Bauer heard herself grunt. "I had that very thought and told my husband of it. Seems a violation of professional courtesy, stealing another's idea."

She twirled around and, holding her head high, marched out the door. At least she had the satisfaction of seeing the girl flummoxed and open-mouthed.

Jessie had been surprised by Mrs. Bauer's visit, and she asked Ralph about it when he returned. He was distracted, she thought, because he tapped his pencil on the desk, looked up at the ceiling before responding to her musing about Mrs. Bauer's charge that Jessie had stolen an idea from her husband.

"She must have been confused... Now, wait." He held his finger up to the wind. "FJ did mention doing something similar to what you proposed. I thought hearing the same idea from two different photographers meant it was probably a good suggestion, but I had to go with the person who approached me first. FJ was understanding. Perhaps he never mentioned that to his wife."

"She did appear upset."

"She can be," he said but didn't elaborate.

Jessie had also probed Gertrude after the woman left.

"That was strange," Gertrude said.

"That she wanted to pick up posters?" Jessie said. "Sounds like a good thing to do, if you ask me."

"No. She acted like she would be seeing Ralph again, just like she usually does on Mondays. But I know he would have told her he was traveling."

"He has a regular appointment with Mrs. Bauer?"

"Oh," Gertrude said. "I shouldn't have said anything. He sees a lot of different people, to counsel them in their spiritual lives. It's all confidential."

The revelation piqued Jessie's interest, and once, when Gertrude could not come in due to a summer cold, she asked Jessie to please file away the folders she'd left on her desk. While tucking them away in the cabinet, Jessie spied a folder bearing the label *Mrs. Jessie Bauer.*

Her heart caught just a bit at seeing her own name attached to Fred's. She'd known Mrs. Bauer's first name was Jessie, but seeing the complete name in writing still unnerved her. Later, she wondered—as she so often did after the fact—if that was why she pulled the file out.

She didn't open the file on Mrs. Jessie Bauer that day, though she longed to. The temptation was great. She fingered the manila edge, stared at is as though she could see through it to the information that lay within. But what would peeking gain her? Insights about the Bauers' life together, proof of disintegration?

She did wonder about the stability of the Bauers' marriage. But Jessie didn't wish an end to it. The pain a divorce would bring to both Mrs. Bauer and Fred, and to the children… No, she didn't want that. She just wanted their marriage to never have been. She wanted to have met Fred Bauer at a time and place when their care could flourish and enrich each other without coming at the expense of others. She wanted to have met him when they could have had a future together.

She started to open the file but had the presence of mind to listen this time when that inner voice said, *Don't do it.* She put the file back and never pulled it out again.

Fred stepped around the cradle he'd permitted Voe Henderson to bring into the studio. What was wrong with him? He'd become weak-minded in his old age, giving in to his employee's request that she bring her child to the studio while she worked. He would turn forty-six this August and ought to have been at the top of his photographic game. Instead he felt stuck with the daily grind of things. He supposed that was why he let Voe bring her little Danny in, to infuse his days with interest. It also helped out the young couple. Allowing it was like making a contribution to one of his benevolence funds, a kind of tithe. Or maybe an act of contrition.

Voe had hoped to hire a girl to look after the baby, but financially the young couple struggled. Daniel traveled on the railroad, so he certainly couldn't stay at home with the boy. They were a team, this couple. When Voe spoke about the family's decisions, she always said *we: we* decided, *we* bought, *we* worked things out. Fred tried to remember the last time he and Mrs. Bauer—Jessie—had decided anything as a *we.*

When the toddler babbled, Fred responded. "Having a good day, yes?" he asked the child. "Not having such a bad one myself," Fred answered the boy's coos. He smoothed the boy's blond hair and let himself remember with fondness those weeks after the mercury poisoning waned, when he was finally feeling better and he'd had both Winnie and Robert close at hand. He loved their presence even though he found himself short-tempered at times. The boy reminded him of Donald, but then, every tow-headed toddler did.

Voe's cheerful spirit never wavered with her baby, and she did well by Fred's customers too. None seemed to think the presence of the child was unprofessional, though one or two did ask if the baby was a grandchild of his. Such comments never failed to disturb him, as he didn't think he looked old enough to be a grandparent, though his hair thinned and he'd noticed new wrinkles at his ears of all places. He also knew that Voe was similar in age to Jessie Gaebele.

"I do have a little to celebrate," he told Voe's boy. In June he'd been elected as an alternate delegate to the North-West States National Association of Photographers representing Minnesota, North and South Dakota, and Iowa. "Only men are allowed to be delegates," he told Danny. It was still something to be noticed by one's peers. The boy offered up his gooey toy. "Already had my breakfast," he said and smiled. He must ask Mrs. Bauer about having Robert spend time at the studio now and then, the way Russell had as a child, and Winnie too. He was in favor of bringing them into the business young.

Why wasn't he content? he wondered. Why wasn't having healthy children, a successful business, and recognition from his colleagues enough to make him look forward to each and every day?

Maybe it was the previous evening's argument with Mrs. Bauer that rankled. He'd finally remembered to ask about Ralph Carleton's strange comment the day he'd stopped by. "Why was Ralph Carleton expecting you?" he asked. "I stopped by there, and he thought I came by to find you. Why would he think that?"

"I have no idea what you mean." She put her needlework down, holding her hands as still as the calm before a storm. He didn't want to be the cause of a thunder burst.

"Not accusing," Fred said. "Just remembered what he said. Nothing of import." He returned to his newspaper and resumed reading of the progress of the breakups of Standard Oil and the American Tobacco Company. He chewed Cuban cigars so didn't imagine the latter would affect his supply, especially since marines had landed in Cuba to protect Americans and their property. Congress had established an eight-hour workday. He wished he had to work only eight hours, but the law would mean Voe couldn't spend more time at the studio than necessary. The senate had also passed a bill allowing for the direct election of senators rather than appointments. He wondered idly how that might work out. World news was less aimless: tensions in the Balkans increased; American troops had been sent to Tientsin in China to protect American interests, but the article didn't say which ones.

"What? I'm sorry, I didn't hear you," he said when he became aware that his wife spoke. He lowered the paper.

"I said, I saw your Miss Gaebele at Reverend Carleton's earlier this week, since you mention the reverend. I went there to pick up posters for his tent meeting. Your Miss Gaebele worked on a poster using a photograph, just as I once suggested you do. You agreed it might be a new revenue source for the studio."

Your Miss Gaebele. He stepped over the remark. "Did you?" he said.

"Did I what?"

"Stop at Ralph Carleton's."

"That's what I said. But of more importance is that the young woman we so kindly mentored those years ago has now stolen our idea. You should be appalled."

"Oh, I wouldn't say that," he said.

"But you told me—"

"Yes, yes, it was an idea. I did tell Ralph about it—"

"And he told her, and now she's doing it." Her voice had risen to its warning note and pace. "That woman can't be trusted. I don't know why we ever hired her—"

"I did stop by to talk with Ralph about his proofs, and I mentioned your idea then. But he said he'd already been given that very suggestion by Miss Gaebele. A mere coincidence of good ideas expressed at the same time."

"You told the girl. You shared your idea with her."

"I didn't…Jessie. Don't arouse yourself over this. I just didn't get to Ralph first," he assured her. "Nothing to worry over."

"A source of revenue is taken from us, and you say there is nothing to worry over? Are we so wealthy, then? We have money to send Russell on to school?" By now she was standing, her hands gripping the needlework. "You're blind, F. J. Bauer. Just blind. That woman is trouble. Mark my words."

She stomped from the room as he said to her back, "It was just poor timing. That's all it was."

Such was the story of his life, which, as with photography, was all about timing.

Twenty

Recipients

Jessie liked traveling to places like New Prague, Northfield, and Red Wing, seeking the parks and watching weather roll in across the fields of corn and wheat or tremble low over the bluffs. The reverend's entourage usually stayed with parishioners, and Jessie became adept at saying kind things about a meal provided, even though she might have had the same boiled cabbage and pork roast at the home they'd stayed in the night before. Ralph rested in hotels, as he needed his private preparation time, but the local people put effort into their hospitality and took extra pride in hosting those involved in the ministry. They wanted to nurture and give sustenance. The best way to assure the reverend's success was to accept the hosts' generosity.

It surprised Jessie that she enjoyed helping with Ralph's evening services, handing out hymnals, standing next to people at the altar to assist them if they fell to their knees with the weight of emotion. Fireflies danced around the tent opening to the outside, competing with the tiny lights strung along the tent ropes. Cigarette smoke drifted in through the opening as men took a final puff before being pulled inside by their wives. Oh, a few came of their own accord; Jessie could see that as they slipped quietly toward the side aisles, eyes downcast. But most needed the encouragement by sticks or sweets of another to get through that tent opening so they could hear the good news.

The music, too, soothed and inspired Jessie—and others, judging by the expressions of rapture as the pianist pounded out the hymns. Jessie hoped one day she'd take piano lessons, but for now, all her resources went into the bank. She didn't have a strong voice like Selma or an apparent gift for playing instruments like Roy. She was more like Lilly, able to enjoy music without having to produce it. But sometimes she wanted to make music too. She surprised herself in a small country church outside of Lake City one afternoon while Ralph and his men stood beneath elm trees shading their discussion. She pulled up the stool and played a tune that rolled through her head and directed her fingers, even though she had no notes before her. Maybe she did have a talent in music; she just needed to hear the song first and let her fingers follow along.

Jessie watched as Ralph spoke to each person who came forward while the pianist played "Blessed Assurance." Maybe taking piano lessons would be the only real dream she could fulfill. George Haas never again mentioned his plans to sell the Polonia, let alone to her, and she hadn't seen his ad in the paper or the photographic magazine. Neither had he mentioned taking her employment to full-time status. He'd been distracted of late with his wife's illness, though, so maybe in the spring she'd ask again.

At least working for Ralph had given her chances to photograph unique people and places. She captured experiences without having to hold on to every detail, knowing she could call up the emotion of the day simply by looking at the image. Her pictures witnessed the face of a woman filled with the joy of forgiveness, or the gnarled hands of a farmer grasping his hymnal. They evoked feelings of her own, and others told her the photographs moved them as did a work of art. It was an added bonus that some of those photographs appeared on posters the advance men hung around town, a chance to share her efforts, what every artist needed. It was not enough to paint a beautiful picture or write a glorious song: someone else must see it or hear it for the work to be complete. She didn't sign her pictures the way many photographers did. She noticed that a recent postcard of the canoe races on Lake Winona contained a tiny embossed seal. On close inspection, she saw it bore *Bauer Art Studio* and the date. She smiled. Fred made sure people recognized even his "tramp" work. Maybe she should do that too…one day.

Still, she made gains in her profession, if not fame. And on her list of achieved goals that allowed her to live and work in Winona for the rest of her days, she could say that she managed her emotions better now. She didn't engage in conversations with men she didn't know, and she'd had no encounters that she hadn't handled well, while being careful of the man's dignity…and her own.

The helpers were taking up the collection in the tent now, the movement bringing Jessie back to the moment. Baskets passed down each aisle. She watched as people put pennies and a few bills into the felt-lined oak. At the end, Jessie collected the money and tomorrow would take it to the bank. She'd asked for that privilege just so the tellers became accustomed to seeing her as one of their investors.

Ralph often preached about how giving that resulted in receiving was a way to encourage people to hope for the joys that came from generosity. "We must offer ways for the less fortunate to be generous or they'll be deprived of the blessings," he said when he talked of the offering portion of the evening service. Jessie supposed that maybe her blessings came in the form of the extra time she gave to Ralph's work. She wasn't paid for such time, but she found joy in helping people feel more comfortable as they entered the tent.

A woman began to wail as she told Ralph about her life. Her hat was simple and her dress dark and patched, and she looked tired as she turned to tell her story to those gathered. She'd had so many opportunities given to her, and she'd wasted each and every one. "I had good parents, and I spurned them," she told Ralph loudly enough for all to hear. "I could have worked in a hospital, taking care of people, but I found the cabinet where they kept the laudanum, and when I was discovered, I was sent away. I married a good man who finally left me when I fouled our marriage bed, and I've found more ways to abuse myself I shall not share. I am penniless, broken, standing before you with nothing left but an unworthy heart and these tattered rags I wear."

Jessie thought the woman dramatic in the telling of her tale, but Ralph treated her as though she spoke truth. "You have much more than that left," he said. He told her she had a choice now to do the right thing, to garner her courage to live in the world where all was not predictable or right, but where she would never be alone again if she chose a safe haven for when the storms hit her.

The woman fell to her knees, and Ralph's helpers and local church men laid hands upon her back and head and prayed over her, their words indistinguishable. Jessie imagined those gentle hands being pressed against the woman, soft as raindrops, and she felt tears well up. Perhaps God had willed her to be there, to receive a message that she, too, had choices to make. Perhaps her dream was not yet lost. The music, the soft summer breeze, Ralph's words, and the woman's bright eyes as she took them in infused Jessie with the wish to take her own next step.

It was that confidence that took her Monday morning into the Winona Savings Bank to make Ralph's deposit but also to seek yet another meeting with the bank's president.

It was a gift. Fred saw it that way. He hadn't intended to be walking past the bank on that day or at the time he did, but there he was. Jessie fast-walked past him out the door, maroon netting from her hat covering her face, though not enough to hide the tears on her cheeks.

Without a thought, his hand went out to her elbow, stopping her. "Jessie," he said. "Are you all right?"

"Oh, Fred. No. It's… I'll be fine, really I will. I'm just so…so… disgusted with it, that's all."

He coaxed her into a café not far from the bank and ordered hot tea for both of them. It was perfectly innocent, them sitting there, and if anyone should come by or ask about them, he'd introduce her as his former student. No one would think anything wrong with that. He let her talk, though her words didn't make much sense—they were all wrapped up in something Ralph Carleton had said and her visit with the bank president. She'd been denied a loan, again. That was the gist of it.

"He had the gall to lecture me about *commitment* being a banking term meaning 'a deposit against which one can later draw.' I knew that. I've put money into the bank, and I'd hoped to have them match it, so I could make a down payment on a studio. But they won't even consider it."

"Not even if your father agreed to honor the loan if you couldn't?"

"My parents are in no position to do that," Jessie told him. "They have their own expenses… Roy and everything."

"Perhaps I could—"

"No!" She actually looked alarmed at his offer, and that pained him.

"I didn't mean anything by it," he said. He raised his hands in protest. "I wanted to be helpful."

"I know, I know. But I have to do this on my own, or it loses meaning," she said. She stirred a lump of sugar into her tea. At least she hadn't said it was *his* offer that so astounded her. *Any* offer of such support she'd likely spurn.

"Maybe Ralph Carleton could—"

"No. Please." She took a deep breath and smiled at him. "I'll be fine. Thank you for the tea. It was just what I needed. I'll work out something else." They exchanged small talk, he telling her of a fine photograph Russell had taken of the trumpeter swans on Lake Winona and Winnie's latest tale, which she'd had him write down as her "story." She'd illustrated it herself with her colored crayons. Robert was growing tall as corn, he told her. She asked about Voe, and he told her young Danny now spent time with her while she worked.

"I'm pleased to hear it," she said. "All of it."

"You ought to stop by and see them at the studio," Fred encouraged.

She ignored the suggestion, stood instead, and thanked him for the tea but did not offer her gloved hand. He bumped the table as he stood, dropped his cane, which she bent to pick up for him. Their eyes met. She nodded, turned, and walked out.

His hand shook when he paid for the tea. He wanted to help her accomplish her dream, but she'd defined a border. He could walk beside her; that was all.

"I've decided to sell the studio to you," George Haas told Jessie a few days later. "I assume you can acquire the funds?"

Jessie swallowed. She didn't dare ask, "Why now?" She'd gone to all three banks, and none had been willing to match her investment. The presidents lectured her about a woman's place and about the unstable market for new business and about how photography was still a young profession. She countered with how long people had been taking photographs (the War Between the States had been captured with a camera) and explained that just this year a French photographer named Charles Pathé had produced a new film that captured people *moving,* not just the stillness of a subject's face. They'd been unimpressed.

She walked out into the sunshine after meeting with those bankers, the warmth doing nothing for her spirit. She loved Winona with its bustle and bluffs, yet her efforts to make a life here as she wished seemed thwarted at every turn. At this rate, the Gaebele girls were destined to grow old in their parents' home, working at the edges of professions but never excelling within them.

Now before her stood George Haas, saying he wanted to sell the studio to her! It was the opportunity she'd longed for, and she didn't have any way to bring it about. *Why now?*

"I'm not certain I can purchase the studio," she told him.

"Oh, well." He stepped back. "I thought—"

"If I may ask, why now?"

"Elizabeth continues to grow ill, and I can't imagine her spending another harsh winter here," he said. "I don't relish a Winona winter while she wiles away in sunny Tampa either." He'd made a small grin at that comment. "You've done a fine job here, and I see your dedication, working for Reverend Carleton and me too. The tenants are secure, so they'd bring income for you. It seemed an opportunity for both of us."

Credit was the only way she could conceive of this working, to buy the business and the building. "Would you allow me to pay you over time?" she asked.

He put his stubby finger to his lips, tapping as though thinking. But he shook his head. "I need the additional income to secure a house in Tampa. We might keep one here too, for a time, but with two homes to contend with, I'd need cash up front."

"Of course," Jessie said. "Would my savings up front be enough as a down payment?"

"How much do you have?"

"Nearly six hundred dollars," she said. "Though it's not even twenty-five percent of the purchase price, I know."

"I don't know... If you could increase it a little...then maybe I could carry the remainder. With three percent interest."

"Give me a day or two, would you?"

He agreed, and Jessie spent the night lying awake on her pallet on the porch, imagining what she might do. She could contact the Harms family in Milwaukee. They'd been generous to a fault and might be willing to lend her the additional sum. She could contact Joshua Behrens. His father worked for a bank in Milwaukee, and maybe Joshua could put in a word for her. Asking Fred was also an option, but she quickly put that one aside. There could be no linkage. Nothing to bind them together.

In the end, she decided to go back to the first bank she'd spoken with. Maybe with her history in both Milwaukee and Eau Claire, and her local Winona connections—"You can always find me if I miss a payment," she'd joked—maybe they'd reconsider now that Mr. Haas was willing to sell. This time, she wouldn't be trying to start a photographic studio from roots, but to grow one already in business, and she had a businessman willing to trust her ability to do it. She wouldn't be asking to borrow the full amount, only to increase the down payment amount. It was her best hope.

"We're quite pleased that you've found an existing studio to consider," the banker said, not looking at Jessie but staring at his notes. "That's much wiser than starting up your own. With an existing studio, you'll have customers waiting, prints to be made of existing plates, items you mentioned yourself when you first came by last year." Jessie nodded. *When you first turned me down.* "But nothing has changed about our concern related to a young woman proprietor being successful. I'm sorry."

"But George Haas is willing to carry the loan himself. Your risk is minimal."

"Individuals ought not to be in the bank business," he said, his lip curling up. He adjusted his glasses. Jessie thought idly that any portrait of him would need to tone down his wild white eyebrows, which looked like the cowlicks at the back of a baby's head. "George Haas should think twice about carrying a loan for a female photographer."

"Many young women are proprietors," she told him. "Look at Lottie Fort. She's a successful milliner. My sister works for her. And there are female photographers, just not in Winona. You could be the first, be innovative." He shook his head. "I am committed, ready to keep the promise that I know borrowing money means." She hoped in her frustration she wouldn't cry. She didn't, but he remained unmoved. Jessie stood, thanked him for his time, and walked out. She was so close, and yet the dream fluttered beyond her reach.

If she sent a telegram to the Harmses, they might be willing to make the loan, but she feared they'd tell Fred. And Joshua, well, she hadn't been in touch with him since the day she'd left Milwaukee. Surely business connections that would pay a dividend to both parties had to be nurtured over time, and she'd done nothing to make that happen. Maybe that was her next step, to reacquaint herself with Joshua, but results from that would take time. George Haas wanted to sell now. Maybe she had to face facts: it was not in her future to own her own studio.

Would working for another be so terrible? Yes, it would. She longed to achieve this dream, to decide the small things, like which brand of glass plates to purchase, how many ads to place, to prosper or fail on her own merits, not just to uphold the decisions of others. She ached to be the one to feel success or disappointment from her own efforts. It was her destiny to do this, to use her talents to bring joy to the faces of patrons by the loving portraits she made of them. Surely her gift—if she had one—was meant to nurture her and be enough to give away. What else could that proverb mean but that a desire could be realized, and that's what brought such sweetness to the soul? Maybe her sweetness was to come in another way. She closed her eyes that night but did not sleep.

"I'm so sorry," she told George the next morning. "I just couldn't work things out. Unless you'd take what I've saved as a down payment and allow me to make payments along the way, there's no way I can purchase the studio. I'm so sorry."

"I am as well," he told her. He patted her shoulder. "I ought to have taken you up on it earlier in the year, when things seemed more possible." She'd been more hopeful then too, but likely it would not have mattered. He shrugged his shoulders. "I'll advertise again in the photographic journals," he said. "I'll work something out. Don't you worry about us."

Jessie felt a twinge of guilt that she hadn't worried about George or his wife. She'd thought only of herself. Though she didn't want Fred to make another offer to help—and she feared he would if he knew of her predicament—she still wished she could talk with him, share her disappointment with one who understood the dissolving of a dream. But even that was out of the question. She thought of him as her closest friend, yet one she didn't dare confide in.

She didn't share her sadness with her family either. She acted cheerful. Nor did she tell Gertrude or Ralph when she went to work that next day.

At the Polonia, she buried herself in the retouching room and worked late into the evening. She'd fallen behind, having taken time off for all the bank appointments, and she found the time moved swiftly as she took the blemishes from a woman's pocked cheeks and trimmed the eyebrows just a bit from the man who seemed to scowl. There was artistry in what she did, and that soothed her. She ought to be grateful to have a job she liked. So it was dark when she left Fourth Street, locking the back door. The studio had a small apartment, but George never used it; he rented the upper offices to a doctor and an optometrist so the building had "professional" tenants. Jessie wondered if she ought to approach one of them about loaning her the money to buy the building and studio. Perhaps that's what George would do next: sell the business separate from the building, though clearly that wasn't what he wanted. The rents from the tenants provided income during slow photographic times, which is what made the investment such a good one. Why hadn't she emphasized that to the banker?

She walked swiftly in the November wind, brushing fallen leaves as she moved along the street to her Broadway home. She pulled the muffler up around her neck and face, careful not to steam her glasses as she breathed hard in her swift cadence. The air smelled of snow, a brisk wind swirling the fur at her cheeks. She liked walking at night, though this wasn't a full-moon evening. She could usually see just the steps ahead of her, reminding her that most of life was like that: taking one step at a time and following the light at hand rather than worrying about the steps in the darkness beyond.

She scampered up the stone steps and at the door stomped her feet of the leaves and mud, then peered into the window through the lace drapes to read the clock in the hall. Its chimes struck ten times. She'd have a cold supper, that was certain.

"Well, it's about time," Lilly said when she opened the door.

"I worked late."

"You might have let us know," Lilly said, arms crossed over her breast.

"I'm sorry. You're right, I should have called you."

"Or at least answered the studio phone when we called it," Selma said. Her sister's eyes sparkled. Her parents stood there. Had they been waiting for her? Was something wrong?

"The darkroom is in the back, away from the phone," Jessie reminded them. She hung her coat on the rack, sat on the bench, pulled the rubber boots from her shoes. Her parents said nothing, just stood there. "Were you calling to see why I was late?"

"We wanted to tell you to go to the bank before they closed!" Selma screamed.

"Selma, ladylike, please," her mother corrected.

"What?"

"The-the-the b-b-bank c-c-called," Roy said.

"They did? Why didn't anyone tell me! What did they say?"

"You're to contact them in the morning," her mother said. "They want to discuss your business proposition apparently. They wouldn't give us any details, of course. Will you?"

"They do? They called here? Oh, Mama, this might mean they've changed their mind and will actually make the loan!" She grabbed her mother's stiff shoulders and danced around her, the woman's apron lifting in the swirl.

"What loan?" her father asked.

"How will I ever sleep?"

As she told them of George Haas's change of heart, her father looked both encouraging and sad. "I wish we could put up the money for you," he said.

"I don't expect you to. I want to do this on my own, Papa. Me and the bank and George Haas. You have good places to spend your hard-earned money." She looked at Roy.

Her father patted the back of her hand. "I'll say a prayer for your meeting with the bank," he said. "I can do that and would have done it all along if we had known."

"I didn't want to embroil you in another possible disaster."

Having them share her hope was nearly as good as imagining that Fred, too, would be cheering her on—if he knew.

A small voice in the back of her mind wondered if Fred might have intervened, but there wasn't any way he could have known of George Haas's intention to let her buy the studio from him or of her latest visit to the bank. It had all happened too quickly. No, this was strictly a gift—as Ralph said when she told him the next morning. She asked him for an hour's time to keep an appointment at the bank and blurted that she might be moving on at last to a studio of her own. He grinned widely. "You see. Prayers are answered."

She didn't tell him that she hadn't prayed for something so selfish as a studio of her own. Prayers were reserved for important things, like the healing of her brother's speech or her father's strange stomach ailments or forgiveness for poor choices.

Concentration eluded her as she waited in the bank's reception area. She scanned the headlines, a few stories inside the paper, another article about the affair of the architect Frank Lloyd Wright and his paramour. She looked at the personals in the *Republican-Herald,* read the story of the surprise birthday party for their neighbor, Arlan Duff, which she'd attended. The paper reported on the guests, the games they played, refreshments served. The reporter gave credit to Ellen Plantikow's lovely solo sung to Mr. Duff's musical accompaniment. And there was Jessie's name along with Selma's and Lilly's, and the mention of Bertha Fisher, Ella Gussman, Emma Roeling, and Art Roeling—Selma's beau, whom her parents knew nothing of. No Joseph O'Brien. Lilly had failed to invite him to the surprise party. It had been a fine evening nonetheless, and Jessie had winked her approval to Selma as Art brought punch to their table. Jessie watched him press Selma's slender hand just a moment longer than needed.

"Miss Gaebele? Mr. Horton will see you now," the secretary announced. Jessie stood, took a deep breath as she absently slipped the newspaper into her folder, and walked toward a hopeful dream.

TWENTY-ONE

A Turning Toward Yes!

After all the saving, all the frustration and begging, after nearly offering up her firstborn child as collateral, all that had previously brought her no now turned into yes. The bank president in his gray suit, white collar stiff above a bluish shirt, sat behind the desk telling her he'd had a change of heart, had reviewed his notes and her work history and professional presentations, spoken with George Haas again, and the bank was now willing to enter into the entire amount of the loan. She would have to move her savings to First National, of course. And she would need to keep her tenants happy so their rental payments could help reduce the principal of her loan.

"Anything at all," she told Mr. Horton. "Anything."

"We'll expect quarterly reports of your earnings and expenses." His white eyebrows lifted as he stared at her over his glasses. "You should consider us your partner in this, Miss Gaebele. For we are. Every successful businessperson has a wise banker, a skilled lawyer, and an accountant, honest all, working on their behalf. If you do not yet have such people—well, you have a banker now, of course—but you must finish out your team with an accountant and lawyer. Keep them apprised of all your efforts so we can foresee potential problems and forestall disasters. Do you understand?"

"Yes, yes, yes!" she nearly sang it out.

As she signed various papers, she asked if she should have her lawyer look the papers over first, and Mr. Horton smiled. "Our lawyer has. It's the standard form, but certainly, when we've finalized things, have your new lawyer review it and come to us if he has any concerns. Using our lawyer here is also fine." Jessie wondered if that might not present a conflict, a lawyer looking out for the bank and a bank's client at the same time, but she didn't argue. Nor did she want to delay and perhaps have him change his mind while she chose a lawyer and accountant. Besides, she intended to wait on the accountant. She'd kept the books for the Bauer Studio and for the Johnson Studio, so she could save money by doing the bookkeeping on her own. Three thousand dollars was an enormous debt. She'd have to manage her finances carefully.

Mr. Horton offered his hand, and she took it and shook it once, then again, not letting it go until he pulled away. He walked around from behind his desk and escorted her to the door. "We wish you the very best, Miss Gaebele. Will you change the studio name?"

"No. I'll keep it as the Polonia. But I'll put an ad in the paper telling people it's under new ownership. I want to assure people who already have proofs that the good work George has done will be continued."

"You'll do well," he said. "I have every confidence in you."

Impulsively, she turned to the grandfatherly looking man who had just handed her the future she'd longed for and unprofessionally planted a kiss on his cheek. "Thank you so much," she said. "Thank you, thank you, thank you."

His white eyebrows raised and lowered, and he cleared his throat as Jessie waved good-bye and stepped out into the light of her new world.

Her enthusiasm brought smiles from the receptionist and other patrons waiting to deposit their money. She approached the street, which looked cleaner, brighter than it ever had before. She looked inside her folder to touch once more the papers signifying this day. "Oh, their newspaper," she said, realizing she still held the bank's *Republican-Herald.* She turned to take it back and place it on the wicker table. As she laid it down, her eye caught the last item in the personals column: "F. J. Bauer has sold parts of lots 2 and 3, block 12 in Sanborn's Addition, for $3,000."

Jessie paused at the amount. But it was business news; it surely had nothing to do with her.

That day, Jessie made contact with each of her tenants. In the several months she'd been working for George, she'd only nodded to them in passing as they went up the stairs. She told them that for now the rents would remain the same, feeling quite generous as she did.

The optometrist said, "Good, because if you raise the rent, I'll have to ask you to turn the heat up."

The doctor said his lawyer would be in touch about the need for a new privy. "I've spoken to George about that often enough," he said. "My patients need to be reassured that they are in professional surroundings."

She realized she'd never seen those offices. That probably wasn't very wise of her. Of all the research she'd done, she hadn't asked to look at the entire building, had accepted George's word that the structure was sound. She swallowed. "Do you have a water closet in your suite?"

"Of course not. That's why the chamber pots must be taken out frequently, though patients often choose to use the privy, which needs, well, tending to, especially in summer."

When she ran the Bauer Studio, she'd asked her father how to keep the privy smelling bearable. She'd have to see if George had lime in the garage and make sure it got added regularly. Maybe he hadn't spent much of late on upkeep, thinking he'd soon be selling, or perhaps he was distracted by his wife's poor health. She'd have to make sure her investment was well cared for.

"I'll make sure things improve," she told the doctor, who grunted as he returned to his work. Had he mumbled something about female landlords?

They'd all been tenants for as long as she could remember—at least three years—so George must have been attentive at one point. Their leases went for two more years, so that was good. She had time to make improvements and get accustomed to being a landlady in addition to running a studio. She just didn't want that doctor's lawyer coming her way before she even had a lawyer of her own.

That night her stomach ached. Maybe she'd bitten off more than she could chew. *Ha,* she thought. *I finally get what I ask for, and I'm still not happy.*

She wasn't alone in this. The bank had approved it. They wouldn't have gone along with making the loan if they didn't have confidence in her and her abilities. That's what she'd remember when she felt nervous. She'd set goals, meet them. This was just another step toward improving, being a professional photographer, investing in the currency of her talent.

She planned to attend the big photographic convention next summer. Only men could be delegates, but female photographers participated. She wanted to meet Belle Johnson of Monroe City, Missouri, whose portraits of kittens were her claim to fame. Oh, she did other fine work too, but Jessie had seen the cat portraits and wanted to tell the woman in person how much she admired her technique. Jessie might even meet the infamous Frances Johnston of Washington DC. Miss Johnston had been asked by *Collier's Weekly* to photograph Admiral Dewey on his way home after the war in Manila, so she had gotten to travel as a part of her professional life. And then there was her inspiration, Jessie Tarbox Beals, whom Jessie had seen standing on that twenty-foot ladder at the St. Louis World's Fair, first sparking her interest in photography. Jessie saw possibilities ahead if she was willing to work for them, and she was.

After everything was signed and George had headed to southern sunshine, Jessie cleaned out the back room, which had a small sink and a daybed, a table, and a chamber pot. From the prop room, she brought one of the folding screens to separate the bed and chamber pot from the table and sink. It bore a Japanese print of a large white bird within greenery. She found a small Frigidaire icebox and Monarch stove, along with a cabinet for her dishes and staples. She did all this in between taking photographs, developing them late at night, and then hurrying home for a few hours' sleep before heading back in the morning, until the studio's living space was ready for her.

"This is like a playhouse," Selma said when she stopped by as Jessie put the finishing touches on the wainscot. The room smelled of paint, and Jessie warned her not to touch the door frame, as the cold November weather kept it from drying despite the open windows. "Will you really live here, all by yourself?" Selma asked.

"That's my plan," Jessie said. "All by myself."

"But I can stay over sometimes."

Jessie hugged her, careful to keep the paintbrush from touching her sister's dark hat and coat. "Anytime. But first, let me get the paint smell out and see what it's like on my own. I heard the steam heat in the radiator the other night and nearly jumped out of my skin, thinking it was an intruder."

"You'll need a cat," she said.

"Why do you say that?"

"I just saw a mouse race across the floor and hide behind that box."

"I guess I'd better look for one then. It'll be good company and, between you and me, a better companion than Roy's chickens. I haven't enjoyed sharing the porch with them all that much." Jessie wiggled her nose. "But don't tell our Frog that."

"I'll find you a cat," Selma said. "It can be my house gift. People give gifts when someone moves into a house. Lilly told me that."

"Do they?" Jessie remembered her grandparents and uncle bringing food when the Gaebeles moved from the Wisconsin farm into Winona. "That would be swell."

She ran ads announcing that the studio was under new ownership: "Jessie A. Gaebele, Proprietor." She loved how that looked. But in the second ad she used "Jessie A. Gaebele, Photographer" instead. It suited her better. She was a professional woman more than a businesswoman; it was the artistry of photographs that fueled her passion.

Then she planned a tea at the studio to welcome her patrons. That's what women photographers in New York did, to ease people's concerns about a female-owned business. Having it before Christmas might bring in additional clients too. Her sisters helped by hanging bunting and greenery, and her father and Roy brought in a small tree they all decorated. Her mother baked cookies. "You can't have a tea without food," she told Jessie. "It does concern me that you've chosen to live alone here, when you're perfectly welcome to stay at home," she added.

"I know, Mama. But here I can work late without troubling anyone else."

"You're not eating well, thin as a shoe hook," she said.

"I'm fine," Jessie told her, secretly pleased that her mother missed her company.

"I suppose you noticed the ads," Fred's wife said.

Fred sighed. "What ads would those be?" He'd just come in from shoveling the walks of snow. He had to be careful since his heart could *thud-thud-thud* when he exerted too much, and he'd have to stop, lean on the handle, and take deep breaths. His lungs resisted bringing him air; they expanded, but it caught in his throat. He ought to get Russell to do the shoveling, but the boy was often busy in his room making things, fixing things. He did a good job of repairing electric lamps and changing cords when they became frayed. Besides, Fred liked being outside in the fresh air when he could. It was what he longed for at the ranch in North Dakota, where the wide prairie grasses looked like water as the wind rushed up and down the swales. He'd planted shelterbelts of trees, rows that outlined the fields and broke up the winds near the big house before it burned, and a few had survived the fire. But he didn't like the necessary windbreaks because the trees also interrupted the expansive views. It seemed he could inhale more easily in North Dakota, even though the place carried with it the suffocation of loss. On a morning like this in Emmons

County, Fred imagined hoarfrost layered like lace against the barbed wires he and his partner, Herman Reinke, used to pen the few sheep. He didn't relish his partner's having to work in this sort of weather; maybe it was best the cattle had perished in the fire, turning Fred mostly toward farming rather than ranching.

He inhaled, sat, began taking off his boots. He was here in Winona, in his own kitchen.

"The ad for Polonia Studio," his wife insisted. "Didn't you see it?"

"They've advertised for years," he reminded her. "Why should I notice them now?"

"Your star pupil is the new proprietor, or didn't that come up at your lodge meetings? Surely you knew that George Haas moved with his wife to Tampa and sold his studios to Miss Gaebele."

He'd known of the studio purchase. He'd seen the ads. But he'd found no sense in bringing it to his wife's attention.

"I did know of that, yes," he said. "On days like today with the snow piled to the rafters, I wonder why we don't do the same," he said. "Go to Tampa."

"And leave my mother and sister here alone? Why would you think such a thing?"

"Your brother could come by and look after them…if we went for a few weeks. He acts like he lives far away. And your sister does have a husband."

"Orrin has a business to run, repairing jewelry and such."

"As do I," he reminded her.

"Well, Ellsworth is miles from here. And Eva isn't the easiest to be around," his wife reminded him. "Mother counts on me." She waved her hand, dismissing him. "I don't wish to talk about my family. I wanted to know what you thought about the ads."

"What's there to think? She bought a studio. She's a photographer. Am I supposed to do something about that?"

"I'd think you'd be distressed, that's all. I am. You trained her, and see what she does?"

Fred sighed. "She served us well in our time of need…Jessie. Let her be."

"Let her be. I declare. That's all you can say? A competitor steals clients from under your nose, and you say, 'Let her be.'"

If only he could.

Jessie danced around the room in the white eyelet dress she'd saved so many months to buy when she and Voe worked for Mr. Bauer. Dancing alone was surely allowed.

The apartment stood ready. Selma had given her a cat, all black with four white paws and white whiskers. Roy named her Negative for the glass plates exposed in black and white. Jessie called the cat Neggie, telling her, "Today is my big day!"

She'd named the tea Polonia's Party, planning a festive occasion. She'd placed general invitations in the paper and sent several picture postcards to addresses of people she knew and local businesses, including other photographers. It seemed wise to let the competition know what they'd be up against. Selma addressed the cards, as her elegant penmanship looked more professional than Jessie's, so Jessie didn't really cull the address list as she might have, which is likely how Mrs. Bauer got the invitation she held in her hand on that December afternoon.

The invitation read "One O'Clock to Three."

Mrs. Bauer arrived precisely at one o'clock.

"Mrs. Bauer, come in," Selma said. "Jessie, look who's here."

Jessie stepped away from the reception table, which was now covered not with ferns but a lace tablecloth and dishes of cookies and candies. A silver tea set, a loan from the church (along with extra chairs), sat at the other end of the table. Lilly prepared to pour.

Jessie wished for the presence of other guests. She wished she had asked Selma to sing or Roy to play his banjo softly—anything to absorb the presence of this woman Jessie never imagined she'd see inside her studio, let alone as the very first guest. Would she remain until the end?

"Welcome. I'm so pleased you could come," Jessie said while her stomach turned somersaults. *Why is she here? What does she want?*

Neggie purred her way from beneath the table, heading for their guest. Jessie looked at Selma, who read the eyebrow message, whisked up the cat, and locked her in the apartment.

"I needed to see what you've done with all that training my husband gave you years ago. Or have you forgotten that we gave you your start, my husband and I?"

"I... No, I certainly haven't forgotten. I'm very grateful."

"As well you should be." Mrs. Bauer gazed around the room. "Not likely you'd be here today without the Bauer Studio."

Jessie saw her studio as she might for the first time: older furnishings left by George; no awards such as those hanging at the Bauer Studio; a smaller reception area without as much lovely light pouring through, even on this blue-sky December day; props of peacock feathers and scarves; a toy train and dolls Jessie'd added for child portraits. Compared to the Bauer Studio, the Polonia looked more like a second thought than a defining dream. Yet the woman's words suggested that Jessie threatened. Oh, she'd be competition, but surely not more than George Haas ever was.

Mrs. Bauer eased around the room, her gloved hands crossed on her umbrella. She studied each of Jessie's framed works: portraits of Minnie Raymond, Marie Harms, the Russian baby, Misha, the Marquette girls. She'd hung the colored character study of Patricia Benson too, and it occurred to Jessie as she followed Mrs. Bauer around the reception room, telling her stories of the different pictures, that only females graced her walls. Maybe she'd begun to specialize without realizing it.

"Would you like a tour of the rest of the studio?" Jessie asked when they'd completed the circle of the reception area.

Mrs. Bauer snorted. "I guess I know what a photographic studio looks like."

"Oh. Perhaps tea then?" Jessie said. "Lilly?"

Mrs. Bauer allowed herself to be directed to the table. Lilly poured a cup, asked if she'd like sugar (she did) and cream (she didn't), and offered her cakes and cookies. She pointed to one of each, then chose a chair close to the door. Jessie followed with the teacup balanced on the plate. She took the umbrella and put it in the brass stand near the door while Mrs. Bauer slowly munched.

"Your father was a photographer, wasn't he?" Jessie asked, sitting beside her. *Will she be the only person to come?*

"How would you know that?" Mrs. Bauer asked. She turned stiffly to look at Jessie's face.

"I believe you told me," Jessie said, "years ago, when I'd come by to confer about photographs and such while Mr. Bauer was ill. We spoke of your own training, retouching, that sort of thing."

"Yes, he was. A good photographer too. I've skills myself, you know. I practically trained Mr. Bauer."

"You did well then," Jessie said.

"Yes, I did," she defended. "He'd have been lost without me and my father to guide him. Papa's passing allowed him to build the studio on Johnson. Did you know that?"

"I didn't," Jessie said.

"Well, it did." She sipped more tea. "My mother's supposed to come by. My sister, Eva, too." She looked toward the door. "Don't know what's keeping them."

"I hope they make it," Jessie said.

It was a truthful statement, but Mrs. Bauer's stiff posture, the practiced eating, and the tortured expression in her eyes when she looked at the door told Jessie of this woman's fragile state, a brittleness that left a mist of fear above her lip that wasn't from steaming tea. Jessie lost her own discomfort then, stopped wondering at Mrs. Bauer's motives for stopping by. Jessie felt instead compassion for this woman whose losses settled in the creases of her face.

Other guests arrived, but Jessie never lost awareness that Mrs. Bauer filled her studio. Once or twice, when the door opened and neither Jessie nor Selma stood close enough to greet the new guests and receive their cards, Mrs. Bauer, looking with anticipation for her sister and her mother, would say, "Welcome to Polonia's Party. Jessie Gaebele's the new proprietor, trained by the Bauer Studio, don't you know."

It would be a long afternoon.

Voe surprised Jessie midway through, showing up with baby Danny on her hip. "Mrs. B.," Voe said. "Didn't expect you here. Isn't this the sweetest place?" Mrs. Bauer raised her teacup as though making a toast. Voe hugged Jessie with one arm while Danny kicked to be set down. He waddled over to Mrs. Bauer, who startled and leaned back in her chair.

Jessie handed the boy a cookie, and he trailed after his mother as she moved slowly along the gallery of photographs.

"All your pictures up here on the walls. Just like a real photographer, you are," Voe said.

"I am," Jessie said. She grinned.

"We'll give you competition, Mr. Bauer and me," she said, winking at Jessie. "Won't we, Mrs. B.?"

"Indeed," Mrs. Bauer said. Voe and Jessie exchanged glances as she led her friend to the table for tea, then completed the tour before Danny's racing around forced Voe to pick him up and prepare to leave.

Voe's brief visit reminded Jessie of the absence of friends in her life. She had busied herself with photography, helping Ralph, and getting this new studio ready, but Jessie knew her distance from Voe wasn't all about work-related issues. Friendship meant sharing what mattered, the struggles and salutations, and she couldn't really tell Voe of her moments of great joys or sorrows without also commenting on the man most often in them.

"Come by anytime, Voe," Jessie said at the door. Voe had Danny in hand.

"Likewise," Voe said. "You know where we live."

"When I get things under control here, I'll do that." Jessie waved into the cold December air.

"There's little to control in a studio," Mrs. Bauer said, still holding the seat by the door. "You should already have learned that."

Mrs. Bauer's mother and sister never arrived, but three dozen others did, including curiosity seekers. Several scheduled portrait appointments or family sittings at their homes; many left calling cards for Jessie to call on later. The party was a success by any estimation.

Fred came by just before five o'clock.

"Welcome to Polonia's Party," Mrs. Bauer said. "Jessie Gaebele is the new proprietor, trained by the Bauer Studio."

"You've come for the tour?" Jessie said. She hadn't realized she'd been waiting for him, but she had.

"Not today," he said, tipping his hat to her. He seemed to know that Mrs. Bauer sat just inside the door because he turned immediately to pick out her umbrella from the stand and said, "Come along now, Mrs. Bauer...Jessie." He extended his elbow to his wife. "I've come to drive you home."

Jessie watched them leave, an odd ache at her heart. She ignored the questioning look in Lilly's eyes as she turned back and began the cleanup.

She set the dishes in her small sink and heated water for washing. The hot sudsy water felt good on her hands. She would allow herself to be pleased for having met her utmost goal at last. The party was a success. Her business would be too. She hadn't done it alone, she knew that. George had accommodated; the bank had been convinced; her family had added furnishing accoutrements. She'd worked hard for this desire, pointed her nose in the right direction, kept herself from stepping where she'd stumble. She could truthfully say that now she was on her own.

She just couldn't describe the reason for the emptiness that grasped her when she told her sisters good night. Even Neggie's purring at her feet couldn't penetrate it.

Twenty-Two

The Absence of Two Chairs

THE LAST CLIENT FINISHED EARLY, and Jessie wanted to do the dirty work, as she called it, before dusk and the awful settling in of January cold. She went to the coal bin and filled up a bucket. Unfortunately, she hadn't negotiated with George Haas to fill the bin as part of the sale, so here was yet another expense she hadn't accounted for. No matter; it was needed. She set the pail on the back porch, then picked up her chamber pot and took it to the newly refurbished privy out back. She walked around to the front, checking the foundation, making certain the tenants had shut their windows. Dusk hovered over the snow-crusted lawn. She entered the studio, still carrying the now empty chamber pot.

Fred met her in the reception room.

"You…startled me," she said, her fingers at her neck. "Did you come in through the back?"

"No. The front." He pointed with his hat he'd removed. "Just there."

"I didn't hear the bell ring."

"You were in the coal bin, likely," he said and took a step toward her, touched her cheek with his fingers, wiping what must have been a smudge from her face. Her skin trembled. He reached for his handkerchief, but instead of dabbing her face again, he handed it to her, let her do it herself. "Let me take the chamber pot," he said.

"No. Please. It's fine. I… Please, sit. I'll fix us tea. Did you want the tour now?" She wiped her cheek and handed him back the handkerchief.

He smiled at her. "I came by to congratulate you," he said, "since I didn't have time during your reception. I hope Mrs. Bauer...well, that she didn't..."

"She was fine," Jessie said. "She seemed—"

"I'd be pleased with tea."

"Tea? Oh yes, certainly."

Her face grew warm. Her neck probably colored, but fortunately she wore a high-collared shirtwaist beneath her apron, and the collar pulled tight around her throat. She took a deep breath. "Thank you," she said. "Let me put this...back." She motioned to the chamber pot. "My rooms, or rather my room, is back here. I'll put the teakettle on."

"May I join you?"

She hesitated, then said, "Of course."

She chattered to him about the studio rooms as they walked through, pointed out the character studies. She mentioned the tenants upstairs. He commented on the helpfulness of the additional rent. "Yes, though renters have their needs," she put it. "I hadn't really counted on the extras." She placed the chamber pot behind the Japanese screen, then reentered the small kitchen area, tightening her apron strings in front as she moved past him to turn on the cooking fire, careful not to touch him. She poured water into the basin and washed her hands, the lavender-scented soap tickling her nose.

This would have been easier if he'd come during her party, when it wouldn't have been just the two of them, and she wouldn't have shared her small quarters with him either.

She took out pickles, a loaf of bread, jam and butter, a chunk of cheese. Neggie eased out from behind the screen and sashayed toward Fred, her black tail twitching as she swayed beneath his legs. He sat on one of the two kitchen chairs at the square table.

"You don't like cats, do you?" she asked, as he seemed to fidget a bit. He nodded agreement. "I've heard they're drawn to people who don't like them much."

"Or to those who'll give them their independence and not smother them with petting, let them be themselves." He stared at her and she turned away.

"I named her Negative, or rather Roy did, for the black and white of the glass plates. She's Neggie for short."

"It's not that I don't like cats," he said to her back. "They shed, and the fur makes me sneeze. Or has in the past. Maybe this one is different. And of course the fur can be a problem in the developing room."

"I have mice," Jessie told him. "Neggie brings them in as gifts to show me. But we make a good team. I dispose of them for her, leave her to her vices, and she leaves me to mine."

"I can't imagine a single vice you have, Jessie," he said. "Not a single one."

She ached with the kindness of his words, made light of them by puttering in the cupboard getting tea leaves out, locating the sieve, picking out the cups and saucers, and pouring when the teakettle whistled.

"How are things at the studio?" she asked. She'd keep this strictly business, ignore the stirring of her heart. "It was fun seeing Voe at the party. And that Danny is a husky one, isn't he?"

"Going well," he said. "Going well. Yes, Voe told me that day that Mrs. Bauer was here. It's why I…came. I feared she might—"

"That's good. She was fine, just fine." She served the tea, kept standing. "Sorry I don't have any sweets or anything. Was your Christmas season good?"

"Adequate," he said.

She lifted her cup, sipped the tea in silence, still standing. "Business," Jessie said. "The new Kodak lets everyone think they're an artist." He nodded. "Would you like to see the operating room? I made a few changes from when George had it."

"I would," he said. "In a minute."

"Oh, of course. I didn't mean to rush you." She set her teacup on the porcelain shelf of the sink, fidgeted with the lace at her neck. The clock ticked. Neggie flicked her tail back and forth, made quiet cat sounds. Jessie drummed her fingers on her elbows, felt the thubbing, put her hands in her apron pockets, took them out. She picked up the cat, watched as her tail twitched.

"I won't bite," he said with a smile.

"Are you talking to me or the cat?"

"Both."

"A girl alone can't be too careful," she told him, keeping her voice light.

"Well said. The tea is very good, very good," he said. He lifted the empty cup to her, and the cat leapt to the floor. Jessie reached for the departing animal, nearly toppling Fred's teacup.

She laughed, a nervous sound even to her own ears.

"The tour," she said as he stood. She led him through the prop room, then the operating room, where her camera waited for the morning setting. She showed him the darkroom, where the lights were on, as she wasn't developing anything. They discussed the merits of orange versus red developing light as they walked back out into a small print room, where she also did tinting and retouching. "The salesmen become enamored with certain brands, don't they?" she asked.

"They always have the next best thing to sell us," he said. "The perfect answer without telling us of the real complications."

She wondered if he spoke of photography or of something else.

He slowed as he noted the series of photographs she'd enlarged lying on the table. She'd decided to change a frame or two. He picked up a photograph of the Russian baby, Misha. "This is good," he said. "Inventive."

"They wanted only the child photographed, and the mother chose the plant stand. It was tricky. From what I could gather, the mother was leaving with the child, going back to Russia or the Ukraine. They came in so the father would have a photograph of his son. It was sad actually, seeing the family separated like that. They must have loved each other once. I could tell that he would miss the child more than the woman."

He stared at her while she talked.

"It's what I see in their faces, their eyes," she explained. "Maybe I add more than is there." *I shouldn't be talking about this with him.*

"You have good insights, Jessie. You always have." He put the photograph down and picked up another. "This is beautiful." He held the portrait she'd made of herself in her "kept-woman dress," as her mother called it, the white eyelet layered two-piece gown she'd saved to buy. "You're beautiful. And wearing the locket—"

"Please, don't," she said, taking the photograph from him, careful again not to touch him. She crossed her arms at her waist, keeping the print between them. She inhaled deeply. "I think it would be best if you left now. I appreciate your coming by to wish me well, I do."

"Jessie." He took a step closer to her, but she put the table between them.

"Please," she whispered, fighting tears. "Don't make this any more difficult. I have what I always wanted, a studio of my own. Celebrate that with me."

"I salute you," he said. He bowed at his waist. "I never…not ever did I imagine that I'd—"

"Please. Just leave."

He stood for a time just staring, then he put on his hat and left.

The black ink he used made the words bold. He'd gone back to his studio to be alone, to think. He wondered if she shared his longing. Probably, but she also knew the impossibility of it, better than he did, most likely. He'd forgotten to tell her that he would send over his *Camera World* each month. She'd always read them more thoroughly than either he or Voe. He'd send Voe over with them. He wouldn't go there again. Being alone with her, unable to express his care for her, was simply too much. His presence unnerved her; he could see that. He'd brought her enough pain.

The clock in his studio struck the late hour. He would pour himself into his work, recommit to his children, his wife. He hoped he and Jessie could be friends, colleagues, share a passion of a talent, but perhaps not even that was possible. He'd truly intended only to stop by and have her show him around, to honor her hard work and dedication to her course. Unlike his own journey from carpenter to cavalryman to medical corpsman to photographer, she'd stayed true to what she said she always wanted.

Now, all he could think about was Jessie. He didn't have a salve to heal that wound. Words came to him in a rush, and he simply wrote them down.

Two Chairs

You scurry across black and white linoleum squares, pouring
milk from glass bottles into porcelain cups with canary yellow daisies,
filled now with black tea.
I watch as your glasses steam from the heat.
You pull apron strings tighter against your whalebone
corset, a device you do not need,
as it molds to your slender frame.
From the Frigidaire you whisk chunks of cheese,
piled high on the tea-leaf plate shaded
by African violets blooming
in the windowsill despite
the cold.
Through the window, Russian grasses gather snow
in the garden beyond.

You place this feast before me.
A pickle crunches, ripe with vinegar, one you put up yourself,
no doubt.
It seeps juices onto my bread and chin.
(My eyes plead.)
But you hustle and bustle about
and won't sit down beside me,
even though there are
two chairs.

TWENTY-THREE

The Essence of Conscience

JESSIE LOOKED ONCE MORE at the photograph of herself in the eyelet dress before throwing herself onto her bed and giving up to tears. A good cry did help, though not as much as she hoped it would. If they could only remain friends, nothing more, she'd be happy, contented. But when he stood near her, she couldn't determine where friendship left off and passion began. "It's nothing I can sort out," she told the cat, "so I'd best not be anywhere near him."

She couldn't talk to anyone, must not. She'd start reading scriptures again, faithfully. That would help her. It had to.

In the morning she rose early, and the doctor-tenant found her unlocking the Polonia's door as he entered the building. "Are you acquiring a cold?" he asked. She frowned. "Your eyes are quite red. I can get you a Watkins product for that," he told her.

"I'm fine. Sneezing," she said. "The cat."

"Ah," he said and went on upstairs.

She would put herself to work, Jessie decided. That's how one set temptation aside. She just needed a new goal now that she'd met this one. As with a garden, she'd harvested and now she must plant again. That explained her uncertain state of mind.

An idea came to her as she entered her studio and prepared to cut a mat for a portrait. Come spring, she'd photograph a garden and print a postcard advertisement, then send it to Winona residents who boasted such plots, offering to make their "garden portraits," as Frances Johnston did. Maybe she'd place ads in faraway cities and get garden clubs to invite her to give presentations on photographing landscapes.

Jessie considered how gardens affected her own life. They brought her beauty, vegetables for sustenance, good memories as well as bad. As a child she'd been distracted from watching Roy by a butterfly, and then he'd fallen down the steps and everything had changed. But as an adult she was comforted by the color and peace of sweet william and gladiolus.

Winona boasted its share of such natural splendor, gardens of the Lairds and Watkinses and beyond. She'd search the city directory and select the possibilities.

She smiled to herself as she measured the mat's opening. It would be for a photograph she'd made of two sisters dressed in Roman garb. It had turned out well. She might do more of those.

She'd heard that Frank Lloyd Wright scouted Winona hoping to design a home there. Other students of his mentor, Louis Sullivan, had designed the Winona Merchants Bank, and maybe the young architect didn't want to be outdone. Wright called his designs Prairie Style, with clean, almost austere lines. There'd been an article about it in the paper. *The architect is only a year younger than Fred,* she remembered, then shook her head of the thought. Wright's use of windows and woods brought the outdoors inside, the papers said, and his work stimulated renewed interest in architecture and landscaping.

A home had been built in Winona last year designed by one of Wright's protégés. Jessie planned to send the owners a card offering to photograph their home and garden. Maybe she'd even venture to Minneapolis, as she'd heard that Wright had designed a "Northome" there. She rather liked the idea of traveling to Minneapolis and St. Paul to secure work she might turn into postcard sales. She'd have to coordinate the travel, though, with scheduling the portrait shots that were her bread and butter.

Her thoughts of bread and butter reminded her that she'd once given Fred a difficult time, telling him he ought to get out of the studio more, take shots of people in action. Now she knew that doing so took up blocks of time a photographer didn't always have. The more that could be done within a studio, the better. One could control the lighting, the shading, and the props, and thus waste less film and finish the order more quickly too. Receiving timely payments wasn't the most glamorous part of being a businesswoman, but it was one of the most critical.

Still, she liked the idea of photographing outdoors, and gardens would permit that. Statues and fountains didn't move, the leafy vegetation and flowering plants could be quite still, and she could assess the lighting and take most of the shots early in the morning, when the light was best and the wind calm.

The idea took over, and she abandoned the mat job. She took the city directory to the kitchen table and began making lists of potential clients. She would go to Minneapolis too. Maybe during the photographer's association convention in the summer. Gardens renewed themselves each season, she reminded herself. Increased exposure to the light, the lengthening of days—those brought on the bloom. She had to remember that.

Now that spring had arrived and she didn't have to maneuver the snowy roads and messy streetcars, Mrs. Bauer resumed her visits with Reverend Carleton. Tulip greens pushed through the latent snows, and the earth smelled musty and moist with new growth. All the shrubbery along the bluffs had been burned as scheduled, and the hills looked darkly naked in the reflection of Lake Winona as she took the streetcar the long way around to Reverend Carleton's office.

Upon arriving, she waited, nodded to Gertrude, thinking she might cease these appointments. It seemed to her he arrived later each time and had to leave earlier. Besides, she found reluctance in sharing anything important with him since Jessie Gaebele had once worked for him. With summer coming up, Mrs. Bauer wondered if he'd reemploy Jessie Gaebele for photographic work. The girl would likely need the contract, as Mrs. Bauer couldn't see how she could operate the Polonia successfully on her own.

It concerned her, too, that Reverend Carleton might have formed his own opinion about the girl, different from her own. He'd found ways to minimize her concerns about the girl competing with her husband's business. She'd noticed that he seemed distracted when she told him of her worries, of the absences of FJ, of her own aging and being unable to gather up any zest for life. He'd prod her by saying, "Yes, yes, we've been over that. Have you worked on the suggestions I've given you? Have you made a list of good things in your life and read it when you feel particularly sad? Have you found a service you can do for others? You know that always makes a person feel better, doing for others. What about your children? Are you able to have an evening with them without becoming upset?"

She'd tried, she really had. Soon the children could play outside, and that would help ease her discomfort. She'd given a quilt cover to her sister and offered to come by and stitch it with her, thinking the two of them might find things to talk about. But Eva had feigned illness. At least, Mrs. Bauer assumed it was feigning, though Eva was often "out of sorts," as their mother put it. Eva and her husband had no children, and Mrs. Bauer thought Eva acted like a spoiled child herself. Mrs. Bauer never expressed as much to her sister, or her mother. Still, Eva hadn't made any time for her. Eva could be unpleasant, and Mrs. Bauer wasn't sure she even liked spending much time with someone like that. Eva would have more friends if she behaved a little more cheerfully. Mrs. Bauer'd said that to Reverend Carleton, and he'd grunted his assent.

Mrs. Bauer had been spending more time with the children, letting Melba off a couple days a week and doing the work of tidying up herself. She thought FJ would be pleased with the savings in expense, but he hadn't seemed to notice. They'd had fewer fights, but that was because he stayed at work even longer and attended more than one veterans' meeting a week, plus took a meal weekly with his Scottish Rite Lodge, which was raising money for projects related to stammering schools. And then he'd agreed to teach a class on photography at the YMCA. The latter surprised her because he had little patience with people who disagreed with him or didn't do what he asked the first time. He'd gone through more than one assistant before hiring Miss Gaebele and Mrs. Henderson. She supposed she should be grateful that the girls had lasted as long as they did. But then, so had she.

It was a cutthroat business, her husband called it. At times she wondered who cut whose throat in the process, with more than one of the girls they'd trained going on now to compete with him. She tried to remember the name of the woman who had worked there before those two girls. A single woman, she was.

"The girls." Mrs. Bauer still thought of Voe Henderson that way, though the woman now had a toddler running about the studio. Mrs. Bauer didn't think it very professional, but she'd said nothing. Winnie stopped there after school and seemed to enjoy the time with the child and her father. He'd bring her home after work, have a quick supper, and then go back to his meetings and whatnot, talking to Russell and Robert more than he did to her.

As for Miss Gaebele—Jessie—her studio looked good. She'd furnished it well with lovely curtains and all, likely made by her sister or mother. The party had been pleasant. Still, the only reason the girl got the loan to buy such a studio was because of her record working for Mr. Bauer all those years past. Such experience would make a banker sit up and take notice. She hoped the girl understood what the Bauer Studio had done for her career.

Where is Reverend Carleton? Mrs. Bauer was about to leave when she saw him pass by the window. He was alone. Good. She'd have plenty of time to tell him of her latest concern. She just had to think of how to put it—in a way she hadn't expressed before—without exposing too much. She had to keep Reverend Carleton engaged, after all. She couldn't afford to lose the interest of yet another man.

Jessie finished hand coloring one of the lantern slides of the Laird garden, annoyed with herself that it took her so long to do this close and careful work. Frances Johnston made a good living coloring slides and giving presentations; she had to remember that. A business wasn't all passion and art; a good portion was just plain tedious work of planting seeds and pulling at weeds. She intended to offer the slide show when she had photographed six or seven different gardens, but the follow-up work took longer than she'd anticipated.

As she approached these wealthy people and successfully commissioned the work, however, she gained more confidence and considered more gardens to include. City parks, for example. They'd make fine penny postcards. The cities themselves might purchase prints to promote their growing communities. She remembered a few interesting parks and gardens that had appealed to her when she'd traveled with Ralph Carleton and made notes of the streets they were on in Red Wing and New Prague. River towns she especially liked, and she preferred gardens with Japanese influences, attractive fountains, or hillside locations.

Newness appealed to her. Perhaps that was why she loved to travel to new places, to take in the complexity of a site beyond familiar. But each garden season bloomed its beauty. Even in winter, the fluff of snow or sometimes ice that formed on fronds collected sunlight in artistic ways. Their black and white images represented the purity of photography. Color could enhance the memory, but black and white captured nuance, crystallized it like a painted portrait.

She finished the slide work and was glad for it, removing her glasses and rubbing her eyes. Coloring required careful attention. She ought to make an appointment with the optometrist, but she couldn't afford the expense right now. Besides, she had a dozen things to do before she could leave for the convention. She'd made enough in commissions to consider hiring help, and at times she wondered how she had managed doing so much all by herself these past months. But she liked being responsible, liked telling stories of her accomplishments when she joined her family weekly for supper, didn't really want to share those personal successes with an assistant just yet. She also liked all aspects of the work. What would she delegate to an employee anyway?

Her tenants provided her with enough "personnel problems," as the articles described issues dealing with workers. The physician wanted remodeling, and the optometrist wanted a skylight. Burning trash was a constant problem, as the smoke irritated the doctor's patients, yet if she waited until Saturday, large piles grew like giant gopher mounds in the backyard. Her tenants had no idea of the expense and didn't want to put any of their own hard-earned income into fixing a place owned by someone else. She worried that they might find a building to buy and leave her. But they could just as easily do that after she remodeled, and then she'd have to find very specific tenants to take their places. It was all much more confusing than she'd ever imagined. But she persevered, made her payments to the bank. That was what mattered.

And she was giving herself a present: attending the Photographers Association of America meeting in St. Paul. She'd been working full time for the past six years, and it was hard to pass up a conference when it was so close by.

She took her valise from the attic and set it on the bed, Neggie following close behind. Her eye caught the photograph Fred had taken of her so long ago, when she'd turned sixteen. He might attend the conference. She swallowed. She could handle it. Not going wasn't an option. She would make good contacts there, meet other female photographers. Her emotions didn't rule her any longer. She and Fred had had no contact since he'd come to her studio last winter, and that was just as well. "No sense dwelling on a relationship that can never be, right, Neggie?" The cat crawled into her bag, purring.

Jessie had told her parents she'd be leaving for a week and asked Lilly to come by after work to feed Neggie and see if the tenants needed anything while she was gone. Her mother chided her about traveling alone, but there wasn't much heart in her worries anymore. Jessie had made a number of trips now without incident, so she guessed her mother either trusted Jessie or relied on prayer. Maybe mothers did that after a time.

"Could I come along, Jessie?" Selma had asked. "It would be such fun to visit a big city."

"You'd have to take off of work," Jessie told her. "I'll be working while I'm there, going to lectures and finding new gardens to photograph. Maybe next year," she said, giving her sister a one-armed hug. "We could plan an extra day and just visit shops and see the latest fashions."

Lilly gave her a lecture about the evils of big cities and whispered a warning about whether Fred Bauer would be attending.

"I have no idea if he'll even be there, Lilly. And it doesn't matter. I'm going for professional reasons."

As much as she anticipated the conference, Jessie also looked forward to surveying those new gardens and parks. She decided that people liked viewing gardens from faraway places more than in their own locale, where they could saunter down the street and see that garden for themselves. So she'd made up her mind to branch out, maybe travel as far as Chicago to get photographs, and perhaps even shoot interesting architecture or ornate building facades and doors. Photographs of objects could be quite artistic, and people might buy a print just for the creative way a common item had been artfully presented, a study of shadow and light. She'd begin with subjects in Minneapolis and St. Paul.

Jessie counted her coins as she finished packing, allowing a twinge of guilt over the expense of her travel. She could have paid more on her loan. She'd made good investments, she thought, and had spent her money wisely. But if the heating went out at the studio building or an unattended lamp caught a curtain on fire, she'd lose everything. She'd read an article in the *World* about insurance to cover disasters in which her cameras and enlargers might be destroyed, but it seemed a strange thing to do: send money to someone who would keep it until you needed it, and if you never did, they'd have the coins and you'd have nothing. She wasn't yet convinced in the merit of insurance.

It was that sort of business issue that made her want to call Fred, or made her irritated that she couldn't go to the lodge and listen to the men discuss such topics. She supposed she could contact a lawyer, but whenever she did, he charged her for an answer! She'd decided to make more business decisions on her own. She hadn't done badly so far; it was only in affairs of the heart that she had such poor return on her investment.

On an August morning in 1913, she petted Neggie good-bye, made sure the cat had a bowl of water and a box of sand for her chamber pot. Then Jessie caught the streetcar for the train station. She boarded the train, sat in the seat beside a man who nodded and tipped his fingers to his hat at her. She smiled nervously, aware of a flutter in her stomach. She pressed her hand to her corset. It was the excitement. *I'm taking a working vacation,* she told herself. *That's all. New things to see.* She was a professional woman, a businesswoman. This is what such women did.

The man turned back to his newspaper as she stuffed the valise under her seat but held the camera case in her lap. The train puffed its way out of the station. The butterfly feeling in her stomach caused her to take a deep breath. Trips always made her more alert, gave her a jolt of interest in the world around her. She looked at the passengers, didn't recognize anyone at all. *I've never been this way before.* She'd taken the train but not to this destination. Her hands shook.

Why was she nervous? What had she read recently in the magazine the physician received and then tossed out to be burned? That German doctor Freud wrote it. *Anxiety is the essence of conscience.*

She wondered why she remembered that.

The Giroud sisters
August 2, 1913, Polonia Studio, Winona

Fragility

I shot this pose prior to the photographers' meeting in St. Paul, when everything was under control, when I felt strong and capable and certain.

It was all the rage, taking photographs of lovely young women wearing Roman togas. The Giroud sisters had seen such a photograph when they traveled to Chicago to visit their aunt and wanted one for themselves. I didn't object in the least. I'd thought of posing such a picture with Lilly and Selma, but what happened after that month made the idea moot.

Amelia, the older sister, stands in this pose, her hands laid gently on her sister's shoulders. They're lovely hands, and their lightness on Clarice's back reminded me of Ralph's tent meetings, when elders gave their blessings and prayers onto new believers through the weight of their hands. Kindness, compassion, love flowed from those hands.

I arranged the curtain to be partially open so that the backdrop wasn't fully textured with lace. When I developed it, I thought I might cut out the darker curtain in the background, but I liked the contrast. The same was true of the carpet. The tapestry gives balance to the photograph. A viewer's eye travels both upward from the girls and then down to flowers on the floor.

They were to be thoughtful poses, as though their minds were full of future dreams, of what they longed to be one day, who they hoped to marry, or how they planned to live their lives in service to their families or faith. The Giroud girls were known for their churchgoing.

The belts they wore I purchased from a catalog. The rings were intended for curtains, but I saw the possibility in them. Clarice suggested weaving them into the girls' hair.

I like the simplicity of their arms, the pale, smooth skin that speaks of purity.

The girls dressed at the studio and giggled over who would stand and who would sit. They already knew what the pose was supposed to be, having seen it in Chicago, but they allowed me to choose the backdrop and props. The girls posed on their own, didn't need much support except for the facade they'd sit on.

"The facade they'd sit on." As I write that, I'm reminded of the facade I created for myself before that journey to St. Paul, how thin the veneer of certainty I carried with me.

The studio prop is made of layers of wet newspapers and plaster, dried, then painted and decorated with embellishments made to look like marble. It's all quite elegant, hiding the fact that there is no real value behind it. Just paper, easily crumbled. As props, the seats can be moved around, and we created this scene reminiscent of a Roman room, but of course it was all pretense. It was nothing but two fine people from Winona pretending to be what they weren't.

It turns out such was true of Fred and me in St. Paul.

Oh, it began without pretense or show. I knew exactly why I'd gone to St. Paul. After arriving, I took several shots of gardens and made my way quite easily around the city on streetcars and on foot, keeping myself aware at all times of how far I'd meandered from my hotel, getting myself back well before dark. I enjoyed meals in the restaurants and didn't feel at all alone despite being the only person at my table in a room filled with men or couples.

I went to church and relished the music. I felt grateful for all the grace heaped upon my life and prayed my thanks. I felt as full as at any time in my life, sure, strong.

On Monday morning, I went to the hotel center early and purchased the Association program. "Criticism and Lecture," a Wednesday program, would be given by Miss Lena McCauley for the Federation of Women Photographers. I hadn't even realized there was such a federation, and this woman, an art critic for the Saturday Evening Post, *would be speaking of it. My investment in this trip had already been paid back! I did chuckle when I saw the program note to that session: "All members are invited to this," as though a group of women meeting alone might be seen as fodder for tyranny. Apparently "all members" were needed to keep us females in line.*

Lectures on adding backgrounds to negatives, on uses of artificial lighting, and on applying "Scientific Salesmanship" and "Modern Publicity" methods filled the program. I noted that a "coaching party" for the ladies overlapped a scientific meeting, and I thought I might never find out what that was about since I planned to attend the salesmanship lecture instead. A theater event and a boat ride on the lake were scheduled for later in the week. The program also carried portraits—mostly of women—and a drama portraying issues of our art.

Outside the auditorium, in the lobby area, booths advertised new cameras, Photo-Era *magazine, and Eastman Kodak and their sign, which read, "Active Chemicals tested by experts bear this mark." Ads in the program helped remind the reader of the booths. Salesmen hawked their wares like they were at a street fair, though dressed in fine three-piece suits instead of straw hats and patchwork vests. Manufacturers offered suggestions for new mounts and lenses, papers including Sprague-Hathaway Company's promotion of sepias for "portraits that never disappoint," and chemicals like duratol and hydroquinone for those "susceptible to poisoning by other coal tar developers." That ad made me think of Fred and his susceptibility to illness.*

I especially liked the program quote from Pirie MacDonald, a well-known photographer from New York City, which read, "Success is not getting the best out of the other fellow—but from getting the best out of yourself."

I was overwhelmed by the majesty and abundance of it all but intended to get the best out of myself as a photographer because of it. That first day, I did well. I took in the lectures, made notes in the program, and attended a reception that evening. I delightfully inhaled the smells of the shrimp and garlic hors d'oeuvres, took in the stage decorations, and milled around noticing the fashion of women—not only of the photographers but of the wives. I wondered once if Mrs. Bauer ever came with Fred, then put the thought aside.

We photographers wore ribbons to distinguish us from mere guests.

I've saved my ribbon, though it now reminds me more of sadness than of those first hours when I felt that I truly belonged at such an event, knowing exactly what would develop in my life and that I had the strength and faith to correct any unwanted exposures. Ah yes, I thought later: certainty shadows the face of temptation.

During the reception, strolling musicians played, and I introduced myself to a cluster of men and women, garnering my courage to enter conversations already underway. I even made the others laugh, talking of my tenants. Many of them nodded, commiserating with what a photographer must do to bring out the best in themselves.

Then I felt a warm hand on my elbow. The circle of guests and members gathering with me widened, and Fred Bauer entered in.

TWENTY-FOUR

Self-Deception

FRED SAW JESSIE DURING THE DAY, just a glimpse as she moved between lecture rooms. He hadn't thought she would attend, being so new to her studio; but then, she'd been in the business since she was fifteen, and now she was what? Twenty-one. She wasn't new at all. But he made no move to try to say hello, not sure he trusted himself to honor the distance she'd set up.

He'd decided to go to the conference—he was a delegate after all—even though finances pinched and the conference always cost him more than he intended. In addition to the expense of the conference itself, he usually picked up new supplies, placed orders for Seed Company's dry plates, and considered different developing chemicals. Those were business expenses. But he also managed to visit the shopping sections of the host cities, where he'd purchase sweets and toys for the children, order a tailored suit, and maybe pick up a piece of jewelry for his wife. Minneapolis and St. Paul weren't new to him, as he'd lived there for a time when he and Mrs. Bauer first married. But he hoped this conference would infuse him with new interests, resurrect that spark he needed as a photographer. He wouldn't spend any more than was required for the hotel and the conference registration. Not this time.

That first evening, he left his cane in his room. When he entered the reception area beneath the hotel's gas chandeliers and heard the music of the string ensemble, his eyes immediately found her: she wore a cream-colored gown in the slender new style, revealing white rounded shoulders, the satiny material molding her tiny waist and flowing in straight lines to the floor. The back of the dress exposed ivory skin, and a shawl hung artfully across her waist and draped around porcelain arms. He made himself take a glass of ginger ale from the tray being passed around by white-coated servers before he did anything foolish, trying to decide if he ought to approach. He watched the faces of those around her, heads cocked to her soft voice, followed by a spurt of laughter and nods. She could do that to men—or women—make them laugh, feel good about what they did, and it was never at the expense of others, only herself. She had not a mean-spirited bone in her delicate body.

Their laughter is what made him decide to join. He felt envious that the luster of her presence shone on others. The very closeness of her is what made him reach with familiarity to touch her arm as he stepped beside her.

"Oh, Fred," she turned, glanced at her elbow. "Mr. Bauer." He dropped his hand. "I'm sure you know the Lewises from Toledo, Mr. Steffens from Louisville, Miss Carnell from Philadelphia, Gertrude Käsebier from Denver."

"New York," the elegant photographer corrected.

"Of course," Jessie said. "I'm sorry. You have that incredible portrait of the sailor printed in the conference program. Truly wonderful use of light. The skin tone is exceptional."

Gertrude graciously acknowledged the compliment, and Fred was certain the New Yorker would hold no grudge over Jessie's having given her a different city for her studio. Jessie introduced three others in the group and never missed a name. He was impressed with her memory, her apparent comfort with these new people. *Something else to admire.*

"Mr. Bauer was my first employer in Winona," Jessie continued. "He introduced me to the art nearly seven years ago."

"And now she has her own studio," Fred told them. "In Winona."

"Ah, competition," Mr. Steffens said. He had one hand stuck

into his white vest; a champagne glass sparkled in the other. "Always makes us better men, competition does."

"You must have been a mere child when you began your career," one of the women said.

"Fifteen," Jessie said. "When did you start, Miss Carnell? I've long admired your portraits of children. Phillips's book *With Other Photographers* highlights your work so well." She was deft at moving past any subject that might distress, he noticed, and turned people to talk about themselves. Always the best policy. The mark of a fine salesman.

"I didn't really like the print work on the plates in that book," Miss Carnell said.

"The quality still sang through," Jessie told her.

"I'm glad you think so. Are children a specialty of yours?"

"I don't think I have a specialty yet," Jessie said. "I love gardens and landscapes, female character studies too. But I do admire those who can capture the essence of a child without making them appear stiff for the posing."

Miss Carnell agreed and spoke of her early years and encouraged Jessie to pursue her talent. Then the subject turned to the events scheduled later in the week, but Fred didn't hear much of that. He was aware only that he stood beside this woman, and being there was unlike being in any other place in his life. She was the source of his renewed energy, the source of his feeling alive. It was enough simply to stand beside her. He'd almost passed this moment up by not coming. What a foolish decision that would have been.

Jessie felt his presence even when she separated herself from the gathered group and left him behind in it. She knew he wouldn't follow her, and she acted as though she had somewhere else to go, even though she would have loved to spend the evening with Miss Carnell. It irritated her that Fred had joined them, because now she was conscious of him instead of gleaning all she could from the other professionals. Fred's presence, the smell of tobacco on him, the textured linen weave of his suit against her bare arm, distracted.

She didn't attend the concert, fearful that with the rush of music in a darkened auditorium, her eyes would seek his. She was unsure if she'd be troubled more to find him or miss him. She went to her room that night without further interaction, but she remembered his presence in the reception room along with those anxious flutters in her stomach. Those thoughts annoyed her sleep.

On Wednesday she slipped into the lecture with the art critic and was relieved to see that Fred wasn't there. That evening another lecture by the director of the Toledo Museum of Art, about photography as art, held her attention even though she saw Fred enter, watched as he sat and began talking quietly to a matron beside him. The gentleman next to her was most gracious, a salesman from the Lieber line of frames—he gave her his card—in Indianapolis. They exchanged comments about the conference, and he asked about her studio. She told him of her interest in garden photography and also candid shots.

"You ought to go west," he said. "North Dakota. Colorado. Pikes Peak attracts people, and photographs are developed on the mountaintop!" At intermission, she listened intently to the frame salesman while she kept her back toward Fred.

An illustrated lecture by Mr. Phillips, whose book Jessie had referenced to Mary Carnell, provided the second half of the evening's event. His subject, Constructive Criticism, held her attention, though that night in her room she wondered if the words weren't contradictory. She never felt she gleaned anything about how to construct a better photograph before hearing what was right in a photograph first. She hoped he'd gotten permission to use the enlargements in which he pointed out problems. She'd die of embarrassment if one of her photographs had been critiqued in that way. It had been difficult enough when Fred did it all those years ago.

She thought she'd survived the week when on Friday morning she arrived early and sat near the front so she could see better and hear everything that was said. Afterward, though, Fred waited for her. "Would you take lunch with me, Jessie?" he said.

Don't do it.

She did it anyway.

They nearly missed the next event because the meal was so pleasant. They laughed and talked "lectures" and got into a debate about the role of photography within art circles. For the most part, her fluttering stomach ceased as they carried on a perfectly normal conversation, like two old friends catching up. It was as she hoped it could be: professional. Then, after the second lecture about lighting, during which Jessie sat next to Fred, he invited her to join him that evening for the theater party.

"Surely you're going, aren't you? I was sad to see you missed the concert."

"Just too tired," she evaded. "I'm not sure about tonight."

"You have to come. They do a special performance, and the entire audience is made up of PA & A members." She frowned. "Photographers Association of America. And their guests, of course. I think tonight they're doing a rendition of Scott Joplin's new folk opera. It'll be fun, yes? You can't come to these conventions and do nothing but work." He shook his finger at her as he smiled.

"All right," she said. She could keep this on the straight and narrow. Hadn't she done so all week?

"It's been a while since you've been to Lottie's, Mrs. Bauer." Young Selma Gaebele spoke to her in Lottie Fort's millinery. "I think it was cold outside when you last came in. I hope that muffler worked out well."

"It was adequate. I'm here for a new purse," she told the girl. Her eyes searched the room. She felt alert and aware despite her lack of sleep. In FJ's absence, she'd repeated her invigorating evening by staying up late, first playing a board game with Russell and Winnie while she bounced Robert on her lap, then by talking with Melba over tea until the girl nodded off at the table. After sending Melba to bed, Mrs. Bauer wound up the Victrola. FJ had purchased it almost as soon as they'd been produced, but then he'd had to wait to find the vinyl plates, called records, to play on it. But she put one on and found herself dancing around the parlor to the music. Afterward, she sat smiling to herself on the settee, and then hummed as she went up to bed and read until nearly three in the morning.

FJ was at one of his conventions, but she knew how to reach him if she needed to. She felt quite safe and content and admitted to herself yet again that she enjoyed her own company and how very strange that was.

She decided that when she arose that morning, she'd shop. She called her mother with an invitation to go along, but Mother was busy looking after Orrin's son. Normally that would have set her off, but today she had the enthusiasm to go out and shop alone. She decided on finding a purse and could have gone to Stott's, but Lottie carried a fine selection, and it usually wasn't crowded, so she got good service.

"I'm partial to this one," Selma said. She held up a silver-toned mesh bag with a coral and green and black enameled design that reminded Mrs. Bauer of FJ's Indian art, which he kept in his room. It was as much the fringe as the bold design, but the purse brought memories of North Dakota, where FJ had picked up most of his Indian artifacts. She didn't want anything to remind her of that place.

"What about that one?" Mrs. Bauer said. She pointed to a silver mesh bag with a pleasant frame. The label *German silver* was inscribed inside the clasp.

"Oh, that's perfect for you, Mrs. B.—I mean, Mrs. Bauer. Just the right size for a handkerchief and a compact for when Mr. Bauer takes you to a lovely photographic party. Will you join him tonight in St. Paul?"

Mrs. Bauer sniffed. "He hardly does anything of the kind. And no, I don't attend with him because it's strictly business, as you might imagine. I wanted one for our after-dinner drama productions."

"Sure. It'll be good for that."

"First it was 'swell,' and now it's 'sure.' What will you young people think of next?"

"I sure don't know." The girl giggled. "Shall I wrap it up for you?"

"Yes, please." Mrs. Bauer looked around. She could use new lacy summer gloves, and Lottie had a butter yellow pair on display.

"Here you are." The girl handed her a string-wrapped package. "I'll be interested to hear what my sister says about the photographic meeting. She said it would be all work, but she packed her silver purse and sheath dress. I sure hope she finds a place to wear it."

Jessie didn't think he planned it. He'd taken her key after the theater, unlocked her door, and then, standing there in the hall, he'd lifted her chin and sighed. "Jessie," he said, then lowered his lips to hers. A kiss, light as fog and all-consuming.

It was as though the years of his absence spilled away like a telescoping rush into history. She felt her legs tremble, heard her heart beat against her cheek, the fluttered kiss now at her neck, which arched on its own. It wasn't her body responding, and yet it was, oh, it was. There was no denying that. The facade she'd worn all these years fell away. This was no schoolgirl crush, no platonic relationship gone awry for a season. Even in the intervening months when they'd encountered each other, she'd done nothing to promote it, had she? Had he? No. She hadn't been strong enough, though she moved away, stayed away, kept the distance. What was happening now was the result of proximity and opportunity.

And his absence having tinted every pose of her life these past six years.

"Please. Don't," she said. "I can't. We can't." She pushed her hands against his open suit coat. "This can go nowhere, nowhere." She could feel the tears rise, and she swallowed. "There's nothing to hope for, Fred."

He still held her key, and she felt it pressed against her back as he moved in closer to her, his arm wrapped around her, his face still just inches from hers. She could feel the brush of his whiskers against her neck now and the prickle on her lips. With her hands holding her purse, she pressed his chest, retreated. "Please," she whispered. She'd started to cry.

He stepped back then. "I'm sorry. I shouldn't have. It's just that when I'm with you, I lose—"

"Shh," she pressed her gloved fingers to his lips. "Just say good night. This never happened and it won't again."

Surrounded by silence, she pushed the door open to her room.

"The boat trip, tomorrow night," he said. He stood straight and stiff, professional. "Please say you'll attend, yes? The scenes are beautiful. I'll be on my best behavior. I promise."

"Fred…"

"As friends. That's all we are, just friends." He raised both palms to her, the key still in one. "We'll be surrounded by others."

She had planned to go. She loved the water, and she was sure they'd see gardens of estates on Lake Minnetonka. Why should she deprive herself of the evening?

Why indeed.

She nodded agreement. "I'll be just one of many," she said, then slipped through the door and closed it behind her. She would have to be careful, cautious. The butterfly in her stomach began to flutter once again, as did Freud's words about conscience.

He was invisible, his feet weightless. He was a boy again, and he had walked off with her key! Fred realized it as he reached the stairway. Maybe he'd call her from his room and leave it at the front desk. But that would be even more disconcerting, with the desk clerk wondering why he had her key. No. He turned around.

One of his colleagues with his wife sauntered by, nodded a greeting. He waited until they entered their room. Maybe he wasn't invisible after all.

He knocked on her door.

⁂

She heard the soft tap.

"It's Fred," he whispered. "Please, let me come in."

Don't do it.

Why did it have to be the way it was? How was it that she had such a desire in her heart—to photograph, to engage with beauty, to bring joy to others with a mentor for her talent—yet here she stood, ready to throw it all away? She waited, as exposed as a blade of grass facing a prairie fire. Should she open the door to a passage of pain and sorrow, not just hers, but for so many others? Her mother and father and Lilly and Reverend Carleton, too, would say it was of her choosing to silence the voice keeping her safe, her turning her back on the desire to do what was right.

He knocked again.

She opened the door. "You forgot something?"

"Your key and my heart," he said and stepped inside.

TWENTY-FIVE

The Absence of Heat and Haste

FRED COULD HARDLY BREATHE FOR HER BEAUTY, the scent of her, the way her hair fell in small, moist curls against her cheek, the inviting softness of her lips, the curve of her hips as he pulled her against him like a violin's bow across a tightened string. She resisted only for a moment, and then the embrace they exchanged told him all he needed to know: that she loved as he did.

"I love you," he whispered. "I love you and always will."

Their arms entangled as he lowered his face to her neck. He could feel her desire melded with resistance; the push-pull of a tryst grown of devotion and passion but tempered with truth.

"Please," she said, and he couldn't tell if she wanted him to continue, to allow what they felt to find respite in each other, or to move back. He slowed, uncertain.

She separated from him, and stood by the cold radiator beneath the window, her hands gripping the pipes and nearly as white, her eyes red. The window opened onto night; a soft breeze pushed the tendrils of her hair, and street sounds broke into the silence. Reflected light from the small lamp highlighted tears on her cheeks. She looked so vulnerable. But when she spoke, she sounded like a woman, certain and sure.

"You have to leave, Fred. I came here..." She looked around the room. "Not for this. I have a business to run. I can't afford an affair of the heart, a scandal, and that's what it would be if you...if we... Please. Your children. Your wife. You have to think of them."

Anger rose in him, he wasn't certain from where. "Leave the children out of this."

"I'd like to. But that means you're left out too. You can't be... We can't be—"

"We could." He felt foolhardy, desperate. "No one would ever have to know. People have done this through the ages, listened to their hearts. I could take care of you. I would. And the children too."

"Fred." She chastised him. "You don't understand what it's like. You're accepted as a professional. What would people think if they thought we were...that we 'traveled' together? It would burden you as well as me. Don't you understand? It's...wrong."

She was right, and he knew it.

"I have my life now, Fred. My profession. It's what I cling to. No, it's what I want to do, to be successful. I need to make this work. People are counting on me." She clasped her arms around herself, shivered. *Is she cold?* "It matters how I live my life, Fred," she whispered. "And I know in the end that it matters to you." He took a step toward her. She put her palm up as though to stop him from coming closer. "I can't live as 'the other woman.' I can't... I won't. It would demean me and you, your wife and your children. It would."

"Jessie—"

"You know it."

Again she was right, and he hated that she was stronger, wiser, that his life was stuck in a hollow, empty place. His hands hung useless at his side. He felt an ache in his heart. And then instead of leaving, allowing another way to be made one day perhaps, or accepting that only he was responsible for the state of his life, he said the worst thing he could say, worse than proposing that she allow herself to be "kept."

"Of course," he said, stiffening. "You're right. Do you think I'm heartless?" He flexed his fists, held them at his side. "I look after my family, and I am capable of more. I have always been there for you, helping as I can."

"I know. I owe you so much." She nearly wailed. "The camera you bought me, your contribution while I stayed in Milwaukee, supporting my efforts with George Haas. But I have to run my business on my own. For my own sanity, my own...integrity."

He spoiled it all then, any future they might have had, however precarious.

"It's not essential that you succeed, Jessie."

"Yes. It. Is." She was angry now; he could see it in the flash of her eyes. She straightened her glasses, which had slid down on her slender nose. "You have no right to tell me that I don't have to succeed, that because I'm a woman I will always have a way out, be picked up by a father or brother or husband or son, be a kept woman. That isn't why I joined the profession. I love what I do." She jabbed at her heart with her fingers. "It's what I've always wanted. I want to do it well enough to support myself and help my family. It's not a hobby. It's who I am. I have to succeed!"

"I only meant that you needn't feel such pressure. I've taken care of things. You can't fail. I've—"

"What are you talking about?"

"The studio. Your studio. I secured the loan at the bank. It was the least I could do. If anything happens, I've covered it. It would simply revert to me if you couldn't make the payments."

"You...you secured the loan?" She looked confused. "I don't... You hold the note? Not the bank? *You* provided the money?" She stopped her pacing, wasn't talking to him now. "That's why the bank called me back. Not because I'd convinced them, but because you had. You and George and Mr. Horton conspired to—"

"I did it for you, Jessie. I did it—"

"Get. Out. Get out of this room."

"Jessie—"

She pushed at him. Tiny as she was, she possessed the force of a tornado. "Leave or I'll call the desk and ask to have you removed."

"Jessie, I didn't—"

She reached for the phone. He obeyed.

⊱⊰

Jessie managed to lock the door behind him, despite her sweating palms. She shook. How could she have been so naive? She sat down on the bed, turned off the light, got back up. She had to think; she had to decide what to do. She listened to the night sounds of St. Paul, the *clop-clop* of a late cab, the *putt-putt* of a car engine moving slowly. Somewhere in the distance, she could hear a church bell, maybe from St. Adalbert's Catholic Church, calling people to an early morning Mass. She sat in the dark; what kind of a plan was that?

And then an old verse, one she'd memorized years before from Micah spoke to her. "When I fall, I shall arise; when I sit in darkness, the LORD shall be a light unto me."

She sat in darkness.

She knew what she had to do.

She changed into her traveling clothes, packed her valise, including the program, and started the walk to the train station. Let him have the studio. It was his money. Let him take it over. She'd…she'd leave. She'd go…west, to Seattle. She'd always wanted to go there.

Walk out on a commitment?

But who was the commitment to? Not the bank. They'd been in on it, patronized her, weren't truthful or honest with the arrangements. Moving her own savings to help cover the loan was nothing to them; it gave them more to loan out to some other unsuspecting soul while they had all they needed from the hands of Frederick J. Bauer.

She stopped. Should she even go back to Winona? She could write a letter to her family. She was sure they'd take Neggie in. Fred could figure out what to do about the tenants, the bank, her clients waiting for their proofs. He could hire some other young woman to take over the studio and make her fall in love with him.

Why hadn't he just bought it and asked her to run it?

Because she would have refused. He'd pretended that she was skilled enough to do it on her own and then denied it by the very act of putting a net underneath her. She thought of circus acts, the high wire, and how much more amazing the feats were when they lowered the nets and the walkers or trapeze artists soared on their own. It was the same physical movement, requiring the same grace and grasp as with the net up, but when the safety disappeared, the act was so much more thrilling, the performers so much more admirable, the success so much sweeter.

He'd put a net under her life for the last time.

⊱⊷⊶○⊷⊶⊰

Fred looked for her in the morning but didn't see her at any of the sessions. Perhaps she'd stayed in her room. He looked for her at lunch, then went to her door afterward and knocked, but she didn't answer. When people gathered for the boat ride on the lake at two o'clock, he joined them and made small talk he couldn't remember. The evening had nothing scheduled, and he knocked on her door again without response. He smiled at colleagues walking down the hall, embarrassed by his exposure. He had trouble breathing as he walked around the hotel grounds, hoping to catch a glimpse of her. Roses bloomed. She so enjoyed the gardens. Why wasn't she here? Why had he told her about the loan? The fact had only hurt her more. *What kind of man am I?*

Her absence haunted him. He loosened his collar, had to sit on one of the benches. The evening felt hot and sticky, adding to the weight on his chest. He fanned himself with his hat. One moment he thought he caught a glimpse of her beyond the reflecting pool, but when he stood, he heard the woman laugh and knew it wasn't Jessie. He would likely never hear her laugh again.

⊱⊷⊶○⊷⊶⊰

Jessie had just enough to afford the ticket to Seattle. It would take her west to places she'd never been before, to mountains and streams and waterfalls higher than anything in Minnesota. Her adopted aunt's half sister had written of the beauty of the "other northwest," as she called it, "where your Mississippi bluffs could be nestled like little pillows in the shadows of Mount St. Helens." It was just what Jessie needed: shelter in shadows, where she could find out what she was truly made of and what really mattered in her life. But she had to do this right. She took the train back to Winona, catching the streetcar to Mr. Horton and his bank.

"I'm sorry," his assistant chirped when Jessie walked in, demanding to see him. "You need an appointment."

"I'll see him now," she said, then fast-walked past the desk and opened the door. Mr. Horton was on the phone, but her expression must have told him he needed to end his conversation, for he hung the phone in its cradle and pushed it aside, clasping his hands on the desk.

"Miss Gaebele. What can I do for you?"

"You can tell me the truth, for once," she said. "Is my loan secured by my savings and my record, or is it secured by F. J. Bauer?"

"Well...both, I'd say. Of course, we have confidence in your abilities. And the rents assist in making this a good business loan."

"And Mr. Bauer's involvement? Is there any?"

"I'd need to look at your file."

"It looks like my name on that folder, there on your desk." She pointed. Fred must have called him, assuming she'd show up here.

"Yes," Mr. Horton said, opening the file. "Yes, he has placed money to help secure the loan."

"The full amount? Three thousand dollars?" He nodded. "Then F. J. Bauer has just bought himself a studio," she said. "I'll have the tenants send their payments to the bank from now on; I'll leave a portion of my savings to cover the interest incurred thus far and withdraw the remainder. Apparently you don't need it."

"But you can't walk away from—"

"Why can't I? You made the loan under false pretenses. Maybe you were right. Maybe I couldn't make it without its being secured.

We will never know. You can write me off as a bad risk, but you still have your money."

"Mr. Bauer meant nothing but goodwill," Mr. Horton insisted.

"And I wish him the same," she said and strode out of the bank.

PART 3

FINAL POSE

TWENTY-SIX

Separations

AFTER THE BANK MEETING, Jessie walked immediately to the studio, met with each tenant, and told them to send their rental payments to the bank. She didn't give them any other information except to say she'd enjoyed having them as tenants and hoped they'd like their new landlord. Then she went inside, turning the key for the last time.

The studio felt cool, darkened by the drapes drawn for several days. She walked through the reception area, picked up the small book on the appointment desk. She'd call each client and refer them to Voe or maybe to Van Vranken's studio. She could finish up the orders she had, would take care of them before she left.

She moved slowly through the prop room, memorizing. What pictures should she take with her? Maybe none. This had all been hers and hers alone, she'd thought, but it wasn't. It had never been. Maybe nothing tangible ever was. "So much for independence," she said out loud. She heard a sound. *Neggie.* "Is that you? Mama's home."

Chairs scraped. She expected to hear the cat's meow, but it was muffled talk that greeted her, then Lilly's voice that called out to her. "Jessie?"

"Oh," Jessie said when she entered the kitchen. "I didn't expect you here."

Lilly stood quickly. So did Joseph O'Brien. At least Jessie assumed the gentleman having coffee with Lilly was her beau. "This is Joe. Mr.

O'Brien. My...friend. I hope you don't mind. I mean we didn't do anything. He just stopped by—"

"Have you been staying here, Lilly?"

"I was just leaving," the young man said. He picked up his hat, bent to kiss Lilly on the cheek, thought better of it. Lilly blushed scarlet. "I'll catch you after work tomorrow, Lil," he said. "Miss Gaebele." He nodded to her and swiftly shut the door.

"We didn't do anything, honest we didn't."

Jessie pushed her hand to silence her. "You've no need to confess anything to me," she said, and she sank into the chair Joe left.

"I only stayed one night." Lilly sat back down. "I told Mama you wanted me to...to help Neggie adjust." Jessie raised an eyebrow. Lilly groaned. "I just wanted to see what it was like not to have to share a bed with a sister. I wanted to see what you liked so much about being on your own."

"What did you find out?" Jessie asked. She removed her hat, gloves, then stood to heat a pot of tea.

"It wasn't nearly as nice as when Joe stopped by to have coffee. That's all we did, honest, Jessie."

"I don't mind your being here, Lil. It'll save me time. I've got to pack anyway."

"The conference isn't over, is it? I didn't expect you back until Sunday."

"Things have changed," she said. She didn't look at her sister. She forgot about the tea and began pulling things from the hook on the wall: her linen suit, her simple shirtwaist, the blouse Lilly had given her for her birthday years before that still fit her perfectly.

"Can I help? What are you doing?"

"I need the trunk from the garage in the back. If you can bring that in—"

"Jessie, stop!" Lilly grabbed her hands. "What's wrong?"

Jessie grabbed up the picture Fred had taken of her, held it momentarily, put it back beside her bed. "It's all wrong," she said. "I've... Just get the trunk for me, please?"

"That man," Lilly said.

"No. It's me," she said. "Please. The trunk, if you want to help."

While Lilly raced out the back door, the cat sauntered into the room. Jessie stuffed dresses into her bag, special earrings her parents had given her. Her Bible. "I definitely need to spend more time with it," she told the cat. *I won't think about leaving the cat.* She chose two pair of shoes.

"What… Where are you going?" Lilly said, returning with the trunk.

"He…" She didn't know how much to tell Lilly. Lilly had never trusted Fred, always thought he had his own interests at heart. Perhaps she was right. "It's Fred. He was at the convention, and—"

"Oh, Jessie, I worried about you living alone here, how convenient it would be for you and…anyone. I mean, look what just happened with Joe."

"Your beau stopped by for coffee. There's no sin in that, Lilly. He seems nice enough."

"But he does drink, Jessie. And I doubt he'd give it up for me."

Jessie sat on the bed, felt the weight of her life sucking out her backbone. Neggie jumped onto her lap and let Jessie pet her. "We're a pair, you and I," she said to Lilly. "We've fallen in love with men we cannot have, knowing full well what we were doing all along. What's the matter with us?"

"*You* are in love with that man. I'm not, at least I don't think I am. I'm just…lost in the impossibility of it."

Jessie stifled a sob.

Lilly sat beside her. "I'm so sorry, Jess. I am. Did he… That is, did you…"

She shook her head. "Not that we didn't have opportunity and desire," she said. "But I made him leave. Just not before he told me that he'd secured the loan for this studio and that I didn't need to succeed here on my own at all. He would take care of me."

"He isn't a good man," Lilly said. She crossed her arms over her chest.

"He's not a bad man, though, Lil. He just is. I knew it when I began to fall in love those years ago. It's my fault as much as his. Maybe loving photography too much is the real problem. Oh, Lil, how could I love something so much even though it's brought me misery?"

"Are you talking about your camera or Fred Bauer?"

"Both, I guess." Jessie wiped at her eyes. "Both have consumed me, and I've let them." She sighed. "The only thing I know to do now is to absent myself from both of them."

"Oh, Jessie, don't give up your camera," Lilly said.

"Maybe it's less the camera than the studio, having it all my own way. The only thing I know to do is to move on."

Lilly rubbed Jessie's back as she talked. It was the closest Jessie'd felt to her sister in years. "What will you do?"

"I'm going to Seattle. I'll stay with Aunt Mary's half sisters."

"You'll leave the studio behind, after all you've worked for?"

"It was all a facade, a pose. My whole life has been swirling with illusions. I'll find what's true in Seattle."

"You have to tell Mama and Papa. They'll... You have to say good-bye to Selma and Frog. They'll miss you terribly." She thought out loud. "You should stay. You can find other work, you can. Stott's is always looking for seamstresses." She cried now, and Jessie did too.

"You'll tell them for me. If I go there, it'll just remind Papa of how I didn't learn anything, how I still let my feelings rule. Just tell them I had to try something new. I took care of things at the bank. I'll write. I'll come home again. I just have to get out now. Please. You've got to tell them for me."

Neggie howled and spurted off her lap, and Jessie realized the girls had squeezed the cat between them in their last embrace. "You'll look after Neggie for me, won't you?"

Lilly nodded.

"Just go now, all right? Please? Come back and get the cat after I've gone."

Lilly hesitated, stroked the cat, then left.

Jessie spent the rest of the evening printing the proofs she had to finish, including the Giroud sisters in their Roman togas. Then she wrote letters to her clients, telling them they could pick up their pictures at the Bauer Studio on Johnson Street. She'd leave a note for Lilly to take the prints to Voe after Jessie was gone.

The sun rose as Jessie finished her last cup of tea, closed the trunk lid, then called for a cab that took her to the train and away from home. Again. The steam, whistle, and screech of wheels announced her departure.

Mrs. Bauer wasn't sure she heard the words correctly. He couldn't be saying it. She had no warning, nothing to prepare her. "You want a divorce? Is that what you said?"

"It is," Fred told her. "I've failed you. I've been—"

"Unfaithful." She gasped.

"That, too, I suppose," her husband said. He didn't sound sniveling. There was a tone, resignation laced with warning.

"I knew it!" she charged. "I knew it. Ever since you came back from the association meeting, you've been strange. Why, this past week you've hardly said a word to either me or the children. You were with that woman! Jessie Gaebele. You were with her last week in St. Paul, weren't you? How could you defile—"

"I was not *with* her as you say, Mrs. Bauer. She did attend, as did I, but I did not…I did not—"

"But you wished to! It is the same!" Blood rushed to her face and with it a surge of clarity and strength. Her ears rang, but she could hear each sound in the room; her eyes burned, but they were wide, taking in every inch of this betraying man who sat before her, his shoulders slumped, head bowed, the smooth spot widening in the back of his head where his hair thinned. She knew everything about him. She wanted him to deny her accusations, but he didn't. He shook his head, clasped his hands together as he leaned his elbows on his thighs, staring at the floor between his feet. "Yes," he whispered. "I wanted to. I've been so…lonely."

"We are all lonely," she screamed. "Do you think your life is so special that you expect to be spared?"

"We don't—"

"That's why I've kept you locked out of my room these years. That's why. You can't be trusted. You…you…" She couldn't find the words. "I should have known. I should have seen this."

"And what would you have done?" he asked, more fire in his voice as he looked up. "Just what would you have done if I'd said I had deep affection for Miss Gaebele, a girl young enough to be my daughter? That I felt alive when she spoke of photographic things, that she made me laugh when I otherwise didn't wish to? What would you have done? Locked me out of the house as well? Told the children their father was a letch? Held even greater distance between us? What greater absence could there be…Jessie, than what our marriage has become?" He held his arms out as though to take in the entire room, the world. He looked so thin.

She sobbed then. "Donald. It wasn't so bad before Donald."

"No," he said. "It wasn't, though you'd left me twice by then, you had, Jessie." He didn't let her protest. "But I know you can never forgive me for Donald's death, and if it's any consolation, I'll never forgive myself either. Not ever. Things I wish I would've done." He seemed to be remembering as his eyes flitted around the room. "Set him on the seat beside me. Told him to wait with you. Taken a different road. Harnessed a different horse, for heaven's sake!" His voice broke. He was a man in pain, and she couldn't find a way to relieve it, for her own wounds sliced her heart and bled her dry. "I come up with no answers, and to see your grief daily is to be reminded of my great and tragic failure. There is no end to the sorrow I've given you. No end, and I am so sorry." His voice caught again. "It's why I want to set us both free of it."

"I will never be free," she said.

He nodded in agreement. She didn't want him to be kind now. She wanted to be angry, to scrape at him until the pain in her ceased. But it wouldn't. Ever. "Your sadness is so much deeper than my own," he said. "Donald was a part of your very flesh. And yet his absence leaves a great hole in my heart too"—he patted his chest—"so great I cannot even fathom the time when I did not know it. It so consumes my life. Jessie…"

She looked up at him, but he wasn't talking to her.

"Jessie Gaebele came into our lives—yes, both of our lives—at a time of need. I did not intend for it to become this…what it is. A longing, that to deny any longer means continued betrayal to you and to our children. She will not even have me, but I can't live with this, with us, the way we are. So I am asking for the divorce."

She felt powerful, yet knew that feeling now, at this time, was wrong, very wrong, but it didn't stop her. "You must never see that woman again. Not ever. Is that understood?"

"I suspect she would agree with you," he said. "The truth is that she's gone, yes? I don't know where, but she isn't in Winona anymore."

"Then what purpose is a divorce?" There was such disgrace in divorce, she thought. Such disgrace, though perhaps no more than what had already occurred. She wondered just how many others knew of her husband's philandering, knew of his betrayal.

"You deserve to be free of me," he said. "I know you, too, see Donald's death with every breath you take in my presence. You deserve something other than that."

"You're pawing your own way out," she charged. But a part of her agreed with what he said.

"You can have the studio, this house, the children of course, the cottages on the river. I'll continue to run the studios." She thought he said "studios." She must have been mistaken. "Whatever you need, Jessie, I'll provide it." The train rumbled by as it did this time of day, halting their conversation. "You'll be safe and secure," he resumed, "and free of the weight I've become."

"You'll not get off that easy," she sneered. "I'm taking the children and going home to Mother's until I've had time to think this through."

"As you like," he said.

She watched him rise and walk, beaten, from the room. Her

desire to run after him, to shake sense into him, argued with her need to talk immediately to Reverend Carleton. A terrible emptiness consumed her, almost as great as when she'd learned of Donald's death, and yet a weight had been lifted from her soul. She couldn't understand why.

Jessie slept through the morning on the train. After waking, she watched the miles of prairie and grasses, wheat leaning into wind. Beyond Fargo, in small towns along the Northern Pacific, people waved if the train slowed but didn't stop, and she waved back, watching as they returned to their hoes or to hanging aprons and men's work shirts on sagging lines. She saw a sign with the name of a town and an arrow pointing north toward "Jessie." *Imagine. A town with such a name.* What kind of place was that? A confused, chaotic place, she imagined.

Occasionally dogs scampered beside the train until they saw the futility of it, and while she couldn't hear them, she could see them barking at the invader that rolled through their territory. At one lonely station, she watched a cat arch its back and saunter into the building. Her eyes watered as she thought of Neggie and everything else she'd left behind.

A squeal from a child on the seat across from Jessie caught her attention. Nothing wrong, just a child bringing attention to herself. Jessie took out a slice of ham she'd brought with her, then wrapped it back up. She wasn't hungry. She wondered if she ought to have brought the photograph Fred had taken of her. She'd left it behind, not needing a constant reminder of what could never be, its presence a reflection of their failures. She shook her head, stared out at the afternoon that no longer inspired.

The bank notified Fred of the status of his secured loan and explained he had to make some changes. He hoped to find out from Mr. Horton where Jessie had gone, or at least hear details of the president's encounter with her. Fred grasped for information, wanted it to fill the emptiness. He made an appointment with the bank to discuss the matter and was just leaving for it when Lilly Gaebele walked into his studio. Lilly had the same soft mouth, the same large, alluring eyes as Jessie, but her face was rounder, her hair tidier, and she lacked Jessie's quiet grace.

"Miss Gaebele," he said. "To what do I owe the pleasure?"

"I doubt you'll find my visit pleasurable," she told him. She handed him folders of prints, then stood, tapping her foot. She reminded him of a banty rooster ready to attack. "My sister has told people to come here to get their prints," she said. "I guess you know why." He nodded, looked through the folders without attention.

"I'm glad we can help. Is this arrangement temporary?"

Lilly snorted.

"Would you like tea?" he asked, looking up. "I'll have Voe fix it." He didn't want the young woman to leave, wanted to know where Jessie was, *how* she was. Lilly was the last thread connecting him to her presence.

She didn't answer, looked around, her gaze stopping at the toddler's toys strewn across the reception room floor. She fanned herself. It shouldn't be that hot on this August day of… It was his birthday. The tenth of August. What a way to acknowledge it. "Can I get you a glass of water? Anything at all?"

"I just wanted to see for myself what it was about you and this place that set my sister on her course to degradation."

He winced. "Nothing about your sister is shameful or corrupting."

"She left feeling humiliated," Lilly contradicted.

"And I am sorry for that, beyond anything I could ever say. Where has she…left to?"

The young woman hesitated. "To the West Coast, Seattle, if you must know. We don't know where, or when she'll come back. Our parents are devastated, Roy is bereft, and Selma has cried herself to sleep every night she's been gone. My sister loves her family, and she loved her studio, the more because she thought it was hers."

"It was," he whispered.

"Not the way she wanted it. You took that from her, along with her innocence. You made her want to leave us. *You* should be ashamed."

"I am," he said. "I am."

"Well, that's one good thing to come of this then," she said. She turned and walked out.

As the train moved west, Jessie focused on the wide, treeless horizon. The train like a giant canoe pushed through waves of grasses. Here, Indians once roamed. She had read of that. Here, native artisans now worked. She'd seen a few sitting beside the tracks near the stations, with pottery and colored blankets before them on the ground. Fred had pots like those at the studio. She wondered if he'd bought them near this place, where the train rolled by not far from the reservations. The engine stopped at Medina to take on water, then chugged out again. The sameness of the landscape mesmerized her. It was long and undulating, with no bluffs to break it, no woods or timber, only lines of trees—shelterbelts, she thought Fred called such rows of plum trees, box elders, and ash—planted to slow the winds that roared across the landscape, scooping up soil left unprotected by such borders. She remembered that Fred had told her something his favorite poet wrote: that love was when two solitudes came together to "protect and border and salute." The trees did border and protect the land, and their greenery against the yellow, ripening wheat could be called a salute, she supposed. Perhaps trees were God's way of expressing love to creation. Hadn't Emerson written that flowers were how the earth laughed?

Their love, hers and Fred's, had failed to border, protect, and salute. Maybe only divine love was really enough, a love that gave one longing and the gifts to pursue it without fear of defiling it or, worst of all, losing it and being left alone.

She wondered if she'd ever want to take another photograph again.

Her passion for the art was what had put her on this train. No, that wasn't true. She had lost her way, had "taken the wrong turn," as Ralph Carleton would say. He'd told her a Hebrew word for *sin* that translated as "missing the target or taking the wrong road." That was her, all right. Maybe running away was just another means of taking the wrong road. Her foot bumped the camera case at her feet. Maybe her waning desire to photograph anything was the punishment being meted out for her having lost sight of the light, the very thing every photographer needed for the perfect shot.

The train slowed. "We're approaching Bismarck," the woman across from her announced. "We'll cross the Missouri River through Mandan and then truly be in the West."

This whole landscape felt like the West to Jessie, so big and open, wide with possibilities, nothing to fetter a soul unless one planted shelterbelts against the ravages. As the train slowed she recognized a meadowlark leaning out at the very edge of a bowed grass stem: something familiar.

"They'll let us get out and walk around," the woman told her. "You should get up and stretch, dear. Your legs will swell." Jessie had learned that the couple headed to Spokane and made the trip often to see family in St. Paul. People seemed to think she needed tending. Was it her small frame? Her youth? Being a woman alone? She nodded and thought of Fred. Had he merely been tending her?

She took in a deep breath, and when the train stopped, she stepped off along with the others to stretch her legs and move without having to balance herself between the rows of seats as the train rocked its way west. She'd have black and blue marks on her thighs from all the bumping, even though she'd stopped trying to walk the aisles miles before. Her ankles were swollen, she noted.

"Rent your room at the Bismarck or the Mandan Hotel." A man hawked his way along the station, shouting. "Thirty days residency and you can settle those domestic affairs in a legal way." Jessie noticed a few people taking his fliers. She wondered what on earth he sold.

Inside the Spanish-looking depot, marble walls and floors kept the building cool. She took a drink of water from her canteen. It tasted warm now. She found the privy, then stepped out, opening the stuffy door to an astonishment in the western sky.

Big, billowy clouds rose up over the wide prairie of North Dakota. Had she not noticed them before? Behind the clouds, the sun glowed orange and red, outlining with colored lace the great pillows in the sky. The shapes and colors of the sunset changed as Jessie watched, reminding her of fire. The light filtered and glowed through the climb of them as the sun eased behind. This was a new landscape where clouds marked the high points, as dramatic as the bluffs burned in the spring above the Mississippi. Huge white birds soared above her. Could they be pelicans? She'd thought such birds were only at the ocean!

She turned. Two towers with red roofs rose above the depot. Across the way, Jessie saw grasses waving in the evening breeze and nothing beyond to obstruct her view. There might be bluffs beyond if the Missouri River ran there. There might be hawks and eagles sinking below her if she climbed to such heights. She couldn't always see what lay ahead.

"Isn't it beautiful?" the Spokane-bound woman said. "In the spring, there are prairie potholes that fill with rainwater—"

"Buffalo wallows," her husband interjected.

"—where birds gather. You can walk the prairie and just come upon them, not realizing there are heights and valleys. It doesn't look like it, I know, but it's not all flat. They plant flax south of here and grain as far as the eye can see. There are rock formations in reds and yellows. You just have to travel to see them."

"You know so much about it," Jessie said.

"Oh, you should always pay attention to a place, even if you're only passing through."

Jessie watched as the porter began shouting, "All aboard."

Pay attention to a place, even if you're only passing through.

Hesitation engulfed her like the steam flowing back from the engine.

The clouds beckoned. She wanted to take a photograph; that's how she truly discovered a place. She wasn't taking photographs and thinking of Fred now; she was taking them to remind herself that here was beauty, here were treasures God had given, photographs where a studio wasn't needed. Taking such pictures could restore her wholeness, fill her empty places.

Her mind made up, she jumped back onto the train, grabbed her valise, then pulled her trunk along the aisle. She plopped her camera bag on top, set her hat more firmly on her head, and pushed at the trunk. "Please help," she asked the porter as she neared the steps. She jumped off, grabbing the camera bag. The throb of the engine building up steam forced her to shout.

"There's not much time, miss," the porter said.

"If we can't get it off, can you leave it here on the return run? Here's my name." She fast-walked as he leaned out, handed him one of her calling cards. "I was going to Seattle, but now I'm not," she shouted. She'd started to run. "Remember. Bismarck. Leave it here at the station and I'll pick it up."

Behind him, the Spokane man pushed the trunk to the edge.

"Just shove it," Jessie shouted, running alongside the train now. "Push it!"

The Spokane man and the porter did as she requested, and the trunk hit the ground, toppling over twice, then landing right-side up with the latch broken and the cover dropped back. Jessie's dresses like rag dolls, picked up and dropped, spilled to the Dakota winds.

Steam pillowed around her as she stared at her trunk, her sprawled clothes, then the train chugging in the distance. Before long, silence. The clouds still performed. She got her camera out. Whatever had she done?

TWENTY-SEVEN

Out of Control into Safety

MRS. BAUER WAITED IN HER MOTHER'S PARLOR, the heavy drapes drawn against her growing headache. FJ would take the children for the afternoon. Maybe they'd go fishing on the frozen lake if it was cold enough. Maybe he'd let Russell drive the car. Maybe Robert would beg to stay with her, as he had the last time. She'd been careful not to say disparaging things about FJ to the children, so she wasn't sure why Robert hadn't wanted to go. Maybe it was difficult for a man to entertain a four-year-old for an entire afternoon by himself.

FJ had let Melba go. Of course, the girl wasn't needed, what with them living with her mother, but he also alluded to strained expenses. He'd purchased land in Texas, he told her. Mrs. Bauer shook her head. Her husband had never met an investment he didn't love.

And he'd also taken over the Polonia Studio, of all things. She didn't like the connection that studio had to the Gaebele girl. She guessed it had come up for sale shortly after the girl left town. No one seemed to know where she'd gone or why she'd left, but Mrs. Bauer knew it had something to do with her husband. It had to. The timing was too coincidental, and she didn't believe in coincidences. It had been three months since he'd asked for the divorce and she told him that she'd consider it. He'd made his request after attending the photographer's meeting in St. Paul. Oh yes, there were connections, she was certain of that. She didn't want to consider how much her own emotional absence from her husband had played a part.

Meanwhile, it was quite all right with her the way things were. She knew the children missed their rooms. They missed their father too, but he actually had more time with them now than he did before, spending every Saturday afternoon in their company. Russell said they went to the studio often, but that was all right. The boy had an affinity for photography. Winifred didn't seem to mind either, especially if Mrs. Henderson had her child there. Perhaps that was why Robert didn't like to go; he had to share Winifred's attention with another child. She was quite the little mother, Winnie was. She must have gotten that from her grandmother.

Mrs. Bauer heard the car pull up next to the house, the door slam, and the children rush out to greet him, hopping over the snow banks, she imagined. At least FJ came on time, so the children weren't sitting around with their mufflers and mittens, growing warmer as they waited. She pulled the curtain back. He looked up at the movement and waved his cane in the air. He looked tired. She ought to tell him about Robert's reluctance to go with him, but as she watched, he lifted the boy and she saw Robert's laughter. *Does he laugh that way with me?* Surely she wasn't jealous of her own son's affection for his father.

Maybe they'd drive to Cochrane and Luise's. Russell said they'd done that a time or two. He liked spending time with his cousins, he said. She wished her children enjoyed her sister more, but Eva didn't make them feel welcome. She had her own problems. Mrs. Bauer sighed. It seems they both suffered from these highs and lows of melancholy. Fortunately, she hadn't told her mother yet of FJ's request. All that anyone knew was that she'd come home to be with her mother for a time. She'd done it before. Maybe this visit would come to the same conclusion and she'd find a way to go back to him. Only this time, he had left her first, asking for that...divorce.

Russell leaned into the car and then back out, holding up ice skates. Ah, so they were going skating. That would be good. It was a nice day for that. Maybe she would join them. She used to like ice skating, didn't she?

But then the throbbing in her head began again. She closed the drapes. No, it was best if she used this time away from the children to simply rest. She wasn't sleeping well at all since they'd come here. Even talks with Reverend Carleton brought her no relief. In fact, she'd told him the last time that she wouldn't be seeing him again.

"You're feeling better?" he asked, a frown creasing his wide forehead.

"Not better, just different."

"You had worried over your husband and...Miss Gaebele for a time. Is that worry lessened? Are you giving your worries to the Lord?"

"In part," she said. It wasn't a total lie. "Miss Gaebele has apparently left town. Maybe you know where she's gone?"

He shook his head. "Once she bought her studio, I didn't see her much."

"My husband is running that studio," she said.

"I'd heard that," he said.

"He and George Haas were acquainted. I imagine they worked that out when the girl left George in the lurch down there in Tampa."

"I imagine that was the gist of it," he said. "Of course, if you feel strong enough now, your weakness no longer consumes you, then it's good that you wish to spend more time with your family than dwelling on your sorrows."

Is he patronizing me?

"I shall always have sorrow," she said, stiffening her back. "I lost a son."

"I only meant that it is part of human nature to grieve, and then, at some point, as God sustains us and we hear His words, we are able to move forward. Never forgetting the loss—no, not ever that—but not allowing that absence in our lives to be so great that we no longer see the sunlight for its warmth or fail to notice snowflakes or forget to listen to the laughter of our children who still walk this earth, who can still put their arms around our necks, seeking comfort."

She wondered if he suggested she didn't do those things. He'd be right, of course. But she now had another absence to face: her husband's wish to end their marriage. She hadn't told Ralph Carleton of that, hadn't said she was staying at her mother's either. She wasn't being honest with this man who only sought to help her. But then, she was barely honest with herself.

Even without the constant strain of her marriage—without the bickering, without his evasiveness, without the guilt of locking him out of her room—she didn't feel as though she'd won in this battle of wills with her husband. Why? She wondered about those nights when he'd been out of town and she'd felt safe. What was it that had given her all that verve to stay up late and do needlework, iron, read, and sleep like a baby without a pain? Maybe she needed to be in her own home for that to occur again. With the children by her side and FJ…absent, but on her terms.

FJ should move out; he needed to find another place to be. But that might push him toward other women, might encourage him to find comfort in the arms of someone other than Miss Gaebele. Then everyone would know that he had left her rather than that she had left him.

The scandal. Without anyone to blame for it, there was no way to hold her head up as the wronged woman, the way Mrs. Frank Lloyd Wright could in the midst of biting newspaper reports of her husband's infidelities. His lover had left her husband and her children just to be with him. How Mrs. Wright must be suffering, and yet she had someone she could point to as the cause; Mrs. Bauer had nothing like that. She could blame her husband, but she believed that he had not acted, that he had only wanted to respond to that girl's allure. But if she told people that he had been unfaithful with the Gaebele girl, Mrs. Bauer could hurt herself. She wondered about Mrs. Wright, what would make her husband take up with that woman. She'd seen Frank Lloyd Wright when he worked in Winona on a home, and for a moment then she wondered if that woman might be traveling with him. Maybe her own husband knew of this affair and thought it sanctioned his own bad behavior, and—

She stopped her thoughts. It was one good thing Reverend Carleton had taught her, how to stop a few thoughts before they ate her entire day.

She drank a glass of water. The coldness hurt her teeth and then made her head feel worse. What would Reverend Carleton tell her? She didn't yet have the knack of knowing how to replace these worrisome thoughts with others less damaging.

Skating. She'd think of skating. She hoped the children wouldn't get hurt. Maybe they should have taken the streetcar instead of FJ trying to drive. Had she pinned Robert's mittens to his sleeves? His hands would freeze if he wasn't careful.

She heard her mother's snores; she napped in the next room.

Mrs. Bauer needed to go home, surround herself with the familiar. That's what she needed. That would get her thinking under control, and that was what mattered now. Being in control.

Virginia Butler and Jessie worked side by side in the developing room of Bismarck's Butler Studio. Virginia, a graceful, stately woman, demonstrated good business sense but never failed to listen to new ideas either. It was just one of the things Jessie admired about her. Jessie hadn't revealed her secrets to the woman and likely wouldn't. But here she felt safe, able to put her past into perspective and find pleasure without thinking too far ahead about her future. She'd spent too many years thinking, planning, saving, worrying, trying to control her life, and for what? It had all been a distraction. In Bismarck she'd found respite.

"We should expect a Christmas rush," Virginia Butler told Jessie. "I imagine you had that sort of thing in Milwaukee too."

"We did," Jessie told her employer. "We advertised for it. I went to a conference...earlier this year and heard a lecture about promoting businesses using photography and how to apply it to our own profession." Jessie didn't want to mention St. Paul. "Promoting in studios, of course. It wasn't about turning out more camera girls."

Virginia nodded. "Personally, I find no problem with camera girls," she said. "Their Kodak pictures just remind people that for special occasions they might want a more professional look."

Jessie smiled. "I suppose you're right. That's how I got started, and I wanted something better myself once I saw the possibilities."

"You began in Milwaukee, right?" Virginia asked.

"Something like that. Could I have more of that solution?" Jessie asked, then bent to her work.

A little over three months had passed since Jessie'd stepped off the train in Bismarck, North Dakota, and stuffed her dresses back into the trunk. She'd sat on it for a moment, worried, but then the skyline captured her again. She'd taken a photograph of those clouds that day, arranged for her trunk to be stored at the depot until she found employment. The hawker advertising hotel rooms, she learned, facilitated residence for those applying for divorces. People rented a hotel room, put their bags inside, then got back on a train to return home. Thirty days later they arrived again, proved their "residence," and were thus able to achieve their divorce and a new marriage if they chose. Jessie didn't want to stay at any place like that!

And yet, the little money she'd taken from her savings—the small amount she hadn't turned over to the bank in payment for interest—wouldn't last long. She knew she had to find work.

Less than two long blocks from the depot, she came upon Main Street. The afternoon air felt warm as she purposed through the downtown. Not a very big town, she'd thought. But a bakery might have need of a woman to bake biscuits; there might be a milliner advertising for a saleswoman to sell gloves...not that she had either of those skills. Maybe an evangelist could use her secretarial skills. She visited the newspaper office, the *Tribune,* to look at ads and noted a couple of promising places where she might apply. She still wasn't certain why she didn't get on the next train west, but something about the place—maybe it was the openness, the absolute newness and distance from Fred—appealed to her.

Just before five, she found 311½ Main Street and saw a woman putting a sign in the window. *Photographic assistant wanted. Will train.*

She walked in, showed Virginia Butler her camera, and talked about the photographs she'd just taken. "You have experience," Virginia said. "And a good camera, it appears."

"I've worked in Milwaukee and Eau Claire," Jessie said. She didn't mention the Bauer Studio or her very own in Winona. "I'm a good learner. I understand about the hazards."

"I had thought about employing a man," Virginia said. "My husband, William... He carried the heavy camera, and of course, men like dealing with men. One of my biggest contracts is taking photos at the prison. They haven't been too keen on having me do it. I'm not sure how they'll feel about an attractive young woman..."

"I'm much stronger than I appear," Jessie said. "I've hauled equipment all over Win...Wisconsin, and I've posed many men. I know how to handle myself. I'm sure I can convince the warden too. It is the warden who's concerned, right?" Virginia nodded. "I really can do this." Virginia's eyes pooled with tears. "I'm sorry. Did I say something?"

Virginia dabbed at her eyes. "No. It's just, I'm missing William." She sighed. "We were a good team. Every time there's a change, I have to face it all again." Virginia explained that she had tried to run the studio on her own but just couldn't and so had finally decided to hire someone. "My husband was especially helpful at the penitentiary."

Jessie had no idea what a photographer would do at a penitentiary, but she persisted, telling Virginia that she'd worked with two different women photographers and could provide references if needed.

"Well, I could wait to find a man, but frankly, you're already trained and that's worth a great deal to me. Let's give it a go."

She showed Jessie the small house behind the studio, off the alley, where Jessie could stay. Virginia's quarters were upstairs in the studio. "I'm sorry it isn't more," Virginia said when she opened the musty door to the cabin. "It's hardly better than a homesteader's soddy. It might not even qualify if you had to prove up." She laughed. "I didn't think a man would mind so much. It comes as a part of your wages. I hope that's agreeable."

"It's real nice," Jessie said. It only needed a cat.

It wasn't all smooth sailing in Bismarck. Jessie didn't like being close to a dark alley at night, where feral cats she failed to tame congregated near the garbage container. Sometimes she heard men who'd been drinking too much step out from one of the saloons beyond. But she liked a place to call her own. Not that she had much time to spend alone there. She worked hard, knowing that what she did could make a difference for Virginia Butler. She wasn't working to save money for herself now, nor to capture her illusive dream. What extra money she might spare, she would send home to her family. Once she decided to let them know where she was, at least. She still worried that if they knew, somehow Fred would discover it. He had a summer studio somewhere in the state, but she couldn't remember where. She didn't trust that he would stay away if he knew where she was.

She had interesting photographic experiences in Bismarck, a town that had been known by other names until someone decided to support the immigrant population and name it for the German chancellor Bismarck.

"We'll make just one trip out to the penitentiary this month," Virginia told her.

"Because of the snow?" The state had paved the road two years before, from Mandan to the penitentiary, but most of the other roads were dirt and not easily cleared of the drifts.

"The snow too," Virginia said. "But mostly because they don't transfer people much over the holidays, which is good. It leaves us more time to photograph community people."

They finished up the current project, and Virginia turned on the lamps and opened the door. "Whew. These chemicals do hurt my nose sometimes. Do they bother you?"

"A little," Jessie said. "We need to keep the room ventilated. Mr. Everson in Eau Claire had the poisoning, but he recovered well and I think it might have been because the whole studio picked up breezes. They kept a window open even in the winter," she said.

"I told William that, more than once." Virginia shook her head. "It makes me angry, it just does. I told him we didn't have to make pictures for a living. We could have homesteaded a plot of ground and been farmers. Why, half the people headed for the West get off the train and stay here and prove up their property in no time. We could have done that, been out in the fresh air. But he insisted. It was what he knew, he said."

"No matter what we do, there are risks," Jessie said.

"I'm sure you're right. And he didn't like the idea of farming, having cows and whatnot. Or the way the wind can wreak havoc on a crop. We've carried a number of accounts since 1910, the last good year of rain. People just couldn't pay for their portraits when the rains didn't come. I sure hope the drought doesn't continue. But if we'd be farming now, I'd really be struggling. So maybe William was right after all." She inhaled a deep breath. "The Butler Studio will survive as a way to a good life and not as a business that's all about money."

"The penitentiary work won't likely let up," Jessie said. "No matter what the weather."

Virginia nodded. "There are always people taking wrong turns and ending up in North Dakota's stone house."

When they made the trip to the prison the first time, Jessie saw photographic possibilities in the architecture of the stone house, with its turrets and white painted stones looking like Lilly's fine stitching around what should have been windows but of course weren't. The gray wall surrounded a courtyard that Jessie never saw but only heard about. She and Virginia were taken through heavy gates and bars to another building, then into a room furnished with only a chair and table and the camera the Butler Studio brought in. Good lighting filled that room through the barred widows. A white wall provided the backdrop.

She'd never thought about posing men whose pictures were taken to verify their presence. The numbers they held at their chests seemed larger than their faces in the frontal shot, and then there was a profile too. Most wore their best clothes. Bowler hats, ties, vests. They might be any man wanting his picture taken, but they weren't; each was an involuntary photograph. All their independence had been taken from them. Or rather, because of their choices, they'd given it away.

The state owned the pictures and paid Butler Studio for them, but Virginia said at times family members would seek a copy, so Jessie always made sure she took the best picture she could. She reminded each prisoner that someday someone who cared about them might put a copy of it in a narrow frame for their parlor. That made most of them smile, and that's when she'd click the shutter.

"We don't need pretty shots, Miss Gaebele," the warden told her once, looking at his pocket watch. "No flirting either. These are dangerous men, could easily lose control." He clucked his tongue. "Women," he said. "Don't know their place."

Flirting? She didn't even know how.

A big man, the warden stood close to her as though she needed protection. Two guards bordered each prisoner's pose. To date, not a one had made any motion toward harming her. They looked defeated more than dangerous, which is why Jessie tried to capture pleasant looks on their faces. Besides, she didn't like how he talked about them—and her—as though they weren't present.

She knew how important the contract was to Virginia Butler, though, and Jessie worked efficiently and kept her professional demeanor. She didn't want to do anything to upset the warden even when he scowled and said how much he missed William Butler.

She knew Virginia missed him more.

Virginia called her from the darkroom late one winter morning. "The mail is in, and there's something here for you."

"There is?" Jessie wiped her hands on her apron.

"You ordered the Winona newspaper, correct?"

Jessie swallowed. "Yes, the *Republican-Herald.* I thought I'd subscribe, just for news about Wisconsin and Minnesota."

"I would have thought the *Milwaukee Journal* would give more information, or the Minneapolis *Star Tribune.*" Virginia handed her the paper. "Where did you say you were from originally?"

"Winona," Jessie said. "My family is in Winona."

"Why didn't you say so? I have friends there. We might know some of the same people."

"We'll have to compare address lists. We're pretty private people, we Gaebeles." She kept her voice light. "But sometimes there are listings in the personal section, where I hope to see what my sisters have been up to. I just thought I'd… I should have asked before giving the paper your address." She fingered the newspaper, anxious to have words from home, hopeful there'd be no notice of a lawsuit against her by the bank.

"Nonsense. I don't mind having the paper delivered here. Maybe you'll leave it for our clients when you've read it. We do get lots of people who've come from Minnesota. North Dakota is a state of immigrants." She looked at the appointment book. "And people seeking divorces, I'm sad to say. We have a marriage portrait to take, I see. A divorce is always a tragedy. William held that people shouldn't be miserable for a lifetime because of a poor decision made in their youth, but he lamented the pain. Happy new marriage portraits can't erase that."

"It's so hard on everyone," Jessie said. "Especially children."

"Especially children," Virginia said. "The best plan is to work things out, and if that's not possible, to forgive each other and find a way to serve the children well. That's what I think."

Jessie liked knowing what Virginia thought. Maybe it would be all right to let Virginia know more of her life; she'd be a wise person to offer counsel about whatever Jessie found in that newspaper.

"Are you finished with those penitentiary prints yet, Jessie?" Virginia asked. The warden wanted them back in record time so he wouldn't be disturbed during the holidays.

"The prints?" Jessie looked up from the newspaper, the clock, and gasped. "Oh." She threw the paper from her lap. "Oh, Virginia, I've left them where I was! I didn't put them in the stop bath!"

She bolted toward the darkroom.

"Let's see what condition they're in. Don't hurt yourself," Virginia told her as Jessie stumbled at the darkroom door, caught herself.

"I'm... I got distracted. Reading the paper. I'm... What was I thinking!"

She raced into the darkroom, remembered to close the door before opening the second—though what did it matter now? The film would be ruined, the photos destroyed. She turned on the orange light. *Such a stupid mistake.*

She pulled the film from the solution. Blobs black as a murderer's heart contrasted with shiny white images where cheeks and smiles should have been. Developing solution dripped from the roll. They couldn't be printed, the contrasts too great. Decimated.

"I'll arrange to take them again," Jessie said. "I'll pay you back for the time I spend doing it and for the film. Everything. I'm so sorry. I...wasn't thinking."

Virginia peered over her shoulder. Shadow and light, all in the wrong places. No images of men, not even the wisp of a smile.

"I'll take the full blame for it," Jessie said. "I'm so sorry." She deserved to lose her job.

"I'll make the call to the warden," Virginia said after a moment.

"Oh, please, let me. It's my fault."

"He'll need to hear it from me," Virginia said. "I'll see what I can work out with him." She left the room.

Jessie chewed on the cuticle of her nails. Snow started to fall, and the afternoon grew darker than the overexposed film. "Stupid newspaper," she said to herself. What she meant was, *Stupid me.* "Every time I get close to doing well, making the right choices, I mess up," she said out loud. "Every time. I..." She couldn't find the words to demean herself properly.

The phone call carried muffled voices, and Jessie found herself praying, truly praying that the warden would give her a second chance, that she could retake the photographs. Maybe he'd let them do it in January. It wasn't like the men were going anywhere.

"What did he say?" Jessie said when Virginia came into the parlor where Jessie waited. "Can we retake them next month?" Her employer sat down, arms on the rounded arms of the stuffed chair. Her hands hung limply.

"He said he knew this sort of thing would happen with no man to operate our studio, and he'd find another photographer, that he should have done it months ago. He doesn't need our services anymore, he told me. And then he said how much he missed my husband."

"Oh, Virginia, I can't... What can I do? I am so sorry!"

"Nothing to be done for it, I'm afraid." She stood up and walked to her room, where she closed the door softly behind her.

Forwarded from Winona to Seattle to Bismarck
November 15, 1913

Dear Sister,

How are you? I am fine.

I miss you. Where are you? I hope this letter reaches you. Are you still traveling? Why don't you want us to know where you are? I'd never tell, I wouldn't. Mama is worried about you. Are you all right?

I am mad you left without saying good-bye to us. Lilly acts like she's special because she saw you, and we have to trust her that you know what you're doing. I don't know if I can trust that. Do you know what you're doing? What could you be doing that we wouldn't want to know about and help you do?

Please write and say where you are so we can stop worrying and maybe even come and visit one time. Roy is so sad. He says it's like you've died, and that's terrible.

Art Roeling is going to come to the house for Christmas dinner. Joseph O'Brien isn't.

What's the weather like where you are? I just wonder.

Your loving sister,

Selma

Twenty-Eight

The Nature of News

THE LETTER ARRIVED A FEW DAYS before Christmas, from Winona via Seattle. "Mail for you," Virginia said.

Jessie took it, didn't look at Virginia.

"It's from an aunt," Jessie told Virginia. She'd spoken little to Virginia since the terrible disaster, even though her employer spoke kindly to her, held no chastisement in her voice. Jessie couldn't see how Virginia could not be furious with her, she was so disgusted with herself.

Jessie's aunt included a note with Selma's letter. *Whatever you've done, it can't be that bad. Let them know you're fine and that you'll write soon. It may be all they need not to worry.*

She was right, of course. Jessie'd been selfish to keep her location from them. They'd never tell Fred where she was. She should write to Selma and Roy and her parents, Lilly too, saying she was doing fine, telling them she considered taking piano lessons when spring came. *I can practice at the Methodist Church,* she'd write. *My employer goes there.* She wouldn't tell them the town, just to be safe. *I didn't mean to hurt any of you by leaving. I just need time.*

Time to be worthy, she thought but didn't write. She'd need a lot more time for that.

So far, Virginia had said nothing about letting her go, but she surely would have to. The penitentiary contract had been essential. Jessie knew she should broach the subject with Virginia, but she couldn't. The weight of her action, her memory of terrible distractions, tied her tongue. She couldn't ask Virginia to forgive her; she didn't deserve it.

While a winter wind blew outside her little house—where Jessie spent all her spare time now, too embarrassed to partake of Virginia's kind offers to read by her firelight or take tea with her at the end of the workday—Jessie wrote to her family. She included a few dollars she'd set aside for Christmas presents they could purchase for themselves, then sealed the letter. She would send it to Seattle and ask her aunt to forward it to them. It would arrive late, but at least she'd written.

She could have told them so much more, how she'd kept much to herself these past months, doing her work. She might have shared that at Virginia's insistence she'd attended one of the young people's gatherings after church and met shopkeepers, teachers, ranch hands, prison guards, homesteaders, railroad employees, bakers, and sons of bankers that kept the city booming. She wouldn't call them her friends though. Merely acquaintances, people she spoke to on the street, remembering to ask about their families, their plans for Christmas or Hanukkah. After one such gathering Jessie noted to herself that she hadn't thought of a single way to make money photographing them. The thought made her grin. Her participation wasn't about earning money, at last. It was about doing her best and helping others. She could have told her parents that.

With the letter ready to mail, Jessie stoked her stove and considered Virginia's recent words that "the Butler Studio will survive as a way to a good life and not as a business that's all about money."

"I could use less snow and a bit more coal," Jessie said out loud as the wind swirled around. She shivered even with an extra wool blanket Virginia had provided wrapped around her. The coal stove wasn't much against this Dakota winter, which had already dropped nearly two feet of snow. Outside, the wind whipped the landscape into towering shapes of beaten cream and bulging drifts. Still, she wasn't suffering the way some women did way out there on the prairie, in those fragile tarpaper huts they were proving up, hoping for land in their own name. She poked at the coals, felt warmth flood her face. Maybe she should try to prove up a piece of property. Her teeth chattered as she turned around to warm her backside. She noticed that a soft silt of snow had blown through the wall onto her bed quilts. She shook the blanket and blew out the light, then crawled under the layers of quilts. That's when she heard the sound in the alley. It wasn't wind. It thumped.

She stayed perfectly still, telling herself it was probably a passing cat, or a dog heading home in the storm, though she heard no howling. Something hit the back of her shack. *Are boys throwing snowballs at my house? In this weather?*

She crawled out of bed, stood closer to the stove. Even saloons closed in weather like this, so it couldn't be someone who had overimbibed. She peeked out the window, saw only blinding snow. The door latch wiggled. She'd forgotten to lock it! How could she be so careless?

Fred had lived in the small room in the back of the Polonia Studio since Mrs. Bauer decided to return to the Baker Street home. He found a certain comfort sitting on the chairs Jessie once sat on, brewing tea with her teapot left behind.

He had little time to simply sit though. He poured himself into his work, determined to keep both studios going. Mr. Horton, at the bank, after looking at her books, had already agreed Jessie was entitled to the loan on her own, without Fred's securing it. "Though she did walk away from a commitment," the banker noted, his eyebrows lifted like caterpillars over his glasses.

"It wasn't an honest deal from her point of view," Fred told him. "She made sure that rents continued, satisfied her patrons, and established that your loan was covered."

"At your expense."

"Small price to pay," Fred told him. Mr. Horton raised his eyebrows again in question, but Fred didn't elaborate. How could he? If she didn't return, then perhaps Russell would pursue his interest in photography and want a studio of his own after he finished college.

If she didn't return. He had to prepare for an absence so great as that.

Even if she did come back, his only hope was to have a friendship with her, if she'd allow even that after what he'd done. He would go on living his life, taking care of his work, looking after his children and his wife.

Mrs. Bauer had not agreed to a divorce, but at least their interactions were honest now. When he came to see the children, the time wasn't filled with recriminations or shouting the way they'd been at first. Once, in front of the children, their mother, and their grandmother, he'd lost his temper—threw a lamp at the wall and said things he never should have said. He'd never forget the look in the eyes of his children, clutching at their mother's and grandmother's skirts. Russell's fists had clenched as he'd stepped between him and his mother. Could there be anything more dreadful than being the cause of that kind of fear in your child's eyes? He didn't think so.

He'd spent extra time sitting in the Second Congregational Church after that altercation, asking God for help to crawl out of this pit he'd fallen in to. He felt lower than when he'd wounded Jessie, lower than a snake.

It seemed best, then, to let Mrs. Bauer come back home with the children. He would move out. She suggested it; he agreed. At least the children would have their toys and books around them, if not him.

He would spend his first Christmas alone, maybe see the children for a short time that day while their mother visited her mother. The less time he and Mrs. Bauer spent in the same room together, the kinder they could be to each other. How had it all gone so wrong?

He couldn't blame it all on Donald's death, though that was part of it. No, he'd been an impatient, perhaps even arrogant, man, had pushed his young wife into a marriage and then neglected her for work, for his lodges that did good works for others (they did, but benevolence ought not to be at the expense of one's family). Then she'd moved away from him, building and maintaining a separation he couldn't see how to bridge. They shared a house, children, and memories together, but nothing hopeful toward each other.

It was too much now to rebuild or reshape their lives into a marriage. He could see that. Mrs. Bauer did too, he thought, but she couldn't find a way to grant him the divorce. Divorce was a humiliating thing for a woman especially. All that talk about the architect and his paramour had made the Winona papers too. Fred could understand their desires, their passions, yet he felt sadness for the architect's wife and children, and the woman's children too. Fred could achieve a divorce on his own if he abandoned his wife and the children for a year, but he couldn't imagine doing that, not ever. He could live without Mrs. Bauer but not without his children.

Neggie wound her way around his legs, and he stood to pour milk into the cat's bowl, add pieces of bread. "If I feed you too much, you'll neglect your duties," he told the cat. "Mice abound, yes?"

Lilly had brought the cat back after "negotiations with Roy's chickens failed." In the return, Lilly hadn't conveyed any information about her sister nor about her parents' views of his now running "Jessie's studio." He assumed such words as might be said by Jessie's father wouldn't easily pour from Lilly's tender lips.

"I have no news," Lilly said as she set the cat on the floor. "And I wouldn't tell you even if I did."

He nodded, deserving of her scorn. "I hope she's all right. I do care for your sister, very much. You must know that. I only wanted the best for her."

"It's not enough," Lilly said. "Love is not enough."

She said it with a firmness meant to convince herself as much as him, or so he thought. She'd surprised him, though, in recognizing that what he felt for Jessie—what Jessie once felt for him—was more than fleeting fancy but in fact nearly consuming love.

As the cat lap-lapped her milk, Fred rinsed the cup with yellow daisies, then reread the letter from his ranch partner, Herman Reinke, in Hazelton, North Dakota. He reported that the winter had been fierce, long before its official beginning, yet he hoped for an early spring so they could get the wheat planted. He'd agreed to Fred's suggestion that they plant more acres in flax next year and suggested he come for spring planting if he could make the time.

Fred laughed at that: there was no time for him to travel, not with two studios to operate. He'd probably never travel again. Maybe he should sell the ranch there come spring. It held all those painful memories. He should close his seasonal studio there too. "I'm running three studios, Neggie. No wonder I'm tired." The cat stopped, looked up at him, then continued with her meal, hunched over the bowl like a troll.

He could keep the forty acres he'd bought not far from Minneapolis. Maybe he'd travel that far once in a while, just to see its woods and rolling fields, a good investment that hadn't caused him grief. He should sell the Texas lot on Mill Creek in Montgomery County though. He owned it free and clear, and it might be developed at a later time. He didn't imagine he wanted to ever live in Texas, despite the claims of the real estate brochures that the land could grow cauliflower "as big as oak barrels."

He took out his cigar cutter, chopped off the cigar end. He didn't smoke cigars, just held them and chewed the tobacco. Mrs. Bauer didn't like him smoking, but he was free to do that now. He imagined that the Gaebele family didn't approve of smoking either. He held the small cutter in his hand, fingered the embossing. A keepsake from the St. Louis World's Fair. Jessie had given it to him. Too many memories lurked even here, Fred thought, slipping the cutter back into his pocket. How could a man reclaim his future when the past held such sway? Neggie meowed for more milk.

Jessie's cat.

Even the present offered no respite. "I live in limbo," he told the cat. "As the old Latin describes it, that region 'on the border of hell.' I'm just sorry you have to be here with me."

⟻⟼

"Who is it?" Jessie said to the wiggling door handle. She looked around for a weapon to defend herself. The frying pan sat on her stove. Could she reach it? She mustn't panic. No sense borrowing trouble, as her mother would say. Maybe her Seattle aunt had already told her family where she was, long before she forwarded Selma's letter. Maybe it was her father come to bring her home.

She couldn't make out the image that finally pushed through the snow-laden door. *An escapee from the penitentiary?*

"I'm sorry to frighten you," Virginia said as she pulled a blanket from her head.

"Oh, good, it's you. What's wrong?"

"I'm terribly cold in the studio," Virginia said. "So I knew you must be freezing out here. There's absolutely no reason for you to suffer through a night like this, or me either, all alone."

"Sometimes people deserve to be miserable," Jessie told her as she sank onto the bed.

"Thank you so much," Virginia said.

"Oh, I didn't mean you," Jessie corrected. "I meant me. I'll be all right here, really, I will."

"Nonsense, you come inside with me. You've abused yourself long enough. Here, put the robe around your shoulders. You have neither the proper clothes for a North Dakota winter nor the proper attitude for an enduring woman."

"Endurance applies to horses," Jessie said and smiled at her.

"Women too," Virginia said. "Good to see some spunk back." Jessie curled her back into the buffalo robe Virginia wrapped around her.

"I do prefer my teeth chattering with company," Jessie said. "But I didn't want to, that is, I feel so—"

"Jessie," Virginia took her hands. "You must put the penitentiary behind you. It was a mistake. No one died, and even if they had, while tragic, it would have been unintended. You're human. We humans mess up. It's why we need unwarranted forgiveness. We can never do it right, so we must rely on grace. Please. Accept my forgiveness and forgive yourself. Then perhaps one day, you can pass that on."

Jessie nodded, still not convinced.

"Why were you walking around the back of the cabin?" Jessie asked as they moved toward the door.

"I wasn't," Virginia said.

"But I heard noises like snowballs against the wall, or a shovel, and—"

"Come along quickly." Virginia looked left and right, then hurried through the drifts to the studio, pulling Jessie's hand as she did. "There's another reason you should spend the night inside with me," Virginia said when they safely stomped snow from their boots in the enclosed back porch. She locked the door behind them. "The sheriff stopped by. There's been an escape at the penitentiary. He said we women should stick together."

The women stuck together, turned the whirling blizzard into a background for tea and talking. Jessie told Virginia everything about her lost love—except his name. There was no sense in telling that. Virginia might run into Fred Bauer at a conference, and how awkward that would be!

Virginia didn't condemn her or call her a fallen woman. "We're drawn to relationships for different reasons," she said. "Often there's a lesson to learn. If we don't understand it, I think we find ourselves swirling like flotsam on the backwaters until we figure out how to pull ourselves back into a safe current."

"I'm not yet sure what the lesson is supposed to be...with him. Maybe to plan my life better."

"One thing I've learned," Virginia said, "is that life is unpredictable. Plan as I might, there'll still be a smudge on the glass plate of life to contend with."

"Maybe we shouldn't waste time planning?" Jessie asked.

"Oh no, we have to think ahead. But we need to be ready to

change and not make ourselves flummoxed in the process. We can do what we can, but we don't control much. And wasting time in blame just keeps us from moving forward, Jessie. That goes for self-recrimination too."

Virginia told Jessie then of being married to a man she loved, how they'd planned for a large family but weren't blessed with one, and how they filled their lives with other joys. She described the sadness she felt when people came from all around to get a quick divorce in North Dakota, then to marry just as suddenly and come to her for their photographs. "North Dakota is getting a reputation," she said. "And not a good one when it comes to marriage."

"Don't any of the marriages last?" Jessie asked.

"Oh, I'm sure a few do. People usually move back to where they came from, so I don't know. Some return a few years later to get yet another divorce. I think people who make the choice to divorce and *then* fall in love later have a better chance of making it. There are no greener pastures on the other side of that legal fence, that's what I think. There will always be weeds masquerading as flowers."

"Virginia, I need to talk about weeds I brought into your life," Jessie said. "Without the prison contract, I realize you need to let me go. I do understand."

"Oh, not yet," Virginia said. She reached to pat Jessie's blanket-covered knee. "I've made contact with other photographers in Bismarck and offered our printing services. Some of the seasonal studios in surrounding areas may prefer not to maintain their own supplies and equipment year-round either. I've had interest."

"Have you? I'm glad, truly glad."

"Who knows? We might end up with more business than we know what to do with."

Jessie couldn't imagine that kind of abundance. She filled the coal stove as they talked, and Virginia said, "That was William's job. Keeping the coal banked up."

"You miss him."

"William and I are...were one of those long marriages here in this state." She smiled. "I miss him terribly, as though a part of me is frozen. He was the thaw."

"I think I know what you mean," Jessie said. And she did.

"Will you ever marry again?" Jessie asked. "Maybe that's too personal. I'm sorry."

"No need to be. Perhaps." Her reddish hair had streaks of gray, and she twirled her finger into a strand at her ear. She looked young, Jessie thought. Closer to forty than to the sixty she probably was. "Marriage was a happy state for me. For us. We teased each other that whoever outlived the other would marry again within the year. I knew he would, but I wasn't sure I could. There are so many memories to weave into a new love. So many memories." She stared into the flames behind the stove's glass.

Jessie's parents had a marriage like that, with long years of contentment and love and old memories—joyful and sad—woven into the fabric of their passion. That's what she hoped for, when the right person came into her life, when her thaw arrived. "I hope one day I'll be worthy of a marriage like that," Jessie said.

"Sometimes our prayers are answered before we're worthy," Virginia said. "Don't forget the prophet Jonah and his whale. He wasn't worthy of delivery, having defied God, but his prayer was answered and he survived to tell the tale. Of course, he had to endure a little retching in the process."

Jessie smiled and pulled her feet up beneath her as the two women curled on the settee in front of the fire. Maybe all this disappointment—her misplaced hope to have a studio of her own, falling in love with an unavailable man—maybe that was the spew required, the shelterbelt to border her soul until she found true refuge.

Two days passed before Jessie went back to her cabin, and by then snow had silted onto the bed, around the floor, and across the table too. But Jessie could still see the tracks of a man's boots in the snow on her cabin's floor, and she noticed that while her letter was there, the currency that she'd put with it for her family wasn't.

For Christmas, Jessie embroidered a handkerchief with lily of the valley flowers, framed it like a photograph, and gave it to Virginia. "It's lovely," Virginia said. "My favorite flower."

Virginia surprised Jessie by telling her she had piano lessons waiting for her, once the weather permitted, with the Methodist pastor's wife.

"But that'll be so expensive," Jessie said. "I know. I've been saving to do that."

"I agreed to do their family portrait," Virginia said. "You can help. Or make a donation to the church if you want to contribute."

"I can do that," Jessie said. "I didn't know you knew of my interest in music."

"Mrs. Jefferson told me she saw you at the piano after church one day, after everyone left. She noticed you played without any music and quite well, just the same tune over and over."

Jessie felt her face grow warm. "I only know how to plunk out a few melodies. The music flows into my head, and I can play it, the chords and all. I'm not sure how. But I can't do that with many songs."

"It's a gift," Virginia said patting Jessie's hand.

"I'm hoping to improve on the gift, if that's what it is. My younger brother is skilled on his banjo. And my sister sings beautifully."

"Runs in your family then. You'll do well with Mrs. Jefferson. She can be opinionated, but I've seen you with difficult patrons. You'll manage."

Jessie arranged for her first lesson while she helped clean up after the church's Christmas meal. Jessie noticed several women with young children at the dinner, and Mrs. Jefferson smiled as she served them. She commented to Jessie later that "the prison holds the men, but the community holds their families."

"They move here after their husbands are put in jail?" Jessie asked.

"We don't discourage it. People need to know they're still loved and cared about despite making mistakes. Small sins are as bad as big ones," Mrs. Jefferson told her. "And besides, the prisoners have fewer altercations with the guards that way, knowing they'll see their families now and then. They have little hope if loved ones forget them or live in far-off Fargo or Williston."

The authorities had never found the man who escaped during that raging storm, and Jessie wondered if her money was his ticket to family somewhere far across the prairie. She hoped so. Better that than if he only made it to a frozen drift.

In late February, soon after Ash Wednesday, Virginia took a trip to visit relatives in Denver while Jessie managed the studio for a week alone. The time moved quickly, reminding her of the season when she'd owned the Polonia. She mourned its passing and wondered if grief was the purpose of the Lenten season after all, requiring her to slow down, witness to her losses to make room for what truly mattered in her life.

TWENTY-NINE

Where the Bluffs Speak

SPRING CAME AT LAST and with it high water on the Missouri. Flooding too, as the ice floes jammed, creating giant lakes behind the ice that broke with loud pops and booms to mark the dam's demise. Birds arrived next, many new to Jessie, along with familiar swans and pelicans and geese. They filled the air with the flush of wings, and she stopped her work to go outside to listen to their calling songs—but without neglecting her darkroom this time. Around the city, she saw purple martins and meadowlarks, and when she hiked the bluffs, she watched red-tailed hawks swoop beneath her just as they did when she stood on the bluffs above Winona. Sometimes she took photographs, but more often than not, she simply stood and marveled, twirling around amid the shimmering grasses, her arms to the wind. She danced. She wasn't worrying about the future or clinging to the past. She lived for the day without any plans. It was an odd state to be in.

Easter arrived in April, and Jessie sent a picture postcard of calla lilies to her parents. She practiced the piano as she could that spring of 1914 and pleased Mrs. Jefferson with her effort. She visited the library, tried new photographic shots of butterflies. She read the paper. In Bismarck she lived with the uncertainty of her future, trusting that when the time was right, she'd move forward as God intended.

In June, while reading the latest issue of the *Republican-Herald,*

Jessie noted Lilly's election as treasurer of the newly formed STC, "which is an industrial organization similar to those in the Twin Cities," the article explained. Jessie wondered how things were with her and Joe O'Brien. She didn't dare ask in her letters; they'd be read out loud. And so far Lilly hadn't written to her, though the rest of her family had. Jessie considered telling Lilly about the twelve friends from Minnesota, men and women who had taken homesteading claims close to each other and supported one another's efforts in getting the land proved up. Maybe Lilly and Joe could do that. Jessie smiled to herself. She had stopped planning out her own life day by day, and now she had thoughts of planning other people's.

Then her eye caught the headline "District Court." Usually that section talked of trials and such, and Jessie always read it with trepidation, thinking the bank might eventually bring a suit against her. But this article was about another broken promise.

> *Judge Arthur H. Snow of the District court has handed down findings in the divorce suit of Jessie A. Bauer vs. Frederick J. Bauer, in which he grants Mrs. Bauer an absolute divorce from her husband. No appearance was made by Mr. Bauer at the trial. The divorce is granted on the ground of cruel and inhuman treatment, Mrs. Bauer alleging that on two occasions she left her husband, once fourteen years ago and again in 1912 because of the way he treated her, but each time she returned to him at his solicitation. She set forth at the trial that he called her vile names and made accusations against her in the presence of relatives. By Judge Snow's decree the custody of the three children, Frederick Russell N. Bauer, Winifred E. Bauer and Robert J. Bauer, is given to the mother, who is required to provide for them, for which the court gives her title to the Winona homestead, lot 2, block 2, Wilsie's addition, and the household goods; also the Bauer photo studio on leased land at the corner of Fifth and Johnson streets and the operating equipment, some*

of the furniture being excepted. Mr. Bauer, the defendant, retains title to a 320 acres farm in Emmons County, North Dakota, to another 40 acres farm and to two cottages in Winona.

Jessie laid the newspaper down. Her damp hands shook.

Mrs. Bauer stared at the clipping. Printed in the paper. Now everyone knew. Were all divorces publicly announced? She hadn't remembered seeing any before, but then, so few occurred. She kept the clipping in the recipe book and reviewed it occasionally, feeling successful for her ability to read it now and not fall into despair.

The trial had been wretched, though Mrs. Bauer thought that if FJ had appeared it would have been so much worse. His lawyer had told him to stay away, and hers agreed. So she and her mother had gone through it together.

Mrs. Bauer told the truth. And yes, she'd left a few things out that didn't need to be spoken of in that public way. Besides, Fred was the one at fault. The judge decided it, and she knew it, and she thought FJ knew it too. Now everyone else did as well. His behavior was to blame: his lack of protection of Donald, his hours away from her and the children, his *everything* had caused the severing of their marriage. He'd been absent from them for years, even when he was in the same room.

Yes, she had her part, but it was minor compared to his. Especially his carelessness that led to Donald's death.

She shook her head. They had agreed before the trial that she would care for the children. How disgraceful it would have been if as their mother she'd been determined unable to care for them. He would provide for them through the Johnson Street studio, which he would operate...for her. It was the best way. He would be working for and serving her in return for her granting him release. A fair trade.

If she didn't like the arrangements, she could change her mind. She had a year to decide. He had a year to prove that he wanted out of the marriage, not for any other woman's companionship but because he'd been sent away, for "cruel and inhuman treatment." It was right there in the paper.

The children would be in soon for supper, and she'd told Melba she would prepare the meal today: the last of the canned string beans, sliced beef, her pickled watermelon, and thick slices of bread. Her own appetite had increased since she'd made the decision; well, since the day FJ had yelled at her in front of her mother and the children. She knew then that in a small, perhaps wicked way, she had won. He'd humiliated her, but he'd humiliated himself as well, had lost his orderly way of being, had succumbed to the frustration of her control. She was in charge, and he had come to accept it. A goal she hadn't realized she longed for had been met.

After that, she'd moved back into the house. In the comfort of her own home, with her children around her, and confident that she was right, she invited him to dinner and told him she would grant the divorce. She outlined the conditions, and he agreed.

Yes, he'd sell properties for the children's college. He was responsible for such as that. She hoped he'd sell that ranch. At least discontinue the seasonal studio. He'd have to hire help, she supposed. He couldn't keep running George Haas's Polonia Studio since that Gaebele girl had deserted it and devote himself to the Johnson Street work too.

She was glad FJ had a decent place to stay at least. She'd never been in the apartment, but George's wife had good taste, so she imagined it was nicely furnished—if that Gaebele girl hadn't diminished it. That might not be fair, Mrs. Bauer thought. After all, Selma and Lilly Gaebele both demonstrated good taste. One could assume Jessie Gaebele did too, and besides, FJ shouldn't be expected to live in squalor because of his acts. No one deserved that. But neither should he live in richness either.

She sliced the bread and put out the butter block. *Whatever happened to that Gaebele girl?* Ralph Carleton didn't seem to know or wasn't saying. Voe Henderson hadn't heard anything about her, if she was truthful when Mrs. Bauer deftly brought up the subject. Voe apparently didn't keep up with the girl. Mrs. Bauer shopped at Lottie Fort's millinery several times to talk with Selma without the girl's mentioning her sister once. It was almost as though Jessie Gaebele had died.

Had she? Maybe she had gone away to deliver a child! Mrs. Bauer shivered. No, he'd said they had not...and she believed him. She had to. Certainly there would have been rumors, and if Miss Gaebele had died, her sisters would have spoken of it, if not FJ himself. FJ would have mourned the girl. Maybe he wouldn't have asked for the divorce if that was so.

She did understand that FJ might marry again one day. But she would always be Mrs. Bauer, and when the newspaper reported on her trips to visit family and friends outside of Winona, they would call her "Mrs. Frederick J. Bauer," even if there was another Mrs. F. J. Bauer down the street. She and FJ were linked through the children and would always be. He would forever be her husband first, no matter who else he might give his wounded heart to. No one could ever take away from her the truth: that he had loved her first and, she might venture to say, best, loving her when he was young and on his way up as a professional man. He'd never be either again.

She would never marry again, she was certain of that. The obligations of intimacy simply overpowered her. It was the greatest guilt she felt over this...divorce. A man had a right to expect physical closeness from his wife, shared tenderness of touch, but her nature—she didn't know why—made even the thought of such intimacies turn her as cold and frozen as Lake Winona in winter. No amount of gentle talking thawed her, and she regretted the years she'd subjected FJ to such resistance. Maybe if she had told the doctors in Rochester everything, if she had truly confessed to Reverend Carleton how difficult this aspect of her marriage was, why she locked the bedroom door, maybe it might have been different.

She felt a sob rise in her chest, and she grasped her apron at her heart. She must collect herself. The children shouldn't see her grieve. They'd managed well, she thought, because she'd been strong, talked of positive things with them, how they'd know for certain their father was coming each Saturday, how their parents would both be happier.

"What about us?" Russell had countered. "How come we can't be happy with both of you home at the same time?" Winnie had nodded, and even Robert looked tearful.

"Perhaps you should discuss that with your father," she told them. She had no words to give them further comfort.

She stood, poured a glass of lemonade, and drank it. *What's done is done.* Outside, Robert chased a ring with his stick while Winnie cheered him on. The laughter pleased her. She had her children, her home, her memories. She would live on. Melba was back in their lives, at least for a time. After all, it was work tending children all alone through the summer months. They couldn't go fishing all the time. She didn't drive, nor did she have a car. She must talk with FJ about that. Russell would be fifteen in August and able to drive. A few states required licenses now. She'd have to see if that was so in Minnesota. Russell would like that, being able to drive her and her mother and maybe even her sister around to shop for household things, or out to the cottages. FJ now owned those, but he'd certainly allow her to take the children out to fish and swim. Yes, that would bring the children gladness.

Her work now was to ensure that she made new memories and that old memories did not overcome her. It's what she thought as she sank onto the chair and stared at her glass of lemonade. It was all she had energy for. Reworking old ways fatigued.

Jessie left the newspaper for Virginia's patrons to read. But she copied the article word for word on a separate piece of paper. No mention of the Polonia Studio. She wondered what had happened. Was Fred running it? Had he lost his money over it? She swallowed. She didn't know where the forty acres might be. Possibly he'd moved away since Mrs. Bauer now owned the Bauer Studio. No, he'd want to be near the children, even though, oddly, it said Mrs. Bauer must support them, not Fred. That might be an error, she thought, but she didn't understand divorce issues—nor did she want to.

It was enough that the Bauers had come to a decision about their lives without her being a part of it. Was that a truthful statement? She'd like to discuss it with Virginia, but to do so meant referring to the article, and then Virginia would know. Maybe that wasn't so awful, letting Virginia know, especially if Jessie and Fred had no future. Maybe confession required naming names. She'd only be discussing an interlude in her life, though a valuable interlude, one that resulted in her learning how to seek spiritual peace, learning to lessen the distance between her faith and her future. She'd found those answers in North Dakota. She intended to keep giving those gifts to herself.

In her cabin that evening, Jessie lay awake, being honest. She thought about the women who waited for their men kept at the penitentiary. How many remained faithful to their marriage vows? How difficult it must be to wait. Many of the men would be there for their entire lives, and yet their wives, as Virginia recounted, moved to Bismarck, found jobs, and raised their children, all to be as close to their men as possible. Did they consider divorce, starting over? Would the stigma be worse as a divorced woman than as the wife of a convict?

She remembered an incident that occurred when Virginia was in Denver. A Mr. Brady came by to pick up proofs of his children, and Jessie couldn't find them.

"Mrs. Butler took them last year, and I'm just now able to pay for them."

Jessie looked carefully through the *B* file but found no pictures of young children that might belong to the big ruddy-looking Irishman. "They must have been misfiled. I'm so sorry, I just can't find them. I've looked on either side, *A* and *C* as well."

"Would you mind if I looked?" he asked. His request annoyed Jessie, with its implication of her ineptness, but she stepped back and allowed him to pass before her to the file box. His wide fingers moved the rust-colored holders awkwardly as Jessie stood aside, waiting.

"Here they are," he said, handing her the file. He smiled.

Jessie looked at the photographs and caught herself in a gasp.

"I'm sorry— I wasn't looking for—"

"I know. People don't expect a man pale as me to have children black as coal, but they're mine. And my wife's, of course. Good li'l ones they are, too." His eyes widened with pride as he sifted through each shot.

"Of course," Jessie said. "They're beautiful."

As she took the money for his photographs, she wondered just how much scorn the man must endure, he and his wife and children, for their mixed-race marriage in a world where the races were so clearly divided. She hoped her reaction hadn't added to it. She wondered how the children felt. As he left, she saw them run out from the wagon he'd parked in front, and they oohed and aahed over their portraits like children everywhere. People could live with the occasional raised eyebrows, she supposed, especially when the cause of it was no act of their own.

Maybe that was how the children of the convicts endured. It was no fault of theirs.

She tossed and turned. Why was she considering such things? She had found a new direction in her life; Fred and Jessie Bauer had made their decision. She was not part of it. That, at least, would make it easier for her to remember his children happy, rather than dwelling on the pain they must have gone through—and still faced—before the article in the paper captured details without feeling.

"I have to go to south, near Linton," Virginia told Jessie one morning in late August. "A studio's going out of business, and we might be able to purchase their equipment at good prices. I want to stop at a few others along the way to suggest they let us do their printing. Would you like to come along? We could both use a holiday."

Jessie shook her head. She wasn't feeling well, and a stage ride south did not appeal to her. That's how Virginia planned to go, to save the train fare of traveling east, then changing to the southbound spur. She'd hire a livery wagon to bring back whatever she might buy.

"A group is taking the steamboat over to Fort Abraham Lincoln after church," Jessie said. "I've never been to the Mandan area in the summer, so if I feel up to it, that's where I'd like to go."

"It would be nice for you to see it by steamboat instead of walking across the ice like last winter."

Jessie looked at the appointment book and said absently, "What's the name of the studio going out of business?"

"I believe it's a seasonal, in Hazelton, owned by a Mr. Bauer."

"I've several frames I have no need for," Fred told Mrs. Butler. She was a comely woman with a good business sense, he could tell that. "And the enlarger can go."

"I'm sorry I didn't realize your studio was here," she told him. "I could have done your developing for you during the winter and kept your clients happy." He'd told her he'd been bringing the proofs back with him to Minnesota and then sending them back and forth, answering clients' questions, clarifying the retouching they might want, and the coloring, and so on. She was right; he ought to have checked out surrounding studios. There were a lot of things he might have done differently through the years.

As she fingered different items, Fred's mind wandered. Things hadn't gone smoothly since the divorce decree. Mrs. Bauer contacted him regularly about repairs needed in the houses, about questions regarding the children, about finances. Like most photographic studios, business had waned with the war talk, as people chose not to spend money on what they thought was frivolous. He'd had to make a change, and cutting back in Hazelton seemed the best plan.

He'd arrived on the North Coast Limited, which boasted sixty-nine hours from Winona to Seattle. It was the first electric lighted train, and he'd read the paper through the dark night. While racing across Minnesota, he learned of the terrible Frank Lloyd Wright–related murders of the Cheney woman, her children, and several workmen. A photograph of the architect's burned-out Wisconsin home, Taliesin, he called it, filled the page. The newspaper story suggested that the woman had brought this devastation on herself by divorcing her husband and living with a man she wasn't married to. Fred shook as he read that. He'd once proposed that Jessie live in the Polonia apartment as a "kept woman," as she'd put it. She'd rightfully refused. He felt ashamed again for the suggestion, for what he'd put his family through, for the time it had taken for him to face the truth.

He wondered if he'd ever love again. He'd snorted to himself at that so loudly that a child on the train had pulled on his mother's sleeve and asked, "Does that man have the croup?"

He assured them he did not, that he was healthy indeed, but still, the idea that he would ever love anyone but Jessie Gaebele was as elusive as mist rising up over Lake Winona in the morning.

He hoped for a new start by selling the Hazelton studio. One more loss to face. He'd gotten off at the McKenzie junction and taken the spur line south to where his partner, Herman Reinke, picked him up in the car. But once in Hazelton, he found himself enjoying the landscape, as he so often did. He understood why Mr. Roosevelt said he might never have been president if not for North Dakota, its wildness and bigness inspiring him to do great things. It was to North Dakota Mr. Roosevelt had come for healing after his wife and mother died on a Valentine's Day. Like him, Fred felt invested in this state, and its prairie always brought hopefulness to his heart despite the tragedy. He didn't really want to sell the ranch or the studio, he realized. At least not right now. There would be interest in photographing branding operations or wheat harvests. Maybe he could even sell such pictures for penny postcards.

Could he continue to manage all three studios? Likely not. He was aging.

Mrs. Butler spoke. "We could still manage your off-season work for you, if you didn't sell completely out." Her gloved hand picked up various props, moving the photographer's brace. "I have an assistant who does fine work, especially retouching."

"Maybe we can consider that, after all," he told her. "I made the decision to sell while in Minnesota. But then I arrive here and end up taking pictures, letting the landscape work its magic. Maybe I could work out an arrangement with the Butler Studio." Saying that brought great relief.

"Good." She smiled. "Will you want to reconsider the sales of these items then?"

"I've no need for that particular enlarger or the frames and mats you've picked out."

He'd close the Polonia instead, make it a medical office. He was exhausted managing both studios anyway. It would be better to focus on one business in Winona and operate Hazelton when he came west. "Maybe I'll take pictures out in the countryside. Like one of those tramp photographers." He grinned.

"My assistant prefers that to studio work," she said. "You have something in common."

Jessie played the piano long after her lesson was over. She lost herself in music the way she often did in photography. At least while playing, Fred's words did not come to mind as they did when she arranged a pose, dealt with a patron, matted and framed a photograph. Music had no history associated with Fred.

The bluffs above the Missouri had no history with Fred either, but when she climbed them, she thought of the bluffs of Winona and of the times she'd looked out over her city and lake to the Mississippi River and felt at home. She felt attached to these bluffs too. She missed her family and wasn't sure she wanted to spend another Christmas here, without them. Bluffs made her thoughtful, longing for home, and yet, at the heights, she could surrender to whatever was in store, without planning or posing at all.

Instead of taking the steamboat to Mandan with the youth group, she climbed the hills, hoping the exercise would supplant her stomachache. She knew the paths of Bismarck's parks, had walked them often, but the bluffs set her free. At the top, overlooking the Missouri, she sat and breathed and prayed and didn't carry her camera with her at all. Instead, she wrote notes to herself about what she felt and what she wished for. She often read books, let Scripture speak new ways to her as the breeze snarled her hair.

Today atop those hills looking west, she affirmed that she might never marry, but she could be part of something good if she set aside regrets, if she ceased demeaning and instead admitted that her self-pity, jealousy, and hopelessness were as offensive as her part in another family's separation. Perhaps then she could be available for...love, for the good God intended for everyone. That's what her pastor assured. She decided that self-pity was an even greater transgression than going to a movie theater or attending a sporting dance, even greater than leaving film too long in a developing solution and costing her employer a contract, maybe even greater than loving a man who belonged to someone else or being a child who failed to watch her little brother.

She'd asked and been forgiven for those misdeeds, but she resisted finding solace in the pardon. While Virginia met with Fred, Jessie stayed behind, uncertain of her strength to take the right next path. She'd been absent from her own truths, and that's what kept her separated from her soul. Unless she saw self-pity and envy and despair as acts of willfulness, she'd always feel set apart, never have the Guide she sought to direct her between needed acts of grace.

Separation didn't always tear a heart; sometimes the division made love larger, brighter, more colorful. Her brother's stammering might be with him always, but he'd found joy in music. A marriage had fractured, but she hoped the couple had found a way to serve their children. Fred's child, Donald, was gone forever, yet his family believed one day they'd meet again. Those were tragic trials. But from them maybe Roy and Fred and Mrs. Bauer could find ways to stitch new fabrics from their threads of separation; maybe even Jessie could.

Without knowing why or how, her spirit filled up that day as hawks soared below her and she watched the steamboat on the river. The future, though uncertain, didn't have to weigh her down; it offered possibilities, like the clouds over the flax fields promising a glorious picture if she took the time to notice.

Jessie sauntered back down the bluff, pondering the words "prone to wander...prone to leave the God I love," not as a pronouncement of her guilt, but of the hopefulness that she had found a way to wander back.

On Friday morning, Jessie photographed the Adams family, scheduled clients. They were a Negro family who attended the Baptist church in town. Pleasant people. She'd gone to their home, posed them outside, sitting in rocking chairs behind a bench, with the men standing. They wanted a casual look, though the men wore suits and vests and the grandmother a fine hat.

Later, Jessie took her rugs out and beat at them, hoping the exercise would help push thoughts of Fred from her mind. She considered walking to the bluffs again, but her legs ached from the walk to the Adamses' home, and her stomach hurt. She felt tired and cranky. In the mirror she noticed her face had a blemish. She'd get alum from Virginia's kitchen cabinet and put a paste of it on her chin. Selma often fretted when she had a blemish before she'd be seeing Art.

At least I don't have to worry about a beau seeing me like this. It was what she was thinking, standing in the kitchen, when she heard the bell ring in the reception room and heard Virginia calling out, "Hello. I'm back."

"You're early," Jessie said as she stepped into the reception room, tapping the alum paste to her chin. Then she stared into the startled face of Fred.

Canoeists on Lake Winona
Spring 1913

Hope

I took this photograph in the spring of 1913, when I was the proprietor of the Polonia. By accident, I brought it with me to North Dakota. Before I left Winona in my hurry, I'd slipped it inside my Bible, and it remained there, tucked in the back, letting itself be found one afternoon when I sat on the hills above the Missouri. My discovery was perfectly timed, really, for it happened on a day when I'd admitted my self-pity and despair and for the first time began to taste the fruits of truthful confession.

This photograph represents joy for me. First, it captures the essence of Winona, with Sugar Loaf in the distance, and Bluffside Park. Second, it brings back pleasant memories, for on the morning when I first met Fred, I'd hoped to photograph fires licking up the sides of those bluffs, flames to be put out by snow as part of a spring ritual. Burning the old to make room for the new. One needs those actions in order for joy to rise to the surface. The grasses at the lake's edge attract the trumpeter swans in the autumn, and in spring, summer, and fall, the canoeists slip their crafts into the waters, guided by slender oars.

I don't know who the people in the photograph are. It never mattered. I imagined for a time that one day I'd be in a canoe with someone I cared deeply for, my parasol shading my face from the hot sun, a young man with his straw boater ready to row me out into the middle, where we'd share secrets without fear of being overheard.

The photograph also symbolizes my wish to make images of people in unposed shots in nature. I want to capture moments in time when subjects aren't always aware that they're being photographed, when one has to adapt for clouds that filter sun or cause unwelcome shadows. But that's what life is like, I've found. It isn't the perfect pose that matters at all, but rather how one adapts to the setting and circumstances over which one has no control. It will be a lesson I'll need to keep relearning, for what do we control? Our attitudes, and the choices we make.

The composition turned out well. The lower right has a focal point—the canoeists—and, opposing it in the upper left, a second interest point—Sugar Loaf. The eye needs interest points to know where to focus, and a good photographer provides them. Only after the image holds the gaze for a moment or two will a viewer allow the detail to fill in the space between the picture's interest points. The precision of the grasses, the point of the parasol, even the farm buildings against the far shore are precious details one notices with extended viewing.

There is a flaw in the photograph. Nothing is perfect. The young man looked up at me as I was taking the shot. I regret that. I wanted him to keep looking at his lady friend. An east wind had pushed them toward the shore. You can see by the flags how the wind gusted. Up until then, the young man had been smiling and called out that they were going to beach. She might have surmised that, but with her back to their destination, he prepared her for the jolt. Her eyes focused on where they'd been.

Shortly after I took this picture, she spoke to him and he laughed, pushed the oar into the soft sand beneath the waters, and moved them out again into the wind. She directed, but it was his effort that took them where they wished to go. She laughed out instructions, and then they were beyond my ears. But together they made the journey work. The picture always leaves me feeling hopeful, and surely that's a part of joy.

THIRTY

Worthy of the Wait

FRED'S WORDS STUMBLED ON HIS TONGUE. "J-Jessie. Miss Gaebele."

"You know each other," Mrs. Butler said as she held the long butterfly hatpin in her hand, then removed her hat. "I thought you might."

Jessie hadn't said a word, just stared, those blue-gray eyes behind her spectacles as wide as robin's eggs and looking just as fragile.

He'd come at Mrs. Butler's suggestion that he ought not spend the weekend alone in Hazelton. He wasn't really alone. Herman was at the ranch and fully prepared to have him for a week or more. He had photographs to develop. But she'd encouraged his return so they could finalize how the Butler Studio would assist him in the future.

He declined. He couldn't really afford the additional train trip, and the roads between Hazelton and Bismarck weren't always well maintained, so driving was a risk. In addition, he knew that Mrs. Butler was a widow; she'd told him as much. He had no intention of courting anyone, not for a very long time, and only then if he could by miracle find Jessie. Somewhere in the conversation with Mrs. Butler, though, as she chose a glass cutter she'd buy, he revealed to her that he had children but that he was divorced. She didn't seem offended by his status or threatened by the prospect of traveling with a divorced man. He continued to resist until she spoke more specifically of her assistant, whom up until then he'd assumed to be a man.

"A young woman, quite skilled," Mrs. Butler said. "She used to live in Winona, in fact. You might have people you know in common. It will be a pleasant way to spend a weekend."

He purposely didn't ask the young woman's name. He wanted to imagine that he was traveling to see Jessie. *An old man's dreaming,* he thought, *quick to rise to steam.* Any number of young women had once lived in Winona. Mrs. Butler didn't say she'd worked in Winona as a photographer's assistant, only that she'd once lived there.

Jessie, so far as he knew, lived in Seattle.

No. The assistant wouldn't be Jessie, who was a photographer, not an assistant. She would pursue the higher profession. Maybe he'd go to Seattle in the spring. Of course, Jessie might well have chosen other work, moved far away from anything they'd once shared. It had been a year. She could be married to someone else. *Should be,* he thought.

But what if the Butler assistant was Jessie?

And she doesn't want to see me.

She had not contacted him or come along with Mrs. Butler. What did that mean? He almost changed his mind again.

But a weekend with Herman and his wife didn't appeal either, so he drove Mrs. Butler back in the car Herman kept on the ranch for when Fred visited. He loaded the purchased items into the backseat, and on Friday they headed north on the hard-packed dirt road to Bismarck. He would drive the car back on Monday. Herman had a few ranch supplies he wanted picked up anyway, and they could save the shipping charges. He'd take a room while in Bismarck. Perhaps he'd drive back early.

Then he walked through the door, carrying the enlarger, puffing a bit. He set it down and turned toward the sound of someone entering the room. He was lucky he didn't drop it on his foot.

There she stood. His hope, warm flesh before him. He gasped out her name.

"Yes, we do. Know each other," Jessie said. "I...used to work for Mr. Bauer."

She looked beautiful, fuller faced perhaps. North Dakota agreed with her. Why wasn't she in Seattle? Thank goodness she wasn't in Seattle! He felt an ache in his chest.

"You never said you worked in Winona, Jessie, only that you lived there for a time."

"No… I…" She lowered her eyes, looked at her hands as she clasped and unclasped them in front of her. "Mr. Bauer was my first instructor. Before I went to Milwaukee and Eau Claire."

Like afternoon clouds that pass before the sun, he watched awareness cross Mrs. Butler's face. "Ah… Well… I see."

She knows. Will she ask me to leave?

"This *is* a small world," Mrs. Butler continued. "Very small. Yet gracious too." She motioned for Fred to sit, but he stood, his feet like stone. "I'll fix us some lemonade," she said and turned to leave.

"No, wait," Fred said.

He didn't want to be alone with this answered dream, for fear it might disappear.

Jessie breathed as hard as when she climbed the bluffs, but in this small studio she lacked the fullness when she arrived on top and could simply stand and swirl. Her mind swirled now. What could this happenstance mean? She had imagined that their paths might cross again one day, had prepared for meeting him on the street, being surprised. She'd looked forward to Virginia's telling of her trip, to hearing her description of the man who came to sell the Bauer Studio, what she thought of him and if by description she'd know that it was Fred. But she hadn't prepared to see Fred Bauer standing in front of her now.

"Yes, please wait, Virginia. I'll get the tea. Lemonade. Coffee," Jessie said.

Virginia smiled at her and patted her shoulder as she walked by. "Why don't you see if you can get Mr. Bauer to sit," she told her. "And do so yourself. You both look like you've seen ghosts."

Fred waited until Jessie sank onto the settee, then joined her on a wingback chair across from her. The two sat in silence until Fred cleared his throat and said, "I'm surprised to see you here." She laughed. "That's an understatement," he said. His face burned red. "I meant, I thought you were in Seattle. That's what Lilly said."

"You talked with Lilly?"

"She's had words with me," he said. "Deserved words. But apparently I'm safe enough to look after Neggie."

"You have Neggie?"

"Your Polonia cat," Fred said, "takes care of me."

"So you're running my studio. The studio. I didn't see anything in the paper that—"

"I am so sorry, Jessie. For everything," he said then, confusing her. He leaned forward, grabbed her hands.

"Please, don't," she said, the shock of his touch just as it had always been, fierce with piercing ache. "I left you holding the loan," she said. "That was wrong, but I was so furious with you...men."

"You don't need to apologize," Fred said. "I should have known how you'd see my efforts to support you, and—"

"I should have told you what I intended to do, not just let the bank call you in and tell you. But I just couldn't—"

"Talk about it. I know. That was my fault. It's all been my fault. Everything."

Virginia entered with a tray, and Fred sat back as though stung.

"Mr. Bauer has decided not to close his studio after all," Virginia said, setting the tray on the side table. "Did he tell you that?"

Jessie looked at her, but Fred spoke.

"Yes. I've decided to hire the fine services of the Butler Studio to develop my Hazelton work. That way I won't get letters as I did from one client, who told me she hoped I could get her the prints *before* Christmas this year." He smiled at that. "I do have a problem meeting some commitments," he said. "She has a home in Hazelton and wanted photographs of her parlor, living room, kitchen, and the like to send to people in Vermont. I failed to meet her deadline."

"You took photographs of a parlor?" Jessie asked.

"A man needs to branch out." Deep brown eyes stared into hers.

"Jessie will do a fine job developing prints," Virginia said. "I find her to be one of the best assistants anyone could have. Her retouching is excellent. But I suppose you already know that."

Jessie wished she could make sense of the chaos flooding her. She wished she could go to her cabin and be alone. She wished she and Fred could continue the conversation and at the same time feared where it might lead. She listened for the words of caution, didn't hear them.

"I wonder if you'd care to take a walk with me, Mr. Bauer," Jessie said, standing. "I'd love to show you around Bismarck."

Jessie always felt better when she was moving, even if she wasn't sure what she was moving toward.

They didn't talk. Fred allowed her to set the pace both for strolling and for speech. He remembered she liked to walk things out so saw this as a good sign that she had invited him with her while she sorted. He wouldn't rush this gift. Once out of the business district, she pointed out birds, commented on the raptors swooping in and lifting snakes in their talons. They approached the train depot, and that apparently inspired her to tell him that she'd decided to get off there because of the clouds. "They were magnificent, and I had to take a photograph." He grinned and squeezed her arm, slipped through his elbow. Just touching her hand felt like golden apples in a silver bowl. "I discovered the bluffs long after, because it didn't seem to me there were any in this flat land. Then I happened upon them as I headed for the river."

"It is possible to stumble onto good things through no effort of our own. Like my finding you here."

She didn't comment.

He was being too direct. But he didn't know how much time he had before she bolted or told him to leave, never to see her again.

"I didn't realize Hazelton was so near Bismarck," she said. "Had I known I wouldn't have stopped here. Or stayed."

He swallowed his distress. "I'm glad you didn't know then.

Would you like to sit?" They stood in front of the depot, where white benches blistered in the hot sun by day. But now the building with its Spanish facade shaded them. He felt suddenly weak.

"If we can keep walking, I'll do better," Jessie said. "It clears my mind." But then she looked at him. "Of course. You must be tired after your long drive and all."

Why did he have to have a bad heart? What right did he have to pursue this woman twenty-six years his junior? That question should have been asked and answered when his heart condition and he were young. He stopped himself. This encounter was a gift, and he'd cling to it for however long he was allowed.

Like two old friends, they gazed out at the grasses. He couldn't stop himself from hoping, from wishing that despite their ages, despite what had gone on between them, they could build a bridge over the bad times and begin anew. He tapped his cane and sighed. "Jessie, Jessie," he said. "I cannot reject this gift I've received, so I'll have to take a risk. Mrs. Bauer says I'm known to take such risks with my investments, which don't always pan out well, but I can't afford not to take this one."

Did she wince at the sound of Mrs. Bauer's name?

"I did not expect to find you here, nor did I ever imagine you'd be willing to sit with me if I did. But here we are. I don't know if you know, but Mrs. Bauer and I have—"

"I know," she whispered.

"—divorced." He turned to face her. "Lilly told you?"

"No. The paper."

Their words crowded each other, but he knew: she had known of the divorce and had not contacted him. She had allowed the separation.

He was doomed.

The space between them on the bench comforted. It was a good border, Jessie thought. When he had lifted her gloved hand and pulled it through his elbow, she'd felt the same agonizing ache that had doomed her years before, made her head crazy and her thoughts selfish with desire.

"Did you know that many people come to North Dakota for a divorce?" Jessie asked. Fred shook his head. "Apparently one doesn't have to live here very long before approaching a judge. Thirty days. And then soon after, people can marry. Not like in most states, where you have to wait at least a year."

"Waiting can be a good thing," Fred said. "If one uses the time wisely. Our circumstances will not be final until June of next year. Until then, Mrs. Bauer can...change her mind."

"Oh," Jessie said.

They watched as a rabbit came out of the grasses beyond the railroad tracks, wiggled its nose, then hopped back and disappeared.

"Mrs. Butler says that second marriages last longer if people fall in love after a divorce, rather than before."

"She's likely right. Sometimes people divorce thinking it's for the love of another, but these past years of...strain between Mrs. Bauer and me have taught me differently."

She didn't know if he'd continue, but she needed him to. It would help her answer a question she had carried with her: whether she had fallen in love with Fred Bauer not because he'd moved her heart but *because* he wasn't available, *because* with him she could pursue her dreams of being a photographer on her own, independent. She'd happily imagined what life might be like as his wife, but she never had to face the realities of the less-than-lovely times: the day-to-day demands of fixing meals for two or more; washing clothes for five, perhaps; becoming aware of each other's teeth yellowing, hair thinning; dealing with stomachaches, leg pains, skin blemishes. She touched her chin, brushed off the dried alum paste.

Maybe she'd never been interested in men her age because she would have to risk the maintenance of love, as she thought of it, face the perils of a promise. Maybe she was incapable of that, so she chose to place her heart where such demands would never come. How would she find the answer?

Fred moved his cane, set it between his knees and crossed his hands over it as he stared out onto the grasses that swept toward the horizon.

"And what lessons have you learned?" she urged.

"You might not like hearing the musings of an old man," he said.

"Didn't you just turn forty-eight?" She smiled at him.

"You remembered."

"Russell just had a birthday too, didn't he?"

"August 31," Fred said.

It seemed a good omen that a father remembered the birthdays of his children, Jessie thought.

"I hope to get a car for them," he said. "For him and Mrs. Bauer and the children to use."

"That would be nice."

"What have I learned, you asked?" She nodded. "That I was a big part of what happened between Mrs. Bauer and me. It wasn't only Donald's death and our own engulfing grief that separated us. I can be a demanding person, lacking patience." He removed his hat and fanned his face. The afternoon was warm. "Sometimes I tell myself stories that bend the truth, ignoring what really is, yes? I imagine that's how I have invested in things that weren't all that profitable. My salve, for example. Property in Texas." He looked shy almost, and Jessie could imagine him as a young man, charming and adventurous. He put his hat back on, and the knuckles of his hand on the cane turned pale. "I should have known, too, that when I insisted on driving to Eau Claire that day with Russell, I was using him, denying to myself the true reason for my trip. Which was to be with you." He looked at her. "Telling you of George Haas's job was meaningless. I only wanted to see you. I realized that as I lay there in Luise's kitchen, knowing you were above me and out of reach. I couldn't sleep."

"Nor I," she said. She remembered that night and her own desires.

"But I knew I wanted to have in my life that longing to be with someone, just to sit beside her for a time, like we are now. To cherish her when she was out of sight, to look after her always. I had never imagined it might come to a man more than once in his life. But with you, it has."

She could feel the tears pool in her eyes.

"Will you consider allowing me to...court you, Miss Gaebele? To see what more we might make of this...affair."

"Affair?" she said.

"Confound it, I've done it again." He reached for her hand. "I've offended you. I suspect it won't be the last time, though I will try to learn from my mistakes. What I wanted to say was, will you forgive me, allow yourself to discover if you might truly love me as I am—as I love you—and to do it for the ages?"

It was what she wanted, yet had stopped longing for...until she saw him standing in the studio.

"More than all the grasses in North Dakota, that's how much I love you, Jessie Gaebele. And even if you say no, I will be forever grateful that I've found you to ask."

What would her parents say? How would people in Winona act if she and Fred returned there as husband and wife? For Jessie knew what he was asking without saying it. She was certain she read the message in his eyes.

"You've been gone such a long time," he said then. "It was an absence so great that I thought my life had ended. I'm so grateful it hasn't."

He removed his hat then and leaned into her face, holding the bowler to protect them from any who might pass by, though they were alone at the depot. Just the two of them cradled in the vast expanse of prairie.

She allowed his kiss, returned it, pressed her face against the wool of his chest. She inhaled, and with the breath, the painful separation of the years disappeared, exploding like an ice dam from her heart.

THIRTY-ONE

Abide

FRED WHISTLED AS HE DROVE BACK TO HAZELTON. In nine months, June of 1915, the divorce would be final, and in nine months, they would marry. He was certain of it. But in the meantime, he couldn't push her, couldn't take her on a faster pace than she might wish to go. Besides, he needed time to prepare his children for the changes.

He and Jessie would live in one of the cottages. He'd rent the others out for income. The one-room apartment at the Polonia was much too small for them both. Maybe they'd move to North Dakota. It seemed to agree with Jessie.

But no, that was too far from the children.

He heard himself singing as he drove along, passing the stubbled fields of flax and wheat. Even a flat tire that delayed his return did not deter his good humor. Jessie had agreed to write to him. That promise had taken twenty years off his life. He felt as young as the colts that raced along the fence as he turned into his ranch's drive.

That evening he made plans. He'd invest in those mining stocks he'd heard about, or that aerator. He might sell the Polonia Studio to get the cash. No, that would mean yet more competition. Better to rent the space for offices. His oil station attendant touted a new additive for gasoline to help with fuel efficiency. It had to be sold door to door, but that was how Watkins made his money. It might be the time to invest in such things, what with the war likely to include America before too long. These were all possibilities that would enable him to support his children and Jessie in the style he wanted for them. It wouldn't be easy, but investing was the only way to move ahead; one had to take risk. That's what his life had been all about. He'd done well with the ranch. The past two or three years had seen less rainfall, but that trend was sure to reverse itself.

He sat up in bed, suddenly wide awake. Stars winked at him through the window. Maybe he was too old to change.

He must be cautious. He had to be. He'd learned lessons; he'd told the truth when he and Jessie sat on the depot bench and talked. He didn't want to do anything that could be misunderstood or might drive her away, but he was capable of doing it. He tried to imagine how she might see any of those investment options.

Before he acted on them, he'd talk with her. Write to her. It would be good to explore options with a trusted partner. That's what marriage was about. He lay back down, pushed the sheet off in the evening heat. He'd almost jumped ahead, doing what he'd always done. That he hadn't meant perhaps he wasn't too old to learn new lessons.

It was Jessie's idea that she not return to Winona. Instead, she suggested, they should share each other's lives and hopes by letter and in that way come to know each other without the pressures of what her return just then would mean. For her, it meant rewriting her letters to eliminate the mistakes. She'd never have that flowing penmanship Fred had. He'd learned English as a second language yet was better at it than she was. The exercise forced her to think about what she really wanted to say before putting it on paper. They'd discover if theirs could be a marriage that would last a lifetime or disintegrate without the intrigue, the clandestine fantasies. They might discover they had no true love to strengthen while they waited.

She knew they did though. The way she'd felt when he took her in his arms and simply held her before he left was enough to unleash all the feelings she'd set aside these many years. Just the touch of his arms on hers, the scent of his cologne, the twinkle in his eye when he looked at her and shook his head, as though not able to believe his great good fortune, all matched the longing she carried in her heart.

Jessie believed.

They had fences to cross, yes. She wasn't looking forward to meeting up the first time with the other Mrs. Bauer, but she knew she could manage it. She'd found compassion when the woman attended her Polonia tea, and she could find it again. The same with the children. She adored Fred's children, though she'd had little time with Robert. She could change that and set a goal not to be their "other mother," but to find a place in their lives that didn't require them to feel torn between two parents. She was not their parent, but like them, she loved one who was.

Fred said Mrs. Bauer had a year to change her mind. If she did, things could drag on for years. What would she do then? Wait? She thought of those penitentiary wives. But she had someone to abide with her to make the wait so much easier.

She stirred the potatoes, checked the fried grouse the Adams family had given them. Virginia set the table. They took their meals together, though Jessie still liked having her own cabin, her own place to call home.

"What will your parents say?" Virginia asked as they finished their meal not long after Fred left.

The truth was, the only hesitation Jessie had at all in going home was facing her family. She'd have to explain the circumstances of Fred's return to her life and where she expected it to go. She wanted them to be at the wedding. She hoped Selma could sing and Roy play his guitar. Maybe Lilly would sew up her gown.

"I don't know. I'm not their little girl anymore. My father will ask if I'm telling myself the truth."

"Are you?" Virginia picked up the dishes while Jessie turned the stove on to heat the wash water.

"I think I am. No, I am. I've confessed everything," she said. "One day on those bluffs, I had this moment when I knew I was happy. I felt like I did when I rode Mr. Ferris's wheel, when we sat for a few seconds at the top: full of expectation, with a tint of trepidation. But I think trepidation isn't so much the anxiety of conscience as it is the prompting to listen to that inner voice. That's how I feel now, about Fred. That's what I'll have to share with them, to assure them."

She wrote to them that night.

She never got an answer.

October 5, 1914

Dear Sister,

How are you? I am fine.

I miss you. It doesn't help to know that you're in North Dakota, though I'm glad you finally wrote to tell us where you are. But North Dakota is as far away as Seattle when you're stuck in Winona. I want to know when you'll come home. Mama says you and Mr. Bauer are courting. That seems strange to me, because I see him here in Winona and you're way out there in Bismarck. Mama and Papa don't talk about it much, but I can tell they are waiting to "see what happens." At least that's what Mama always says when I ask how it will be if you and Mr. Bauer are married one day. What will his children call you? "Mrs. Bauer?" Where will you live? If you have children, how will they be related to the other Bauer children? "We'll see what happens," Mama says when I try to get answers. Her face looks as sour as Grandma's vinegar pickles. I wonder if she thinks you will get married at all or if she hopes you won't.

I hope you do. Your letters sound so happy! It will be like one of the stories in my Woman's Home Companion.

Art and I are happy. I'm eighteen now, though Mama still treats me like I'm twelve. But Art is courting me openly too. He and a partner opened a grocery. He likes what he does. We might marry one day. Joe O'Brien still visits with Lilly, but she won't agree to marry him unless he promises to stop drinking beer. He claims he has, but Lilly doesn't believe him, or so she says. I think she's afraid to take a risk, but that's what love is, isn't it? One can't be sure of anything in love. Marriage is a promise we don't really know if we can keep. We just have to hope we'll have the strength and faith to endure if the risk we take proves too great. Art says our time of courting builds credit so we can believe in each other after we're married and times get tough. He says they will get tough, but our beliefs will carry us through.

Roy's taken new interest in gardening. He says his chickens are the reason for his huge tomatoes. We canned and canned vegetables this year. He still takes his time in talking, but no one minds. He doesn't seem to either. He says he doesn't mind being who he is at all so long as he has his music and his travel books.

What's the weather like where you are? I just wonder. Please write soon.

Your loving sister,

Selma

THIRTY-TWO

Erasing the Ache of Absence

FRED'S LETTERS FILLED JESSIE WITH ASSURANCE. This Fred she met on paper, across the miles, listened. He responded to her questions and comments as though she sat before him while he wrote, but he didn't interrupt her, didn't jump ahead to finish her thoughts. Words of photography, business, of his lodges, poured out on the stationery with his name printed at the top. But there were always words of tenderness for her, of love expressed, and with them written, she could hold them to her heart.

She began to anticipate seeing him, this time without guilt. She imagined them working side by side, his hand brushing hers, and the joy of what could be now filled her dreams.

For Christmas, Fred sent her sheet music titled "When I Met You Last Night in Dreamland" from Woolworth's in Winona. Her twenty-third birthday came and went. (Fred had phonograph records delivered from Bismarck's Lucas and O'Hara Department Store. She played them on Virginia's tabletop Victrola and danced around the room, imagining Fred's holding her in his arms.) He also sent a photograph of a rose he'd labeled "My Bauer Rose." She wondered if it was a rose he'd nurtured so he could give it his name, or if it was a picture of a rose from his garden at the studio and he was calling her his rose. Either way, the gifts gave words to her feelings, filled her heart with gratitude.

Five days after her birthday, Lent began, and Jessie decided to commit the time to writing in her book each day, marking down things she was grateful for and letting Scripture lead her mornings. The exercise would remind her of how much she had and would help her live through what she didn't have: time with Fred.

The war across the ocean intensified. In Washington DC lawmakers rejected a law giving women the right to vote (even though women in some states already could). Congress designated a portion of the Rocky Mountains for a new national park. All since she'd looked at Fred's face and tried to read their future in his eyes. She'd nearly forgotten what he looked like. As the months wore on, she found letters to be enduring, but not the same as holding a loved one. She'd ask him for a photograph of himself, surprised to realize that she'd never seen one. Longing took on new meaning. She never wavered, never wondered if he'd come in June. She knew him.

"I could put your name up for the Fortnightly Club," Virginia offered. It was the oldest women's group in Bismarck. "It might keep your mind occupied," she said.

"My mind is occupied, all right," Jessie told her. "It's getting it settled that I'm having trouble with."

Old fears threatened, made her wonder if the anticipated joy was something she deserved. She shared them with Virginia, wondering if this nervous dread meant her conscience still carried weights she thought she'd given up.

"It's human nature to mistrust goodness. Part of our exile from Eden, I suspect," Virginia told her as the two attacked Virginia's carpets, which hung on the line behind the studio. "We have to be vigilant in remembering that we all mess up our houses. And with grace we're allowed to straighten things up once again."

"Do you think we can straighten two messed-up houses?" Jessie asked her. "That's what we'll face when we return to Winona."

"If you guard your hearts, yes."

As Jessie walked to her piano lesson later that afternoon, she thought about those two houses. Fred had once messed up his house. Would he be inclined to do so again? Might he one day find some other woman to press his devotion on? She also remembered the wording in the divorce decree about his having used "vile names." Would he change for the worse once they married?

The piano lesson took those thoughts away. Later she decided there could be no guarantee of Fred's fidelity, but at least she had asked herself the question, had admitted the possibility. She'd trust that honesty, commitment, and faith would be the shelterbelt to keep them from succumbing in future storms.

Fred's postcard arrived in late May, but it was dated the fifth. Jessie turned it over in her hand. The picture was of the Johnson Street studio, and he stood in front of it. Voe must have taken the picture, or maybe Russell. Fred had written earlier that Russell followed his father's interest in photography, though he'd already decided that if America joined the war, he'd enlist. Jessie didn't want to think about that. Anti-German sentiment grew even here in North Dakota, especially toward Germans who spoke English with an accent. Even in church, the Burgers and Shultzes kept more to themselves near the back. The very idea that Fred might lose another son was unbearable to consider. She prayed the war would end before Russell was old enough to go.

Fred hadn't even put her name on the postcard when he mailed it, just her post office box of 344 and Bismarck, ND. He'd written: "Just a line. Received word. All is well." He'd signed it *F.,* with the top of the letter making a long line out from the single initial. The line was "allegro," Jessie thought, smiling at the idea of her music lessons making their way into her future husband's handwriting.

Her future husband.

The note did look happy, with its up-tempo line, though she didn't know why or what the words meant. The plan had been for him to return to North Dakota in June, when the year of waiting was over and they could marry. Except that Jessie didn't want to marry in North Dakota because she didn't want people in Minnesota thinking theirs was one of those quick marriages destined to fail, as they would wed just after a divorce was made final. So they would travel back to Minnesota, and then they would marry with her family all around her, proof that theirs was a marriage that would endure.

"I have a mystery for you, Virginia," Jessie said. She showed the postcard to her employer. It had taken several weeks to arrive.

"What word did he receive? That the divorce is final?"

"Maybe, though I think not until June. He looks happy on the postcard, don't you think?"

"A woman in love," Virginia said, squinting at the tiny figure of the man, "is a telescope to amazement." Her smile joined Jessie's. She really would have to get a photograph of him that was larger than a hatpin head. There were so many things to look forward to.

Fred had said they'd wait until mid-June to see each other again, but Herman wanted him out for spring planting. How fortunate. Fred made arrangements to meet Herman in Hazelton, then left Winona a day earlier. He hadn't told Jessie he was coming for fear she'd tell him to stay away until the agreed-upon time, but he'd thought it through. This wasn't impulsive; it was necessity. He needed to show her Emmons County, the ranch, the place where Donald died, and speak of what it meant for them.

The train lumbered into the Bismarck station at noon. His plan: meet Jessie, return to Hazelton with her, be picked up by Herman. He'd booked a room in the hotel. He felt like a child about to enter a candy store without pennies in his pocket. So close, and yet...

Jessie's eyes grew large when she saw him in the Butler Studio reception room. "Fred? What are you doing here?"

He swept her into his arms, and she allowed it. He kissed her, right there in front of Virginia Butler and the surprised eyes of a patron waiting in the reception area. "I think we're ready for that portrait," Virginia said, and she hustled her customer into the operating room.

"Fred, please." Jessie pushed back against his chest. "Goodness." She blushed.

"Hear me out," he said. "I'll, well, I'm..." He swallowed. The room felt warm. He stepped back and removed his hat, held it in one hand, his cane in the other. "I know what I said, about our waiting, but Herman wanted me out this month. And it's almost a full year since Mrs. Bauer and I came to terms. I need to show you the ranch, the place where...Donald died. Maybe as much for me as for you," he said, realizing the truth. "Come with me to the ranch. I'll bring you back tomorrow."

She conferred with Virginia, then packed a small satchel. "Bring a special dress," he said. "We'll have dinner at the hotel."

They walked the two blocks to the depot, and Fred thought the petunias planted in old shoes and the daffodils leaning their yellow heads against picket fences behaved like royal flowers marking their way. He barely noticed the fields as they headed east, then south, his eyes on Jessie, his hand holding hers tucked discreetly between them on the leather seat.

Herman awaited. "You must be Miss Gaebele." Jessie nodded. "*Ja,* well then, welcome." Herman wiggled his eyebrows and winked as he turned toward Fred and picked up Jessie's satchel. "Women in the back. You won't be minding?"

"Not at all," Jessie said.

The men spoke of the crop season, of moisture through the winter, but Fred's thoughts were on Jessie sitting behind him. He turned frequently as though to keep her engaged in the conversation, but mostly he wanted to look at her, take in the outline of her profile, the gentle point of her chin, the chinalike cheekbones and the way her hat feather dipped as she became aware he stared, turned toward him and smiled. His heart swelled.

When they reached the borders of the ranch, he pointed out the fields that had been plowed and seeded. "We had dozens of teams working it," Herman said. Fred wondered what she thought of the vast expanse with so little to break the horizon. At the ranch house, a two-story building without flowers or fences, Fred suggested she rest upstairs. He filled the water pitcher for her. A breeze pushed the lace curtains through the open bedroom window. "I'll finish up with Herman, and then we'll take a drive out to...where it happened."

Sunset waited in the wings as they approached the place in the road where Donald had died. When he traveled to the ranch, Fred often came to this spot to think, to seek comfort as he stood over the wooden cross bearing Donald's name. Sometimes he talked to Donald, though just as often he bowed his head, hat in hand, while the wind blew and meadowlarks quieted, landing on bending grass. The loneliness lessened with Jessie beside him.

He told the story then of Donald's death: Mrs. Bauer's gentle horse harnessed to the wagon; his holding Donald in his lap, then letting the boy stand behind the dashboard; the hooves rising up higher than what could ever be imagined, who knew why—a bee, some other startle; one strike above Donald's eyes. The child died instantly, no lingering, no chance to say good-bye. "I could not believe it," Fred said. "I could not believe it."

He spoke of cradling the boy and noticed his arms wrapped around an empty space all these years later. He felt Jessie's touch on his arm as he spoke. He'd held the boy while Herman drove back to the ranch, with Russell's sobbing and Herman's "Oh no, oh no, oh no" ringing in his ears. His dread deepened as he thought of telling his wife, his dear, fragile wife, and he feared she would die from the shock. She sank to her knees when Fred carried the lifeless form to her, and Russell patted at his mother's back.

"How hard for all of you, for Russell too."

He nodded. "We'd gone out to find a couple of lost horses, yes? At the last minute both Donald and Russell asked to go along. Level ground, it was." He extended his cane out to show Jessie how innocent the landscape looked. He noticed Jessie's tears as he continued, couldn't stop to wipe them from her cheeks.

"If only I'd said no... If only I'd told them to wait, let those horses go!" She patted his arm. "I was angry at everyone, blamed everyone—God, but especially myself. For a long time. A wound formed between Jessie and me. No salve could heal it," Fred told her. "Later, I sought an explanation for such a tragedy. " He bent to pick stems of prairie smoke, the pinkish blossoms curling over his fingers. The entire length of the fence looked lavender bordered by the wildflower.

"Did you find it?" Jessie asked. "An explanation? Meaning?"

He said, "Did you know that these flowers grow most in areas that are overgrazed or just used up? They turned brown the day Donald died." He twirled the stem. "They always marked the end of a season for me rather than a beginning." He handed her one. "But when I see them now, I'm reminded that Donald really had only a beginning. He never experienced more than four springs. Only four." He sighed, stared out over the shimmering horizon. "Donald reminds me that those of us still posed in this portrait we call life must live honestly and fully, take in all there is to its goodness and tell ourselves the truth, pray to lead a better life. That's the meaning I've found." He slipped her arm through his, feeling the warmth of her through the yellow linen sleeve. He thumbed a spilled tear at her eye. "Once, our minister said Jesus told His disciples to go forth, to find worthiness, and to abide until they left. A simple direction. We all stay until we go, of course, but sometimes we're there in body only, not in spirit. Sometimes we don't abide at all, we don't cover and protect. I haven't always abided since Donald's death—haven't sought worthiness, stayed, lived truthfully—but I wish to from now on."

"I remember that scripture," Jessie said. "It's my reminder to listen to what's happening around me, to hear those voices before I make a terrible mistake."

"That too, I suppose," Fred said. "I want my life to be a memorial to Donald, to live fully and faithfully because he couldn't."

"Are you… That is, are you having second thoughts about leaving Mrs. Bauer?" she asked. "Because if there is anything you feel you can do to put the pieces back together, you should do that. You must do that."

He thought he heard a quiver in her voice. How brave she was to speak those words.

He laid the prairie smoke on the ground. He had to finish what he intended before he lost his nerve. "I will be there for the children and for you. And yes, even for Mrs. Bauer as she needs. I hope you understand that, Jessie. It's not an easy house I'm inviting you into, but I will do my best to make it a faithful house despite what's happened. With you in it, it'll be a good home. You will marry me, won't you? Live with me in Winona, come here at times, despite the complications?"

"I bring complications of my own," Jessie said.

But none of them were as complex as what he asked her to marry into. He took both hands in his, looked at her. "Mrs. Bauer… She makes demands," he said. "I'll have to go there now and then, tend the house as needed. She's not always well, and we may have the children at times." He faced her, held both her hands in his. "The truth is, Jessie, she won't be out of the picture."

He waited for her response.

"She can't be," Jessie said finally. "She's the mother of your children, all your children, including Donald. I bear responsibility for some of this…undoing. I've thought it might be my punishment never to be able to love you fully because I came between you and your wife."

He shook his head. "We all had our…poses, if you will. You stayed away as you could, and painful as it was, I'm grateful for that. It forced sense into my head."

"I'll do my best to be kind to her, I truly will. And I love your children, I always have."

"Thank you," he whispered. "You are more gracious than I have any right to expect."

Fred kissed her then and tasted sweetness, all the sweetness of a candy store with plenty of pennies in the waiting. Prairie smoke's whiskery blooms danced in the wind.

His wife will not be out of the picture. Jessie remembered Misha, the Russian child she'd photographed on the plant stand. Only the child was posed in the portrait; his parents stood apart. Whenever Jessie looked at that print, she could see the father's ache of anticipated absence. Fred faced the same thing now, and she knew he'd want to do whatever he could to maintain a relationship with his sons and daughter. She'd be in the middle of that, stepping back when the occasion called for it, supporting from the backseat, keeping herself from feeling disappointed when plans changed because of Mrs. Bauer or the children. It was part of what she'd be inviting into her life with this marriage. Was she strong enough? Was she taking the right path? She must not allow self-pity or the future's uncertainty to erase present joys. *Abide until you leave.*

Fred spoke. She looked at him. His eyes showed apprehension. She loved him: the gray in his mustache, the thinning brown hair she reached to soften as the wind lifted it, his passionate eyes, the broken-down body. She loved it all. She asked him to repeat what he'd said.

"I said, will you marry me tomorrow?"

"Tomorrow? But—"

"I don't want to wait another moment to call you my wife, to hold you without guilt or shame. I want to take a new picture of our lives without posing as anything other than what we are to be forever: husband and wife."

"But you know how I feel about a marriage in North Dakota—"

"We'll marry a second time in Minnesota, I promise. When everything is arranged back there. To be certain we're legal. But we've waited long enough. And besides, we have work to do as soon as we return to Winona. I've had word, as I told you on the postcard. Things have sold."

"The Polonia, I imagine?"

She'd held hope that the business would be their way to begin again, the two of them in her studio, because Mrs. Bauer owned the Bauer Studio now. She prepared for his words.

He shook his head. "I've sold property so we can keep the Polonia. But you've got to run it, make it pay, Jessie. I know you can. Your specialty of photographing women... It distinguishes you. You're missed in Winona."

"But you won't be there?"

"Yes and no. Mrs. Bauer agreed to exchange the cottages on the river for the Johnson Street studio lease. I've rented us an apartment not far from the Polonia, the Bauer Studio, and the children."

"What? But how will she provide for the children? Wasn't that part of the—"

"She has the houses near the railroad, three of them, and she can rent them out to boarders if need be. She can sell the cottages if she chooses. It finally made sense to her that I keep the studio. It's my profession. We reworked the terms of the divorce, Jessie," Fred said into her confusion. "The court just recently accepted it. I'm asking you to work beside me at Bauer Art Studio, though one will be on Fourth Street and one on Johnson. We'll be partners, working side by side."

"I'm to have the one I love *and* a studio of my own? This I don't deserve," she whispered.

She didn't warrant her own studio, but in truth, nothing was just hers or even theirs. They were stewards of the talents, the gifts they'd been given. She looked down at Donald's marker. Especially the gift of life.

This was what Virginia must have meant by *grace,* an unwarranted opportunity to begin again, this time with assurance that she walked a lighted path.

She waited to hear that inner voice tell her not to do it. *Abide in me,* is what she heard, and she took it as assent. She hugged him, then stepped back and shook his hand. "Partners," she told him. "We'll make this family portrait together."

⁂

They married in Hazelton at the minister's home, his wife acting as a witness. Fred spoke the vows clearly and loudly and told her later that he really understood them now. They dined later at the Hazelton hotel while storm clouds rolled in, looking like feather pillows spread open across the sky. In the distance, dark rain streaked the landscape, but in Hazelton, sunlight fractured the clouds like shards of melting ice. Except for the rumble of thunder, Jessie noticed only the man sitting across from her.

"Let's go," Fred said.

Jessie lifted her skirts as they ascended the carpeted steps to their room. He opened the door, and she stepped inside to the fragrance of roses. "Where did you...?"

"Ordered them in. Herman picked them up yesterday."

"You were pretty certain of yourself, Mr. Bauer," Jessie said.

"Always one to take a risk, Mrs. Bauer. And apparently"—he wrapped her in his arms—"so are you."

It was what love required.

Jessie Ann Bauer, wedding portrait
November 15, 1915

Contentment

December 1939. My husband, Frederick John Bauer, took this photograph of me on November 15, 1915, in Winona. We married a second time on November 2 that same year in Anoka, Minnesota, but we took a honeymoon rest in Minneapolis for a few days before our nuptial party. My family did not attend either of our wedding ceremonies but joined us later at our apartment on Broadway, a few blocks down from where they lived and from where I spent my childhood. It was quite a gathering. Even my uncle August, who bought me my first camera after the St. Louis World's Fair in 1904, greeted us both with a handshake for Fred and a swinging lift at my waist for me. My mother's eyes grew large with worry as her brother swung me around. I knew her look wasn't over Uncle August's dancing with his niece. She worried over the baby. I was five months into carrying our first child when we officially remarried in Minnesota.

I didn't return with Fred after our weekend wedding in North Dakota. I stayed on at Virginia's because we thought it wise for me to wait until after June, the official year's end to the divorce waiting period, and also because Virginia needed me until she could hire another assistant. I thought I'd return in July but "things" seemed to keep happening, a state of affairs that followed my loving husband.

Mrs. Bauer did not leave the picture of our lives by any means, and getting her settled with boarders, helping her sell one of the cottages on the river, keeping up the studio... All of that took time. That's what Fred wrote. I hadn't been aware of his tendency to put things off, because we'd married sooner than planned. But like all perfectionists, he waited for the right and perfect solution to a problem before saying it was finished, forgetting that perfection means "complete" and not "free of mistakes or snags." This divorce from his wife would never be without challenge, and neither would our marriage. It was what living looked like, I decided.

I could have helped him if I'd been there, operating those two studios all that time. But he wanted to settle things down, as he put it, before bringing me home. Of course, he'd added new investments to his duties, ventures that didn't always turn out, but we'd discussed them together at least. We'd made the decisions together.

I wrote to him in August telling him of my condition and urging him to come and get me. In September I told him Virginia had a new assistant who needed the cabin I still occupied, though Virginia certainly wasn't pushing me out.

A part of me worried that Fred had changed his mind and didn't know how to tell me! Virginia said that was nonsense. She'd seen a man in love, and Fred was certainly it. I scolded him about that at one point. He wrote back with full assurance. But he didn't come to get me.

I continued to help with the studio work, though Virginia and I thought that developing prints in my condition wasn't wise. I had to tell her of it, because my morning illness wasn't confined to the morning. I spent most of my time photographing, even carrying the heavy camera and tripod to the bluffs one day. Nothing so filled me as when I captured a bit of God's creation to preserve it for when I left it behind. I talked to my baby about my day. And when I curled into my bed at night, I held the child inside, leaving loneliness behind.

By October, though, I'd had enough. Winter threatened, and I told Fred if he didn't come for me soon I'd have the baby in Seattle, since he'd obviously changed his mind about wanting to live with me in Winona. I made it sound like I'd always wanted to see Puget Sound—which I had—but I also wanted him to know that I was capable of moving on if in fact he'd found reason to reconsider.

He arrived three days later to help me pack and put trunks onto the train. I never was so joyous!

We arrived in Minneapolis late in the evening. He'd arranged for a minister to marry us in Anoka, not far from the city, the next day. He'd planned ahead and already possessed the marriage license.

I dressed in the hotel room, wearing what I have on in this photograph, a dress Lilly sewed for me, and we repeated our vows at the parsonage. We didn't ask the minister to take our photograph together; in fact, to this day we have few pictures with both of us, as one of us is usually standing behind the camera.

We relished our time together after so long an absence, visiting Minnehaha Falls and driving past gardens. This marriage, this life with Fred, was what I'd always wanted. That was the truth. But to have this marriage, my love of making photographs, and soon a child...well, this was abundance indeed.

Fred drove me out to show me the forty acres at Pine City (which I loved for its rolling hills and woodlands) before we boarded the train to Winona. There, we took a cab to the apartment he'd rented for us on Broadway and began planning to celebrate our marriage. Marriages.

For the photograph I stood in the parlor of our second-floor apartment in front of the piano Fred gave me as a wedding present. It was there, waiting for me when I arrived, a gift better than roses. I squealed, I know I did, and kissed my husband. He did know what pleased me; he hadn't procrastinated about the piano or finding new sheet music to display either.

On the day of the portrait, Selma did my hair up for me, twisting pearls in the roll and adding a string of them to the shoulders of the gown. Lilly had embroidered roses on the sheer shoulder veil. She adjusted the waistline, as she'd tailored the dress in early July, when I'd written to my family that we were married and would be married again in Minnesota because I just didn't trust those North Dakota weddings. She'd sent the package with Fred when he traveled out to get me. My belt is a ribbon clustered with cloth roses. I carried chrysanthemums that Roy grew. "Fer-fer-fertilized by my chi-chi-chickens," he told me, his dimples deepening into a smile.

The meeting with my parents had caused me worry. They'd failed to answer my letter telling them where I lived and about the marriage; only Selma, Roy, and Lilly kept the channels open. I imagine they struggled to find a way to explain to themselves and perhaps to their friends about my part in the story of the Bauers. But they arrived, all of them, shortly after the delivery men carried our trunks up to the apartment.

"Roy's been riding his bicycle by here every day since FJ left for North Dakota," my father said. "FJ told us he was heading out to get you."

It surprised me that Fred had spoken with my parents. I would chastise him later for not telling me, but then, I'd failed to let him know I was worried.

"It's good to see you, Papa," I told him. I listened for criticism in his voice, prepared for a stern response, but received neither. Instead he pulled me into his chest, which smelled of leaf burn. "It's good to have you home, girl," he said. "Good to have you back safe and sound, and now just down the street."

Roy hugged me then, and I exclaimed about how tall he'd grown.

"N-n-nearly as t-tall as you." He beamed.

Selma asked about the trip as I fussed in the cupboards, found tea, and put the kettle on to boil. "I don't know what's here to serve you," I said.

"Hush now," my mother said. She stood with her hands stuffed in the pockets of her knitted sweater, buttoned up nearly to her throat. "We brought cookies. Selma, put them on the table, please. Now come here, Jessie, and let me hold you."

I sank into my mother's arms. "It's been so long," I said. "Thank you for coming." She stepped back, still holding my shoulders, a glisten in her eyes as she stared at my waistline. "Yes," I whispered, taking a deep breath.

"You'll be grandparents in March," Lilly told them.

"How did you know?" Selma charged.

Roy clapped, and I winked at Lilly, who had kept the secret. "I had to tell Lilly because she made the dress."

"And had to keep altering it."

"Because your husband didn't bring you back as fast as he should have," my mother said.

I heard annoyance in her voice and intervened. "Fred had a lot to take care of before it made sense for him to travel out to get me," I said. "It's not easy running two studios, taking care of his children..." I realized I'd stepped onto a path of discussion I didn't want to be on during this first day back. But it would be the path that weaved through the rest of our lives. Fred had two families. I didn't want us to sidestep what was so, either. Perhaps it was best to talk of such things. "He'll take care of them and of me. Us," I defended.

"That he will," my father said.

"As I've vowed to," Fred said.

Both men stood like feuding dogs, jaws set, tails up and still. Then my father stepped back and nodded his head. "As I've vowed to," Fred repeated and reached for my father's hand. It was taken and clasped, the beginning of two men having settled a score.

And so Fred did take care of us until his death earlier this year, 1939. He cared for all of us, me and the five children I bore him, beginning with Fern in March of 1916. Grant and Pearl brightened our Winona days further, and then in 1920 we moved to Minneapolis, where I gave birth to two more children, Stan and Corinne. Fred was sixty-five when our youngest, Corinne, was born. His lodge gave him cigars on the occasion.

When we moved to the Twin Cities, he brought my entire family with us. We ran a new Bauer Studio in Minneapolis, mostly retouching and coloring, making contracts with dozens of other photographers in the area. We kept the Hazelton Studio for many years, with Virginia Butler doing the local work until we sold the studio in the thirties. Then Fred had another heart attack, and hard times fell upon the country. We sold the ranch then, too, and the Pine City property, because we could not pay the taxes. That one broke my heart. I loved those rolling woodlands that reminded me of Cream, where I'd grown up.

The wedding photograph I look at now is filled with memory. That morning my mother gave me the necklace I'm wearing. It had been her mother's, given to her to wear on her wedding day.

Fred's sister, Luise, and her husband came on that celebration day too and treated me like family. I was so grateful. We'd decided ahead of time not to include Fred's children. It might be confusing for them, and there would be time enough for the pull and tugs that would stretch our threaded family into the comforting quilt it became.

I try to remember Fred's first children's birthdays. Winnie's is easy since it's the same as mine. Often, when Mrs. Bauer needed caring from her mother, the children came by in the morning before school, and I'd braid Winnie's hair and talk with Robert about his lessons and his interests in building things. They're good children who have been good to me as well.

Mama died in 1930 and Papa two years later. I was always grateful that the snags we felt those early years did not ruin the garment of our lives. My mother never mentioned again my being a "kept woman" or how much older Fred was than I. My mother must've held the philosophy of letting the water of past decisions flow under the bridge, as there was no sense trying to get it back.

I did encounter Mrs. Bauer soon after the Republican-Herald *reported that "Mrs. and Mrs. F. J. Bauer" had given birth to our first baby, a girl. The paper added that "Mrs. Bauer is the former Jessie A. Gaebele." Mrs. Bauer surprised me by knocking on the apartment door. I'd rarely seen her when I shopped or ran errands. She never came to the studios. You'd think as small as Winona was back then that our paths would have crossed close enough to have a conversation. But they didn't. Fred went to church with me at the evangelical church, though we made certain to attend the congregational recitations, where Robert and Winnie often spoke. Mrs. Bauer and I nodded feathered hats to each other on those occasions but didn't speak. I had not talked with her since the Polonia Tea.*

I opened the door to her, holding Fern in my arms.

"So it's true," she said.

I stepped back. Not that she looked wild-eyed, but she hadn't greeted me, and I didn't know the social graces for speaking with a husband's first wife as she stood in the doorway. She was finely dressed, and I felt a bit dowdy. "Yes," I said. "Won't you come in?"

"It's not his first child, you know. Russell is."

"I know. Won't you have some coffee or tea?" My heart pounded as she crossed in front of me. She glanced around.

"Those Indian pots." She pointed. "I never did like them."

"Fred appreciates the designs," I said.

"Always reminded me of that ranch. Flat. Takes too much money for whatever gain there is. It took Donald from us."

I nodded. "A place can hold hard memories," I said. "And farming of any kind takes work." I thought of my father, who had left the dairy in Wisconsin because of his chronic pain.

"Especially when you're an old man," Mrs. Bauer said. "And FJ is. An old man. You know that, don't you? You'll be a widow before long. Alone like me."

"Maybe," I said. But who could predict a life's end? Donald's young death was the reminder of that. "He could outlive me," I said. "Until then, I'll appreciate the time I have."

She'd grunted then and sat down.

"I want to know something," she said. She pointed to a place for me to sit. Fern started fussing, probably in response to my own loudly beating heart. I continued to stand, patting her diapered bottom. "Before the divorce, did you and my husband... Did you...?"

What could I tell her? What wouldn't I tell her? The silence felt explosive, and I took a breath to speak.

"Never mind," she said to my hesitation. She flapped her hand as though swatting at flies. "I don't think I really want to know." She shook her head with certainty. "No, I do not wish to know. Reverend Carleton told me I should just forgive, not for your sake but for my own, so I can make the best of what is. I just wanted to see where he lives now." She scanned the room cluttered with laundry, newspapers, and prints I hoped to frame during any spare time. "I'd like that tea."

Shaking, I prepared it, and when I returned she drank it slowly. We sipped in silence. Finally she offered, "I'm retouching again. Did FJ tell you? I suppose not. Something to fill my days. I use FJ's old bedroom. Doing it for a few studios in town. Could do it for you Bauers if you wanted. Didn't know I'd miss it. I can make my way too, you know."

She rose to go.

"Thank you for the tea. I will always be his wife," she said with her gloved hand on the glass doorknob. Gloves. A protection and a cover; we all wore them. It reminded me of Selma's letter sent years before: "If that from Glove, you take the letter G, then Glove is love and that I send to thee." I did send love to Mrs. Bauer, but I've never known if she received it. "He will always be the father of my children, and he will always take care of us," she added.

"That won't be challenged or discounted," I told her. I didn't want to argue the intricacies of words like wife.

"Good. Then we have an understanding. I am in this family portrait until the day I die, and then maybe even after." She left then, as abruptly as she'd arrived.

I pulled this wedding photograph out of the album today to remember. Using the magnifying glass, I checked to see who was in the framed picture on the piano, and then I remembered. It was Donald, his absence filling a space perhaps larger than had he lived.

There's a smudge on this photograph of me, off to my right shoulder. I should rewash the print to get rid of the teardrop, but I haven't yet. It reminds me that Donald and his father are together at last. We buried Fred in March, on Pearl's twentieth birthday. We had twenty-four good years together, Fred and me. I never regretted for an instant my decision to marry him, despite the hard financial times, the health problems of Pearl and Stan as children, and Fred's deteriorating health, these past eight years especially. We almost lost the house after he died, but I convinced the banker to give me more time, and he has. I took a job as a nurse's aid, and I still do retouching for several studios in the city. Virginia Butler even sends me work. We remain good friends. I rent out rooms, just as the other Mrs. Bauer does in Winona. I do so to help support my three children still at home.

Our children see their father's older children, and all think of themselves as family. It's as it should be.

When I'm feeling low, I pull out my photo album and remember as I did that day that photography was my life only until I discovered what life is really made of: the settings, props, and poses we encounter, then put aside so we can cherish family and faith, live fully, and abide until we go. It's what I was thinking in that wedding portrait when my husband made me look more beautiful than I am. His caring eye behind the lens captured a love that now helps fill an absence so great I could not have prepared for it on my own. God remains my guide.

AUTHOR'S NOTES AND ACKNOWLEDGMENTS

While I alone am responsible for the words, errors, and omissions in this text, I still send acknowledgments on wings of gratitude to Craig and Barbara Rutschow—my brother and sister-in-law—Ron and Corinne Bauer Kronen, Helen Kantorowicz Bauer, Molly Bauer Livingston Hanson, Patricia Bauer Butenhoff, Jeanne Bauer Strand, Joanne Bauer Krejca, Bruce Bauer, and posthumously to my aunt Fern Bauer Griffin, especially for her family book researched and written in 1985 about the lives of Jessie Gaebele Bauer, Jessie Otis Bauer, Frederick John Bauer, and their descendants. The Portraits of the Heart series based on my grandmother's life could not have been completed without the care and support of each of these relatives and other cousins, who read drafts, made comments, looked for answers, and sent me missives that gave authenticity to the story. I am deeply grateful.

Marianne Mastenbrook of the Winona County Historical Society provided constant access to archival documents, answering questions ranging from toboggan slides to streetcar bridges. Her devotion to original research and her positive spirit made asking for help an easy task. Audrey Gorny read an initial draft and offered insights about early Winona. I continued to use the digitalized records of the *Republican-Herald* newspaper, which provided me material of daily life in Winona for the first book, *A Flickering Light.* Similar digitalized city directories of Eau Claire, Wisconsin, provided ways to authenticate Jessie's time in that city, as did audiotapes made by family members when she was in her advanced years. The *Milwaukee Journal* archival material provided information about early photography in that city, the sporting dances, the journalist Robert Taylor, and the North-Western School for Stammerers.

Providentially, Lori Oser, a volunteer for the North Dakota State Library, contacted me while reading one of my books to thank me for writing words she loved to read. Imagine my delight at finding someone living in Bismarck who loved history, is a writer herself, and who was willing to paw through archives and other musty places to locate information for me about railroad timetables and land grants. Lori suggested a reading list I followed to get to know North Dakota better. Roxanne Henke, another writer and North Dakota lover, made trips and notes of landscapes—as did Lori—so that along with the photographs in my grandparents' collection, I could capture the prairie richness of this north-border state so beloved by Teddy Roosevelt and my grandparents. I thank Oregonian Bette Wright, who grew up in Bismarck, for her copies of newspaper articles, clippings from her own scrapbook, answers to questions about the state, and good cheer as I wrote this story. Florence Thompson, whom I see each Sunday morning in Moro, Oregon, also spent her childhood in North Dakota. She offered insights as I came to know the state that stole my grandfather's heart and brought my grandparents together. I'm grateful to each of these special women. I'm also grateful to Susan Andrews, general presbyter of Hudson River Presbytery, for her words, "Joy is the fruit of despair truthfully confessed and providentially transformed," written as part of a Lenten reflection in *Christian Century* magazine (March 24, 2009), which provided insights for Jessie's journey from despair to forgiveness, from self-recrimination to joy.

Many events described in this book, including Jessie's Milwaukee and Eau Claire work and the events in North Dakota, are based on family stories. The encounter of my grandparents in North Dakota was inspired by audiotapes made with my aunts and uncles, and by my grandmother's remembering of events. She told the story as though she and FJ were introduced for the first time by Virginia Butler, though she had worked for him many years before that. I took this discrepancy as evidence that between story and history lies memory. We don't always remember the facts and details; we remember the emotions of the experience.

That Jessie loved the Ferris wheel, high bluffs, daily exer[illegible] travel is remembered by her children, even if it meant merely ri[illegible] the streetcar to the end of the line and back.

The two marriages are a part of the family story. During the audio interview when Jessie was in her eighties and still sharp as a hat-pin, she was asked by my genealogically astute aunt to explain about the two marriage licenses. There was a pause. "Did you have to get married?" one of her children asked. She quickly said, "No, of course not." Still more pause. Then my uncle said, "Maybe Minnesota didn't recognize North Dakota's marriage license at that time." "That's right," she said, happy to move on to another question. We'll never know the why of the two marriages. But given the dates of other events, the story portrays my speculations.

Both Jessies outlived F. J. Bauer. The children of both Jessies and their children have kept the extended family as one, sharing in family gatherings. I always admired my grandmother for her part in making that connection work during an era when blending families perhaps had greater challenges than today. Jessie's family did in the end accept her decision to wed FJ, and as portrayed, when they moved to Minneapolis, *all* of Jessie's siblings and her parents moved with them. As sisters, Lilly and Jessie had their disagreements, but the family remained close throughout their lives, Lilly acting as the older-sister protector. At least, that's my explanation for her sometimes strident behavior.

I doubt that my grandmother would describe herself as a feminist, though she urged all of her grandchildren, regardless of gender, to seek their dreams and not let the discouragement of the past, fear of the future, or others' opinions stand in our way. I do think Jessie would have argued with the bankers; she did argue with the banker when they nearly lost the house during the Depression years. In her elder years, she fought off two muggers, one while taking her daily eight-city-block walk, and another who attempted to storm her door. She played music by ear, and the piano was her wedding gift. I have no doubt that after FJ died the greatest joys of her life were her children and her church.

Some of the rest of the story that I frequently include in the author's notes are presented in the interview that follows. But I'd be remiss if I did not thank my publisher, WaterBrook Multnomah Publishing Group, a division of Random House, which has been faithfully publishing my work for the past fifteen years. Editors Shannon Marchese and Erin Healy, production editor Laura Wright, marketing and publicity staff—especially Johanna Inwood, Staci Carmichael, Melissa Sturgis, and Lynette Kittle—and the production and sales staff have all gone beyond the call to present this duet of books about Jessie with family photographs in the way that I envisioned. I'm grateful. To my long-time agent, Joyce Hart of Hartline Literary Agency, we have done it yet again! Thank you.

I am also deeply grateful to five special women who actively support my work and prayer life: Judy Schumacher, Carol Tedder, Gabby Sprengler, Susan Holton, and Loris Webb hold special places in my heart. Equally important in supporting my writing life are Arlene Hurtley, my niece (who, along with her two precious girls, Rylee and Dally, take care of the mailings for me), and friends Sandy, Kay, Blair, Nancy, and others whose names I won't list, though I hope I've told them personally how much their encouragement means to me.

Finally, to my family: I am grateful for my stepdaughter, Kathleen Larsen, stepson Matt, and their families for making it possible for me to write and for encouraging my days. And of course I am deeply grateful to Jerry. These books would not be without him.

Last but not least, I thank my readers, who make room in their lives for these stories. Thank you for the unexpected words of encouragement you send me just when they're needed and for continuing to anticipate that next book.

With gratitude,

Jane

You may contact me at www.jkbooks.com, www.janekirkpatrick.blogspot.com, or 99997 Starvation Lane, Moro, Oregon, 97039. To sign up for my newsletter, visit www.jkbooks.com.

AN INTERVIEW WITH THE AUTHOR

How did you become interested in writing stories based on the lives of actual people?

As a child I loved reading biography—Laura Ingalls Wilder's *Little House on the Prairie* was set not far from where I grew up in southwestern Wisconsin. But there weren't many biographies of women, and even fewer of ordinary women. I read Irving Stone's novels and Anya Seton's books about famous people and loved them. Then I learned about a historical couple who lived in Central Oregon in the 1860s. I wanted to tell the woman's story but couldn't find much information about her. Records existed about her husband, father, and brothers, but not much about her. When I found her obituary, which demonstrated such love for her, I knew she must have lived an extraordinary life. So, despite having never written fiction, I decided to tell her story in a way that allowed me to explore the truth of her life. I call it speculative historical fiction because I speculate about the why of things after researching the more factual what and when.

What novel was that?

A Sweetness to the Soul. It was followed by fifteen others, including this Portraits of the Heart series: *A Flickering Light* and *An Absence so Great.*

***Where did you get the title* An Absence So Great?**

A friend and writer, Linda Lawrence Hunt *(Bold Spirit: Helga Estby's Forgotten Walk Across Victorian America),* wrote of the death of their daughter Krista in a bus accident in Bolivia while on a mission trip some years back. As a comfort someone sent her a line from poet Mark Doty: "How could I ever prepare for an absence the size of you?" She felt it captured the great gulf of grief her daughter's death created. She and her husband went on to establish The Krista Foundation (www.kristafoundation.org) to support young people around the world doing important social and environmental work. I adapted the lines for the title, as Jessie was managing the loss of integrity, the loss of a dream, and the loss of a great love while learning to trust in God's guidance. The loss of the Bauers' child I thought contributed to the absence of love that occurred within their marriage. Grief and loss take their toll on each of us, and the absence of spiritual support is perhaps the most devastating loss of all we humans face.

How was writing about your own family different from writing about other historical people?

What was similar was a great desire to memorialize and honor the lives of ordinary people, especially women. As with my other novels, I also found and listened to descendants' recollections. Grandchildren and great-nephews might each have a different take on their ancestor, but each story lends credibility and helps shape the character. I could talk to aunts, cousins, and my brother and his wife, who all had experiences with Jessie, so that was different and helpful. I recalled stories my mother, Pearl, shared. My mom, by the way, was the third, or middle, child.

I was also able to talk to others who knew this woman. She wasn't just someone in a historical record. The subtext for me as a writer was also different, knowing that this woman's story shaped my heritage, my mother, my life. I wondered about what kinds of values, thought processes, trials and tribulations, and strategies for enduring might have been handed down. There's some evidence that DNA carries more than just physical characteristics, possibly emotional ones as well. I think I see patterns of my life in hers, but then I also saw universal patterns in her life, and those are the ones I most wanted to write about. I didn't write the story to be a voyeur into an ancestor's past but rather to explore the life of a woman I loved and wished to honor, while believing that her story could inform in positive ways the lives of those who never met her.

I also had audiotapes of my aunts and uncles interviewing my grandmother when she was in her eighties and another when she was ninety-three. She played the piano on one, and on others her children asked some of the questions I would have asked. The family collection of glass photographic plates was another treasure I didn't have with my other novels. And of course, I had my own memories of her, which shaped the story as well: picking blackberries together, watching her shed her whalebone corset in hot July, laughing with her at my brother's wedding reception.

To help me dig deeper into what I thought were the truths of the story, I asked myself more often, *What aren't you writing about?* And of course I worried a bit about whether I'd be invited to the next family reunion after the relatives had read the books!

Did you uncover any interesting subtexts you'd care to share?
Like Jessie, I tend to deal with disappointment by first avoiding then acknowledging the truth. I struggle with unworthiness, distancing myself at times from spiritual support, and have to work at seeing what's past become water under the bridge. How I deal with absences of the heart gained dimension in the writing of this book.

Another subtext is the number of ancestors—cousins of mine, aunts and uncles, nieces and nephews—who have artistic passions with degrees in art, music, literature, and design, as well as the sciences, such as physics and engineering. In addition, there are a surprising number of relatives who count their faith life (me included) as an important part of who they are and who have served as pastors, nurses (my mother was one), writers, social workers, and missionaries. Many contribute their time, talents, and treasures to their respective churches and communities. I think my grandmother influenced those acts of artistry, science, generosity, and faith.

I also explored my own issues related to marrying an older man (my husband is sixteen years older than I) and the complexities of divorce and its impact on children. My husband of thirty-three years and I were both married previously. He brought children into our family picture. That made for interesting conversations within my immediate family, and of course, blending a family made me admire my grandmother even more. The idea of how grief affects a marriage (my husband's son died the first year of our marriage), what ex-wives think about each other, and the way fathers stay attached or not to their children after a divorce also intrigued me as I explored this story.

Considering talent as a currency and seeing ways that gifted people (young and old) sometimes harm themselves by their poor choices intrigued me as the story developed as well. As Pulitzer Prize–winner Willa Cather once noted, we writers most often find material in those experiences we had before we turned fifteen. Lots of grist for thought as I wrote this book.

How did you do your research?

Pretty much the way I always do: I start with an interesting character, for example, a woman who had done photographic work, which was considered to be a man's profession at the turn of the century. I was an adult when I learned that my grandfather had been married before, because the children from his first marriage were always known to me as my mother's "older brothers and sister," without the distinction that they were half siblings. Considering the time period, I thought that remarkable and wondered about it. I also knew of something strange—the two marriages to the same man. My grandmother never answered that question on the audiotapes.

Along with these unanswered questions, I create a time line of actual known events in the person's life and then talk with descendants. I look at census information, social histories of the time period, then contact historical societies—in this instance the Winona County Historical Society was of huge help to me, and so was a friend, Lori Orser, in North Dakota. I read histories of the areas I'm writing about and read first-person accounts of growing up during the time period I'm researching. Magazine articles written by hunters and fishermen are rich with landscape detail, and the storytellers of antique shops bring fascinating details to the manuscript. I also had dozens of original glass plate negatives to study and work into the tale.

Finally, I ask myself three questions from a book called *Structuring Your Novel* by Meredith and Fitzgerald: *What's my intention in writing this story? What's my attitude? What's my purpose?* I work those answers into three sentences, which I post on my computer to help me when I get lost. Then I identify what I think are the significant life events, the turning points in the character's life. I ask myself what each of the characters wants, then begin to write, trying to find out what motivated the characters to be where they were in the historical record and to do what they did. How did that affect them? I weave landscapes, relationships, spirituality, and work into the story and keep researching, talking to photographers (for this book) and other specialists as I go. I'm still asking questions, making corrections, until just before the book goes to press!

How did you research Mrs. Bauer's part of the story? Was her first name really Jessie too?

Both women had the same first name! That's why I used Mrs. Bauer as the character name, to distinguish her from my grandmother, Jessie. To learn about Mrs. Bauer, I had the wonderful help of cousins Molly Bauer Livingston Hanson, Bruce Bauer, and Patricia Bauer Butenhoff, who answered questions, read drafts, and were generous with their time and memories, including details such as that Mrs. Bauer loved to fish. Several descendants spoke of her emotional difficulties, which her sister, Eva, also had. I also had several photographs of Mrs. Bauer as a young woman and with her children. I find photographs to be quite revealing. My aunt Fern Bauer Griffin, who did the genealogical work a number of years ago, also transcribed interviews with all sides of the family, including Mrs. Bauer's. While I didn't have access to those transcriptions, I did have access to the book she wrote for our family in 1985, *Frederick John Bauer and His Ameri-*

can Wives, as well as several stories she sent me that my grandmother told her. Some included references to Mrs. Bauer. The consensus is that Mrs. Bauer was a troubled woman, and I attribute much of that to her great grief over the death of Donald. She may have suffered from clinical depression, but she also was known to hold the retouching brushes in her mouth to keep them moist, and the chemicals in the fluids and paints were not safe. Some of her descendants speculate that metal or chemical toxicity might explain her erratic behaviors. She died two months after the death of her mother in 1941, two years after the death of Fred Bauer.

I wanted to portray all three main characters as three-dimensional people with flaws and strengths so they could inform our own lives more fully.

Did your grandmother own her own studio as you portray in this book?

She did. It was called the Polonia Studio. Oddly, she never mentioned it in the audiotapes or when my aunt Fern, her oldest child, interviewed her years before and wrote that family history. On the audiotapes she asserted, "I took photographs too," and spoke of the character study she photographed in Eau Claire but not of the studio ownership. I discovered it through the *Republican-Herald* archives. Earlier, while going through family records, I'd come across a single page with the logo for Polonia Studio on it. It was not part of the ledger accounts, and when I asked, none of the relatives knew what it was doing there. So when I found the news announcement that Jessie A. Gaebele was the new proprietor of Polonia Studio, I did the happy-dog dance. Then the speculation began about how she might have come to purchase a studio from George Haas at the ripe young age of twenty, a woman in 1912. The news account of the sale of some of FJ's property about the same time gave me direction to speculate. Also in the family collection is a hard-bound program for a Photographers Association of America conference. Rides on a lake, the theater and lecture titles, and presenters described in the book were taken from that program, so it's likely Jessie did attend at least one of these gatherings, where she could have found female mentors.

Are the photographs used in the book of the people you claim them to be?

Some of them. The photographs of Jessie and of Roy with his chickens are. The portrait of Minnie Raymond and the sample photographed in Eau Claire are part of the labeled family collection, as well as the wedding photo. But the others were part of the collection received at her death labeled "don't know, don't care." But I did. So the stories Jessie tells about them—Misha, the Marquette girls, the Giroud sisters, the canoeists, for example—are purely fictional. I had dozens of other glass plates from other family members to choose from. It was difficult to decide, and I've put many of them into a PowerPoint presentation I sometimes present at book signings and events and on my Web site. They are really quite remarkable.

Did your grandmother really travel to different states to help run studios?

Absolutely. In addition to her work in Winona, she assisted in Milwaukee, Eau Claire, and Bismarck. She had plans for Seattle too, but apparently those changed. The studio in Eau Claire, Wisconsin, and the Butler Studio in North Dakota were both identified in the family record; the Milwaukee studio was not named, but she was there and she did live with the Harms family, relatives of Fred Bauer. Incidentally, the studio in Eau Claire was the Johnson Studio, not the Everson Studio. I had to change it because in my aunt's book, she said the Milwaukee studio was run by "Mrs. Johnson," and I used that in *A Flickering Light.* But during research for *An Absence So Great,* I found no studio by that name in Milwaukee but one in Eau Claire instead. It was too late to use the correct studio, so the name was changed to Everson. I don't think Jessie knew the reporter Robert

Taylor, but the story of his motorcycle and the type of photography he inspired for newspapers is accurate.

Did your great-uncle really stutter? Was Lilly actually a seamstress? What about Selma; did she sing well? What happened to them?
It's all true! Roy was also a musician and later became a clock repairman who came home to look after scads of plants and who loved to watch travel programs on television. I remember visiting him and my aunt Lilly and loving his roomful of African violets and orchids and all sorts of tropical plants he kept alive through the Minnesota winters. It felt like a hothouse. Lilly worked at the glove factory, and when the entire family moved to Minneapolis in 1920, she worked for the drapery section of Boutell's department store until her retirement. When I was young, she and Roy and Art—who survived Selma—would come to our Wisconsin farm and collect black walnuts they later cracked and dried. Selma and Art married in 1918 but had no children. Roy never married.

Lilly never married either. The story is told that her long-term beau finally convinced her to marry him after years of asking. She'd resisted because he had a tendency to drink. The night she agreed to marry him, he celebrated with pals and drank the first beer he'd had in years. She found out and called off the marriage. I do have a postcard written to her by a Joseph and signed "Joseph 4 Ever."

After my uncle Stan married, he helped build two houses side by side in the Minneapolis area: he and his family lived in one, and Roy and Lilly lived in the other.

Many of the smaller details are true as well: Lilly was the secretary of the Stott Company Young Women's Industrial Association; the North-Western School for Stammerers was in Milwaukee (a piece of history I discovered on a penny postcard, and later I found the winter program for the school on eBay); my grandmother worked for "a healer in Winona," and Ralph Carleton was such a minister, whose activities were reported in the paper.

Russell married a woman who had gotten his name when, like many soldiers, he wrote his name on a piece of paper to toss from the train window. Young women then wrote to the soldier whose paper they picked up. He lived in Winona all his life and was an electrician who loved photography. One of his children, Patricia Butenhoff, worked for the *Republican-Herald* as a proofreader. Winnie married and had children and also lived along the Mississippi River near Winona. Robert, too, worked as an electrician and raised his children in Winona. One of his daughters, upon her marriage, lived in the house near the railroad tracks, and both Molly and Bruce, two of his children, were wonderful resources for this novel.

My grandmother Jessie died in 1990, at the age of ninety-eight, leaving numerous grandchildren, great-grandchildren, and even great-great-grandchildren to mourn her passing.

What do you hope a reader will take away from this book?

I hope they hear a story about listening to one's heart, learning from missteps, and redeeming grievances—though not without cost. I hope people consider the talents they have and how they've invested them. I hope this story affirms that accepting the gift of forgiveness is the hardest yet most meaningful work of the human spirit. And I hope that readers might use the story to consider the absences in their own lives and hearts and to examine what actions they can take to fill them and thus cherish more deeply the relationships in their lives.

What's next?

More stories about remarkable men and women, ordinary souls perhaps, but people who lived lives worthy of remembering. I feel so fortunate to have both the passion and the support necessary to research and write these stories. I hope readers keep reading them!

READERS GUIDE

By appointment, the author is available for phone interviews with book groups. Visit www.jkbooks.com to arrange a thirty-minute conversation with Jane, or visit www.waterbrookpress.com for more information.

1. This book is titled *An Absence So Great.* What were the absences revealed in this story? How did each character attempt to fill the void? What worked? What didn't work?
2. How would you describe Jessie Gaebele's efforts to be an independent woman working in a profession that largely excluded women in the early twentieth century? Do businesswomen today face similar challenges? How have things changed, and what has remained the same?
3. What kind of isolating experiences did Jessie Gaebele impose upon herself while in Milwaukee and Eau Claire, and even in Winona when she had her own studio? Did she rebuild those barriers in Bismarck, or did she learn from her experiences?
4. How would you respond to Mrs. Bauer's remark: "Maybe that was the way for women: having time without a man around offered relief, but they didn't ever dare say so, not even to themselves, for fear the thought violated heavenly law"?
5. Do you think Jessie overreacted when she learned of ways Fred hoped to advance her career, to be helpful, as he put it? If talent is in part a currency meant to be invested, how did each of the characters invest their talents? Did Jessie misuse the "credit" and "meaningful deposit relationships" she'd established in her life? How

else might she have handled the men who offered to assist her?

6. What did each of the main characters want? Why is it so difficult for us to name our desires? What did you think about Jessie's reliance on the proverb, "Desire accomplished is sweet to the soul"? What does that proverb mean to you?
7. How would you characterize Fred Bauer? Was he unfaithful? Was Mrs. Bauer unfaithful to her vows? Was Jessie? How does emotional infidelity affect a relationship? What actions did the characters take to find new directions? Were they successful?
8. Virginia Butler says, "It's human nature to mistrust goodness. Part of our exile from Eden, I suspect. We have to be vigilant in remembering that we all mess up our houses. And with grace we're allowed to straighten things up once again." Do you agree with Virginia? Why or why not? Have you mistrusted goodness? Messed things up in your life? What brought you through to "straighten things up once again"?
9. On top of the Missouri bluffs, Jessie says, "Unless she saw self-pity and envy and despair as acts of willfulness, she'd always feel set apart, never have the Guide she sought." What do you think Jessie means? What sorts of acts keep us from spiritual wholeness? Is the trail back to wholeness from self-pity and envy different from the way back from other hurtful and self-destructive decisions we make in our lives?
10. The author told this story through Selma's letters, through Jessie's photographs and her commentary about them, and through the third-person narratives of Jessie, Fred, and Mrs. Bauer. How did each of these elements move the story forward, or did they? Did you find that the letters or photographic commentary distracted from

or enhanced the narrative? Did you see things revealed in the photographs that Jessie missed in her telling?

11. When preparing to write this book, the author said her purpose was to prove that "accepting the gift of forgiveness is the hardest yet most meaningful work of the human spirit." Did she accomplish her aim? Why or why not?

INDEX OF PHOTOS